About Gra

MW01264755

A courageous book that breaks new ground, *Gray Rainbow Journey* dares to depart from what the public is accustomed to reading as it presents yet another facet of the Native American in his many struggles. A fascinating story by a new voice in Indian America.

> PRINCIPAL CHIEF WILLIAM "RATTLESNAKE" JACKSON
> American Cherokee Confederacy

Native American Christians have long known what a struggle it is to live in two worlds, torn between traditional beliefs and the Christian faith. The characters in *Gray Rainbow Journey* speak for so many of us.

> BETTY MAE JUMPER, TRIBAL ELDER
> Doctor of Humane Letters, author of *Legends of the Seminoles*
> Seminole Tribe of Florida, Inc.

An enlightening peek into contemporary Native America that portrays reservation life clearly and compellingly. It gives a window into the challenge of making spiritual choices for today's native person.

> CRAIG STEPHEN SMITH (OJIBWE)
> Native American Evangelist, author of *White Man's Gospel*

A fascinating peek at a different facet of Native American life: that of Christian Indians, and the many challenges they face. *Gray Rainbow Journey* is a heart-thumping face-off between good and evil that will keep you in suspense until the very last page!

> DANA K. CASSELL
> Writers-Editors Network

An exciting coming-of-age novel. I can definitely relate to this book's characters. I can't wait for the second book.

> CARLA MCKAY
> *Indian Life* newspaper

GRAY RAINBOW
JOURNEY

K. B. SCHALLER

INCLUDES
BONUS FEATURE

Taking It Deeper
Helps for Teachers and Leaders

OAKTARA

WATERFORD, VIRGINIA

Gray Rainbow Journey

Published in the U.S. by:
OakTara Publishers
P.O. Box 8
Waterford, VA 20197

Visit OakTara at
www.oaktara.com

Cover design by David LaPlaca/debest design co.
Cover images © 2008/iStockphoto.com/Chase Swift, Kris Hanke, Vladislav Gurfunkel

Author photo © 2008 by James Schaller

All Scripture quotations, unless otherwise noted, are taken from *The Holy Bible* (London: Eyre and Spottiswoode Limited), with grateful thanks.

ISBN: 978-1-60290-087-5 (novel)
ISBN: 978-1-60290-220-6 (novel with helps for teachers/leaders edition)

Gray Rainbow Journey is a work of fiction. References to real people, events, establishments, organizations, or locales are intended only to provide a sense of authenticity and are used fictitiously. All other characters, incidents, and dialogue are drawn from the author's imagination.

For my husband,

JIM,

for his patience, assistance,
and encouragement
during my long labor to give birth
to *Gray Rainbow Journey*

And also
In loving memory of my sister,
DORIS,
Whose beauty, strength, courage, and faith
Inspired us all.

Acknowledgments

My heartfelt thanks are extended to the following persons who, by word or deed, encouraged or contributed to the creation of *Gray Rainbow Journey:*

Native Believers everywhere in their unique struggles;

All the members of my cherished family;

Jeff Nesbit and Ramona Tucker, cofounders of OakTara, for their guidance throughout the finalizing of this project;

Carol Cypress, Seminole Tribe of Florida, Native speaker, Mikasuki Language, for her assistance and who also delights the world with her beautiful beadwork;

Maritza Canizares, friend and colleague for her word processing suggestions so freely shared;

Mr. and Mrs. Stephen A. Lamont, for posting my biography on their Transformed Lives Mission Services website: www.tlms.org;

Beloved mentor and retired missionary to the Seminole Tribe of Florida, Gladys A. Wigden;

Rev. Paul Buster (Seminole) for his enlightening anecdotes and homilies;

Rev. Wonder Johns (Creek) for his frequent words of encouragement;

Rev. Salaw Hummingbird (Cherokee) for his dedication to Native ministry;

All my wonderful friends in the Seminole Tribe of Florida, especially

Sally Billie and Judy Baker;

The Oklahoma and North Carolina Native congregations, especially D.B., H.B., R.P., and Alma Johns (Cherokee);

To the memories of H. Pepper Harris, retired missionary to the Seminole Tribe of Florida, who was an outstanding teacher and also a loving mentor;

Annie Stallworth, my beloved friend and prayer partner over the years, who was always about her Father's business;

And Judy Ann Osceola, a cherished friend.

Sincere thanks also to my two consultants on *Taking It Deeper: Helps for Teachers and Leaders*:

Bettye C. Bryant, Ed.S., **Reading** (Retired), Elementary School Principal, Palm Beach County **School** District;

Donna Meredith, **English and** Journalism Instructor (Retired), Leon County School District.

Jesus saith unto him,
Rise, take up thy bed and walk.

—THE HOLY BIBLE

.

I

Bitterroot
Angry at the Sun

April 11, 1980
Cheha sat on her screen porch enjoying the sunlit morning as she
worked at her bead loom. The annual Powwow and Indian Crafts
Show was not very far off, and her beadwork always brought a tidy
sum.

But suddenly the soft brightness disappeared. In its place, a
gigantic shadow oozed across the small patch of ground that was her
front yard. Startled, Cheha looked up.

The great winged creature was straight out of the nightmare
world. Its menacing eyes petrified her, held her spellbound; and he
was soaring straight toward her....

My hands shook as I sat there holding the journal at the small table in my mother's breakfast nook. As I strained to see in the rapidly fading daylight, I dreaded what more these pages would reveal. Yet my curiosity was overpowering.

I drew in a shuddering breath, because as I turned each page of the spiral notebook, it was like opening a door where you knew a Horror was hiding somewhere in the room—a Horror you knew that, without warning, would leap out and grab you.

My muscles ached from hours of sitting and poring over her baffling words; so I stood, stretched my back, rotated my head, and kneaded my shoulders. For all my fervent searching, I thought with dejection, so far there was little to add to the facts I already had: three months gone without a trace, without a word; journals—eight spiral notebooks—left behind, although it was obvious that writing was a ritual for her.

I was tired. I had a mid-term nursing care exam coming up and I needed to go home. Yet I was unable to pull myself away from this new discovery, because it held the first promise of a break in the mystery of Cheha Youngblood's disappearance.

How close I had come to not discovering the journals at all! Even now, I had no idea what prompted me to look beneath her mattress. But look I did, in yet another search of this tiny house where I had spent much of my childhood. And there they were, spread out end-to-end, written in pencil in her unusual third-person way of speaking.

I breathed in deeply and mustered all my reserves of courage. I needed them in order to continue exploring the dark reaches of my mother's mind:

> *Its wings spanned the width of the house! And, suddenly, the creature ripped through the side of her screen. Cheha leaped up then, screaming in Terror!! Her loom clattered to the floor. Hundreds of tiny, brightly colored seed beads scattered across the cement....*

I tore my eyes away from the text. Were they dreams—night terrors—or was it madness?

> *...she stood with her back against the wall, horrified, as this—thing!—glared at her with his fiery eyes. And though it was a gigantic owl, strangely, it hopped about like a buzzard on a carcass. The stench of death clung to it and fouled the air...*

The next passage caused my heart to thunder and my mouth to go dry:

> *Then the owl-creature hissed: "You will follow the way of the black hat!" And with a terrifying screech it shot upward. This time it ripped off Cheha's entire screen roof and quickly disappeared into the blinding sunlight!*

I pondered the words, and whispered them into the quiet stillness: "*The way of the black hat.*" Like the trademark black Uncle Joe that Mama's grandmother, and my great-grandma, wore?

This nightmare was so like the stories Hannah Glory Cypress, Mama Hat to all who knew her, relayed around the evening campfires. They were told in the blackness of deep nights in the South Florida Everglades: tales that were as old as the Indian nations.

But my Christian mother had forbidden Mama Hat to pass them on to us children, so they were therefore instilled in us secretly, during casual conversations and family gatherings. Little snippets. Seeds. One here, a few there, planted, and nourished by stolen waters from hidden springs. They were seeds she hoped would germinate in us and keep the ancient ways alive, for they were tales Mama Hat feared would become like many perceived the Indian people to be: existing, yet somehow extinct.

Even I had thought them long dead, those stories that Mama Hat, before she moved to the Bitterroot Confederacy, told beneath her Seminole *chickee.* But the owl-buzzard night terror had exhumed them. Now those memories were peeking through the cobwebs in the crypts of my mind, slithering through the crevices, poking out their tongues and making ghoul faces at me—those tales of death-speaking owls and night spirits that roamed the earth. They were told when the moon, stars, and campfires were the only lights, and they still maintained their power to terrify.

My heart began to drum in my chest and my skin to prickle in the dying moments of day. But try as I might, I could not tear my eyes away from the jagged remnants of my mother's anguished life:

Cheha cried out then, and bolted upright in the pitch darkness. Her blood pounded in her ears. Sweat drenched her face, streamed down her neck, and soaked her nightshirt. Where did the sunlight go...?

She switched on the bed lamp. As the Horror skittered away with the fleeing shadows, she remembered. It was night. Morning, really—3:00 a.m. Heart hammering sickeningly, trembling, she crept over to the window and pulled open the curtain. It made perfect sense that the yard that was so shockingly bright in the dream was now as black as she remembered the Everglades nights to be, so many memories ago....

The ten-year-old girl that still cowered inside me shuddered. No doubt my mother's Terror was an extension of those long-ago tales; but even so, I realized that, during the day one could rationalize specters and shadows—things that haunt our dreams. But in the quietness of night, when the floors of our deepest fears creak beneath their unseen footsteps, they are real.

As I continued reading, I glanced about now and then with mounting uneasiness:

The giant winged creature spoke of a black hat. It has been over a decade now, but did HE also cause Mama Hat to disappear? If so, why? Was it because my grandmother discovered the truth about US and therefore had to be silenced? Oh, the strength of HIS wickedness! And if HE sent the owl-buzzard, can HE also work evil in Cheha's children—even her Dina?

Cheha's life is all gone! Like water poured out on the ground that cannot be gathered up again...

April 13, 1980
Cheha feels detached—strangely empty—so empty; like when her mother passed to the other side. Empty, like when she married, and when she reared her children. Only one thing is worse than this emptiness: The terror. HIS Terror!

Now I was really perplexed: "*even her Dina?*" Did she think that I was cursed or something? My mind was spinning; even my thoughts seemed to echo off the walls of the empty house. Did she leave us because she believed that somebody was working evil in all of us children—even me?

Other than her feud with my kid sister, Shania, what had any of the rest of us—my two brothers or I—ever done? My stomach was churning with its usual bitter heaviness that stress induced. And I could almost hear my mother's hopeless sigh:

April 12, 1980
Now Cheha must fly, and without a word, because if HE knew, HIS
Evil would be there waiting for us!

I was literally scratching my head as I pondered the words: *He—us?*
The following entry in bold angry letters screamed from the page:

April 15, 1980
DO NOT COME UP TOMORROW, SUN, BECAUSE CHEHA IS
FURIOUS WITH YOU. YOUR RAYS DANCE ONLY ON THE
OUTSIDE WORLD, WHILE INSIDE THESE WALLS, CHEHA
WAITS IN THIS DARK STILLNESS. LET THE DAY THAT SHE
FLIES BE AS BLACK AS THE NIGHT AIR THAT STOLE HER
DREAMS!!!

Enough!
I closed the journal and sat there with my face buried in my hands.
"Where are you, Mama?" I whispered in the quiet emptiness. "Why
didn't you tell me what was going on in your life? You are *Christian.* You
went to church. Couldn't you have shared your fears with your pastor,
the elders, a friend—*somebody?* You always were ashamed of the
traditions of the people, rejecting them as limiting. Backward. But the
truth is, you're a caricature Indian yourself—the stereotype the White
man portrays—closed-mouthed and stone-faced!"
I cried then, because the cold reality was that nobody seemed too
concerned about Cheha Youngblood anymore—nobody, that is, except
me. Foul play was not suspected because her suitcase and personal items
were also missing, so she was just another Youngblood that took off to
parts unknown. In fact, one of the investigators, a big, blond-headed guy
from in town, had even joked as he fingered her picture on the dresser:
"You say she's your mom? She's quite a looker. You sure she didn't just
run off with one of those good-looking Injun road workers in town?"
Not even her big brother, my Uncle Donnie, seemed all that
concerned, I thought, as I dried my tears.

"Cheha was born and raised on the reservation," he said. "She moved here to Bitterroot, but The Root is pretty much part of The Rez—only yelling distance away. If anybody did anything to Cheha, somebody would have seen it. She'll come back when she wants to—*if* she wants to."

His next comment even held a hint of amusement: "Besides, taking off seems to run in this family's veins—especially the women's!"

Well, I did have to admit that Mama Hat was included too, in this increasing clan of runaways, but that did not excuse the family's lack of interest in my mother's whereabouts. Didn't they care where she was and how she was doing? Didn't anybody ever wonder why our runners took off to parts unknown? Didn't anybody care if Mama was still alive or not?

Even my brothers, when they dropped by the house, were almost casual in their concern: "Any news about Mama?" And all the time they were nonchalantly stuffing their faces with sandwiches, dragging on a cigarette, or chugging a beer.

I stacked the journals. The day was all but spent, the walls were closing in, the shadows were starting to whisper, the house to creak. Also, Uncle Donnie was no doubt beginning to worry because I hadn't come home directly from school. I picked up the telephone—the only thing we kept working in the house—and dialed. Uncle Donnie picked up on the third ring.

"Just calling to let you know I stopped off at Mama's to check on the house. I'm on my way," I said.

"When am I gonna eat? I got diabetes. You know I need my meals on time. So you need to get home and cook something so I can eat!" Uncle Donnie said, sounding exasperated.

I sighed. *Learned helplessness.* There was an edge to my voice. "There's always food in the refrigerator you can heat, Uncle Donnie. I do go to school, too, you know. I can't always keep banker's hours."

"You never said anything about working in a bank!"

As usual, any figure of speech was lost on him. "Look. I'm on my way, okay?" I replied resignedly.

"You should have been home two, three hours ago. And mind how you talk to an elder, aaay!"

When all reason fails, play the Respect Card, I thought. "I'm on my way. Sorry I'm late." I hung up before I really mouthed off at him.

I searched for a bag for the eight journals and entertained my favorite fantasy: that of disappearing also, like my dad, a North Carolina Cherokee-Apache did when he walked out; then my Seminole mother; and before her, Mama Hat, my great-grandma. And if an old Indian woman had the courage to flee, I wondered, why did I feel obligated to take on the problems of Bitterroot and my family of disappearing Youngbloods and vanishing elders?

It had been after a rousing revival meeting in town that Mama Hat had disappeared. It was hard for folks to accept, because my Traditional great-grandmother had been a fixture on the reservation, and later in the Native enclave of Bitterroot—The Root, as everybody called it—for generations. She was always barefoot. She wore a black hat, dozens of strands of brightly colored beads around her neck, the Seminole cape and patchwork skirt and, of course, although she was Seminole, the signature pipe in her mouth, like a female Sequoyah. A Rez grandma for as long as most folks could remember, it just did not seem possible that she had quite simply *disappeared.* The last anybody on The Rez or in The Root saw of her, Mama Hat was standing in her yard talking gently to the fireflies and the fat lizard that made its home under the loose stones that led to her doorway.

Weeks of intense searching turned up nothing. Many stories followed. Sightings were reported in places as far away as Arkansas and Oklahoma. Follow-ups ended in confusion and conflicting accounts, but no Mama Hat. Among the most bizarre of the tales was that she was out West hosting her own television talk show. Some even hinted that she shape-shifted into an eagle or something, and flew away.

Only one thing was for sure: my great-grandmother had simply vanished. Away from it all.

I wondered sometimes, even though I felt guilty doing so, what it would be like to disappear too, away from Bitterroot, from caretaking, all of it; and move into a world of my own choosing, which was to finish school. Get a good position somewhere. Buy nice clothes. Go to parties and have a good time for a change, without being spied on and gossiped about, via the Rez-Root grapevine. And more importantly, meet somebody special.

As I headed for the door, journals wrapped securely in an old Winn Dixie grocery bag I found beneath the kitchen counter, I heard a thump from somewhere outside. I tensed—my nerves were already on edge. I listened intently.

"Who's out there?" I called out.

My answer was the hammering of my own heart and the pounding of the blood in my ears.

I peered outside. Still nothing, but I banged on the window anyhow. "Is anybody out there?"

Still no answer.

I was feeling more and more edgy being alone in Mama's deserted house, with Night creeping in and Fear, the cruel prankster, causing havoc in my mind.

II

Home Before Dark

One final quick inspection—even under the rugs—assured me that there was nothing more to be discovered in Mama's house. Besides, I wanted to be out before the owls came—the pair that took up vigil in the mango tree outside the kitchen window each time I visited and spoke terrifying night parables in throaty whispers: *"Don't go to sleep tonight, Dina. Bad dreams—bad dreams..."*

I shivered. Then one more thing caught my eye—a small black book on the bottom shelf next to some rejected can goods. I dusted it off and read the title. *The King James Bible.* Mama's. But I seldom saw her pick it up after her hiatus from church and, consequently, mine from Sunday school. It was a real oldie. She had left it behind, but it might come in handy tonight, I figured: Jesus was in it. And evil night spirits were scared of Him. After all, didn't the Bible teach that He cast out demons? That had to mean He could make owls beat a hasty retreat too, I thought as I placed it in the bag with the journals.

I was about to close the door behind me when the telephone rang. It startled me, because other than Uncle Donnie—who knew that I was here?

"Dina, how long are you going to be there?"

Her voice surprised me.

"Shania? Well, well, when did you get in from Oklahoma?"

"Maybe a couple of hours ago." She sounded urgent—as usual. "So, how long are you going to be there?"

I glanced at my Timex. "Actually, I was about to leave. What's up? I mean, can't it wait? And how did you know I was here?"

There was a shrug in her voice. "Uncle Donnie said to check. Look, don't leave. I'll be over as soon as JohnnyHawk gets change for a ten so he can lend me some cash. My Greyhound ticket left me busted, and I needed a few bucks to water the pony. Wait for me, okay?"

"Well, gas up in a hurry. The lights are shut off, and I'll be standing here in the dark soon."

I hung up and paced about as I glanced repeatedly at my watch. *Shania. Back.*

Gone for over a year and now she was back. I was always glad to hear from my confrontational younger sister, but I was also on edge around her—every word I spoke could be like stepping in quicksand. For the first few weeks after Mama disappeared, she peppered everybody with telephone calls from our Aunt Bett's home in Broken Bow. Headstrong and uncontrollable almost since the minute she hit puberty, she had fled there as a fifteen-year-old runaway and self-proclaimed emancipated minor after an all-out verbal combat session with Mama.

Shania demanded updates, but when asked why she wouldn't come home, her reason was the usual center of her concerns—money. As much as she could lay her pretty, manicured hands on: "I just got this job, see? I can't ask for time off 'cause they'll replace me…"

She then went through the phase of making sure she got her share of the pickings, meager though they were, even though Mama could reappear at any time: "Don't take anything, because whatever Mama left belongs to all of us equally!"

No doubt she was short on cash and home for a visit to find what she could to tide her over and to finance her grandiose life plans. It was different, though, when we were growing up. Shania was sweet-natured then, a free-spirited, happy child. And nobody was like her big sister. There were nearly five years between us and I was her idol. I could usually persuade her to do things with only a suggestion that Mama couldn't get her to do without a fight.

But all that had changed after her fifteenth birthday when she started hanging out with the party crowd at South Florida Public and it drove a wide rift between her and Mama.

"This White boy football player that you let keep you out late—why won't he come around and show his face?" Mama asked. "What will you do when he gets tired of playing with his little Indian Barbie doll and dumps you for a White girl?"

And the fight would really heat up. I knew Shania was spinning out of control, but I didn't want to lose favor with her. So I admit I sort of took her side: "Lighten up, Mama. Shania's a good kid. She'll come around."

But there were times she didn't come around, literally. During those times, when she stayed out all night, we would be frantic, and Mama would send JohnnyHawk and my younger brother, FrankieEagle—FrankE—to look for her. Sometimes they would drag her home screaming, protesting, cursing; on other occasions, she would leave for school on a Friday and straggle in sometime Sunday.

Her blazing sunset hair also drew Mama's disdain:"You look like a Rez apple—like somebody lit a campfire on your head. Aren't there enough real White people around that you don't need to try to be like them? What's wrong with looking like what you are: an Indian?"

Well, Shania did and she didn't. She had golden skin, but the narrow skull and retroussé nose were more Caucasian than Indian; and she'd always had a natural hint of auburn in her hair that none of the rest of us had. But fiery tresses and all, she was still my little sister, so, yeah, I stuck up for her. If she wanted to dye her hair a hue that screamed for attention, so what? She was a kid. What was the big deal?

But my laidback attitude always raised Mama's ire. She'd fire off at me and accuse me of standing against her:"You ought to be helping me tell her that what she's doing is wrong, but all you ever do is take sides with her!"

Things really came to a head one morning before breakfast a couple of months or so after Shania began her wild streak. Mama heard her retching in the bathroom and found her with her head hanging over the toilet. She'd had it with her rebellious daughter and was at her wit's end: "Heaving up, huh? Did you finally get what you've been working toward—a big belly?"

Shania's face was flushed and hot-red with anger. "Would you please just get off my back? I had too many drinks and ate something greasy at the party last night, okay?"

Mama shook her head in resignation: "Dina never did these kinds of things. Drinking. Smoking. Staying out. Sleeping around, like you do. Dyeing her hair that strumpet color, talking back to me, like you do!"

Shania then turned her fury on both of us: "Maybe it's easy to be Miss Perfect when you're almost twenty, never had a boyfriend, and don't have a life. And maybe you're just jealous 'cause Dad walked out and you don't have a man. Well, I'm not going to sit around and dry up like the two of you!"

For the first time ever, Mama slapped her hard across the face. Shortly afterward, Shania ran off.

But even now, nearly two years later, my sister's comment still sliced deeply, mostly because it was the truth. Perhaps the status of my life was determined even before my birth, I mused. When my grandmother MaryJim's diabetes worsened, Mama, as her only unmarried daughter, had had to drop out of school in tenth grade to care for her. And now, the lot had fallen to me to drop out, too. So, two months before I completed tenth grade, complications from Grandma MaryJim's diabetes worsened, and I left school to accompany her to dialysis three times a week. And from then on, it seemed a carved petroglyph that my life would also drift into the same caretaker's pattern as Mama's: "She's a fine girl, taking care of her grandmother like that," the elders would say.

"I'll send Dina over; she'll stay with him till he gets better," Mama would promise when any of the neighbors got sick.

"You littler girls could learn a lot from Dina about a woman's role," Pastor Ward said one Sunday. "You need to pay attention and follow her example."

But that was the way it was on The Rez and in The Root—we took care of each other. In the meantime, there were no eligible young men beating down my door, so, although I was screaming and panicking inside, I continued to smile outwardly, and in my quietness, perform all the duties that my mother had.

There was one difference, though. Mama always wanted to be a writer. She won school competitions for her poems, essays, and short stories. But once she quit school, her dream died, and what was left of it cried out piteously from these journals. I, on the other hand, completed my diploma in the night program after Grandma MaryJim passed on, and after graduation, enrolled in Community College. Diabetes was epidemic among Indian people, so with my background, a nursing degree seemed natural.

Therefore, love, for Dina Youngblood, continued to wait. All through grade school, though, I did have a huge crush on Marty Osceola, a firebrand who dropped out around the same time I did and kind of disappeared after that. He sort of had the eye for me, too, but neither of us ever really acted on it—that is, until The Footraces.

Although taught to be demure, the more adventurous of us girls made up an after-school game called "Girls Against Boys." We'd choose a destination—a tree, a building, anything—then challenge one of the boys. The game was rigged from the start, because each girl would only tag a boy she figured she could beat. And he didn't dare decline because he would risk losing face with his friends. Most in my circle were pretty fast then and were also at that pre-puberty stage where we were even stronger and faster than most of the guys.

Except for me, that is. Unlike Katey Huff, Mellinda Billie, and Emellda Tommie, I was not particularly fleet of foot, was on the shy side and always hung back. But one day they just would not stop egging me on.

Emellda called out my nickname: "Hey, Deenie, you never run. Pick somebody." She was still panting after defeating Shane LuckyMan, a skinny kid with a terrible overbite, whose name belied his defeat. She nudged me. "How about Marty over there? He's skinny. I'm sure you can outrun him."

Then they all joined in the chant: "Go, Deenie. Go, Deenie" till finally I had no choice.

"Beat you to the oak tree!" I said with false bravado. I tagged Marty and the race was on. I took off as fast as my legs would go, while Katey, Emellda, and the rest of the girls shouted me on. And I was winning, too. Marty was lagging at my heels and that tree was no more than a body-length away. My first race, and I could just taste the victory. But at the very last minute Marty sped up—barely—just enough to ease past me to win the footrace.

After that, the girls kept after me to race him until I beat him. So after school, that became our ritual and our obsession: beat Marty Osceola. But each time, he would hang back and then at the last minute cruise past me with a smirk on his face and that slight dimple in his left cheek.

Soon the challenge was unspoken. Whenever we met, I would simply tag him and we would start running—destination to be announced. But wiry and deceptively strong, Marty *always* won.

Before long, though, the competition developed into something else—a delicate dance of two young hearts, with our eyes saying what our lips could not yet speak. Marty lived out in the hummocks with his stepdad. but unless you sought his services, people seldom saw Jack Turner. And it was rumored that as the area's most feared, most powerful witch, he could shape-shift into an animal, a bird, or even a snake at will; and that he could sicken or even kill you from miles away with his terrifying powers.

So for most people, my girlfriends included, the name *Jack Turner* struck fear in their hearts; and most, my girlfriends included, were half-scared of Marty too, because everybody took it for granted that he was being schooled in Jack Turner's craft.

As for me, I was more awed by Marty than anything else. He was incredibly good-looking; my crush on him was almost a physical ache. But I'd never let on because my friends—Mellinda especially—would have teased me unmercifully.Although I sometimes caught Marty's shift-eyed glance at me and fantasized about being in love with him, that was as far as it ever went. When Marty's mother married one of the Apache construction workers that came each year to work on roads and bridges, they moved West. I lost contact with him after that.

As time passed, however, now and then his fiery letters to the editor appeared in *Indian Herald,* our community paper, and I would wonder idly what he looked like after so many years. But other than that, so ended the "love" life of Dina, *aka* Deenie Youngblood.

I glanced again at my watch. Just as I'd decided that I'd give Shania only five more minutes, I heard another sound, soft and rustling. This time, between the break in the curtains, I glimpsed a shadow—a figure—peering inside the house.

I rushed over and banged on the window: "Who's out there? Speak up, or I'll come out there and kick your little butt!"

My mild threat should scare off any kid, I figured, as I let up the kitchen window and glanced out. It wasn't a kid, but a man, and he was walking briskly across the yard. He held up his hand and, deliberately it seemed, dropped a piece of paper.

I watched as it fluttered to the ground and settled on the sparse lawn. But when I looked up again, the man had vanished. One minute he was there, the next, gone.

And just then, an owl appeared, perched on a limb of the mango tree near the kitchen window. He locked his two yellow beacons with my gaze, then slowly wafted away into the dusk. A chill jolted through me. I slammed the window shut and locked it.

After a few minutes to collect myself, I mustered my courage and eased open the front door. Perceiving no immediate danger, but keeping an eye on the mango tree, I ventured out and, with trembling fingers, picked up that piece of paper.

A Snickers wrapper? It was pressed flat, carefully preserved. I studied it briefly. Was there some hidden message in this? I stuck the candy paper in the pocket of my jeans. It was time I locked up and headed for home.

Just as I rummaged for my keys, Shania rumbled up in JohnnyHawk's old Impala—the pony—and jerked to a halt, crunching shale rocks under the nearly bald tires.

Relieved to see another human face, I ran to meet her. "Hey! Did you see anybody—a man—running down the street when you pulled up? He was wearing a dark shirt, a hat, Western boots, and he dropped—"

"Nope. Only a couple of old guys down on the corner sitting around, just looking on. Am I the FBI?" Shania swung her long, slender legs outside, flung her purse over her shoulder, and strode toward me.

"Is that Full Blood Indian, or Frybread Indian?"

"More like a Flat Broke Indian," she said.

They were old Rez jokes. Stale. Lame. But they relieved some of the tension that hovered in the air, so we both laughed.

"Seriously. Somebody was peeking in the window," I said. "I thought you may have seen him. You think we should call the police? I mean, Mama was living in this house and she disappeared. It might be a clue..."

"The cops care about a peeper in The Root or on The Rez? Get real," she said.

We started toward the house. She was seventeen now, and her skinny blue jeans revealed a much thinner figure than when I had last seen her. She was taller, more willowy than any of the Youngblood women, and her formerly waist-length hair, auburn-tinged to start with, and once dyed to rival a blazing brushfire, was now bleached a kind of moonlight silver and was only a bit longer than a buzz cut.

We were approaching the front door when suddenly an insistent and urgent thought popped into my head: *Hide the journals. If Shania gets her hands on them, she'll pick them over like a vulture on a roadkill.*

I planned quickly as I hurried inside. The oven. Never the domestic type, it would be the last place Shania would look. So I shoved the bag inside. Hot on my heels, she strode through the doorway. She was now almost a full head taller than both Mama and I. Her pale hair and white shirt glowed against her unblemished tawny skin. In the rushing twilight she looked almost magical—a Peter Pan beauty who'd leapt out of a book of the White man's fairy tales.

"You didn't take anything, did you? Because everything belongs to all of us equally. We've talked about it before," Shania said as she examined odds-and-ends pieces of flatware in the kitchen drawers.

"There was nothing to take," I said.

She placed a chipped cup back in the cabinet and gave only cursory attention to a few ancient plastic plates, cups, and saucers. "Junk. Why didn't you just throw this stuff out?"

"You said not to take anything. The boys and I passed on it, so it's all yours." I sauntered over to the oven and stood there casually, hoping against hope she would not look inside. I breathed with relief as she swept past me without a hint of interest.

"Where's all the patchwork and the bead jewelry Mama always made for the Tribal Fair and powwow? They're having one of those multi-cultural things in Broken Bow. Indian stuff sells for a lot of money," she called out from the bedroom.

"Listen, Mama took her personals and all her crafts, the things she could market. I told you. There's nothing here and it's getting dark. Look, how long are you going to be in town? Maybe we could get together—do something before you head back," I said. "How does

16

tomorrow afternoon sound? I don't have classes."

"Tomorrow's good. But no rush. I'll be hanging around for a week or two. I'm between jobs." She glanced about the house one last time, decided that there were no pickings, then studied me briefly. "So. You went back to school for a nursing degree. That took some guts."

"Yep. Earned my diploma taking evening classes and went on to Community College. And the scholarship I got sure helps."

She was pensive. "Well, whatever keeps your dugout floating. Me, I'm going to be the first Native American super model." She postured expansively: "something glamorous, exciting. Maybe later, I'll become an actress. As soon as I save enough for a portfolio, Tracee and I are heading for California; we can room together and share expenses. I've got big plans for great things, big sister. I'll leave the puke and the bedpans to you do-gooders of the world."

I ignored her putdown. "It's good that you and Tracee are still friends after all these years. But what about tomorrow? Are we going to get together for a burger and fries—my treat?"

"A veggie burger and a diet Coke sounds good, so long as you're paying. I have to make sure I have enough cash for my trip back to Broken Bow."

Veggie burgers, diet Cokes, and hold the fries, I mused. No doubt that was how she stayed twig-thin. "Okay, what about noon? You could pick me up in the pony," I said.

"Sounds like a plan." She gave the room another quick sweep with her eyes. "Well, let's go. Come on, I'll give you a ride home."

"Uh, thanks, but I'll walk. I need the exercise so I can get as skinny as you," I answered quickly.

She smiled. "You're skinny enough. Anyhow, don't say I didn't offer." Without insisting, she swung deftly into the pony and started the engine. "Oh, by the way, Marty Osceola's in town. JohnnyHawk said he was asking about you." Then with a wink and a knowing smile, she was off.

Marty Osceola. Back in town after all these years, and he still wants to know about me? My skin prickled and my pulse quickened.

My heart must have skipped two beats as I locked the door. But as I glanced up at the tree in the backyard, I shuddered. Not one, but both owls were there now. And they were starting their menacing duet: *"Dina, Dina, you will follow the black hat—bad dreams are coming—coming through the doorway of the night."*

My blood pounded in my ears. I picked up my pace.

III

The Scent of Twilight

The fragrance of night jasmine perfumed the air, but I was barely aware of its sweetness as I walked briskly down the street. I held the bag with the Bible side close to my heart and hoped for protection. Like in the movies. And I gulped back the nausea of Terror.

"Dina—Dina Youngblood? Hey, hop in. I'll give you a ride."

The dark green Ford pickup, old but very well maintained, pulled to the curb. The occupant leaned over and opened the door. And I didn't have to guess his identity. I knew. Even after all these years, even though time had deepened his voice, even before he turned on the dome light.

"It's me, Marty Osceola. Panther Clan. Girls Against Boys. Remember me?"

I wondered if he heard the owls as I glanced quickly over my shoulder. I shuddered again because they were still there. "I remember," I said. "Thanks for the offer, but I can walk. It's only a block or so more."

Marty inched along beside me anyhow. "Come on, hop in. It's hot tonight."

I could have used a ride, but I was really kind of embarrassed. Why, of all nights, I wondered, did my secret heartthrob pick now for an Up Close and Personal, with me all wilted from the heat and wearing scruffy jeans and a tee shirt?

But he either didn't notice or didn't care as he pulled to a stop. "Hey, I know we haven't seen each other since we were kids, but you can trust me to drive you a block to the corner."

"Okay, thanks," I said, and climbed in. As I did so, as suddenly as they appeared, the owls wafted slowly away and faded into the dusk. I sighed with relief and blotted my face with a Kleenex from my purse.

He glanced at me. "You okay?"

"I'm fine, just a bit winded. I haven't walked in a while—a little out of shape, I guess."

His eyes slid deftly over me. "You look pretty put-together to me." And he smiled that Marty smile that had been buried in my memory for a decade—that smile with that slight dimple in his left cheek.

My face grew hot and my heart fluttered the way it had ten years ago. I avoided his eyes. "Are you flirting with me, Marty Osceola?"

"You said it, I agree, and I'm too inexperienced at it to be subtle, pretty Indian woman. So, what are you doing for yourself these days other than going to school to be a nurse, taking care of your Uncle Donnie"—he grinned mischievously—"and saving yourself for me, I hope?"

I glanced at him. "How do I know I even *like* you? We haven't seen each other in a hundred years."

"Oh, you like me. You can't help it. You see, I have my ways of knowing."

"You've been away from Bitterroot for ten years. How could you know anything about what I feel?"

He smiled. "Maybe I use medicine; send owls to spy on you."

"Or ask my brothers?"

He threw back his head and laughed. "Okay, I value their input, but that's secondhand information. I have my unique ways of checking things out for myself to see if you're as good as you seem. And you are. Most people aren't, but you are. I've been plotting this, uh, chance meeting for a couple of days now, ever since I got back."

"Oh, have you?" I stole a quick glance at him: dark, bright eyes set in the bronze, perfectly sculpted face; hair, delinquent and gently nuanced by the sun; and his voice, his words, his smile—all exuded the sweetness of ripe mangos. His nearness drew my heart and my reason away and every red light in my brain started to blink frantically: *A man for you, yes, Dina, but are you mad? This one is that lush ripe fruit in the Garden of Eden—the son of a witch, the most powerful one on the East Coast. What if he isn't joking? Suppose he really does command the owls?*

"...so, I'm not directly involved with the Natives United Movement," he was saying as I quickly refocused my mind, "but I have

20

many friends in it. They were a big moral support to me while I was fact-finding—traveling around, visiting as many reservations as I could. The conditions on most that I visited are deplorable."

He inched along, drawing out, I knew, the short distance to Uncle Donnie's house. "I can't rest thinking that I made no effort to alleviate the suffering and the broken spirits of my people."

"By now, it's more or less a generational thing. So there's nothing much that one man can do about it, is there?" I asked.

His words were firm with resolve. "No. Because one man is only one voice. But many voices? They are a force. I want to create an intertribal nexus, a forum that would unite all the tribes under one standard. You know how the Blacks—the African-Americans—got their power in the American system? By thinking and acting as *one.* They never separated themselves by tribes or nations. They're one society. One people. And it's time we banded together, too. Time we brought back the old ways and infused them with the new so far as it benefits our people. We need solidarity—political power. It's the only thing the White man respects!"

I shrugged. "That's—quite a vision."

"But not impossible," he replied. "Either we unite, or all that most of us will ever get are scraps from the our oppressor's table."

Shale rocks crackled beneath the tires as he pulled into the driveway of the small tan house trimmed in brown and bordered by purple bougainvillea shrubs. Though it was past sundown, Uncle Donnie was standing outside, water hose in hand, sprinkling some scraggly cuttings in a yard largely devoid of grass.

"Dinner's way late," he called. "You know I got diabetes and need to eat on time!"

Marty got out, opened the door for me, placed his hands about my waist, and lifted me to the ground. When our eyes met, with our faces so close together, I was breathless.

"Down you go," he said, smiling that smile. "How you like my White man's manners?"

"Chivalry is a positive—White or Indian," I said and quickly snatched my gaze away. I headed for the house as he sauntered toward Uncle Donnie.

"Need some help with that heavy water hose?" Marty asked.

Uncle Donnie was in no mood for jokes. "Do I look like I need help?"

Marty laughed. "Whoa, they need your spunk in Natives United to help revolutionize status quo thinking!"

Uncle Donnie eyed him. "That's a radical group for radical people—rabble rousers!" He turned off the water. "Nothing but trouble," he murmured as he tramped into the house.

Marty just shrugged. "Well, I guess you'd better go and feed that feisty old warrior. But why don't you and me get together tomorrow—go eat. We could drive down to Chickee Choices on the Tamiami. It's been a long time since I had their frybread and gator nuggets."

Though my reasoning screamed *No!,* I heard myself saying, "Okay, but not tomorrow, though. I'm having lunch with my sister and afterward we'll probably hang out for a while."

"Can I call you tomorrow evening?" He stood at the foot of the steps with his thumbs tucked casually in the beaded belt of his Levis, and his eyes swept gently over me.

"Sure, Marty," I said. "Around seven would be good." I tried to sound casual, but my heart was drumming so I could barely hear myself speak. I tried to ignore the thin, faded scars on his firmly muscled arm—the scratches from the Green Corn Ceremony, no doubt. I didn't want to deal with them. And because of his interest in intertribal brotherhood, I wondered if he also had piercing scars on his chest from the revival of the Sun Dance. Once considered so bloody and pagan a spectacle by White onlookers, it was outlawed as inflammatory by the U.S. Government.

The screen door swung open, and Uncle Donnie stood there with a scowl . "Am I gonna eat anytime tonight?"

"I'd better go," Marty said. "Look, I'm working at the housing authority and I get off around five. Why don't I call you then? If I don't reach you, I'll just keep trying."

"Okay. Well, see you," I said with as much nonchalance as I could muster. And I avoided Uncle Donnie's eyes as I swept past him and into the house.

"I don't want you seeing that boy," Uncle Donnie said simply.

"He only gave me a ride home. I'm not seeing him."

Eddie Was, who had been bird-dogging the front door, maiowed loudly. He shot past us and into the house, ringed tail held high, and sat by his feeding dish. It seemed that lateness with dinner landed me protests on both fronts.

Uncle Donnie was at his waspish best: "Well, I'd like to eat before midnight!"

I placed the bag with the journals on the kitchen counter. "Didn't you see the note I left for you, dear Uncle? Your dinner is on a plate in the refrigerator. All you had to do was heat it."

"Can't read notes without new glasses. When you gonna take me to get new glasses? And mind how you talk to an elder!"

Oh, here we go with the elder bit, I thought with resignation. But I knew not to go there with a comeback. So I just focused on his exam. "What good are glasses? You never wear them."

He walked away without answering. The crinkly furrows around his eyes, he had to know, were consequences mostly of many years of squinting—because he conveniently "lost" every pair of eyeglasses he ever owned. When his ophthalmologist asked why he refused to wear them, he muttered once, "'Cause they make me look old."

As I heated his food in the skillet, he poured Purina Cat Chow into Eddie Was' bowl.

"That's right, E.W., eat, boy," Uncle Donnie said and gave the cat a gentle scratch behind the ears.

While the cat relished his meal with feline gusto, Uncle Donnie switched on the TV, removed his ever-present alligator boots, and propped his callused feet on the living room coffee table. From there, he had a beeline eyeshot to the kitchen and nonchalantly dictated the preparation of his supper. "Put a little flavor in the cabbage," he said and motioned with his leathery brown hand toward a cellophane bag of pork rinds on the counter.

I knew he would worry me until I did, so I sprinkled in a few. "You know they aren't good for you. Too much fat and too much sodium."

"Sam Waters said sodium is better for you than salt."

"Well, you just tell Sam Waters that sodium *is* salt."

"A little bit won't hurt me. And check my toe after dinner. Looks like it's turning. I don't want it to get black and rot like Sam Waters' did. And that rot traveled all the way up. They had to take off his whole leg below the knee."

The Toe again, I thought with weariness. It was his way of either getting attention, diverting it from a non-preferred subject or task, or after he'd lost a verbal sparring match. "If your toe had turned colors as many times as you said, you'd be minus a foot and on crutches by now. You should wear sandals instead of those smelly old boots anyhow. I have a mind to throw them out. Anyhow, you're going in for a complete physical and eye exam day after tomorrow. I've already set it up, so don't argue."

He hated doctors' offices, so he demonstrated again his expertise in changing the subject: "So, what's in that bag—books?"

"Right. Books."

"Good. When you know what Indians know, and know what the White man knows too, you're ahead. But the White man, *he* only knows what *he* knows."

"Well, so far, the White man's still tops on the leader board, so it looks like he's doing pretty good with what he knows," I said.

"'Cause they cheated," he grumbled, as I placed his dinner before him. For a long moment there were only the sounds of his fork on stoneware, and the noise of running water as I filled the sink and washed the frying pan.

Presently he spoke. "Don't you throw my boots out. You do, and you gonna be in big trouble."

I suppressed a smile. "Oh, they're going into the trash can, all right. One of these days."

"Better not. And don't spray anymore of that powder stuff in them, either."

"It's the anti-fungal deodorant powder or the trash can. Just as soon as I hear you snoring, they're going straight into the trash can one of these nights."

He eyed me. A hint of amusement tried in vain to hide itself beneath the layers of gruffness in his playful threat. "You mind how you talk to an elder!"

Another long silence ensued. And as he neared the completion of his meal, his mood shifted to contemplative. I looked up and caught his eyes resting on me.

"Marty is Jack Turner's second wife's kid. First wife died. Don't know what from," he said without preface…and let the statement hang as if for full impact before he continued. "Anyhow, Marty's real dad is a good-looking half-Apache-half Navajo guy, Allan Begay. Liked the night life. A mean, violent sort. So Marty's mama ran off. Met Jack. Married him. Then ran off again, *back* to Begay. They left Marty for Jack to raise. And he loved that boy like he was his own."

"I've heard of Jack Turner—never met him to know him, though," I said.

"Um. Well." Uncle Donnie's eyes narrowed. "He's *bad* medicine—a witch. Everybody in Indian Country is scared of him. He has a lot of power. Can shape-shift, they say."

I shrugged. "And Marty's his stepson. So what does that have to do with him? But tell me this: how did he get the name Osceola? That's not an Apache name. Not a Navajo name, either."

He glanced up at me. "Marty's mama is Seminole. RaeEllen Osceola. She wasn't married when Marty was born, so she called him by her own name. She and Begay didn't hitch up and move to Arizona till after Marty was maybe two years old. But his name remained Osceola. Anyhow, Allan liked the partying life. And when it got worse, with the drinking and skirt-chasing and all, RaeEllen split. Left Arizona, and came back here to The Rez. Well, she and Jack met up, took a liking to each other, and they married. But Begay came back here to work on the roads one summer, and he and RaeEllen took off together.

"Anyhow, Marty ended up staying with Jack, and you wouldn't have known he wasn't his own kid. Never had any sons himself, so I guess that's why he fought so hard to keep that kid. And by the time—"

I cut Uncle Donnie off. "Look, none this stuff is Marty's fault. He was a kid. He can't help who his parents were, or who raised him."

"No, it's not his fault; didn't say it was. But one summer, Allan quit partying long enough to persuade RaeEllen to give their marriage another chance. Well, she did, and they decided they wanted Marty back. He was a big-sized kid by then, maybe six or seven. Anyhow, Jack wouldn't give him up, so Sam Waters says…they used to be neighbors, he and Jack. And he would hear them arguing:

"'I told you before. I've had it with this swamp, and with your spying and trying to control everything I do. I'm not coming back to you, Jack Turner. I'm taking my kid and don't you try to stop me. Marty, go and get your things!'

"'You go wherever you want, but don't take the boy, please. What kind of life can you offer him? For his sake, I'm begging you, RaeEllen!'

"She laughed: 'Jack Turner—with some of the most powerful medicine in Indian country, who can call up the spirits to do his evil work—is begging?'

"'RaeEllen, Allan won't quit partying long enough to drive to town and back sober, let alone to Arizona. He's making a fool of you, so you're not taking the boy!'

"'He's my son—not yours!'

"'I'm more his daddy than that drunken skirt-chasing pig you ran off with. Go on, get out, RaeEllen. Meet your lover boy, if that's what you want. But take Marty, and I'll make both of you wish you'd never been born!'

"But one day," Uncle Donnie continued, "she and Allan secretly scooped up Marty after school and snuck him back to Arizona—Tsaile, I think. Allan soon hit the bar scene again. By then, RaeEllen had fell into that life, too. They would leave little Marty alone for days at a time—scared, hungry, wandering from house to house for food.

"Anyhow, news travels in Indian country, and it got back to Bitterroot. Next thing you know, Allan's mind is gone. Even till now, I hear, he just sits, drools, rocks back and forth, talks to himself—and screams at things nobody can see except him. After that, RaeEllen took Marty and hid out, scared to death of Jack!"

"Why?"

"Medicine—it's what took Allan's mind!"

I rolled my eyes to the ceiling: "Oh, here we go. It was probably the alcohol."

"Nope. It was Jack's medicine. That's what took that Navajo's mind!"

I shook my head and sighed. "Is there a point in this somewhere?"

"Point? Yeah, there's a point. Allan's mama is Apache, but his daddy was a Navajo. A witch, too—like Jack. *That's* the point. He didn't have

Jack's powers, but who knows what he might have taught the boy? So Marty could be into his grandpa's stuff *and* Jack's stuff; and since you're half Christian, don't you get involved with either of them!"

"You're making an awful lot out of Marty's just giving me a ride home."

"Yeah, well, that ride is just the beginning. Sam says it was Jack who put medicine on his toe, 'cause he got drunk and beat up one of Jack's sisters he was messing around with. Now Sam's sick all the time." He jabbed the air with his forkful of cabbage for emphasis: "It's Jack's medicine!"

"Oh, stop it. Sam Waters lives off Spam sandwiches and mayonnaise, drinks way too much, and doesn't take his medication as prescribed." With more bravado than belief, I continued: "Besides, they say that medicine—curses—are only in the mind. They can't work unless you believe they can!"

His eyes held bridled fury. "Is that what they teach you in those nursing classes? Then they don't know what they're talking about! The spirit world is *real*. Bad medicine is *real*. Powerful. Terrible. Every true Indian knows that!" He spoke around his mouthful of cabbage and chicken without meeting my eyes. "Besides, I've heard—other things."

"Like what?"

He riveted his gaze on me. "Think hard on what I'm saying to you. Why would your mama leave without saying anything?"

I shrugged. "Who knows? She just up and left. Like Mama Hat."

His eyes narrowed. "She left 'cause she was scared to death of Jack's powers!" He sopped the last bit of chicken drippings with a corn cake.

"But what would he have to do with my mother's disappearance? I don't think she even knew Jack Turner. At least, I never heard her mention him."

He continued on his own trail. "Marty's a mighty good-looking fellow. Full Indian. Unlike Jack Turner—one-eighth White, I hear; not enough to call his honesty into question, as they say—but look at his nose. Narrow. Turned up like a White man's. And up close his eyes have got green and gold sparks in them. And his hair's got a little fire in it. He won't admit to it, though. And you. You are a beautiful girl, Dina. You and Marty would make some real good-looking kids together."

My face flushed hotly. "What are you talking about? One minute you're telling me to stay away from him, and in the next you have us making babies together!"

"What I'm saying is, if he has medicine you may *try* to stay away from him, but get drawn anyway, into whatever he's into!"

I was thoughtful. "I'm getting conflicting messages from you. Do you or don't you believe in—this—stuff; believe that it has power over us?"

"Yes as an Indian Way Indian, and no as a Christian."

I cleared the table. "And since when did you become a Christian? I've never once in my life seen you in church except on first Sundays for the fellowship meals. And during holidays to eat and socialize. And flirt with Martha Bowlegs."

"Hmmmph." He was silent for a long moment. "What about The Strut? I came for *that*, didn't I? Participated in it."

"What strut?"

"The Second Annual Alley Cat Strut—that cat contest fundraiser to renovate the fellowship hall. Cost me a lot of money."

"How so?"

"That twenty-dollar entry fee, for one thing. And it took me a whole month to get Eddie Was ready. Bought him all kinds of high-class cat food, shampoos, and creams. Had him looking good, too."

"And how long ago was that—three, four years ago? And I just wonder. If that department store hadn't pledged a new television set to the winning cat's owner, would you have been interested in any alley cat pageant?"

He was pensive. "Eddie Was would've won that Strut, too, if he hadn't bit the judge and got D-Qed. Guess he didn't like some strange old White woman looking in his mouth."

I threw up my hands. "Okay, you helped build the fellowship hall with your twenty-dollar entry fee in a competition for rescued scruffy alley cats. And other than that?"

"Hmmmph. Well. At least ol' E.W. got his picture in the paper." He paused, and as usual when he was trumped, he deftly changed the subject. "Like I was saying, they *made* us go to church when I was in that Indian boarding school. Well, they may have made me a Christian on the outside," he chortled in victory, "but, for sharpshoot sure, I stayed Indian on the inside. So that makes me only *half* Christian. Like Cheha. Like you."

"Then that would make you only *half* Indian, too. Right?"

As usual, he would not admit he was trumped. "Doesn't work that way," he mumbled.

More Donnie Jumper logic. I shook my head. "Look. You can't be half Christian. You have to accept Jesus Christ as your Savior and give up everything in the Indian religions. It's all or none." I paused, wistful. "I almost made the profession of faith once, a long time ago. Never quite got around to it, though."

"But you went to church, so you're half-Christian," he insisted. He pushed away from the table, went to the refrigerator, and filled his glass with ice cubes and water. "Me, I'll die believing in the Indian Way." He took a swig from his glass. "But just to be on the safe side, I keep Jesus as a backup just in case, aaay." He was thoughtful again. "From what I hear, He got a bad rap, but He wasn't a bad fellow, though. Not a bad fellow at all."

It would not do any good to argue with him, I knew. Long ago I had learned just to mentally switch channels. "Tell me what you heard about Mama and Jack Turner. If something was going on between them, I have a right to know. If she was scared enough of him to run, there had to have been a reason."

He kept his eyes averted. "Maybe it's just talk. If you stay away from Marty and don't get involved with Jack, you'll be all right. Remember that." He drank deeply from his glass: "Ahhh, good water." He then went into his room and shut the door.

I banged loudly. "This isn't fair. You can't leave me hanging like this. Please, Uncle Donnie, tell me what you heard. Uncle Donnie!"

I kept it up till finally he turned up his ancient black-and-white television set so loud it drowned me out.

The telephone rang. I stifled the angry tears from my voice and picked up. "Hello?"

"Look, something came up." Shania's voice was urgent. "I won't be able to hang with you tomorrow like we planned. There's some important stuff I have to do."

"What kind of stuff? Is everything okay?"

"Uh, sure. I just have to go and pick out a new pony."

"A car—for yourself?"

"Yep. Isn't it exciting? No more broken-down Indian nags for me!"

"Yesterday you were hitting big brother up for gas money and tomorrow you're buying a car. Okay, who is he?"

"Can't say. That's part of the deal."

My anger flared. "Oh you and Uncle Donnie and your secrets!" I slammed down the telephone.

A few minutes later it rang again. I answered sourly. "Yeah, hello?"

"Me again. What did you say about Uncle Donnie?"

"Nothing, really. I was just upset. Look, I'm sorry I overreacted about the car. It's just that he says he heard something about Mama. Some kind of relationship between her and some guy. Then he just left me hanging."

Shania was silent.

"Hello, you still there?"

"Yeah. It's probably just talk. Look—uh—I have to go."

This time *she* hung up.

IV

Ghost Town Spirit

Isat silently in the crowded waiting room at the clinic, weary and short-fused after two rounds of helping the nurses coax Uncle Donnie into the examination rooms. Each year it was the same scenario. First it was for his physical: "Not getting on that table. There's things you folks do to a fellow that's not natural!" he said to the nurse.

He was no more cooperative with the ophthalmologist who dilated his eyes: "I just needed new glasses. Now I'm blinder than I was when I came in here!"

Well, it was nearly all over for another year, but I was still a bit peeved as I sat there in the waiting room. I was already tired and bleary-eyed from my studies the previous night and from searching through the journals for something—anything—that would shed light on a possible relationship my mother may have had with Jack Turner. But I did not uncover one clue. Zilch. Nothing. Zero.

Sometimes, I mused, taking care of my mother's older brother was more difficult than my studies and all the other drama in my life combined. There was no question that I dearly loved my uncle—he was the dad I'd never had.

But there were times when I could not help but wonder: *what does life hold for Dina Youngblood?* How much longer could I deny the pent-up dreams that shouted, leaped, laughed, and danced inside me, begging to be free; the dreams that did not include The Rez, The Root, or, I thought guiltily, even Uncle Donnie?

With Mama gone, I even entertained the notion of moving back into her house. I could drop by periodically to check on Uncle Donnie. After all, I'd never meant my stay there to be permanent in the first place. He'd had a crisis once, so I'd moved in—temporarily it was supposed to be—to care for him. Well, he got used to the attention, and each time I broached the subject of moving back to Mama's, he'd do something to set himself back.

Then, too, there was the problem of the owls: two of them. Whenever I came to Mama's, they came. And when I left, they would eye me until I reached the corner, then flutter away. I never saw where they came from; they were just *there.* When they left, I never saw where they went; they were just suddenly gone. So there had to be something to the Traditional Indian belief that associated owls with the ominous, I figured, even though my mainstream logic resisted.

In Sunday school, Reverend Ward had said that Jesus had power over all such things. But it had been a long time since I'd had anything to do with church, so I no longer had a sense of belonging in that setting; and even though I attended through most of my teen years, somehow I never got around to making the profession of faith.

Looking back, it was around the time that Mama stopped going to church that I slacked off going to Sunday school. I had no clear memory of exactly why or when I quit. One day I just woke up and realized that I had not been in a while. Although I believed overall what the church taught, the Indian belief system was my heritage; yet, I both denied and feared its power.

I also felt like a traitor in abandoning the beliefs of my ancestors; and my Traditional friends I grew up with never let me forget it.

"You church guys are sellouts. That's not our culture. Christianity is the White man's religion. The Bible is the White man's gospel!"

Those brave enough to make the profession—most of them, anyway—usually returned quickly to the Indian ways. So, spiritually, I was not stable in the beliefs of either culture.

"Miss Youngblood?" The voice cut through my thoughts. "He's all done," the smiling young Asian-American nurse said.

I quickly switched channels. "Was he a good boy today?"

She winked and smiled. "Well—I'd give him a C minus."

Uncle Donnie waved off the staff members dismissively and mumbled something under his breath. He adjusted the dark shields the ophthalmologist recommended for his dilated eyes and headed for the door. It would do no good to chide him for his behavior, I knew, because nobody could change Donnie Jumper's mind once he had it set and there was no way to stop him from having his say. It was easier just to placate him I figured, while at the same time softening him up for the really big item on my hidden agenda.

"Why don't we stop off for some lunch? You like McDonalds. How does a Big Mac and a diet Coke sound?"

He took the bait. "Throw in fries and hot apple pie, and you got a deal, aaay."

Once at The Golden Arches we made our selections, I forked over the cash, and we sat by the window.

"So, how'd it go?" I tried to sound off-handed as I sipped my orange juice and unwrapped my more modest hamburger.

"They do the same thing to you every year—got no respect for a fellow," he said as he dug into his feast. "First they make you pee in a cup. Then they stick you." He held up his bandaged fingertip. "After that, they poke and prod; won't say where."

I cleared my throat. "It's—uh—for your own good."

I ate in silence and agonized over how to broach the subject again. Just as he was polishing off the last of his fries I bit my lip, garnered my courage, and gave it a shot. "Uncle Donnie, suppose you had, say, a dad, granddad, or brother, and she left home…"

"She?"

"Well, he, she—doesn't matter. But, say, somebody you knew had some information that might provide some answers. You would go to that person and ask, wouldn't you?"

"If the person was a true friend, you shouldn't *have* to ask," he said as he gestured with a forkful of hot apple pie.

"Then you're saying that they should offer the information of their own free will?"

He was headed straight for my snare.

"Unless the information would hurt them; get them into trouble," he said.

"But if the person asking is level-headed and responsible, not prone to doing anything rash…"

"Can't ever be sure what a person will or won't do," he said. "If you love them, you protect them from things that would hurt them." He licked his fingers, wiped his mouth and hands with his napkin, and emptied his tray in the trash can without looking at me. "Thanks for the lunch. Let's go."

Once back in the car, he rolled down the windows. He leaned forward, fanning himself, and doing what he did best: directing. This time from behind those big black eyeshields: "Stop sign coming up."

"I see it, Uncle Donnie."

We drove on in silence until we reached the intersection a couple of blocks from home.

"Now, when you get to the light, wait till it turns green before you make that right."

"I've told you; you can legally make a right turn on red. In Florida, it's the law!"

"And I've told you before, it's a *stupid* law, aaay. Red means stop—period!"

I sighed. "Uncle Donnie, I know how to drive. You taught me, remember? And I know the way home!"

Another week slipped by. I sat propped up in bed, trying to study for an exam, but my spirit was in turmoil and my obsessed mind kept returning to the journals hidden in my bottom drawer. For all of my searching, it seemed I was no closer to the truth than when I'd begun.

Also there was Marty, and that exhilarating lightheaded surge I felt every time I saw him or thought about him.

But he was a Traditional, and one more than likely deeply involved in witchcraft. I, meanwhile, was at a crossroad, wavering between the religion of my heritage and the Christian faith as preached by Reverend Ward, the White pastor of Hope for Tomorrow Independent Indian Church: "All Indian religion is animistic—rooted in superstition and demonic spiritism. It causes you to live in fear and doesn't offer you peace. It cannot deliver you from evil, because it is in and of itself, evil. Only Jesus can save you from a burning hell!"

I accepted that simply and without question as a child. But because I wasn't involved in Indian practices or witchcraft, I had felt no urgency to pray the salvation prayer or to be baptized.

And things became even more complicated as I grew older, when, one by one, most of my few Christian friends defected; when Christianity began to seem more and more like a pretty dress one wore to church but took off when the service ended. Too, there was Hope for Tomorrow's unstable congregation—about thirty total, largely women—and even they filtered in and out. Their families and friends were, for the most part, either non-Christian or infrequently attending members who came on first Sundays for the fellowship meals and to socialize with friends.

Church-sponsored holidays were also big crowd pleasers for Christians and Traditionals alike: there was the Christmas pageant, loosely organized, with lots of food and presents for the kids; the egg hunt on Easter; and on Thanksgiving the community meal. Afterward, however, the crowds faded until the following year. Then the cycle would repeat itself.

I sometimes thought Church of the Revolving Door would be a more appropriate name. And it raised Reverend Ward's ire:

"You can't practice Indian Way religion and Christianity!" he would bellow from the pulpit and pound his fist on the lectern. "And how many of you people are still hanging out and dancing and drinking at the Swamp Rats Tavern? If you're doing the same things you did before you got saved, then you're in deliberate rebellion against God!"

So those who still attended Green Corn, participated in other Traditional ceremonies, or stopped off at the tavern felt like hopeless sinners and drifted even farther away, until trouble hit. Then they'd show up at church for prayer. Tearful. Repentant. Promising to serve the church better. They would then attend for a few Sundays straight—more than a month would be a record. Afterward, they would almost invariably drift away again as they continued to walk in two worlds.

It could be argued that, within the confines of Traditional Native principles, one takes only what one needs for now, and no more. Sometimes I thought Indian Christians carried that belief over into church attendance also: come only when you have a need; otherwise, don't bother God. Or the church.

But now and then, they came for other reasons. Like one Sunday when a group of strapping Rez men—four of them to be exact, plus Tobias Tigertail's teenage son, together nearly a ton of Red humanity—rumbled into Hope for Tomorrow. They sat shoulder-to-shoulder in the folding chairs on the back row.

The few regulars suspected trouble, so they nervously shifted in their seats and stared straight ahead; for only the most intrepid dared to hold the gaze of the formidable row of unsmiling Traditionals. It was well-known that Reverend Ward, with his blazing John the Baptizer's eyes and his thick shock of coarse auburn hair, hated all Indian Way practices. Some even thought he hated Indians—and drunk Indians in particular.

Anyhow, the word was out that he was delivering a series of sermons on moral living. Today's subject, everybody knew, was on the evils of alcohol; and these Traditionals, Tigertail especially (whom, it was rumored, drank heavily and occasionally beat his wife), took offense.

Reverend Ward, clueless, was only too happy to see his sparse congregation bumped up by five unfamiliar Native faces—and men, yet. The attendees were scarce enough in number, even on holidays. So when he spoke, he was smiling from ear-to-ear. "Stand up and introduce yourselves," he said.

Tigertail all but leaped to his feet, hitched up his pants over his generous paunch, squared his shoulders, and fairly bellowed out his response: "Tobias Tigertail. And this is my son, Mackenzie." He also introduced his friends, then sat ceremoniously, his beefy arms crossed over his chest. Waiting. Looking for an opening.

Reverend Ward launched into his "Evils of Drinking" sermon, citing among others Proverbs 20:1: "It states here *specifically* that wine is a mocker!" This time he banged his fist several times for emphasis, and his eyes blazed. "This isn't my word, people; it's *God's* Word!"

Tigertail nudged his son and gave him the signal. "Go."

Mackenzie raised his hand. "Uh, Pastor?"

Reverend Ward's face lit up. "Yes, young man?"

"Uh, doesn't it say in, uh…" He faltered and glanced at his father.

"John, chapter 2," his father whispered behind his hand.

"Doesn't it say in John, chapter 2, that the first miracle Jesus performed was turning water into wine?"

"Yes, it does *say* that, but..."

"If it's true that drinking any alcohol is a sin, then wouldn't that make Jesus a sinner, who was causing all the other people at the wedding to sin also?" Mackenzie shift-eyed his father again, who by now was convulsing with suppressed laughter.

"Look at that White-eye's face!" The elder Tigertail snickered to his friends.

Reverend Ward's face had reddened. He nervously popped a Kleenex from a nearby box and dabbed the sudden beads of sweat from his brow. "Oh, don't *misunderstand* me, son. Jesus *never* sinned—uh, why don't you come to Sunday school next Sunday? We'll fully explain—"

"But if drinking *any* alcohol is a sin, then isn't that what you're saying?" the boy asked.

Tobias Tigertail elbowed his friend. "Looks like a White-eye can't even tell the truth from the pulpit, aaay!" So great was his suppressed laughter that, by now, tears flowed down his round cheeks. His cronies snickered loudly also, and there was so much buzz going on afterward, both pro and con, that whatever else Reverend Ward said was lost in the din. After the service ended, I noticed on the way out that somebody had turned backward the picture of the blond-haired, blue-eyed, rosy-cheeked Jesus that had hung in the vestibule for as long as I could remember.

The story made the front page of *Indian Herald:* "Mackenzie's Question Stumps Preacher." A posed picture of father and son grinning triumphantly accompanied the article. Next to it was a file photo of a fiery-eyed Reverend Ward. A sidebar stated, "Indian religions evil, Ward says." After that, the church's attendance dropped even more.

By the following summer, however, the small Christian population was finally buzzing again with excitement. For the first time in three years, the Creek Indian evangelist, Aaron Burning Rain, was coming back to The Root. It was July, I was in my late teens, and everybody in my circle had a boyfriend. Except me. Because by then, I was caring for my Grandmother, MaryJim, almost around the clock and taking her to dialysis three times a week. So I was ready for anything that would break the monotony—even a revival meeting. And who knew but that maybe some good-looking guy could be in that entourage.

Every night for a week the evangelist thundered the message of the Christian gospel. By the second night, the word was out that this Creek preacher was saying that Jesus was not a White man, and therefore not just the White man's God, and that the gospel He taught was for everybody, not just for his own people. So maybe that old saying was true: that God made man in His own image, and that man, the White man, in this instance, anyhow, returned Him the favor, because the only Jesus we knew had pale eyes, blond hair, and rosy cheeks.

Anyhow, Tobias Tigertail and two of his cronies came to see if any truth lay in this odd rumor. They sat on the back row, as was their custom, and leaned forward, as if evaluating every word. It seemed it was the first time they—like most Traditionals—had ever heard that Jesus was not a White man, as they had assumed, and that maybe His gospel was not just for White people alone.

Burning Rain was telling them, "Jesus was a Jew, an olive-skinned man, dark-haired and brown-eyed, like you and me. He belonged to a tribe, like you and me—the tribe of Judah. His earthly ancestors descended from tent-dwellers, much like those of us who lived in the tipi. And, my beloved brothers and sisters, His Gospel is not just for the White man. The good news of salvation is for everybody!

"Romans 3:23 says, 'For all have sinned, and come short of the glory of God.' But, my dear Indian people, you don't have to die in your sins and go to hell. Just step forward. Pray the prayer of salvation. You can walk away tonight—cleansed, redeemed, saved!"

I took him at his word that summer. Even though I did not know of any sins I had committed, like lying, stealing, cussing, or boyfriend stuff, there was something in his voice, something in those sincere and blazing eyes that made me not want to say "no" to this Creek preacher, something that kept urging me to walk down that aisle and receive this salvation he said Jesus promised. So I stood up and took a tentative step.

But without warning, out of nowhere, a Fear, all but palpable, overshadowed me. A voice in my head began urging me, "*Don't do it,*

Dina. Turn around! If you try to walk The Jesus Way, you won't be Indian anymore. And if you fail at it, you'll be worse off than before. You do not really know this God. So it is best not to anger Him!"

Burning Rain seemed to sense my dilemma, for his eyes were riveted to mine as, trembling, I sat back down in that folding chair.

"Don't be afraid," Burning Rain said. "Let Jesus take control of your life. And if you stumble, get back up. Remember that we all fail at times. But you can always repent—come back. Jesus will forgive you. Beloved children, He knows we are flawed and weak!"

Despite those reassurances, however, I could not will myself to come forward.

His next words were nothing short of a plea: "Don't reject His gift of eternal life. He died for you so you won't have to go to hell. You could drive away from here tonight and get creamed by an eighteen-wheeler. There is no guarantee any of us will see tomorrow! Listen, young Indian people. Don't think that only old folks die. The reservation is the only place in America where funerals for the young equal funerals for the old—deaths out of season. From suicide. Drug overdoses. From alcohol-related traffic accidents, and from murdering one another!"

But it was what he said next that all but froze my heart in my chest as his finger panned the room: "This may be your last chance, you—and you—and you. Don't put it off. Your eternal life may depend on the decision you make here tonight!"

Young Mackenzie's attention was focused on the evangelist's face that summer, and Tobias Tigertail fidgeted in his seat as one by one his two cronies went outside. Through the open tent flap, one could see them smoking, pacing. At length they ground their cigarettes beneath their boots and returned. Their faces were wet with tears. Neither met Tigertail's eyes as they came to the altar. One, crying out in repentance, fell prostrate; the other to his knees. Burning Rain knelt and took the hand of each as they rose to their feet; and like a father welcoming errant sons, he embraced both as they shook with sobs, made the profession of faith, and accepted Jesus Christ as their Lord.

Tigertail's face clouded at this defection. By now, he was sweating profusely. His eyes darted about like those of a trapped animal. But he did not go up.

Burning Rain's words of warning echoed through my head: *"This may be your last chance, you—and you—and you..."*

His last "you" seemed to sear my very soul. I did not want to go to hell. I wanted this bronze-skinned, dark-eyed Jesus, who had black hair, was tribal, and who loved even Indians to save me and to love me...like He did White people. Who knew, but that perhaps one day He would show us favor, too? Maybe He would even make the Whites give us back what they stole.

My heart was drumming so hard I felt almost faint as I stood to my feet once more. But as I took that step forward I froze again: this time, through a maze of people in folding chairs like mine, toward the pulpit, from the corner of my eye I glimpsed a figure—an old woman in an Uncle Joe hat, with many strands of beads around her neck, who wore a Seminole patchwork skirt and was barefoot, as was the Traditional way. Her eyes, two smoldering sparks of charcoal, burned through mine. She leaned slightly forward, staring, as if she knew me.

Mama Hat? But how could it be? She had disappeared a decade ago, yet the heart of this old woman—if indeed she were a woman and not a ghost—seemed to speak to mine: *"Did you come to forsake The Indian Way and receive the White man's gospel like your mama, Cheha, did?"*

I pushed my way toward her through the throng. But by the time I reached the place where she was seated, she had vanished.

Time ran in reverse. The echo of drums was in my head; and just as when I was a child, I could see Mama Hat in her regalia and her delicate steps as she and the other Traditionals circled about the powwow grounds. I could even hear the applause again as the crowd of largely White onlookers viewed the dazzling spectacle of the Parade of Indian Nations....

Then as quickly as the memory-dream appeared, it vanished. Still slightly dazed, I left the crowded tent and navigated my way to where the folks clustered at the back. There was a smattering of White people, a few Blacks, but mostly people from the Native communities: Big Cypress, Tamiami Trail, Immokalee, Brighton, and, although it was not a federally recognized entity, the Bitterroot Confederacy of Indians.

Once outside, I searched through throngs of those who arrived too late to get a seat, got too hot and needed fresh air, or were standing

40

around, just looking on. It was then that I saw Tobias Tigertail rush out of the tent too, and leap into his four-by-four. His voice was testy. "Fine—you can just walk home, then!" he said to young Mackenzie, who stood in the tent doorway. Tobias then fired up the behemoth engine and roared away. Apparently, to his father's disappointment, Mackenzie had decided that he wanted to hear the rest of Burning Rain's message.

It was then, just at that moment, on the outskirts of the clusters, that I caught another glimpse of the old woman; my heart leaped with anticipation. I wove my way toward her. But again, by the time I made my way to where she had been standing, she had disappeared into the throng. I wanted to call to her, but my voice froze in my throat.

From the inside, I could still hear Burning Rain's thundering voice, imploring, warning again of the damnation to come for all who did not repent: *"Don't walk away. If you deny Jesus before men, He'll deny you before the Father!"*

By continuing to follow the Mama Hat spirit instead of making the altar call and formally giving my life to Jesus, wasn't I doing just that—denying Him?

"Evil spirits exist. They are real. They have a lot of power. But all power is given to Jesus Christ in heaven and on earth. And it is He who gives us the strength to resist their workings in our lives." There were now tears in Burning Rain's voice. "Hear me, my people! Won't you say 'yes' to Him tonight?"

I wanted to. How I wanted to! But even as I picked up my pace, Burning Rain's pleas followed me as I headed for home. Perspiration beaded on my forehead. I did not want to admit it to myself, but I was really scared to commit to Jesus. What if I failed, as the voice had warned me? But I was also scared not to. So my life was given over to Fear. And owls. And the ghost of a great-grandmother long gone.

By the time I turned the corner on the home stretch, I was no longer walking. I was running. And Burning Rain's words pursued me: *"Only Jesus can save you and give you peace. Don't run away!"*

I was seventeen then—over three years ago. But after that night, I'd had nothing more to do with religion. I had failed. Walked away, in spite of all of Burning Rain's impassioned pleading. Surely Jesus would have no use for me now.

So profound was the impact of that night that, even now, I couldn't bear to walk down Mama Hat's street anymore. The bougainvilleas had grown rampant, and her tiny house with boarded-up windows was now nearly obscured in their bramble embrace. I never told anybody what I saw—or thought I saw—at that last revival meeting. And until now, I'd tucked that memory away in the cobwebbed recesses of my mind...

It was now nearly eleven o'clock, I discovered, as I glanced at my watch. I shuddered. I had not been able to focus on my studies, so I folded the few notes I managed to take from my distracted and sporadic reading and slid them inside the *Nursing Care* text on the table next to my bed.

It was a warm, muggy night, so I turned down the air conditioner as low as it would go and lay restlessly in bed, consumed by my obsession to uncover the mystery of my mother's disappearance.

And suddenly the idea hit me. Why had I not thought of it before? What did I have to lose? It would be a last-ditch act of a desperate daughter, but what could Jack Turner do if I simply called him up and flat-out asked what the deal was between him and my mother?

Across the hallway, Uncle Donnie was snoring gently as I eased open my door, tiptoed down the hallway to the telephone, and quickly looked up several Jack Turners in the telephone directory. Wrong numbers. Each of them. The last was listed simply as *J. Turner.* When I rang the number, a girl answered. "Speak," she said simply.

Shania's voice—unmistakable!

"Mr. Turner, please," I said in a muffled whisper.

"It's for you," she called out.

I hung up.

V

Patchwork, Rainbows, & Hummingbirds

"**D**ina, it's me—open up!"

The knock on the front door the following morning was loud and insistent. I sprang awake and glanced at my clock. Only seven-thirty.

I rubbed my eyes, padded to the front door, and peeked through the curtain. Clad in a brightly hued Seminole patchwork jacket and blue jeans, Shania glanced at her watch and paced back and forth with her usual edginess and impatience.

"Who is it?" Uncle Donnie hollered hoarsely from his room.

"I have it," I called back as I opened the door. "Shania, what's up?"

"I'm on my way back to Broken Bow, and I didn't want to leave without saying 'bye to you and Uncle Donnie. Oh, and I want to give you something." She swept inside, carrying a paper bag, and simultaneously rifled through the snakeskin purse flung over her shoulder. She withdrew a substantial wad of bills from her wallet and pressed them into my hand. "Now you can't call me selfish anymore. Sorry we didn't get a chance to hang out, but do something nice for yourself, big sister. Tribal Bingo dividends get pretty thin by the middle of the month."

I stood there goggle-eyed. One hundred dollars. In twenty-dollar bills. "Wow—thanks. But where'd you get this? I mean, a couple of days ago you were all but the FBI who couldn't afford feed for the pony."

Her face brightened. "Speaking of ponies, step outside, please, so I can introduce you to my new filly."

I followed her into the driveway. She had left the engine running and the candy-apple-red Mustang purred gently.

"A two-year-old with only twenty-two thousand miles on her." Shania mimicked her brother's jargon as she slapped the car's hood.

I suppressed my suspicion. *Courtesy of J. Turner?* "Really nice," I said as I folded my arms across my chest. "But tell your big sister what's going on."

Shania glanced again at her watch. "Maybe next time. I told Aunt Bett I'd be back Thursday night. I'm running late, I don't want her to worry, and I want to say 'bye' to Uncle Donnie."

She dashed up the steps, into the house, and by the time I caught up, she was already in Uncle Donnie's room, sitting on the side of his bed.

"It's been such a long time. Stand up and let me see you," he said.

Shania drew herself up full height and stood there beaming, smiling down at him.

"Hardly look like yourself under that butchered General Custer hair. But you're still pretty. Still a beautiful Indian girl."

Shania pranced about. "I agree—glad you think so too, 'cause I'm going to be the first Native American supermodel. And I have something for you, also." With a flourish, she withdrew another wad of bills from her wallet. "This is for my Uncle Donnie. You go and buy yourself something nice."

She kissed his craggy cheek, then withdrew a bag of Snickers candy bars from the paper bag. "I suppose you can have one once in a while. A friend gave them to me, but I'm not into candy bars anymore. Have to watch the cals." She laid the candy on his nightstand and glanced at me. "I know he's diabetic, so make sure he doesn't pig out."

A friend gave her Snickers. Why Snickers? I wondered. I tried to appear casual. "This friend—is he anybody I know?"

She smiled and shrugged. "Maybe. But I doubt it."

Uncle Donnie raised himself up and sat on the side of the bed. He counted the bills, stared at them momentarily then wedged them beneath his bed lamp. "Ump. A lot of money, aaay." He looked up and motioned her to sit. "Why you in such a hurry? Sit down. Eat something. Dina, go fix her some breakfast."

"Oh, no, no, I can't stay. I left the engine running," she said.

"Then go turn it off. You need to eat something. You know we

Indian men don't like our women too skinny."

She flashed her pearly smile. "But rich White guys do. That's one of the reasons I'm going into modeling. There's big money in it. Later on, I'll probably move on to acting. I'm going to be on the cover of *BP* magazine. And a rich White guy would have the cash and the connections to help get me there."

"A rich White guy," Uncle Donnie mused. "Well. They usually prefer the she-Custer types, don't they?"

"In acting and modeling, it doesn't matter so long as you're skinny and pretty."

He sighed deeply. "Well, that you are. But the type of man you want will grind up a *tay-koo-che* like you and spit her out like a sugar-cane chew."

"Cut it out with that Mikasuki talk. You may as well wear an Uncle Joe hat and say 'ugh.' And stop worrying. I can take care of myself. And I'm not a *tay-koo-che*. I'm a young adult. An emancipated minor, if you will."

Uncle Donnie raised his eyebrows ever so slightly: "Ump. Big words, aaay."

"Show him your new pony," I said. If she wouldn't tell me its origin, maybe Uncle Donnie could wrangle it out of her.

"So, a new car, too." He sat in silence and deep thought, and at length took the wad of bills, studied them briefly, and stuck them back beneath the bed lamp.

Shania's eyes seemed to be pleading for him to accept the cash but to ask no further questions.

His reply sounded resigned. "Well, your Uncle Donnie is glad you got a job that pays a decent wage." He then got back in bed, turned his back, and pulled the covers over himself.

"Don't you want to see it—my new car?"

"Later. I'll see it next time," he said.

Shania stifled the sudden tears that sprang into her voice. "Okay. Later, then. And watch for me—I *will* make the cover of *BP* someday. I *will* be a model or a movie star!" She was quickly out of the door. Her bright jacket held my gaze as I watched her pause only long enough to give Eddie Was a fond scratch behind the ear. Then her long legs conquered the distance in easy strides. She swung into her new pony and pulled out of the driveway.

Gone. Again. So quickly. To be the first Native American supermodel. Or movie star. And to make the cover of *Beautiful People* magazine.

She was just like a hummingbird. Or a rainbow. Dreamlike in beauty, appearing at whim in our lives, staying only long enough to briefly dazzle our senses, but forever beyond our grasp.

Rainbows and hummingbirds were like that. You could not summon them to appear, could not dictate how long they stayed. In their brief moments, you simply enjoyed them; for when they were gone, they were gone.

I pulled my nightshirt around me tightly, sat on the front steps, and Eddie Was leaped on my lap and purred gently. I stroked him absently, remembering the scraggly, starving, little four-legged that had shown up on our doorstep so many summers ago.

Shania was a tongue-tied six-year-old who helped nurse him to robust health. He had no name then. He was simply The Cat.

When Shania got into mischief, as she frequently did, she would usually blame The Cat. And Mama would scold her: "He couldn't have done it. The Cat was nowhere near!"

Her "yes he was" lisped out as, "eth he wath!"

Shania's rendition morphed into Eddie Was, and that became his name. It seemed a hundred years ago. And like those years, the pretty little girl with the bright brown eyes and round chubby cheeks quickly disappeared, too, like so much smoke. In her place an untamed beauty sprang full-grown from the flames—a she-creature who did not seem in any way related to my little sister. Sometimes it seemed as though a stranger were wearing her face.

But when it came down to it, did anyone really know anybody else? Mama Hat—what made an old Rez grandma run? And Cheha Youngblood...apparently the fact that she was my mother was the only facet of her I was privileged to know for, like Mama Hat, her heart evidently had many secret places—unexplored lagoons hidden in tangles of mangroves, sawgrass, and cypress trees.

And Donald Jumper. Who was he, really? Did a young man just go to sleep one night and wake up an Uncle Donnie? Were there dead hopes and dreams enshrouded within that weathered flesh? And what of regrets—how many did he entertain? And in the blackest part of night, did he ever desire a woman anymore?

I heard him stirring in the house. Duty was calling me. It was time for his breakfast—his oatmeal. And time for his medication.

VI

Painted Horses

A couple of days later as I was walking home, JohnnyHawk rumbled over to the curb, reached over, and opened the door.

"Hey, hop in before you fry."

"Thanks. It must be a hundred degrees today." I climbed in and tossed my bookbag on the back seat. Once the pony was moving, however, the cross ventilation through the open windows provided some relief. Still, I fanned myself with my hands.

"This is a solemn promise: with my first paycheck as a nurse, I'm buying myself a car. Brand new," I said.

"What—with this kind of service?" JohnnyHawk said with mock incredulity. He glanced at me sideways. "So, how's school?"

"Tough. Just came from the library. I have a test tomorrow, and I couldn't find a book I need."

"Ah, you'll make it all right. God looks out for do-gooders." He spotted a smoke shop. "I'm going to pull in for a pack. You want something?"

I reached into my purse. "Maybe a Coke? And as an aspiring nurse, I recommend that you quit smoking."

He waved away my dollar bill. "Hey, I'm not Rockefeller, but I can buy my sister a soda," he chided gently. He ignored my cigarette warning, pulled onto the blacktop, and threw up a salute. "B.J. How's it going?"

The proprietor flashed a broad-faced smile from the open window of the single-wide trailer. "Can you do something about this heat?" He tossed him a pack of Winstons.

"I *like* it hot," my brother said and fished a five from his jeans. "And throw in a Coke for my sister."

B.J. exchanged the merchandise for the five and handed over the change along with a flyer through the window. "Have a good one."

JohnnyHawk tossed the change into a tray on the dashboard and glanced at the flyer: **REVIVAL** screamed across the top of the yellow sheet. He regarded it casually: "Since when did you start advertising The Jesus Way, ol' pal?"

B.J. shrugged. "Some lady from the Indian church came by and offered me five bucks to hand them out," he replied as he idly stuck a toothpick into his mouth. "Looks like they're having that Creek fellow down here to preach again."

"Tall guy—big—like a pro linebacker?" Johnny Hawk asked.

"Yeah. Him. Looks like an oversized Tonto. Wears a lot of beadwork. Bolos and belt buckles and stuff. His wife used to make them. I remember her selling them at the powwows before she crossed over."

"He really draws a crowd. Did you take the five?" JohnnyHawk asked.

"What five?"

"You know. From the church lady. The five."

B.J. waved his hand dismissively. "Nah. If people want to go hear him, I figure, hey, if that's their thing, rock on. I'm a businessman. I have to keep good relations with the whole community."

"I hear you, pal."

JohnnyHawk scanned the flyer. "Yep. That's the one. He was here two, maybe three years ago. Burning Rain. Now, if that's not a hellfire and brimstone name for a preacher, I don't know what is." He looked up at B.J., and a twinkle was in his eye. "Let me ask you something. Suppose this Burning Rain fellow starts telling folks that smoking will send them to hell. Would you still pass out his flyers?" He let loose a loud belly laugh as he pulled away.

From the rearview mirror, we could see B.J. dismissing us with a good-natured wave of his hand as his round face broke into a laugh also.

"Can I see that?" I reached for the flyer.

REVIVAL
SOUTHSIDE ARENA
July 15-19 * 6-9 p.m.

AARON BURNING RAIN, EVANGELIST
*Testimonies *Gospel Singing *Fellowship
*All Are Welcome
Salvation is FREE!

In spite of the sweltering heat, I was suddenly shivering. Aaron Burning Rain. The evangelist that thundered damnation for the unchurched and the unrepentant—the night I pushed through the crowd to give my life to Jesus…the night I turned away to chase the Mama Hat ghost. Aaron Burning Rain was coming back.

JohnnyHawk was talking, but I was so focused on the flyer and my thoughts I was not even aware when he pulled into Uncle Donnie's driveway.

"…I hope he won't be too mad at me. But work keeps me busy, and I just don't have time to visit him like I ought," he said and was quickly up the steps and into the house.

Uncle Donnie, having espied us coming, stood holding the screen door open, a wide grin on his craggy face. Eddie Was twined around his feet.

I gave my uncle a perfunctory greeting and headed for my room. My old Fears were resurfacing, and I was feeling queasy. I popped open the Coke and took a slow swallow. Maybe it would settle my stomach. I set the can on the nightstand, tossed the bookbag, and threw myself across the bed next to it.

Why the edginess? I could not figure. After all, if I did not want to go to hear Burning Rain preach, nobody said that I had to. I remembered Rev. Ward saying that only 5 percent of Indians are Christian anyhow; so what would be so unusual if I remained in the other 95 percent—could God condemn us all?

Besides, the Traditionals said you could not be a real Indian and a Christian at the same time. And according to the more radical of them—Marty included—to adopt the White man's religion was the ultimate betrayal of an Indian's heritage. In fact, one of his editorials in *Indian Herald* I had clipped and read over and over so many times I could recite it almost word-for-word:

Some accuse me of hating the White man. I do not hate him. I hate his arrogance and his lies. I hate his brutality and his treachery. He is an illegal occupant in this nation. He came to us with a Bible in one hand and a rifle hidden under his coat in the other; but the God of these invaders from Europe and the gospel that they brought with them are for their people, the White people; for they alone have benefited from it. The word gospel is supposed to mean "good news." But to the aboriginal peoples of this continent, the words in that black book came through deceitful lips that brought only darkness. The end of our nations. And death to our people. And if there was ever any good in his original intent, the innate greed of this marauding and predatory race soon overshadowed it—so thoroughly that his real objective became genocide—to wipe us from the face of the earth. Why? We did not look like him, or speak his words, or believe as he did, because we did not know his God.

And we had something that he wanted: Land. Gold. Our natural resources. All of it. But we would not give it willingly, and were splintered and powerless to defend it. We prayed to our gods, but even they were weak before his. So these brutish and rapacious invaders simply wrested what they wanted from us with the force of their evil and destructive weapons. And they wrote the history of this illegitimate nation in our blood.

We had great wisdom but no technology. He had great technology, but lacked both wisdom and compassion. For wisdom does not deface the earth, does not misuse its resources, decimate its peoples, or wantonly destroy its creatures.

So knowing all this, you Indians who call yourselves Christians, how can you believe that the White man's God regards your souls as equal to theirs before Him?

And therein lay my conflict: the church preached that God created all people and that Jesus died so that all may have a chance at salvation. Yet, the tragic history of our nations was hewn in stone and forever in our faces.

The telephone rang. I snapped out of my reverie and padded down the hallway to answer it.

"Dina—Marty. Got a minute?"

"Sure. What's up?"

Immediately my queasiness left. My edginess left. My tiredness left. The raging diatribe that exploded from the newspaper was quickly but a distant echo, and I was instantly wrapped in the aura that engulfed me every time I heard his voice.

"I need you to do me a favor. Can we go someplace where we can talk? I'll pick you up. You eat yet?"

I tried to answer in a matter-of-fact tone. "No, I just walked in."

"Good. I'll come for you in a few minutes."

Gone were the doldrums and Uncle Donnie's dire warnings. I borrowed Shania's courage: wasn't I almost twenty-one, and wasn't it way past time I started choosing my own path? If Marty were only a fever, then it would have to run its course. Besides, he was Panther, I was Otter—different clans. So what was the big deal about us seeing each other?

I hurriedly laid fresh jeans and a crisp white shirt across the bed and was immediately in the shower. Close to waist length, my wet hair was heavy on my head. I would have to cut it soon or it would cause headaches—at least, that was what some of the elders said.

I dressed quickly, lightly powdered my T-zone and smoothed on lip gloss; neither Marty nor I liked a lot of makeup. And the more I anticipated seeing him, the more my heart thundered with excitement...but also a sense of Dread.

Other than to write scathing letters to the editor, I wondered what else he did all those years after we drifted apart. No doubt he knew lots of girls. Was I only one more silly young woman who drooled over his classic good looks and trembled in the excitement of his nearness?

Yet wasn't life about taking chances? If I couldn't take care of myself now, when would I? I would just have to be careful and not get drawn into anything.

From somewhere outside, Uncle Donnie's sullen voice sounded. "She's inside. Go knock on her door."

I slipped on my sandals and glanced at myself one last time. Could Marty hear my heart drumming all the way down the hallway? Before he could knock, I opened the door; and there he was—tall, firmly muscled, with newly cropped hair just past his shoulders. He was freshly-scrubbed handsome—no, Male Beautiful. What other words could adequately describe Marty Osceola? But he was so focused on his life's mission he did not even seem to realize that he drove women crazy.

His clear dark eyes oozed over me like warm honey.

"Looking good, Indian woman." He flashed that disarming smile, and that dimple in his left cheek added to his individual magnetism and mystique.

"Thanks," I said. "Not bad yourself."

But my throat was dry, my heart was pounding, I felt lightheaded. Giddy. Was this what love felt like, or was I, as Uncle Donnie had warned, under his spell? Because right then I would have thrown myself in front of a freight train if he had told me to, for I had no power over myself: *Run, Dina, my reason warned me. Run!*

Marty's eyes seldom left my face as we sat in the booth, straining to hear above the din in Chickee Choices Indian Restaurant. In the span of two hours, we had gone from being long-lost childhood friends to his toying with my fingers, my hair.

"So, do I get an answer tonight?" he asked.

"Let me think about it," I said. "An international forum newspaper sounds like a good idea. Who knows? Maybe it could unify all the Indian nations—connect us together. But I have my schoolwork, Uncle Donnie, and this business about my mom's disappearance. It bothers me a lot. I don't see how…"

"Talk to my dad. He may be able to help you find your mom."

"Oh—how?"

He sort of shrugged and avoided my eyes as he spoke. "He has his ways. Talk to him, okay?" He was kissing my hands again, muddling my thinking, so I deftly withdrew them.

"Thanks, I'll keep that in mind," I said.

Uncle Donnie's hint of a relationship between Jack and my mother began to nibble in earnest at the edges of my consciousness. But right then, the tingle of Marty's touch and those smoldering eyes sublimated everything else.

He reached over and took my hands again. "Just give me the okay, and, hey, I'll ask him for you myself, if you want."

I seized the opportunity. "I was wondering if he told my sister anything. I heard they talked, that they were uh—friends, or something like that? And…"

He released my hands then and his voice was incredulous. "What? Shania and my dad friends? Who in the world told you that?"

I shrugged. "I just heard some—uh—rumors. It's probably just talk." I took a sip of *sofkee* to disguise my nervousness. "But tell me, how did you get to call Jack your dad since he really isn't? I mean, why do you call him that?"

He was pensive for a moment. "He always insisted on it. And I've always felt that he was. Whatever was on the stove or in the fridge—I never had to ask for. If I needed shoes or clothes, he was the one who took me shopping. I got in trouble a couple of times as a kid and he was right there." He lowered his eyes as he continued. "He told me a few days ago that he felt cheated when my folks took me because it caused him to miss that time watching me grow up. I never saw a man who wanted a son more than he did. He even wanted me to have his name, but Mama dug in her heels on that one.

"So, if caring about a kid like me the way Jack did—and still does—is what being a father is all about, then I'm proud to call him my dad. But what you heard about him and Shania, that's not a rumor. That's a tall tale, to put it kindly."

We both sat in silence for a long moment before he spoke through a sigh. "Well, I hope you'll consider working for the paper, Dina. It's for the survival and empowerment of all Native people. Just think. Indians will have a chance to become a commanding force again—not just splintered bunches of tribes and nations, many depending on scraps from the White man's table for their existence. We can be greater and grander than before. There is a lot you can do for this project." He took my hands again. "And for me."

The heady feeling was too much; things were happening too quickly. The red lights in my brain were blinking frantically, so I deftly withdrew my hands once more and shifted the conversation:

"Look, over there. It's B.J., my brother's smoke shop friend."

Marty glanced over. His face clouded. "He's a scourge, like all Indians that sell tobacco, and all the White scum that sell liquor to our people. They're only helping to cut our lives even shorter for a few filthy dollars!"

I shrugged. "Don't be too hard on B.J. He's a businessman. Supply and demand. Maybe it's all he knows how to do."

"Then I say it's time he learned some other way to make a buck!"

"If people really want to smoke, they'll find a way. I mean, it's legal. So if not through B.J., they'll buy from somebody else," I said.

The cheeriness left his face then and he pondered the comment for a long moment. "I think I'll have a cup of coffee. How about you?"

"Sounds good." I opened my purse. "Look, we've been running up quite a tab. I don't mind…"

He placed his hands over mine. "Two things you should never worry about when you're with Marty Osceola, pretty Indian woman—money and time. Because whatever I have is yours, too." He signaled the waiter. "Two coffees, please."

The eyes of the young waiter with the scalp lock hairstyle were awestruck. "Yes, *sir*, Mr. Osceola. Two coffees coming up."

As we awaited our orders, I sat back in the booth and just studied Marty. I noticed then that he was not wearing a watch; and because his arms were evenly tanned, I speculated that he probably did not own one. So, as he said, with him, there was no worrying about time.

The waiter placed our cups of coffee on the table and his starstruck eyes never left Marty's face. "Anything else, Mr. Osceola? More gator nuggets, fry bread, some dessert?"

I patted my stomach. "Not for me. Another bite and I'll bust out of my jeans."

As the waiter retreated, Marty gazed at me with a soft smile toying at his lips. "You would look charming with a big belly—the kind that lasts for about nine months. Maybe soon we could work on that?"

I blushed. "Don't start that, Marty."

He leaned back in the booth, still smiling softly. "Stop it, why? I'm talking marriage, Indian woman, not just hanky-pank. I'm talking Mr.

and Mrs. Marty Osceola."

"We're nowhere near that stage in this…renewed friendship after all these years. People have to have a lot in common before they start talking about the M word."

"I believe any marriage can work after any span of time if you want it to. You just need to stay faithful and give the other person their space. It would be hard for anything to go wrong in that."

"Faithfulness and lots of space aren't the answers to everything that can go wrong between two people in a marriage."

"How would you know? You've never even had a boyfriend." There was an amused twinkle in his eyes. "Now, don't look at me like that. Virgin of Bitterroot." He laughed and kissed my hands again. "Right?"

I withdrew them. "You've done a pretty good job of prying into my life. And I can't say that I appreciate that."

"Marty Osceola never has to pry. He has other ways of finding out what he wants."

"Let me guess; you send owls to spy on me," I said.

"Of course. They do whatever I ask them to." His deadpan expression was soon replaced with a burst of laughter. "I wish you could see your face right now."

I didn't know whether to take him seriously or not.

At length he signaled the waiter with the scalp lock hairstyle again. "Hey, Nightrain, my lady wants to take her *sofkee* home. Be *extra* careful with it."

"I understand, Mr. Osceola. I'll take real good care for you." He scurried off and returned with a lidded Styrofoam cup that was wrapped securely in a foil-lined bag. "That'll keep it nice and warm. Anything else, Mr. Osceola?"

"Not tonight," Marty answered. He paid our tab, left a tip, and the young man grinned with wide-eyed appreciation, as though beholding royalty as we left the café.

"So. Since when did you become 'Mr. Osceola' around here?" I asked as we walked across the parking lot to the truck.

His response was nonchalant. "He's a young kid—looks up to me. I know his family."

"So you're like a big brother. His idol."

56

His taffy-stretch grin revealed a clan of even white teeth that glowed brightly against skin bronzed more deeply by the sun. "You got it, Indian woman—like a big brother."

He gave me a boost into the truck. "Up you go. White man's manners." He was again smiling that Marty smile and softly dismantling my resolve, eradicating my reason and my common sense with effortless efficiency. And there was nothing I could do to stop it.

Uncle Donnie's bedroom light was still on even though it was well past midnight when Marty pulled into the driveway, switched off the ignition, and turned to face me.

"Well, we practically spent the night together and you still didn't give me a firm answer," he said.

I had to do something with my hands so I opened the *sofkee* and took a sip of the still warm corn drink.

"Look, I did okay in writing in grade school, but for an international newspaper like the one you want to launch—I don't know if I have the confidence for that," I said.

"Oh, quit doubting yourself. You have the skills. Let me worry about the confidence, and let's team up."

"I don't know, Marty. I'm distanced from all politics and religion right now. I've read some of your opinion pieces in *The Herald,* and they were written with fire. Thunder. Conviction. Certainly not by a lukewarm fence-straddler like me."

"But your calm voice can bring balance and be just as effective, so long as you get the point over. We have to wake the people up. We have to find a way to establish a society where we take care of one another. The rich tribes—we have to convince them that they have a moral obligation to help eradicate the grinding poverty on some of these reserves.

"Besides, when you ask people for their money, you have to ask softly. Eloquently. You can do that. I can't. You can speak words almost like you were reading a poem. White people—the ones that sympathize with us and support us—they like that."

I raised my eyebrows. "More scraps from the White man's table?" I asked with a wry smile.

He threw up his hands. "Okay, okay, score one for Dina. I know there are some...well...okay Whites out there. I guess my point is, we shouldn't be totally dependent on their handouts."

"Got it," I replied. "But I'm just an ordinary Rez-Root girl. I don't speak poetry. Your dream is too big for me. And my concern is that only a few firebrands like yourself will be convicted enough for action by reading your paper. The folks I know who get community papers are interested only in who got married, who had a baby, who died, and when's the next powwow."

"Then we few firebrands will have to wake them up." He gripped the steering wheel. "Yes, the dream is big, Dina. We *need* big dreams—something other than our common misery to unify us.

"But you can dream big too, if you take the shackles off your imagination and say 'no' to your unbelief. There has to be a Native Martin Luther King somewhere out there. Your words can rouse him from his apathy and his silence and wake up the greatness in him. Then we can follow the pattern of the African-Americans and not give up until we throw off the last vestiges of bondage from our necks.

"And we can't do that unless we think and act as one, like they did. They didn't hold on to their African tribal identities. They became *one people*—a powerful political force!"

Even in the half-light, I could see the resolve in his brushfire eyes.

"I met Minister Khaleed-X of the Second Nubian Nation at the annual Rally of the Non-white Peoples a couple of years ago," he continued, "and every fiber of him exuded confidence and strength as he stood there on that podium—tall, eloquent...like a carving from ebony wood. The very air around him was electric when he spoke:

"'...and so, my brothers and my sisters, with your beautiful skins of yellow and black and red and brown, I say to you: stand tall. Be proud. Everything is yours now, everything for the taking. The day of the White man's tyranny over your lives is over—forever!'

"The people must have applauded for twenty minutes after his speech," Marty said as he relived the memory. "I went up to shake his hand, and later when we had coffee together, I discovered that the Second Nubian Nation has powerful communities—their own hospitals with state-of-the-art equipment, staffed by some of the nation's most skilled physicians and surgeons, all people of color. They have their own schools, farms, grocery stores, universities, banks—everything. Right here in the U.S.A. But they accept nothing short of excellence from themselves.

"They apprentice their young people from an early age. They don't ask the Whites for *anything*. They don't walk among them, or seek to learn their ways; and I thought, *If only I, or somebody, had the kind of power to unify the Indian people!*"

Marty's entire being was now pulsing with energy, his hands animated. "We, on the other hand, are Apache, Seminole, Creek, Cherokee—scattered remnants, shadows of our former glory as powerful nations. I say, let's do away with these divisions and be known as one people—*Indian*. Then we too will again have strength as a people within this nation and on this continent.

"It's time we all came together, Dina, as one. If Little Big Horn taught us anything, it is that if we stand together we can *win*. He stretched out his hands, then clasped them: 'Fingers spread apart are hands. Clenched together, they are fists!' I need you, Dina, to help me rally the people!"

I sighed. I did not have the heart to tell him that I had no place within this grand design. "Okay, Marty. I promise I'll think about it and let you know." I checked my watch. "It's late. I have a test tomorrow and I have to read over my notes."

He took the cup from me and placed it on the dashboard "Dina, would you look at me, please?"

"Marty, it's getting really late."

"This won't take long. When I told you that I watch you and tonight when I mentioned marrying you, I wasn't just kidding around." He smiled softly. "I could have let you win one of those footraces when we were kids. I wanted to. But it would have ended the competition and my chance to be near you. I've always loved you, Dina. And I'll do whatever I have to do to win you."

"Please stop it, Marty." I clasped my hands in my lap so he couldn't see that they were trembling.

"You must hear me out. I admire you, respect you. You're the only woman who can be my companion, my lover, my friend, the mother of my children—our children. You are what I need in my life—your stillness, your intelligence, your beauty, your commitment to something other than yourself."

"Don't do this to me. It isn't fair. It's too soon. I have to go. I really have to go!"

"I'm not playing with your feelings, Dina. I wouldn't do that. Please trust me—I wouldn't!"

"I have to think about this, Marty." I placed my hand on the handle of the door.

"All right, all right. You have to go. But finish your *sofkee*."

He took a sip from my cup. "It's a toast to make our love grow big and strong," he said, smiling, and handed the cup back to me.

"All right, so long as it's love that grows and not my waistline," I said lightly and drained the cup. "There. Satisfied?"

He smiled. "*Very* satisfied." He pointed toward the light still on in Uncle Donnie's room. "Well, looks like I've kept you up way past your curfew. But think about what I've said. Give us a chance. I know I travel a lot. But from now on when I go, I want you with me. I want you to be a part of everything I do." He kissed my hands and smiled again. "Have-um *chickee*. Need-um squaw."

"Now who's being a caricature and a stereotype? You're making me *On-na-hak-bee-pek*, Marty Osceola."

He brightened. "So you speak some *Mikasuki*—hey, that's great. But your problem is that you're resisting what you feel for me. *That's* what's making you crazy. I love you, pretty Indian woman. But you're afraid of me, and I would never hurt you."

All I could do was sit there studying him in the dimness. There were so many stories about Jack Turner's command over the dark powers—and the common belief that Marty was heir to it all. And if it were true, could I walk the narrow bridge between the two worlds and not fall into that darkness or, better yet, could I lead him out of it?

Finally he threw back his head and laughed. "You think too much, Dina Youngblood. Why does my past matter? When a day is over, it becomes like a shadow—a dream that you remember. Yesterday and tomorrow are just words. There is only *now*. Let's live the rest of our moments, whatever we choose to make of them, together—you and me."

I sighed. "That's a lot to throw at me so soon. But I promise I'll think it over. Thanks for the evening. And give me my garbage." I took the empty cup, stepped out of the truck, and started toward the house.

"Dina?"

I turned to face him.

"Do you know what I dread the most?"

I shrugged. "Death? Most of us don't like to think about that."

He shook his head. "A good death is desirable. What I fear most is dying without my being here on earth ever having mattered—without having done anything to better the condition of the Native people. I need you, Dina, for meaning in my life, for the children I leave behind that must come through you to carry on the struggle."

Without any further words I hurried away. I could not explain my tears that came without warning. I scaled the steps quickly and the screen door squealed on its hinges as it slammed behind me. Uncle Donnie, empty water glass in hand, stood in the kitchen doorway. I dried my tears and avoided his eyes as I swept past him.

"He's got you crying already. I told you he was no good," Uncle Donnie said as he followed me into the kitchen. "What did he do?"

"Nothing happened, Uncle Donnie!"

"I may be an old man, but I can still handle myself. I can still kick butt if I have to. If he ruins you, I'll drop-kick him over the moon!" He refilled his glass with water and ice and shot a scornful look as Marty's tail lights retreated into the night.

"I'm not a *tay-koo-che* anymore. I told you, nothing happened. I can take care of myself."

He waved me off and went to his room. But he tossed one last warning over his shoulder: "Whatever that boy told you tonight—don't believe a word. All lies. He's a troublemaker and a rabble-rouser. And remind me tomorrow to oil the hinges on that screen door." He then took his glass into his room and shut the door after him.

He would never understand. I tossed the Styrofoam cup in the waste can and headed for my room. And I wondered: how could I concentrate on my studies with all the stuff going on?

As I kicked off my shoes and began to unbutton my shirt, a sudden inexplicable tiredness, a weariness I had never before experienced literally crushed me in its heaviness. With the last of my ebbing strength, I crawled into bed fully clothed.

"Lie still. They are coming," a small voice whispered. I sensed that I was smiling.

My dress was dazzling white, the intricate patchwork designs also iridescent and brilliant in their whiteness. I tried my best to feel the grass beneath my bare feet, but I was suspended in air, wafting just above it.

In the distance, several horses—each mottled with the same prismatic colors that changed as they moved—galloped toward me.

The rider, his bronze skin clear, shimmering, translucent, sat astride the most spirited of the paints and soon outdistanced the two more docile colts. As they approached, the riderless horses grew smaller and smaller, and faded into the background until I could no longer see them.

The rider—Marty, and yet he was not—was shirtless, shoeless, and riding bareback; he was clad only in shimmering white trousers with a drawstring at the waist; but instead of shoulder-length hair, this dream-Marty's flowed past his waist and streamed behind him like fingers of ebony silk in the wind. As he neared me, oddly, his horse suddenly grew flaming red.

This strange Marty was laughing and rode around me in a circle, teasing, taunting me. I laughed too, but it was a nervous, frightened titter; when I looked down, my dazzling white dress had turned as red as that spirited steed.

The rider galloped away then returned. This time, as he neared me the horse was a dazzling yellow, as blinding as the sun, and so was my dress. He rode away again. And again.

Each time he returned, his horse was a different color. This time it was a shimmering horse as black as pitch. And my dress changed accordingly.

I cried out: "Why do you keep making me change—don't you like my dress?"

He did not answer. His mare reared up on her hind legs and all the colors raced across her, rapidly changing like in a dream sequence.

When I looked down to see if my dress reflected the same shimmering hues, this time I was standing there stripped bare, as a giant shadow descended from the sky. The great wingspan shut out the sun as the owl-creature soared toward me; lightning shot from its eyes and ripped across the sky. Thunder shook the earth. Giant drops of rain and hail pelted me.

Terrified, I sank to my knees and screamed out, "Marty, make it stop!"

He galloped toward me, threw back his head and laughed, then turned around and rode away again, his horse's hooves kicking up clumps of turf. I lay there curled in the fetal position, trying to cover myself, ashamed, too terrified to open my eyes, while the storm raged around me.

But as suddenly as it appeared, the gigantic owl creature shot upward and disappeared into the now brilliant sky.

A death-stillness then settled over everything. When I opened my eyes again, I was once more clad in the white dress; only now it was soiled. Filthy. A rainbow, with different shades of gray, arched across the now clear sky. I scrambled to my feet and ran after Marty. But he only laughed and charged toward that strange rainbow, with those ribbons of raven silk streaming behind him. If I did not catch up, I would be left alone in this forsaken place.

"Marty, don't leave me here—wait!" I cried out. I ran until I had no more strength or breath left, but he never once looked back and his laughter faded with him into the horizon.

Somewhere in the distance hammering—knocking—shattered the silence. Did somebody besides me exist in this forsaken place?

"Hello, is anybody here?" I called out.

Silence.

Then, suddenly, the earth shook; icy rains drenched me. I dug my nails into the ground and held on. And somewhere in the distance somebody was calling my name.

"Dina, Dina, wake up! Open your eyes!"

Through the haze that separated the real world from dreams and nightmares, Uncle Donnie gradually came into focus. He was prying my fingers from the mattress.

Icy water drenched me again. "Wake up, Dina—can you hear me now?"

I reached out. "Marty, come back—please. Don't leave me here!"

It was my voice, yet it was somehow detached from me, disembodied, coming from someone else.

Uncle Donnie nearly collapsed with relief. "You're awake—back with us!"

I struggled to raise myself up and sat on the side of the bed. Cold rivulets streamed from my hair, down my face, and formed a puddle beneath me. I brushed away a smattering of ice cubes and wiped dripping strands of hair away from my face.

Uncle Donnie stood in front of me holding a pitcher, water still trickling from its lip, a few ice cubes still inside. "I've been trying to wake you up for fifteen minutes! Are you all right now?"

My confusion lifted, but I was still gasping for breath. "You didn't have to drown me," I murmured. "I—guess I had—some kind of nightmare." I trembled uncontrollably so Uncle Donnie rushed for a blanket and wrapped me securely.

"Nightmares happen at *night*. It's three p.m. You've been sleeping all day. I thought you were in school till I heard you screaming!"

"Oh no, my test. I missed my test," I said.

He tilted my face upward and impaled me with his piercing gaze. "Tell me where he took you. *What did he do to you?*" It was the first time in my life that my uncle had ever yelled at me.

"We just went out to eat—to talk. You have to believe me. That was all!"

He grasped my shoulders and shook me. "Did he give you something? Peyote, liquor, drugs?"

"No—no! Don't blame Marty, he didn't do anything!" I pressed a trembling hand to my forehead. "Maybe I'm coming down with something." I rose unsteadily to my feet. "I want to go to the bathroom."

Once done, I threw more cool water on my face, then sat there on the bathroom floor with my face buried in my hands.

Marty's words oozed through my memory: *"Drink your sofkee—it's a love toast."*

Was it possible? Everything in me rebelled. Marty would never put anything in my drink. No matter what people thought of him, I just knew in my heart that he was telling the truth when he said that he would never hurt me.

Would he—*would he?*

Still unsteady on my feet, I stepped cautiously into the shower and turned the water on as hot as I could stand it. Some of my tension and tingling numbness washed down the drain with the froth of Palmolive Gold.

Just as I was wrapping myself in a towel, Uncle Donnie knocked on the door.

"I made you some soup. Come eat. Get some food in your stomach. You'll feel better." The telephone rang and Uncle Donnie called out, "Get that. I got my hands full."

I made my way down the hallway and sat on the floor. "Hello?"

Silence.

"Who's calling?" I asked again, holding the towel around me with my free hand.

"Dina?"

The voice was soft but unmistakable. Blood pounded in my temples. My voice choked and was barely a whisper: "Mama?"

Another silence. "Cheha needs to talk."

I could hear an infant's faint cries in the background and voices—a woman's and a man's. Maybe I was dreaming again, hallucinating. But who else spoke of themselves largely as though they were on the outside looking in?

"Mama, are you still there? Where are you?"

She started to say something but again, hesitated.

By then I was almost hysterical. "Tell me where you are. Are you all right?"

"Cheha will call back," she said softly. "She—can't speak right now. Please forgive me, Dina." And she hung up.

I stood there momentarily, unsure of what to do. Still wrapped in the towel, I padded into the kitchen leaving wet footprints in my wake.

"It was Mama, Uncle Donnie. She's alive. She didn't say where she is but she's okay—she's alive!"

"Already knew that," he said without as much as looking back at me.

Barely able to contain my excitement and renewed hope, I made my way back down the hallway. "I'll stay close by. She said she would call back!"

He just kept on stirring the pot. "Cheha will come home when she's ready. You're a Youngblood woman. Deal with it, 'cause running's in your blood, too. And come eat some soup while it's hot."

"If only I knew where she was. Why would she *do* this to us?"

"She let us know by her leaving that it's not about us. It's about her. Wishing her back here may be rushing her into danger. We better listen to what those owls have been trying to tell us." He glanced at me. "Now go get some clothes on—walking around in the house like that. And come. Sit. Eat."

I dried my hair, donned a bathrobe, returned to the kitchen, and sat at the table toying with my fingers in deep thought.

"Uncle Donnie, is Mama running from Jack Turner? Tell me what you heard. I'm confused. I mean, knowing how much Jack loves Marty, I don't really see how he could be as—"

Uncle Donnie's eyes blazed. "Jack Turner loves Jack Turner. He had no sons of his own to pass down his evil to, so he used that boy. So you stay away from him." For the first time in his life he pointed his finger at me. "Leave it alone, Dina!"

"I won't leave it alone! Because you know something. I think you know exactly why she left. Something was going on between them, wasn't it? And you think you have the right to hold it back from me!" I waved my hands expansively. "After all, you're an exalted elder, and you think I'm too much of a stupid kid to handle the truth. Well, if none of the rest of you care what happened to my mother, I do. If I have to—to—walk through hell in gasoline underwear to find it out, I'll do just that!" Okay, the statement was childish. But I was mad.

He ladled soup into a bowl. "Well, gassy underwear or not, you keep nosing around and you just might end up in a hell of your own making. Now I know what I can do, and what I can't!" His voice softened. "I can't go any deeper—without going too deep. It's bigger than me. Bigger than you." He set the bowl down before me. "Now eat." And without saying anything more he retreated to his room.

I tried to, but I had no sense of taste, so Uncle Donnie's can of chicken and rice soup was like watery sand in my mouth. Tears stung my eyes. I was closer to Uncle Donnie than I was to anyone else in the entire world—even my own mother, though I loved them both. He knew this, knew how this whole thing was eating me alive, so how could he keep what he knew from me?

And my accusing inner voice spoke immediately: *"Like you are keeping those journals from him—and everybody else?"*

VII

Truth Crushed to Earth

The night skies were just giving way to the first blush of sunrise the following morning when I rolled over and turned off the alarm before it went off.

Mama had not called back. Uncle Donnie remained close-mouthed, and the journal lay right where I had left it before sleep overtook me.

By now I was skipping about in the notebooks and connecting time frames to see if anything she wrote offered any clue as to why she feared Jack Turner—or anybody else for that matter—enough to run.

I wanted to tell Uncle Donnie about Shania's being at Jack Turner's house, but somehow the time didn't seem right. Besides, why should I tell him? Wasn't he keeping what he knew secret? Resentment was building in me, so engaging him in further conversation only to have him to persist in being close-mouthed would only fuel the conflict that was now seething between us.

I switched on the light and continued reading where I'd left off the night before:

March 12, 1986
So sick in the mornings. Cheha's husband(!) and she are barely speaking now. Everyone on the Rez knows about him and her. With her flaming hair. But they are so busy with their gossip they are not looking at Cheha—do not know about her revenge against him and the fire-haired woman—and it is sweet!

Yet Cheha knows: the day will soon come when the sweetness will turn to bitter gall in her mouth and she will wish she had chosen a different path...

So my father was involved in this, too? I did not really remember him. He was a fable to me. A tall warrior chief—handsome, strong, with boundless love for his family. He had gone away to find work just like Mama said, and one day he would return. It would be like Christmas—and like when Uncle John used to come around, when there would be presents and feasting.

My child's mind never doubted why he left. And now this entry in Mama's diary had destroyed my concept of this mythical Indian man; had stripped away the Christmas paper in which I had wrapped him. Now, for the first time, I was faced with my feelings in the glaring light of reality. And what were they?

Rage. Suppressed rage. Raw and bitter in its starkness. Those were my feelings. He had left my brothers and me for this fire-haired woman—with my little sister still gestating in Mama's belly.

He apparently did not even care if we had clothes, shoes, or enough food to eat. Yet Mama never spoke against him to any of us. She just kept it all inside. As for this vengeance my mother spoke of—I could not even begin to speculate what it was. But whatever she had the courage to devise gave her a sense of empowerment. And it showed a dimension to her strength that I had never before observed through my child's eyes.

I heard Uncle Donnie stirring in the kitchen and glanced at the clock. Only 6:45—unusual for him to be up so early. Maybe he wasn't feeling well. I closed the journal, tucked it beneath the mattress, slipped into my bathrobe, and padded down the hallway.

He was pouring oatmeal into a small pot.

"How come you're up so early?" I asked. "You okay?"

He did not look back at me. "I'm fine. Want some oatmeal?"

"No, thanks. I still don't have much of an appetite. I'll probably grab something at school in the caféteria later on. I have class at nine. I'll say I was sick. Maybe they'll let me make up my test." I watched him as he busied himself. "I usually make your breakfast. You sure you're okay?"

He still refused to meet my eyes. "I feel fine. Just got a lot of things to do today. I figure I'll get started early before the sun heats up."

I sat with my elbows on the table and my face cupped in my hands. "So. What's so important that you're up before seven doing what you hate the most?"

His face was set as he stirred his oatmeal. "Rather keep it to myself."

A brief silence hung between us. "About last night when Mama called…"

"*You* don't know anything. *I* don't know anything. So leave it alone."

He poured the steaming oatmeal into a bowl, added sweetener, and pulled up his cane-back chair to the table. He blew on a spoonful to cool it down, took a careful mouthful, then continued to avoid my eyes as he spoke. "You need to quit seeing that boy."

"He's not 'that boy.' His name is Marty," I said. "And stop jumping to conclusions. We're just friends—for now, anyway. But I am meeting him this evening. It's about the paper he wants to start. And don't blame him about yesterday. He likes me a lot and I like him. He's really a nice guy. You just have to get to know him."

"Oh. And you think in your limitless wisdom that you do. What time are you meeting him?"

"Six-ish. He works in Rez housing—gets off around five."

"Cancel it. Call him up and tell him you can't see him."

"Why?"

"'Cause I have something I need you to do. So call him up and tell him. Now."

I threw up my hands in exasperation. "Will you please tell me what is going on in your head?"

He did not respond.

"This is getting crazier all the time. You know I don't mind doing things for you, Uncle Donnie. But why does it have to be tonight?"

"You'll know tonight when I tell you tonight," he said as he pushed away from the table. "Got to take care of some business first. I need to be in town as soon as the stores open."

"Alright, I'll call Marty. But he's going to want to know what's so important!"

"Not his business."

I glanced out of the window at the old truck—after nearly a year, it was still propped up on cement blocks. "Why don't you get that thing fixed? It would sure beat walking—or having to borrow JohnnyHawk's old clunker. And I wouldn't have to take the bus to school."

He rinsed his bowl. "Indians walked long before trucks and horses were around. And don't talk down about Indian cars, calling them clunkers." There was a hint of levity in his voice: "They're part of our culture—the Native experience. Like Rez dogs. Besides, walking is good for you. Makes you strong. Clears your head. Gives you time to think. And another 'besides' is that they want too much money to fix that truck. All it needs is a new starter. And some tires."

"Ask JohnnyHawk. Or FrankE. They should know where to buy used auto parts. And tires—some retreads."

"Might have to do that." He poured himself a glass of ice water and drank deeply. "Ahhh, water. Good for you." He set the glass on the counter. "And remember what I told you. Tell that boy you can't see him tonight. Do it now before you forget."

He closed the door after him and I stood at the window watching as he turned down the street toward town.

I called Marty, but he had already left for work. He was probably still en route, so I left the message with the housing secretary. Back in my room once more, I turned listlessly through the pages of the journal. And suddenly something caught my eye.

There, scribbled on the margin next to a November 1978 entry, a telephone number leaped out at me:

New number—555-7809—Need to call HIM.

Immediately I compared it with J. Turner's number in the telephone book. Bingo. Confirmation. Just as I thought. One and the same.

The mystery guy.

Mr. Terror himself. He whose soul was consumed by darkness had so filled my mother with Dread that her only recourse was to run.

Now I would have to confront Mr. Terror and meet him face-to-face. He was the only one who could tell me what I needed to know. Mr. Terror owed me some answers. And whatever it cost me, I would demand them from him. The timing? TBA...

"Thanks for the ride," I said as Sheila Marston's Beetle pulled into the driveway that afternoon after class.

"What are friends for?" she said. "And hey, don't forget the book you wanted to borrow. It's on the back seat."

"You saved my college career," I said. "They didn't have any more copies at the library. And I'm also lucky they're letting me make up that test I missed."

Her blue eyes sparkled as she spoke. "It's mine from last term. *Hated* it. And now it's yours to enjoy!"

I waved as Sheila's school-bus yellow Beetle disappeared down the narrow street. I tossed the mail—the telephone and gas bills I collected from our mailbox—onto the kitchen counter.

It was a little past three and I had just enough time to make dinner, get dressed, and finish all that Uncle Donnie had lined up for me to do. Maybe I would even study if this constantly unfolding drama did not consume all of my time.

It was unusual for his door to be closed during the day, so I rapped lightly. "Uncle Donnie, are you okay in there?"

"Uh, yeah," he said. "Just doing some reading."

Reading, Uncle Donnie?

This whole thing was becoming more bizarre all the time, I decided, as I took some cubed steaks from the freezer and placed them under running water for a quick thaw.

He had always been eager for his meals, but when dinner was done, this time, I had to call him twice. As the saying goes, there is a first time for everything; but more curious yet, when he finally did emerge, he closed his door behind him.

"So what did you buy today?" I asked as we sat at the table.

He avoided my eyes as he cut into his steak. "A book. Bought myself a book."

I leaned back and beheld him with awe. "Oh? What's the title?"

"It's a book. That's all. Need to read it to find out some things."

"*The How-To Book of Conjuring?*"

"I don't ask you about your books."

We allowed the brief silence.

"Well if you did ask me, I would certainly let you know. But I'm proud of you, though. Reading is the door to learning, they say," I replied.

"They taught me that in boarding school—how to read. They would beat the red off our hides for speaking Indian or praying our prayers, but they did teach us to read." He took a sip of the rice *sofkee*—the kind he liked best. "But remember that you can learn in ways other than reading. Like from the old ways by listening to the elders." His eyes held mine. "By listening to *me*."

"Okay, agreed. But when are you going to let me know the title of this book that's so interesting you got up early and walked all the way to town to buy? It isn't *Playtime*, is it?" I wiggled my eyebrows.

"*Playtime* is a shameful magazine. For a few filthy dollars, White men degrade their women and market them like you would sell a melon or a pound of hamburger. Glad they don't put any Indian girls in that piece of trash." He took his time before he spoke again. "You will know the title of the book in due time."

He quickly finished his supper, poured himself a glass of ice water, and headed for his room. "Don't be late getting dressed. We need to leave here by six."

I followed him down the hallway. "May I know where we're going, since I'm to be part of this great adventure? I mean, what do I wear—jeans, patchwork, old-fashioned Traditional?"

"You can wear what you got on if you want."

And not only did he close the door in my face; this time, I heard the click of the lock. So I knocked.

"Uncle Donnie, will you please tell me what's going on? You're not hiding Martha Bowlegs in there, are you?"

"I'm *reading*. And I don't want to hear anymore of your mouth!"

Some things you have to accept, I decided, but it was reassuring to know that in this house that was growing nuttier all the time, I was not the only one who was a bit *on-na-hak-bee-pek* around here.

I readied myself for the Great Escapade and, pouting, sat on the couch in the living room waiting for Uncle Donnie to emerge from his sanctuary.

At five sharp he was dressed: jeans, crisp white shirt, and those ancient ever-present alligator boots. The mystery package, wrapped in a brown Winn Dixie grocery bag, was tucked protectively under his arm.

The Book, I surmised.

"Let's go," he said, stern-faced.

I sighed. "Whatever you say."

Down the road we traipsed through Bitterroot, past the Seminole Reservation, in total silence. I noticed others either walking or driving in the same direction—too many to be a coincidence. Finally, at the edge of town, on the large vacant lot, the gigantic letters of the banner screamed out its message: *REVIVAL.*

I stopped dead in my tracks and shook my head. "Oh, no you don't. Uh-uh. I'm not going in there. Not this, Uncle Donnie. You can't do this to me!"

He ignored me as he proceeded into the giant tent.

Several huge fans circulated the air and provided some relief from the sweltering July heat. Assistants were still checking the microphone system: "Testing—one-two—testing…"

Uncle Donnie searched around for the ideal place to sit and chose the front row, smack in front of the pulpit.

"You could have told me. Why such a big secret about going to a revival meeting?" I asked.

"I didn't tell you 'cause you would have mouthed off."

"But why do you need me here? You go just about everywhere else by yourself."

"'Cause I need to know some things. And only the preacher can tell me. I figure since he's Indian, he'll level with me and tell me the truth."

"Great. *You* need to know something, but *I* don't need to know something. So why am I here?"

"You're here 'cause you're the one who's gonna go up there."

"I will not!"

"You will. You're gonna go up there for me and ask him what I need to know."

"Oh, great. *I* have to go up there and ask him what *you* need to know!"

He took a pack of Juicy Fruit from his pocket, popped a slice into his mouth, and handed one to me. Fuming, I took it and vented my quiet rage on the stick of gum.

The tent was gradually filling up. In spite of the fans, it was uncomfortably warm inside. I picked up a flier on the seat next to me and idly fanned myself. Workers from the crusade brought out more folding chairs and placed water coolers at the four exits.

When the tent was at about three-quarters capacity, a loud applause peppered with a lot of amens suddenly erupted from the back.

Aaron Burning Rain strode in and was just as I remembered him: tall, bronze, broad-shouldered, and yes, like a pro linebacker. Maybe there was a strand or two of silver at the temples of his hair, which he wore pulled back in a bun like Tonto of the Lone Ranger, that had not been there before and, just barely, a hint of a thickening of the waist since I saw him last. But he still wore his trademark beaded bolo and belt buckle. Actually, he was pretty good-looking. Some of the older single ladies were pretending not to notice, but I saw them secretly checking him out from the corners of their eyes.

Uncle Donnie nudged me. "That's *him*—the Creek fellow. Now, they say he can *preach*."

And preach he did. Just as I remembered. And if a man's voice could mimic thunder, Burning Rain's did just that. On and on he went about getting saved and accepting Jesus as your Lord. I spent much of the service glancing about to see if any of my old friends were there, and if any gorgeous guys were around. I was totally infatuated with Marty, but it couldn't hurt to look, I figured, for who knew which way this new relationship-of-sorts was going to go?

Burning Rain then began again to live up to his reputation and started preaching about dying and going to hell if you did not accept Jesus as your Savior. I began to fidget. Choosing The Jesus Way was no small thing—it took faith and commitment to stand in the face of criticism and sometimes rejections from the people closest to you. I had learned that in church. But after I had quit going, it became easier and easier to tuck The Jesus Way and dying and hell into the cobwebbed recesses of my mind.

I had lived a pretty good life, I figured, yet, all the preaching about hell was downright scary. I couldn't wait for this service to be over with.

When it finally did end and Burning Rain gave the altar call, I breathed a sigh of relief, because I felt somehow that God was impressing a message on my heart—some kind of calling that, if answered, would turn life as I knew it upside down. Right then, I was walking more the Indian Way…well, halfway anyhow…and I couldn't handle anymore disruptions in my life at the time. There was Mom, who had not yet called back. School. Uncle Donnie. And Marty, who was definitely *not* Christian.

Aaron Burning Rain stretched his hands out to the congregation: "If you want to receive Jesus as your Savior, just step forward. Don't look around to see what your friends are doing or to see who's watching. This is your time, your moment of decision. You don't have to die in your sins and go to hell. Say yes to Jesus *tonight!*"

His booming voice, amplified by the microphone, jarred my eardrums: "Jesus said that if you are ashamed of Him, He will be ashamed of you when He comes in the glory of His Father with the holy angels. Mark, chapter 8, verse 38, tells us that!"

Uncle Donnie nudged me. "Go on up. Tell him I need to talk to him about something."

I set my teeth. I would *not* go up there. And I would fix him for tricking me into coming to a revival meeting in the first place. I raised my hand.

One of Burning Rain's assistant's eyes brightened; he tapped the evangelist on the arm and pointed to me. Immediately the preacher's intense eyes rested on mine. "Yes, yes, come forward, young sister, and receive the Lord as your Savior."

But I pointed to Uncle Donnie. "My uncle wants to ask you some questions," I said.

Burning Rain whispered something to the assistant, who then came down. Now it was Uncle Donnie's turn to squirm in his seat.

Good. You put me on the spot. Now take a taste of your own medicine, I thought.

"If you tell me what your concerns are, perhaps I can be of help," the assistant said.

Uncle Donnie shook his head while holding the tightly bagged Mystery Book close to his chest. He pointed to Burning Rain. "I need to talk to *him.* In private."

The attendant rubbed his chin and pondered the words. "Well, the pastor doesn't usually have private conferences during revivals, and right now he's involved in the altar call."

"How long is that gonna take?"

"It's hard to say. There's a long line of folks. Tell you what—let me see what I can do, and I'll get back to you."

Uncle Donnie sat back in his seat, protectively grasping his treasure. "No hurry. We'll wait."

In a surprise move, Aaron Burning Rain glanced at Uncle Donnie and then at the assistant. "Brother Bushyhead, what does this brother need?"

Bushyhead, wearing a beaded bolo with the words *Cherokee Nation,* went forward and spoke in Burning Rain's ear.

I heard him say, "I'll just have to *make* the time, Brother Nate. I'll just have to make the time."

Uncle Donnie pulled himself up higher in his seat. "Learn this, *tay-koo-che*—when you want something, you have to keep on asking," he said with a triumphant ear-to-ear grin.

"Okay, okay, you win, you stubborn old redskin," I said. "And I'm a woman, not anyone's *tay-koo-che* anymore."

As the service wound down, I glanced about. Maybe the Mama Hat spirit had returned. But this time, it—or she—was nowhere to be seen.

I kept glancing about and fanning myself with the flyer. I spotted Mellinda Billie of Foot Racing days. I waved at her and several other Rez and Root friends. All of us once attended Sunday school together. And I hoped that would win points with Jesus, because we had all quit attending without any of us praying the salvation prayer, making the profession of faith, or being baptized. Yet after all of Aaron Burning Rain's impassioned preaching and threats of hellfire for the unrepentant, none of us heeded this altar call, either.

Our days of dusting the boys in footraces seemed a lifetime ago as I watched one of Mellinda's kids lying asleep across her lap. Two were fidgeting. Her swollen belly suggested that yet another child was on the way. Talk was that she and Mickey Sixkiller had split—they had never married, anyhow—and that he was now seeing some White girl in town, but apparently still came around often enough to father yet another little warrior.

So I wondered idly if she were here scoping the guys, too. None of the Traditional women would ever admit it, but in The Root, it was sort of common knowledge that a lot of them secretly wanted a good Christian guy. And if he were Indian, all the better. They made the best husbands because they were afraid of going to hell if they ran around or mistreated their wives. Of course, Christian guys varied too, so even with them, relationships did not always work out favorably.

The altar call was winding down, and Uncle Donnie began to shift nervously in his seat. What, I wondered, could be so important to him that he would attend a big tent Christian revival?

When we kids were small, Uncle Donnie sometimes attended Traditional observances like the Green Corn Dance. And there was a Pine Ridge Lakota guy, a friend of somebody's friend who was a *yuwipi* man—an *iyeska*—who interpreted the instructions of spirits that others could not understand, hear, or see. He visited the Rez and The Root off and on, and each time he created quite a stir.

During one of these visits, somebody sponsored a *yuwipi* healing meeting and asked the *iyeska* to conduct the ritual. Uncle Donnie, though Seminole, was also a pan-Indian idealist back then—always curious about the practices of other tribes. So he, Sam Waters, several of his friends, and some other local men decided to attend.

Maybe because the ritual was performed in the dark, with the *iyeska* wrapped, mummy-like, in the center of the room; or maybe it was because when the lights were turned on again and the *iyeska* was sitting and holding the blankets and ropes that bound him, claiming that the spirit beings to whom he prayed freed him, it was too much for Uncle Donnie.

I never knew what—Uncle Donnie was close-mouthed as to specifics—but something happened there, because the next time the *yuwipi* man came visiting, Uncle Donnie said he was busy and did not attend the ceremony. Whether or not he actually was busy, I do not know. But he never attended any such ceremonies again.

And from then on he did not actively practice anything. Whatever he believed, he carried around within.

Now, nearly a decade later, here he was at a Christian big tent revival meeting; so something really important, something remarkable, had to be going on inside him.

As I sat musing, I idly perused the flyer I had been fanning with. It was mostly pictures from former crusades with appeals for contributions to keep the revivals going.

But one picture caught my eye: a group of people sat in what appeared to be a rodeo stadium, with Burning Rain in the makeshift pulpit. An old woman sitting in the bleachers in the far corner, her face turned slightly away from the camera, wearing the Seminole cape, many strings of beads and a black hat could have been my great-grandmother.

I did not remember Mama Hat clearly. But did I need to? Gone was the signature pipe; but how many old Indian ladies wore Seminole clothes and an Uncle Joe hat? I folded the flyer and stuck it in the pocket of my jeans.

By the time I refocused on the present, Burning Rain was seated next to Uncle Donnie and giving him his undivided attention while the tall, rawboned Nate Bushyhead took over the altar call.

"I don't want to rush through anything this important," Burning Rain said. "Why don't we meet and talk tomorrow. There's a We-Hop restaurant close by, and…"

Uncle Donnie's face lit up. "Nope. No We-Hop. My niece here can put any cook to shame. So You-Hop on over to our house, and Dina here will have a good meal ready," he said, smiling, pleased with his clever play-on-words. "Frybread or *lapalee*—you choose. Or have both if you want. She can make *sofkee*, too—corn, rice, any kind you like. And I'm pretty sure I can get us some venison. And Dina here even makes good coffee."

Burning Rain laughed gently and raised a hand in polite protest. "Don't have your niece go through too much trouble." He patted his stomach. "I guess you can see by the looks of me that I'm close to carrying around my own spare tire. And a traveling preacher needs to be lean. Just some decaf would be fine. Caffeine keeps me up at night."

I resigned myself. I was part of Uncle Donnie's plans so I figured I may as well make good of the situation. In fact, there were some questions I wanted to ask the preacher, too, about owls and curses, social drinking and dating; specifically, I wanted his take on my seeing Marty, the son of a witch.

If things took off between us, would he tell me that I should give him up? I mean, I liked Marty. He was fun to be with. True, he was idealistic and maybe on the radical fringe, but wasn't what he wanted for the Indian people, and not for himself? So I was not ready to end our budding relationship, because I did not believe that Marty was the fearsome ogre Uncle Donnie and others made him out to be.

But my discussion would have to wait for a future date, I knew, because now was Uncle Donnie's time.

"Could you give me an idea as to what I can do for you, Brother Donnie? It would help me to focus my prayers as I prepare for you," Burning Rain said.

"Well, mainly, it's about this book," Uncle Donnie said.

At long last, I thought. *The Great Unveiling.* My eyes were glued on his eager hands as Uncle Donnie peeled away the heavy brown grocery bag.

And I sat back in my seat astounded. Dumbfounded.

So this was Donnie Jumper's great secret—a King James Bible.

"I bought this today, preacher," he said. "Never really read one before, but I heard in boarding school and here and there, that stories about this Jesus fellow are in it. They say He could touch the sick and cure them. Could make the blind see. Probably could cure my diabetes too, if He took a mind to. They also say he brought people back to life after they died, and that he walked out of His own tomb after three days.

"They also say He can still do that." He glanced at me. "So I guess what I'm asking is, what can He do about bad medicine? You know. Owls. Curses. Nightmares."

I glared at him, my mouth agape: *Why, you crafty old redskin. So this was what all the mystery was about.*

Uncle Donnie obviously thought witchcraft had caused my sleep Terror episode. He wanted Jesus to take off the curse and he thought the Bible would tell him how—like Jesus was some kind of *yuwipi* man.

I shook my head in embarrassment, disgust, and disbelief. But apparently Uncle Donnie was dead serious as, with the engaging eyes of a child, he held up his Bible. His words were measured: "I need to know if what the White preachers have been saying is the truth, or if they're just more of his forked-tongue double-talk. You are an Indian like me. If you tell me that what they say about Jesus is the truth, and that it's in this book, I'll believe it."

Burning Rain paused in deep thought. "Dryden, a great thinker, said that truth is the foundation of all knowledge. Bryant, another great thinker, said that truth crushed to earth would rise again. Pilate asked, 'What is truth?' And Jesus Himself said, 'I am the way, the truth, and the life.'"

He placed his gentle catcher's mitt on Uncle Donnie's shoulder. "So let's get together tomorrow night and talk about where Jesus is in this book, what Christians believe, and why we believe what we believe. Then you will understand why that wonderful volume you bought today is the greatest investment you ever made. And what you do with what's in it will affect your eternal destiny."

Uncle Donnie chuckled as he thumbed through the gilt-edged pages. "Well, looks like we're gonna have a pretty long talk, preacher. If everything you say is in it, then this is truly *naa-ken-chaok-choo-bee*—a very big book."

"Agreed, brother, agreed. Why don't we do it this way," Burning Rain said. "Let's skip the Old Testament for now and get back to it later. When you go home tonight, read the Book of John—over here in the New Testament. I call it *The Love Book*. Tomorrow, go to Romans—right over here." He placed slivers of paper as markers. "I call this one *The Salvation Book*."

Uncle Donnie appeared a little confused. "When I read these—uh—books in this *naa-ken-chaok-choo-bee*, I'll know about Jesus, and what's truth and what's not?"

Burning Rain's eyes were compassionate, warm, and he spoke gently. "Belief is based on faith. As you read about Jesus and why his disciples chose to die rather than to deny what they saw with their own eyes, you will have to decide whether they would give up their lives for accounts they knew to be a lie; or if they died because they could not deny what their eyes had seen."

Uncle Donnie pondered his words, and at length, stood up. "All right, Preacher Burning Rain. I'm looking forward to learning more about this Man and His Good Medicine. Dina, here, and me will see you tomorrow evening. And come with a big appetite!"

Burning Rain took my hand and his smile was soft. "Miss Dina, it was a great pleasure meeting you and your uncle. But don't tire yourself out doing too much for my visit tomorrow night. Just some decaf would be fine."

And in the nanosecond that his hand touched mine and our eyes met, something ignited between us. Something that somehow lulled my restless spirit while at the same time set my heart pounding.

He stood there, solid, strong, like a cypress tree, like a giant that thundered, but only when he preached the words of his God. His eyes flamed, but only when he thundered.

I withdrew my hand quickly. Men of God had always scared me, but this one managed to send a strange rush through me that was different from what I felt with Marty, yet just as powerful; and its effect on me was giving me stomach cramps.

"I'm glad to meet you too," I murmured as I snatched my gaze away from his, turned away, reached into my purse, and popped a couple of Tums into my mouth to quiet the roaring in my belly.

As the tablet slowly dissolved in my mouth and Uncle Donnie and Burning Rain continued their talk, I sat there and quietly reflected on my role in this drama: *Well, Dina, it's a good thing you don't have classes tomorrow, because you'll be cooking all day. The preacher is coming to dinner, amber caution lights are flashing all over the place, and you want to run away from it all. But you cannot. It is too interesting to pass up!*

VIII

Speaking Spirits

It was nearly eleven o'clock by the time we arrived at home from the revival meeting, way past Uncle Donnie's usual bedtime, but he was *wired.*

"Make sure you get everything cleaned up, now. Dust off things in the living room. Put fresh towels in the bathroom and a new roll of toilet paper—the one in there now is about used up. You don't want the preacher having to ask for toilet paper.

"Sometime tomorrow, go find some of that coffee he likes. Not the store brand. *Good* coffee. Maxwell House or something. I'll ask around about some venison." He looked about ponderingly for a few moments. "Well, I'll be turning in now. Got some reading to do, aaay."

Convinced he had covered all the bases, he went through his nightly ice water ritual; then with his Bible tucked protectively beneath his arm, he went to his room and shut the door.

Clean. Shop. Cook, I thought. It was just like Uncle Donnie to make these grandiose plans and leave all the grunt work to me. But he was my uncle and I loved him. Besides, although it was difficult to admit even to myself, I was looking forward to spending the evening with Aaron Burning Rain. Yes, I, Dina Youngblood, had lived to see the day that she would be excited about meeting a *preacher.*

I spruced up the house, marinated some Spam in canned tomatoes, put fresh towels and a new roll in the bathroom, and made a "do" list for the following day: most I would carry out, but some, his Bible reading notwithstanding, I would insist Uncle Donnie pitch in and do.

The telephone rang, and I half-wondered who would call so late. Probably Marty, wanting to know what was so important that I had to postpone our meeting.

I cleared my throat and used my most pleasant "Hello."

After a short silence, a tentative voice spoke: "Dina, please don't say anything. Just listen. Your mother needs your help. You're the only one Cheha can trust!"

My heart leaped. I held the receiver with both hands. "Mama!"

A sob caught in her throat. "Please don't tell anybody, not even Donnie. I—I want to come home!"

"Where are you? I'll come and get you. I'll find a way!"

"No, Dina. You must not get openly involved. Cheha has to work this out alone and once she is at home we cannot let anybody know where she is. But where can she go? You have to find your mother a place, but not on the Rez and not in Bitterroot. Something in town. An apartment, but not too expensive."

"Mama, please tell me why you have to hide from Jack Turner. It's killing me. I have to know!"

She was silent. Again, I could hear an infant crying and she soothed it softly. "So you know about him," she said with a resigned sigh. She sounded defeated, but at the same time, relieved to be rid of this great burden of secrecy.

"I hear a baby. Where are you? What's going on?"

A door closed in the background and I heard a woman's voice.

"We can talk later," my mother said urgently. "Cheha has to get back to work."

"Give me your telephone number. I can call you…"

"No!"

"Mama, listen. Shania was over there, at Jack Turner's house. But she won't tell me what's going on between them!"

I could hear her labored breathing, could literally *feel* the Fear in her voice. "How long ago did this happen?"

"A couple of nights ago. She came in from Oklahoma, having to budget her money for gas and food. And the next day, she's buying a car. A Mustang. With only twenty-thousand miles on it. Also, she was handing out hundred-dollar bills to Uncle Donnie and me like Halloween candy. She wouldn't tell me who bought her the car, or who gave her the money. Or—listen to this—a bag of Snickers candy bars. But I'm sure it was Jack Turner. Like I'm sure it was him that dropped the same kind of candy wrapper in your yard a few days ago!"

"Snickers." There was an interminable silence and a long sigh. "No—no—this cannot be happening. It has to stop. Cheha needs to talk to her. When can I talk to her?"

"I don't know, Mama. She left for Broken Bow already, going back to Aunt Bett's."

She sighed again. "The reason your mother cannot give you the number is that if you called, it would show up on your telephone bill. Jack Turner has informers. Spies. They watch everything. And everybody knows Donnie's in and out, and that he never locks his door before bedtime. I cannot take that chance!"

Again, there was a stirring and voices in the background. Mama's tone grew anxious. "Look for a place for your mother in town. She has to go now. She will call again—soon!" Without saying more, she hung up.

I held the receiver, reluctant to break the connection between my tragic mother and me. When I finally replaced it in its cradle my mind was spinning with a million thoughts that collided with each other.

Did I dare go to the hummocks alone and confront Jack Turner? And what about Marty? Did he know anything? Was he a part of this Terror campaign against my mother, merely a bystander, or worse, a pawn?

Furthermore, what about the night of the kaleidoscope horses, and Marty, and the strange rainbow of differing shades of gray? Nevertheless, I still resisted believing that Marty would drug my drink—make me hallucinate. After all, why would he? And yet…

"Sure, Mr. Osceola. I'll take real good care for you."

Kind of strange, I had to admit in retrospect, as I remembered the worshipful eyes of the kid with the scalp lock hair. People usually said they would take care *of* you, not *for* you.

And there was Marty's promise: *"I will do whatever it takes to win you."* But too, *"I would never hurt you, Dina…"*

Mine was a black sleep that night. Deep. Without dreams. And when I woke up the next morning, I felt curiously empty—like one whose spirit had been hijacked. There was lots to be done but already, it was a struggle to hold on to my thoughts, to remain focused.

It was only a bit past six, but I was already up and dressed. And as I started toward the kitchen I was surprised to see Uncle Donnie there in the hallway dialing the telephone.

"Hey, sorry I had to wake you up so early, Tobias....Right. Listen, what can you do about some venison and gator? If you could bring it by the house, that would be fine...no, didn't get the old truck fixed yet, but I will. And one more thing—that Creek preacher's gonna be here. There'll be lots of food, so you can stay for dinner, and bring your wife and your boy..."

The conversation hitchhiked its way to the kitchen and I could not help but smile at my predicament: *Oh, fine, Uncle Donnie,* I thought. *That's right, invite the whole Rez and all The Root folks. We've got lots of space in our six-bedroom-three bath home and four Native gourmet cooks....*

Our old asthmatic air conditioner was doing little to dispel the heat as I kneaded dough for the frybread and lapalee. But at least lapalee was pan-baked, and unlike fry bread, would not further add significantly to the closeness in the small, already overly warm house.

I noticed then that I was low on cooking oil and therefore would have to traipse down to Pik'N'Git on the corner for more, plus some Maxwell House decaf since the preacher could not tolerate caffeine. When would I find time to do it all? As I set the dough aside, the doorbell rang.

Uncle Donnie hollered cheerily from his room: "Come on in, Tobbie. The door isn't locked."

But after the screen door shut, the footsteps stopped behind me. I turned around, and my heart leaped with a mix of elation and embarrassment, for it was not Tobias Tigertail, Uncle Donnie's church-hating venison and gator friend that he was expecting.

"Marty!" I said in a barely audible voice. I glanced down at the flour dust on my hands and jeans. Barefoot, my hair tied back in a Gypsy scarf, I was a sweaty mess.

He seemed to read my thoughts: "No, you're not a mess. I would count any man lucky to have you in his kitchen," he said with that smile and that slight dimple in his left cheek that always left me weak-kneed and blushing like a fifteen-year-old experiencing her first real crush.

I rinsed my hands and wiped my face with a paper towel. "I apologize again for not having time to explain why I had to cancel our meeting last night. Uncle Donnie needed me to…"

"…go with him to the revival meeting. That's okay. Family always comes first," he said.

"How'd you know he went to the revival?"

"You don't realize yet that nothing happens in The Root or on The Rez that everybody else doesn't know about?" He handed me a grocery bag. "Here's the stuff you wanted," he said, then settled himself at the table—unknowingly in Uncle Donnie's chair—opened a folder he had with him and withdrew some papers.

I peered into the bag, and looked up at him, my mouth agape, puzzled. "Cooking oil, Maxwell House decaf, and a bag of—Snickers candy bars?"

"It isn't what you wanted?"

"The oil and the decaf, yes, but how did you know? And what's with the candy?"

He shrugged. "My dad said to stop off at the store and bring you the oil and the decaf, and to make sure the candy was Snickers. For Shania in case she showed up. I figured you talked to him." He leaned back in the chair and smiled guilelessly. "So I take it he's coming to this gala too. And frankly, I'm hurt."

A cold chill raced through me. The entire time he was speaking, I was shaking my head in denial. "I—haven't spoken to—your father…" I backed away, fearful of him. "Just—tell him thank you for me."

I thought, *One of you is toying with me, like a shadow-walking panther stalking its prey. Uncle Donnie was right. Apparently, we are players in this show—and only the writers of this Horror script know how it will all end.*

I tried to appear composed when I spoke again. "Uh, I guess I may as well put on a pot of coffee. You—uh—drink decaf?"

"If your hands made it, sure," he said with that smile.

I turned away and quickly busied myself to avoid looking into his eyes. I feared what I would find in them—or maybe that I would lose myself in them.

As I filled the coffee percolator, a movement outside the kitchen window caught my eye: a gigantic owl. It perched on a limb right there in broad daylight and eyed me with a baleful stare.

It spoke into my thoughts: *"Dina, the night's door is open. You will go through it."*

I lost it. In Fury combined with Terror, I banged on the window. "Go on, shoo!"

But it just sat there. Glaring at me.

Marty looked up casually from thumbing through those papers. "What's going on?"

My words were choppy, spiked with Terror: "That owl—I hate owls!" I cried. "It's speaking to me. Make it stop!"

Marty came to the window, and just as he did the owl took off—just flew away. He shrugged. "Okay, it's gone. Whenever Marty's around, he won't let anything hurt you. Remember that." He smiled coolly, sauntered back to the table, sat, and continued sifting through papers as though not a thing unusual had happened.

"So," he continued, "tell me about this in-house powwow you're having." He leaned back in the chair again, smiling that smile. "Maybe your boyfriend's coming. Is that why you didn't invite me? You have a boyfriend?"

My Fear made me bold: "Wouldn't your owls have told you if I did? No, I do not have a boyfriend. The dinner is for Burning Rain, the evangelist!" I fought to control my trembling.

He studied me briefly. "Really? So what's with him?"

I sighed and paused for control. "Uncle Donnie invited him. And as you can see, all the drudge work fell on me."

He threw back his head and laughed, with a hint of relief in his voice. "Your Uncle Donnie is inviting a *preacher* to dinner? Tell me that again. Donnie Jumper, the old sweat-lodging-Green Corn-*Yuwipi*-going Peyote man is having a *Christian* preacher—an *evangelist*—over for dinner? You *are* kidding me, right?"

"He's not into any of that anymore," I said.

The doorbell rang again and Uncle Donnie again hollered from his room. "Is that you, Tobbie? Come on in. You know I don't lock my door."

Tobias Tigertail and his son, Mackenzie, came in carrying two boxes. "Where you want us to put this meat?" Tobbie called out.

"Dina'll take care of it," Uncle Donnie answered.

"Here, I'll give you a hand," Marty said. He took the boxes and set them on the kitchen counter.

Uncle Donnie quickly appeared and examined the delivery. "Ahhh, good—nice and fresh, aaay."

Tobias Tigertail shrugged and slapped his son on the back. "Yep, Mac and me do pretty good. Well, we'll be seeing you around."

"Coming back for dinner with your family? Bring Vera. You keep your wife in the house too much," Uncle Donnie said.

"No thanks. My boy, Mac here, is different, but my wife and me, we aren't into that Christian stuff," Tobias said.

"But this is an *Indian* preacher, a Creek guy," Uncle Donnie said.

"Yeah, but it's the same White man's Bible, the same White man's gospel, and the same White man's God, isn't it? We have our own beliefs. Maybe there are separate—uh—heavens for people who believe differently."

It had been many summers since his son's challenge to Reverend Ward's alcohol sermon that Sunday, but the elder Tigertail seemed as defiant as ever of "White" religion.

Uncle Donnie shrugged. "Well, forget the religion part and just come for the cooking, then. I have to give you something. You won't take any money for all this good meat."

"I never charge for food. If I have it, I give it. Well, call me if you need more. Mac, come on, let's go." With that, Tobias Tigertail and his son were out of the door.

Uncle Donnie spread the generous slabs of venison and alligator on the counter. "Good meat. Fresh, aaay. Fix it up nice for the preacher."

He made no eye contact with Marty—or me, either, for that matter.

"How are you, Uncle Donnie? Warm today, isn't it?" Marty asked from where he sat in Uncle Donnie's chair, the newspaper drafts spread before him.

Uncle Donnie shift-eyed him and started back to his room even as Marty was still speaking. "Well, you look pretty comfortable. I'm doing good. And yes, it is a warm day."

"I hear the preacher's coming. That's an awful lot of food for one guest," Marty said.

"Preachers eat a lot. And they sit where they're told to sit!"

"Uh, Marty's invited, too if he wants to come," I said quickly, to defuse the situation, as I sprinkled seasoning on the venison.

Marty brightened. "Hey, sounds like an adventure. Don't believe I've ever seen an Indian preacher before, or missionary, either, for that matter. Only White ones—and every one of them paternalistic and condescending. If it were not for their intended benevolence, I would despise them all."

Uncle Donnie stopped then and engaged Marty's gaze. "So you never heard of Oral Roberts?" His tone was imperious.

"Well, yes, *him* I've heard of. Some kind of faith healer on television, isn't he?"

Uncle Donnie pulled himself up to full height: "Yeah. And he's Indian *and* Christian."

"Is he? I didn't know he was Indian."

Uncle Donnie grinned in triumph. "Good. Thanks for admitting that you and your owls don't know everything. So tuck that in your belt!"

I changed the subject. "The preacher should be here around five. His assistant is taking over the revival tonight," I said as I prepared the three rows of flour-dusted dough patties for the bubbling oil.

Marty was pensive. "I have a few issues I'd like to discuss with the preacher, so it sounds like this is going to be a stimulating evening." He stood up and tossed a stray lock of his heavy silk off his forehead. "I may run a little late, but save me a spot at the table. Oh—and Dina—when you get the chance, look over those drafts for the newspaper that I left on the table, okay?"

As soon as Marty started toward the door, Uncle Donny immediately shoved his chair back under the table and stalked off to his room.

I stood at the window watching. He was so tall, so gorgeously beautiful, so comical at times, and so devoted to his cause and those he loved. And I wondered: *what, and who are you, Marty Osceola?*

At about three minutes before five, Burning Rain's van rumbled into the driveway. Gospel music blared from his radio. I was already showered and dressed, but I skittered back to my room and gave myself a last-minute look-over.

Already Uncle Donnie was at the door. I could hear Burning Rain's solid footsteps, his greetings, their small talk.

"Come on out here, Dina," Uncle Donnie hollered from the dining room. "Now when you taste her food, Preacher, you'll have to admit she is the *best* cook there is. Only twenty—maybe twenty-one—something like that. And up till now, pretty as she is, *never* even had a boyfriend!" There was a wink and a nod in his voice that was suddenly low and conspiratorial: "And you and me will figure something for that later."

Heat shot to my face. *Why, the crafty old redskin. I could kill him,* I thought mildly. Obviously my uncle had something on his agenda other than Bible study, food, and fellowship; and I made my grand entrance with a face burning with self-consciousness.

He immediately grabbed my hand. "Dina here, my niece, did *all* this cooking," Donnie-the-Lip of Bitterroot said with an expansive sweep of his hand and a proud taffy-stretch grin. "If it wasn't for her, I don't know where I would be. Makes me take my diabetes medicine and eat right, 'cause she's gonna be a *nurse!*"

Burning Rain just stood there smiling at me. His hair was pulled back neatly in that Tonto bun. He was dressed in a crisp white shirt that brought out his sun-burnished glow; with black slacks, and a different but just as exquisitely beaded bolo and belt buckle. He exuded a light fragrance of cologne. I had to admit it. He looked really good. Especially for a preacher.

"Nice seeing you again, Miss Dina." He studied me intently. "But I can't help but think that I've seen you before. At one of the crusades, perhaps, maybe a few years back? I don't recall that you got saved, though. Anyhow, it was a blessing to see you at the revival last night."

"She's coming back tomorrow night, too," Uncle Donnie volunteered, "'cause getting saved is *very* important for a girl!"

Burning Rain diplomatically let the remark slide without comment as he surveyed the table that was set with our modest best, and the counter, a smorgasbord of Indian goodies. "My, my, this must have taken an entire day to prepare. I didn't want you to go out of your way, but I sure appreciate it. It's wonderful—just wonderful."

"All by herself," Uncle Donnie said.

I just crossed my arms and rolled my eyes to the ceiling.

"Food is a hard ministry," Burning Rain said. "I realized that when my wife passed away three years ago, and I had to start cooking for myself."

Again I marveled at his soft tone and gentle manner. It was such a sharp contrast to the big, booming voice that thundered from this giant when he stood in the pulpit. But I averted my eyes, embarrassed by the attention.

"Well, everything is ready," I said.

"You've done a wonderful job, just wonderful," Burning Rain repeated. And his tender eyes revealed that his comments were genuine and not just small talk.

"So let's give thanks," he said and lowered his head. "Holy Father God, we give You thanks for this food. Thank You for providing it, bless the hands that prepared it. Thank You for the hospitality of this home, on which I ask Your blessings, in the Name of Jesus. Amen."

Even as Burning Rain was asking the blessing, Uncle Donnie was focusing on other things on his agenda. "You sit at the head, right here, preacher—next to Dina," he said, all but interrupting the "Amen."

Burning Rain sat obediently and took a sip of the corn *sofkee*. "Ummm, this is wonderful. Just wonderful—as good as my sainted wife used to make."

He then looked directly at me. "So, Miss Dina, tell me a little about yourself. I know you're studying to become a nurse, and that's a great profession. But other than taking care of your uncle, are you involved in church—any other things?"

"Uh, mostly just school. Community College. When Aunt Jessie passed away and Uncle Donnie got sick, I moved in to help. I've sort of been here ever since. His own kids are—away."

"In jail—the house with the iron bars—two of them, anyhow. My boy and my youngest girl. Drugs. Only Star seems to be walking the right way, but she won't come home to see me anymore. She's out in California somewhere, last I heard. Been four, five years now."

"I'm sorry to hear that. I'll be praying for them," Burning Rain said. He turned again to me. "What church do you attend, Miss Dina? Hope for Tomorrow? Reverend Ward is a *fine* pastor, a *fine* White brother."

"I used to but—uh—not for a while now. You know. School and all."

He seemed to sense my discomfort. "Well, any sisters or brothers?"

Uncle Donnie piped up. "Dina's the *only* one who hung around. Her two brothers moved out on their own, then her younger sister, Shania. Nobody can control her. No, sir. Pretty girl, too—just like her sister, Dina, here. Well, not *quite* as pretty, but pretty."

Burning Rain smiled, obviously amused. "You know, a preacher has many sisters and brothers in the Lord, but few friends. And I guess I'd like to feel that you two are my friends. So there's one thing I would like to ask of you."

Childlike eagerness sprang into Uncle Donnie's eyes: "What's that, Preacher? Anything. Just say it."

"I'd like you both to call me Aaron."

Uncle Donnie pondered the request. "I'll need some time to work my way up to that. But we *are* your friends. Yes, sir. And I read those books you told me to. Good stuff. But tell me this: what does the Bible say about our clans—you know, Panther, Otter, Snake…"

Burning Rain took another sip of *sofkee* and paused as if choosing his words carefully. "In my own opinion, it's okay to recognize clans for their family and historical significance. But let us not forget that Genesis chapters 1 and 2 tell us that God created us in His own image. We are speaking spirits, the only beings fashioned by His own hands. The rest

He spoke into existence."

Eddie Was leaped on Uncle Donnie's lap and curled up as he purred gently. "Tell me," Uncle Donnie continued as he absently and gently scratched the little four-legged's chin, "why you as an Indian believe that all this stuff in the Bible is really the truth."

Burning Rain did not hesitate. "These are the reasons I believe." He popped up one finger after another. "Number one, because creation itself is not haphazard. It demands an intelligent creator. Two, because of fulfilled prophecies. Three, because of answered prayer—miracles we cannot explain. And lastly, this is deep: the way God has supernaturally preserved the Jewish people and established the nation of Israel. Just as He promised. That a nation would be born in a day."

Uncle Donnie shifted in his seat. "Oh." He kind of shrugged. "But how do you explain when medicine men—witches—make things happen? Powerful things. You're an Indian. You know. How do you explain that?"

"Power comes from two sources, Brother Donnie. From light and from darkness. I used to go to the medicine man. Sure, he has some power. But what medicine man ever walked out of his own grave after being dead for three days? And certainly no medicine man ever claimed to have died in your place to pay your sin debt so you could have eternal life in heaven."

Uncle Donnie was pensive. "Umh. Well, you ever have a prayer answered?"

"Oh, yes. I have had prayers answered. I have seen miracles, too. I'm one of them. I was literally delivered from death, spiritual and physical, all by the power of God Almighty. Been born again. Hallelujah!"

I fidgeted uncomfortably. I could not help but wonder what Marty would say to all this if he were here. I glanced at my watch. It was almost six-thirty. Where was he?

Uncle Donnie missed nothing. "If you're waiting on that boy, he's not coming. Never intended to come. It was all just talk!"

"We were supposed to have another guest?" Burning Rain inquired.

"I did ask Marty Osceola. He said there were some things he wanted to discuss with you. He's Traditional, but he's...interested in the Christian viewpoint," I said.

Uncle Donnie's eyes blazed. "Lies. That boy's not interested in Christianity. He's just playing you along. I don't think he *can* change. He's in too deep. The powers have too tight a hold on him now!"

He then turned to Aaron. "He comes around here, but he's not her boyfriend, no sir. So don't go thinking that. But he'll say anything to get Dina believing he'll become something other than what he is!" He eyed me then. "The son of two low-life drunks and druggies that gave him away, and who was raised by a witch!"

I leaped to my feet. "And what are you? When did you ever worship inside a Christian church? You're only interested in how to break curses and spells. That's why you have the preacher here. At least Marty doesn't pretend to believe in something he doesn't understand just to get what he wants!"

Uncle Donnie leaped to his feet also, sending Eddie Was scrambling. I had never before seen his eyes glitter with such fire, and he stood only inches from my face. "Oh, no? It's what he believes, girl, that's gonna take you down. It will keep nibbling away at you until it has *all of you.* Like it has your mama—and your sister!"

"Stop it. Marty isn't evil. He had nothing to do with Mama's and Shania's running off. It's Jack Turner. *He's* the witch; everybody knows it. Marty would *never* do anything to hurt me—or anybody. He wants only to help his people. You're wrong about him. You're wrong!"

Tears streamed down my cheeks and our eyes locked for a long moment. Neither gaze wavered.

Finally, Uncle Donnie sat. Still glowering at me. "You went out with him one time." He wagged one finger. "One time—and couldn't wake up till the following afternoon, screaming!"

I sat too, then, wiped my tears with my napkin and tried to control my trembling. "Anybody can have a nightmare!"

Burning Rain reached over and placed a reassuring hand on my shoulder. His voice was tender. "I feel in my spirit that you're deeply troubled. I'm going to pray for you right now that the Lord will put a hedge of protection around you—that He who kindled the stars will also kindle a desire in you to seek Him."

I flung my napkin to the table and sprang to my feet. "Excuse me. I don't feel too well. I just want to go and lie down!"

"You can give all this to Jesus. Just give Him all these things that trouble you. No evil is stronger than the power of God," Burning Rain called out as I headed for my room.

Interest sprang into Uncle Donnie's voice. "What about curses and owls? Can she give Him those, too?"

I turned and faced Burning Rain. "They haunt me, the owls." I sobbed. "They follow me and threaten me. They're making me sick. Someone's trying to kill me—or drive me mad. I don't want to believe it, but I do—I do!" I could no longer control the torrent of tears.

Aaron came over, put his arm around my shoulder, and led me outside. "Let's talk," he said, and we sat there on the steps. He held me close to him, and I could feel the beating of his great heart, feel his strength; soon I felt a security I had not known before. Never had I felt such comfort in anyone's nearness.

"It'll be all right. Just tell it to Jesus," he said gently.

Uncle Donnie peeked out of the screen door. "How do we take care of this, Preacher?"

"Aaron. just call me Aaron. I say this to the both of you: confess Jesus Christ as your personal Savior and believe in your hearts that God raised Him from the dead. Tell Him you know you're a sinner. Ask Him to forgive your sins and to come into your heart."

His arms were still wrapped about me as if as if he were protecting me from the unseen forces. "Do that," he said, "and you can command those owls or any other demon spirit to depart and it will *have to go.* But you must have faith and believe that Jesus can do these things."

"That's all?" Uncle Donnie asked as he came outside and stood next to us. "No burning sage—sweats—smudging?"

"Jesus does it all," Burning Rain replied. "But God is not a cosmic butler who exists only to do your bidding. He wants a personal relationship with you."

Uncle Donnie seemed a bit let down as he pondered the words. "God wants a relationship with me? Umh. That's a big thing to think on, preacher Aaron. Kind of scary too, aaay."

"Nowhere near as scary as hell, brother Donnie. Making up your mind to follow Jesus is a life-altering decision—the most important you will ever make. If you feel the Lord pulling you, hear Him calling you, don't put it off."

He stood up then and held my hands. "I know what you're going through. I know. I've been there. Jesus is as close as a whisper. But He is also a gentleman and doesn't force Himself on anybody. You have to *ask* Him to be the Lord of your life."

"Sometimes I want to, but then I'd have to give up being who and what I am. I don't want to give up being Indian. We have practiced our traditions for as long as we have been a people. Why can't Jesus just love us the way we are?" I asked.

"He does. He died for all of us, while we were still in rebellion against Him. And you don't have to give up all traditions—only the ones that teach us to place our faith in anything other than God." He glanced at his watch. "I do thank you for the supper. It was wonderful. Just wonderful." He cupped my face in those great hands and looked deeply into my eyes. "And, Miss Dina, I pray that you will make the right decision for the Lord; and that the seed of the Word sown into the soil of your spirit will bear much fruit."

He smiled and turned to Uncle Donnie. "And you—keep that Bible open, brother. 'A bruised reed He will not break, and a smoking flax He will not quench.'"

Uncle Donnie looked puzzled as he accompanied Burning Rain to his van, to resume his leadership for the rest of the meeting. They stood there talking, and shortly afterward Uncle Donnie went back into the house. "Got to get my Bible. Gonna go to the revival," he said. "You coming too?"

I started back up the steps and into the house. "No. I have to get the kitchen cleaned up."

My mind raged as I scraped the plates. Marty had not called—where was he? What was this strange feeling I had for Burning Rain? Mama had not called back, either. And who were the baby and the people in the background?

Wherever she was, she was ready to come back home. But she needed an apartment so she could hide some more. It wasn't fair. And I had no money to speak of, so how could I help?

Also, Jesus was chasing me, and all I wanted from Him right then was the small favor of dealing with the owls haunting my life. Maybe later, after I got all this craziness sorted out, I could consider making a real commitment to Him. Maybe.

But for now, I had to make sure my mother had the peace in her life that she was entitled to. And for that, I was prepared to be more than Burning Rain's speaking spirit. I would also act. In any way I had to...

Sleep came in fitful snatches that night, for not only was my mind torn between Marty and the church, but now there was the matter of Aaron, too. Though unspoken, it was obvious that we both felt the power between us, and his words haunted me: *"Good soil for the seed..."*

I tossed about and compared the two men. My flesh craved Marty; my spirit, Aaron. But what kind of pastor's lady would I make? I already felt cheated out of my youth. Shania had been right. I had never really had a life.

When my girlfriends and other young women my age were giggling about boys and dates and all the other stuff that goes along with youthful crushes and first loves, I was hardly more than a bystander. Even the few times I did garner enough guilty courage to sneak away to a club or dance or something, I was always the first one to have to leave: caretaking duties. Or studies. Not that we were doing anything really wrong. But I always worried: suppose the news got back to Uncle Donnie? He had that way of avoiding looking at me that riddled me with guilt.

"Good soil for the seed..."

But marriage to a *preacher?* Wouldn't that mean having to live under even greater restrictions? Wouldn't I be told what to wear and where to go? Wouldn't people scrutinize my every word and action?

Also, even though the mystery of my mom's disappearance was solved, the *why* of it was not. Then there was the business of helping her establish herself all over again. I was eager to do so, but also secretly angry that it meant quitting school, getting a job, deferring my nursing career, putting my own plans on hold—yet another circumstance that required me to give up something I wanted for the good of someone else.

When was it going to be my turn?

With Marty, there would be none of the constraints placed on a pastor's lady. He couldn't care less what I wore and he enjoyed the social scene. Every gathering was a networking opportunity for him; a chance to push his political agenda.

No, he was not Christian. Yet. And yes, he held Traditional beliefs. But didn't he say he wanted to discuss some issues with Aaron? So all that could change...

IX

Noonday Nightwalker

Whenever something weighed heavily on my mind, I always awoke early; so I was up at six again the following morning. I had searched the journals for much of the night, and two events that happened in the mid-seventies especially troubled me:

Must meet him again tonight. If only Cheha knew a way out...
He will be waiting for me. Cheha needed the help. She could not allow her children to go without. But now she is trapped and cannot escape...

I donned jeans and a T-shirt, closed the front door softly behind me to keep from wakening Uncle Donnie, and tiptoed down the front steps. Eddie Was sat there by the door, home from one of his all-nighters. Ever the opportunist, he shot past me and into the house, ringed tail held high.

What could the classifieds offer me, I wondered, with so few marketable skills? All I knew right then was that, other than me, Mama had nobody else to turn to—and that she had run enough.

School? Hey, life was life, I decided. You just had to take what it pitched your way. I patted the pocket of my jeans for reassurance that I had enough cash for a newspaper and a cup of coffee. I did, barely.

Memories that eluded me throughout the night continued to tease the blank spots in my mind as I walked the three blocks to Pik'N'Git.

I must have been four or so—barely old enough to remember the man that came to our house periodically after our father disappeared. Whenever we asked, Mama always said our dad was away. Working. And that he would return someday. But now and then, I would hear her talking to Mama Hat about how no-good he was for walking off and leaving us, her with a baby due any day.

The man—Uncle John, we called him—would let me "doctor" his left pinky, which had only a half fingernail that was perceptibly darker than the others.

"I was born with it," he explained. But he would allow me to apply "nurse medicine" I made from sand, water, and leaves, and wrap it in bandages I fashioned from paper.

"She wants to be a real nurse," Mama apologized as she opened the paper sacks he always brought. "Look," she would say. "Uncle John brought you sandwiches and soda again. Sit. Eat."

And I remembered how quickly my brothers and I would scramble to the kitchen floor, anticipating the mouth-watering treats that always appeared like magic from those brown paper bags.

And nothing tasted better than those "Indian steaks"—bologna sandwiches—probably purchased at a 7-Eleven or a Pik'N'Git. Mayonnaise dripped down our chins and chests with every relished bite, and there would be Orange Crush soda pop.

For a really special treat, Uncle John would bring us Hershey Bars. But for little Shania, when she was old enough, it was Snickers; and we would laugh and call her Little Chocolate Cheeks for the mess she would make while indulging her pleasure.

And for Mama, Uncle John would bring housewares, cuts of meat, and occasionally a blouse or a bottle of cologne or something. Small dividends from Tribal Bingo went only so far. Looking back, no doubt his generosity was a welcome help to an expectant abandoned wife rearing young children on her own.

Whenever Uncle John visited, it would always be around sundown. And there would be feasting. He and Mama would laugh and talk, and he would play with us for a short while.

But after Shania was born, when the merrymaking ended, Mama always said, "You kids go outside under the *chickee* now. And stay in the yard. Don't go running off." Then she and Uncle John would go inside the bedroom and lock the door.

There was something somehow magical to me at sundown during those times: colors seemed brighter, sounds clearer, whites seemed whiter, and the sky closer to the earth. And my brothers and I would play outside during these somehow enchanted times and would watch little Shania till Uncle John came out and left in his truck. Then Mama would call us in.

If only I could remember his face! I wondered whatever happened to him. Was he still around? If so, was Mama still seeing him, secretly, at the time of her disappearance? Was their relationship the spark that ignited Jack Turner's wrath—and if so, why? Was there a relationship between the two men?

As I neared Mama's house, there were no owls in her mango tree. Yet. But it was still early. Even so, I picked up my pace. And just then, a bird flew down and settled on a limb. My heart leaped, I stifled a scream—and immediately chided myself.

It's only a mockingbird, Dina. Get a grip...

"Morning," the wiry, middle-aged convenience store clerk with thinning brown hair and pale blue eyes said without looking up. He was sorting change behind the counter as I entered Pik'N'Git.

I nodded and handed him a newspaper. "And one medium coffee," I said.

"Fifty cents total, Miss."

I counted out the change.

"Help yourself to cream and sugar and you have a nice day," he said.

I immediately went to the classifieds. "Uh, do you mind if I sit here on the windowsill?" I could take my time, I reasoned, without having to worry about Uncle Donnie's prying questions.

"Not at all. Go right ahead."

I sipped the strong brew and searched through sections that interested me most. At length he smiled up from where he was wiping the countertop: "Job hunting, huh?"

I smiled and nodded.

"You're from the reservation, aren't you?"

"Bitterroot. My mom moved there a while back. But, yes, I was born on the Rez." He did not need to know that Mama, and later the rest of my family, left to get away from the gossip about my dad's affair with the fire-haired woman—and all the sordid fallout surrounding it; for in the Bitterroot Confederacy, people largely stayed to themselves.

102

"Interesting place, Bitterroot. Made up of people from different tribes, from all over, I hear. Founded for those that want to stay connected to the Native community but don't want to live The Rez experience," he said.

I glanced up briefly. "Sounds like you did your homework."

He busied himself rearranging items on the shelves. "I love the Indian people. I think they got a raw deal from this government."

His constant conversation was breaking my concentration, but I nodded politely again.

He seemed clueless, however, as he continued: "A lot of folks from the reservation and The Root come in here. I don't see much of you, though. You live here permanently, or do you come and go?"

"I spend a lot of time in school. Community College. And I take care of my uncle. He's diabetic. I don't have time for much of anything else."

His interest was aroused and his eyes brightened. "A college girl. Hey, great. Not too many of your people go that route. Not around here, anyway. I guess it's especially tough for you, with your obligations. I sure hope you get that job. I know when I was in school, some extra cash sure helped with books and spending change." He was chattering nonstop.

"Me, I was a business major," he went on. "Then I got married. Dropped out after two years—family responsibilities. Always meant to go back." His eyes were wistful. "But I never did. I make a decent living here though, so I'm not complaining. Could be a lot worse."

I lowered the paper. "I'm going to have to drop out too, for a while at least. Something…came up. I need a job. I really need a job. And not day labor picking beans, either."

"I agree—you shouldn't have to pick beans." He sighed deeply. "That's too bad, having to drop out, a smart girl like you, swimming against the tide. Because sometimes when you stop, like I did, you never get going again."

He scratched his chin. "Look, I'm the manager here, and I have a hard time getting reliable help. The fellow that works here regularly has been missing a lot of work. There's talk in the wind that he's using—strung out. He's also been playing fast and easy with the till and coming up short too many times. What kind of work experience do you have?"

He really got my interest then. "Mostly health care, my uncle being diabetic and all. I'm studying to be a nurse."

"I see. Well, we need good nurses, for sure. But I'm afraid I can't help you there. Did you ever work a cash register?"

"Well, I know how to use an adding machine."

"Cash register's easy. I could teach you if you're interested."

I was in no position to bargain. "Sure. I'll take anything. But it has to be full time, because I need to earn some money right away."

He was thoughtful. "Tell you what—uh—I didn't get your name."

"Dina. Youngblood."

He stuck out his hand. "Mine's Rick. Check back with me tomorrow afternoon, Dina Youngblood, if you don't find anything in that paper that you like."

"I don't need to think about it. I'll take the job. Thanks so much! When can I start?"

"Tomorrow. You'll be on the afternoon shift first. You'll shadow me for a few days till you learn the ropes."

Uncle Donnie was seated at the table nursing a cup of coffee. "Just getting home from sneaking out all night—to meet up with that boy?"

I was so elated at the prospect of a job that even his digs about Marty were of no effect. "Nothing like that. Had to run to Pik'N'Git. Important business. I'll get your oatmeal. And by the way, how was the revival meeting?" I poured water into a pot.

"It was powerful. Strange and powerful. Made me feel something in here." He patted his chest. "I hadn't planned on going, but I guess it just snuck up and bit me." He eyed me curiously as he toyed with his cup. "Marty was there."

My entire being seemed to freeze. "He was—Marty?"

"Yep. Didn't get a chance to talk to him, though. Fact is, I didn't see him at all till I was on my way out. He was sitting in the back, kind of looking around." He glanced at me. "Like he was looking for somebody. Sure was a surprise to me, after he didn't show for dinner."

104

"And you didn't ask him why he stood us up?" I asked as I sprinkled the oatmeal into the boiling water.

"He stood *you* up. Wasn't here on my invitation." He took a swig from his coffee. "Tonight's the last night of the revival, but Burning Rain's staying around for a while to help me learn the Bible."

I raised my eyebrows. "Uh-huh." I ladled the steaming cereal into his bowl. "So, my Uncle Donnie really is interested in becoming a Christian. That's a surprise."

He shot me a glance. "Yep. Aaron Burning Rain is staying for a while." He relished a spoonful of oatmeal. "He needs a wife, you know. And he has taken a powerful liking to my beautiful niece."

I measured my words. "Now, wait just a minute!"

He slammed his palm on the table. "And you need a husband, a good man. How old are you now—twenty-two…three?"

"I'm twenty-one!"

"And a half! Near middle age for an Indian—we Natives live an average of forty-five years, give or take. Most girls your age have two or three nice kids by now. You have the chance to marry a good solid Indian man, and you're playing silly-girl games!"

"Uncle Donnie, hear me and hear me good: Aaron Burning Rain is a wonderful person. He believes passionately in Christianity. And that's good. For him. Not for me. Not yet, anyway. "Maybe if he weren't a preacher…I'm just not interested in marrying any *preacher.* My life and his," I shook my head, "it just wouldn't work."

He sighed and his voice softened. "Now, just hold on and think about it, Dina. He's a decent man and not bad-looking. He would treat you good. You would get a chance to travel with him. And listen good now." He squinted and pointed his finger for emphasis: "No owl in his right mind would come near you ever again with the preacher around!"

I filled my own bowl with oatmeal and sat across from him. "And what would the preacher and I live on? Donations people drop in a bucket?"

"He's a carpenter. Can make near anything. Hand-made furniture for rich White people mostly, when he's not traveling. Bassinets—baby cribs—can't forget that. Beautiful stuff. They pay him good money, too, I hear. And even at worst, think of it this way." He waved his hands expansively. "He would be supporting you in the manner to which you are accustomed." He leaned forward. "Be serious, young Indian woman. We're not rich White people or wealthy Black people or billionaire Middle East oil barrels!"

"Barons."

"Whatever. We're Indians, aaay. We have to pull together to survive. It has always been that way. Me, I picked beans till I got too old. You never had to do that. Dividends. And we deserve every penny! But I taught you kids how to survive in good times and rough times. Remember my old *efche esh fah yee kee?* It's still in the closet back there on the top shelf. Go get it. Let's go hunting. Let's see if you still remember how to shoot game."

I held up my hand. "It's etched into my brain. Some things you never forget. Believe me, I know how to shoot if I have to. But I was hoping for something a lot better for myself than eking out a living from the land."

He leaned toward me with burning eyes. "*You do what you have to do to survive!* You and the preacher can have a good life. You can figure out the money part after you get married!"

"Oh, so we're getting married? Well, his carpentry sounds more like a hobby to me, with his travel schedule. And kids? They cost a lot of money if you rear them to compete in today's mainstream world. And that's what I want for myself and my children."

"You're supposed to tie the horse in the shed before you bolt the door. Get married first. You get a dividend check every month. You won't starve. Besides, there's talk that the tribe is expanding into casinos. That'll be more money for everybody. *Big* money. You and I, we live in The Root but we're still Seminoles. Think, Dina. You can't put a price on a good man. You *can't.*"

"You're making me sound like a gold-digger. I just want a future for myself and my kids. And I want a career. And parties. Pretty clothes. Friends that like to have fun. Becoming a preacher's wife with too few dos and too many don'ts just doesn't cut it for me."

He brought the rifle out anyway, and laid it on the table. "When you get married to the preacher, I'll give you this just in case times get hard." His eyes twinkled. "Then you can show him you know how to live like a *real* Indian, aaay!" He roared with laughter.

I didn't find the situation so humorous. "I've thought about it. Aaron's a great guy, but he's a widower and probably already has a bunch of kids at home. I'm not ready for an instant family. I-I love him but not—like that."

Suddenly sobered, Uncle Donnie threw up his hands. "Okay. Your mind is set on that boy. But what can he do for you, other than make you feel good? Oh, he can keep you with a pumpkin under your shirt, but what can the Father of the Year teach your children—how to conjure?"

I leaped to my feet. "You're wrong about Marty. He's not what people say he is, and I don't have to listen to this!"

"You mean you *hope* I'm wrong about him. Open your eyes to the truth, because it's right in front of your face!" The telephone rang. "If it's that boy, he's means nothing but trouble for you. So you don't need to be talking to him, and you don't need to be spending time with him!"

"His name is Marty!" *That boy,* I groused in my mind as I picked up the receiver, *as if he doesn't have a name.* But Uncle Donnie was right. It was Marty.

"Hey, pretty Indian woman. I got off work late yesterday," he said. "I passed your house and saw your uncle getting into the preacher's van. I thought I'd see all of you at the revival. My fault. I guess I shouldn't have assumed anything."

"Well, you could have called. Did you get a chance to talk to Aaron?"

He paused. "So, Aaron, is it? Interesting to be on a first-name basis with a preacher so quickly. Anyhow, no, I didn't talk to him. Too many people were crowding in, and I had to hurry back to help my dad. He was mending the floorboards in his house and wanted to finish before bedtime. He's deathly afraid of cockroaches and was scared some would come in before he was done and crawl over him while he was asleep."

"Your dad's deathly afraid of some insects? I find that hard to believe. It's almost humorous."

"Well, ol' John Turner is near terrified of cockroaches. I can vouch for that."

"I don't think anybody really likes—did you say 'John'? I thought his name was Jack."

"Don't people call all Johns Jack? Like Jack Kennedy, the president, whose name was really John. And Jack the Ripper whose name was probably John." He laughed.

"Oh, stop being silly." I laughed too, but the name stuck in my mind: *This is your Uncle John. He brought you sandwiches and soda. Sit. Eat.*

"I placed your schedule on the refrigerator as a reminder for you to take your meds. And when you're ready for dinner, like I've said before, all you have to do is heat it. Now, it's payday, I'm running late, and I have to go, okay?" Two months at Pik'N'Git had flown by swiftly.

Uncle Donnie sat at the table like a scared little boy. "This isn't working. I always burn my dinner trying to heat it up. Can't get the stove to work right. And it's hard to remember by myself to take my medicine on time."

It was my fault that I had him spoiled, so I felt a little sorry for him. "Look, I bought this timer. When it goes off, it's time for your meds. Hey, I have an idea. I'll be off Saturday. I'll make you the best dinner ever—deal? But for now, I have to go."

"You're promising me, but if that Rick guy calls from Pik'N'Git, you'll go running off to work again," he said. "Why are you working so hard? We get dividends. And I always say we deserve every penny. And you got your scholarship for school. We do okay. And you need to look at my toe. It's turning…"

I ignored The Toe ruse. "I work because I have other obligations that I can't talk about right now. And Rick already knows I'll be taking Saturday off. Now, get back studying that Bible. Aaron will be coming back through here soon, and you can show him how smart you are. Oh. And Marty may call about the newspaper. Tell him I have the drafts at the store. Be nice to him just once, and do that for me, Uncle Donnie?"

I tucked the folder of articles in my purse and was quickly out of the door. I would read them over during my break. The paper still did not yet have a name, so Tanya Willow, a volunteer, suggested *Our Voices.*

Marty insisted on *War Arrow*. I thought that something like *New Phoenix*, symbolizing a rebirth of the people would be more appropriate, especially given the premise for starting the paper in the first place. But Marty thought that sounded too Southwest. So, well aware of his persuasiveness, it would no doubt be dubbed *War Arrow*, I thought as I started the borrowed VW Beetle and headed for Pik'N'Git.

I knew how important the newspaper was to Marty, and I wanted to see it succeed; but tonight my mind was on more important things. It was true that I *was* going to work, but what I did not tell Uncle Donnie was, for tonight, it would be only for a few hours. And then Rick would be coming back in to take over my shift.

He had become a friend and confidant in addition to being my boss. He allowed me to work overtime whenever possible because he knew the extra cash came in handy.

With what I earned, and the small amounts Mama sent whenever she could from her on-premises child-care job as far as I could surmise, I was able to pay for a small apartment in town. It was nothing fancy by a long shot, but it was in an out-of-the-way location near a strip mall with a grocery store—all within walking distance. But I do not believe that either of us really thought that she could elude Jack Turner forever; he had toadies everywhere.

It seemed like a hundred years since I last saw my mother, and my heart drummed with excitement, because finally she was coming home. Tonight. On the 7:50 Amtrak.

When I had telephoned my girlfriend and told her that I would have to drop out of school for a while, Sheila Marston expressed regret, but was preoccupied with news of her own.

"Are you sitting down?" She inhaled deeply. "I'm engaged! He's that curly-haired pre-med student. I figured I'd better snag him now. You and I have to celebrate. My treat. I'll pick you up!"

She arrived in her BMW, and as she chattered almost nonstop, I could not help but contrast our lives. They could not be more different. She was a wealthy Jewish girl, had two cars, and could afford to attend any school she wanted. But she chose Community College "to be with the *real* people."

In spite of her privileged status, however, she seemed blind to color and class. All her close friends were minorities: LaTanya, a Black girl; Deepak, from somewhere in the Middle East, who spoke six languages; twin Chinese sisters—and one Indian.

Only at length, as we were pulling into the parking lot to begin her celebration at Luigi's, did she seem to notice that I wasn't saying much.

"Hey, forgive me. I'm sorry for being so wrapped up in myself. What's going on with you? I mean, what's this dropping out business all about? If it's some cash you need…"

I held up my hand. "Let's not go there. It's too complicated to explain. I wouldn't know where to begin. But I'll say this much. I have to help my mother, and I have to find a way to protect her from somebody that's—how do I say it?—interfering in a terrible way with her ability to live her life."

The hostess greeted us and Sheila requested a booth near the back "where we can talk."

"So why would anybody do something like that to your mom?" she asked as we slid onto the leather upholstered seats.

"It's a lot of Indian stuff," I said. "You wouldn't understand the control witches have over people's minds. She won't tell me what it's all about, but I think one of them has my mother terrified." My anger rose. "I'd like to go out in the hummocks and burn down his house with him in it!"

"Oh, you don't mean that," Sheila said, dismissing my empty-sounding threat. "A real witch, huh? Is that the same as a medicine man?"

I shrugged and avoided her eyes. "I'm—really not into that."

"But I thought all Indians understood everything about Indian stuff."

"I—uh—grew up Christian. I was never really taught anything about witchcraft or medicine. What little I know, I picked up here and there."

"Are you baptized and all that?"

"Uh—no. Not yet, anyway. But I was brought up in Sunday school."

The waitress came forward. "I'm Mimi. I'll be your server this evening. Can I get you ladies something to drink?"

I noticed though that as she spoke, she never made eye contact with me.

110

"A root beer for me," Sheila said. "With a dash of Louisiana Hot Sauce, if you have it."

"We sure do. Root beer with hot sauce. And for your friend?"

"Just Coke," I said and quizzed Sheila with a raised eyebrow. "Hot sauce?"

She smiled. "One of my oddball predilections."

"I'll bring your drinks—and I can put your order in, too, if you're ready." Mimi-the-Waitress' eyes were still glued on Sheila.

"Is a sausage pizza okay with you?" Sheila asked. "I'm craving."

"Fine with me," I said.

The waitress brought the drinks and set them before us: a root beer with a dash of hot sauce for Sheila, but for me, a lemonade.

"Excuse me—I ordered a Coke," I said.

"Oh, I'm sorry," she said to Sheila. "My mistake. I thought you said she wanted lemonade." She grabbed the glass and returned quickly with the Coke and set it sort of in the middle of the table. "Your order will be ready soon." Gaze still locked, I noticed, on Sheila.

The waitress returned shortly with the steaming pie and set it in the center of the table. "Enjoy!" she said to Sheila. "Just signal if either of you needs anything." And she was off again.

By then, Sheila had become aware of Mimi's snubs. "What's with this chick?" she asked. "Am I your interpreter or something?"

"Oh, let it go. She has probably assumed rightly that I'm the FBI and you're the one picking up the tab."

"Flat Broke Indian. I remember that one. Well, even an FBI deserves to be treated with respect. I think she needs to learn a lesson," Sheila said. So when Mimi-the-Waitress with the saccharine smile came back over, Sheila was ready.

"Another root beer?" Mimi asked.

"With hot sauce," Sheila said.

"And your friend—would she like a refill?"

Sheila shrugged. "Don't rightly know. Ask her. She's the one who's paying. And your tip depends on how satisfied she is with your service."

Suddenly I had her full attention. She took my empty glass and wiped the ring of condensation from the table. "I'm sorry. You must excuse me. I'm sort of new here, and it's been a long day. Would you like another Coke, too? And maybe dessert or another appetizer?"

I smiled. "No thanks," I said politely, even though there was a world of subtext in that "too."

She scurried off again and we could not stop laughing, because I had little more than vending machine change in my purse.

A pause hung between us before Sheila spoke again. "You know, life is too short to side-step adventure. Why don't you and I go out to the swamp together—safety in numbers? I could bring my camera and film while you talked. This witch guy, can he really do magic, cast spells, or put curses on people? If he can, I have a professor I'd like to…"

I laughed. "Forget it, Sheila. Try to imagine Jack Turner's face." I gestured broadly. "A strange White woman drives up in his yard; I jump out and give him what-for while you stand there…" I was in such hysterics that tears ran down my cheeks. "…pointing a movie cam in his face! It would be safer and a lot more fun filming the one that's scary and makes me crazy but is so-ooo good-looking!"

Sheila raised her eyebrows and leaned back against the booth. "Oh? Now I'm *really* getting interested!"

"It's the truth," I said. "Well, I'm not sure he's into witchcraft. But his stepdad who raised him is. And he has a thing for me. But I'm scared of him. Just thinking about him or being around him makes me crazy!"

"Well, lead *me* to him. *I* certainly wouldn't be scared of a good-looking guy, regardless of what he was into." She laughed uproariously as she leaned across the table. "Hey—I may even break my engagement to the curly-haired pre-med student for that kind of excitement!"

I squint-eyed her. "Watch it, woman."

Sheila shrugged. "Well, it was a thought." She giggled as she downed a large swig of that adulterated root beer. "But seriously, if you need a car, the Beetle is yours any time. You could keep it as long as you liked. But if you 'off' the old wizard, just don't get witch blood on the seats!"

The evening finally wore down, and we started for the exit. "Hey—want to bar-hop a little bit and scope the guys before we call it a wrap?" she said as we left the restaurant.

"Absolutely not. I've got studying to do and you're engaged. So what would be the point?"

She eyed me and laughed as we hopped into the car. "Of course you're right. What would the world do without sensible people?"

That was two weeks ago, and Sheila had made good on her promise. My mother had called to say she was coming home. And now I would be there in that school-bus yellow Beetle to pick her up.

Finally, after being dead to us for over a year, Cheha Youngblood was coming home. I could barely contain my excitement, but she had sworn me to secrecy, so I had to choke on it. I couldn't even tell Uncle Donnie. Business was brisk and I was grateful. It kept my mind occupied.

At about a quarter of seven Marty swung through the door. He chose a bottle of cranberry juice and sort of browsed the aisles as I completed ringing up a sale.

"How's it going?" I asked, having perfected the art of sounding casually detached. I handed him the folder. "Let me know if you want anything else changed on the new drafts. The others look pretty good to me."

As he took the papers from my hand my heart skipped erratically, the air around me became electric. I feared this power he seemed to wield over me.

He paid for his juice, set his bottle on the counter and flipped through the pages. "Looks okay from here. Thanks." His face brightened as he continued, "By the way, I have some good news. Listen to this: our paper qualified for start-up funding through the Foundation for Indigenous Publications. They'll pay for the overhead in modest accommodations and a stipend for the staff. We can also get additional funding for each five-hundred new subscribers every year."

I bagged another customer's purchases and gave her change. "Hey, that's great. A little extra cash is always nice to have."

He pulled an envelope from his pocket. "Take a look at this; it came in today. It's about a delegation from the Canadian tribes that want to contribute to the paper." In his excitement he leaned across the counter.

I felt suddenly breathless. Lightheaded. I moved away. Uncle Donnie was right. Marty was obviously controlling me with medicine. Because right then, if he told me to kick off my shoes and go gator hunting in the swamp in the black of night, I felt I would grab my purse and be off. And it scared me. My love for him and my Fear of him were so intricately intertwined I could no longer separate the two or determine where one ended and the other began.

So each time Marty came close to me, I hoped he did not notice that I inched farther away. But nothing escaped him. Finally he stood studying me intently, in that casual posture of his, his thumbs tucked in the beaded belt of his jeans.

"Dina, why does your spirit fight so hard against mine?" The question had no nuances. It was simple, direct.

It would do no good to deny it. "Marty, I don't know what's going on with me—between us, I mean. I don't think my spirit fights with yours. I'm trying to resist you, yet I don't want to. Make sense? Not to me either. There you have it. Don't ask me anything else about my feelings."

He took a step back. "Am I doing something to make you feel like you have to resist me, fear me, run from me? I've been pretty straight-up about my feelings for you."

"There's just so much—the owls, so many crazy happenings. I wish it weren't true, but you just plain terrify me, Marty."

He raised his hands in surrender. "Sorry. Tell me how I terrify you, and I'll try not to do that. As for owls…"

"It's nothing that you *do*. It's you—-who you are. No, me. The effect you have on me. Or maybe it's that I don't feel I know you or what you're capable of doing."

He studied me for an instant and gathered his paperwork. "Well, I certainly don't mean to make you feel that way. But the tales you elect to believe about me, well, they are your own choosing. I've made my honest intentions toward you pretty clear. So I'm sorry you've allowed a bunch of wild tales and fabricated legends to come between something that could have been beautiful between us.

"One more thing and I'll leave you in peace," he said. "We already have office space. The Tribal Council is letting us use a room and their newspaper staff as consultants. We can funnel the money we save into a really great looking paper—color, advertisers the whole herd of horses. Well, thanks again. See you around, Dina." He took a swig of his cranberry juice and strode through the door.

The remark sounded so *final*. The scared part of me was relieved. The other part, the part that was intoxicated by his eyes, his voice, his very presence—the crazy-mixed-upside-down part—felt as though he had torn away my heart and left me empty. And it was all I could do to restrain myself from running after him.

I kicked the counter, angry at my big mouth, and popped a Tums to calm my roaring stomach.

Right then, Rick sauntered in with his usual upbeat grin. "'Evening," he said. "Happy Friday."

I greeted him in return, we made small talk, and I completed my shift.

"See you in a couple of days, Rick—and thanks," I said. I was quickly in the Beetle and moving through traffic. Once inside the Amtrak station, my eyes combed the crowd for that one familiar face. An hour passed. I scanned some travel brochures with disinterest to pass the time and kept glancing at my watch: 9:30, then 9:45.

I paced up and down the walkway. Finally, it was 10:20. Two trains had come and gone, and still there was no sign of my mother. I had to know something, so I stood in line behind an elderly gentleman at the information counter.

Thin and balding, his suit was well-tailored but could have used a good dry cleaning. He stood staring at his ticket. When his turn finally came, he handed the seller his ticket, and his voice was apprehensive. "Do I have to get off, change trains, or anything like that before I get there?"

The young Black woman with cornrow braids checked his ticket and answered gently: "No sir, you'll go straight to Washington D.C."

"You're sure we're not going to stop somewhere and I have to get off and change trains?"

"Well, the train will make stops to pick up new passengers, but you won't have to get off till you get to D.C. Somebody will let you know when it's your time. We won't let you get lost." She smiled and handed him back his ticket.

I shifted my weight from one foot to the other and glanced again at my watch. *What would it take for him to understand?*

Seemingly oblivious to the line of people that continued to queue up behind him, the old man, in his private Fear, continued to study his ticket. "Oh, I see," he said. "Well, I'm sorry to have bothered you. But I just don't want to get off in the wrong town. That happened to me before, when I was just a kid.

"It was one summer when I was ten or so and was supposed to visit my uncle in Vermont. I got off in the wrong town, and I just don't want that to happen again. You see, my wife, my Vertie, is waiting, and she wouldn't know what happened to me."

By then, there must have been twenty people lined up behind me as he rubbed the slight graying stubble of his chin. He continued to stare at the ticket as though some cosmic trickster from his childhood were still trying secretly to lure him into some black hole of no return.

When he glanced up again, finally aware that he was holding up the line, he smiled apologetically, walked away slowly, still studying his ticket, front and back. He spotted a redcap and started out of the door behind him.

"Excuse me," he said. "I was wondering if you could help me..."

"Next," the ticket seller said.

I stepped forward quickly and started talking almost before her command cleared the air. "My mother was supposed to be on the 7:50. It's after ten. I was supposed to pick her up and..."

Busy with paperwork, she didn't even look up. "Everything's behind tonight, Miss. Problem on one of the tracks. Domino effect. Just sit tight, her train'll be here."

As soon as the train pulled to a stop at twenty before midnight I was immediately on my feet, and my eyes searched every face as the passengers stepped down onto the walkway. Mama could not have kept me in more suspense if she had planned it; because just when I was about

116

to panic because she was not on board, that familiar face appeared, third from the last passenger.

The conductor helped her negotiate the steps while she held a single suitcase—and a bundle cradled close to her breast.

"Mama!" I cried out.

I dashed over and threw my arms around her and that little bundle she was holding. When she saw me, her face crumpled in tears as she just stood there, holding that sleeping baby. Not caring who saw us, we both wept until we had no more tears.

We finally dried our faces and I took her suitcase. She glanced about with apprehension as we started toward the Beetle.

I pulled the blanket away from the tiny face. "And who's this little guy?"

"My son. Your baby brother. Cherokee Apache Youngblood."

I noticed then that she was thinner, her face a bit more haggard. Though she was still a pretty woman, the stress of more than a year in hiding was clearly etched around her eyes as we walked toward the blacktop.

"His father?" I ventured, somehow knowing, yet fearing the answer even before she spoke.

"He can never know—or he will make his baby into what he is." Her eyes were imploring. "You must help me, Dina. Somehow Jack Turner must never lay eyes on this child!"

I spent much of the next week juggling my work schedule to help my mother get settled in, doing her grocery shopping, and trying to keep her return a secret. But Rick was becoming curious, more and more suspicious. Around mid-afternoon, when he came in to cover for me yet again, only half-joking, he teased, "Are you sure you're not sneaking off to see some rich married guy? You've been asking for a lot of schedule changes and time off. I know you always make it up, but it sure would make me feel better if you'd tell me what's going on."

"I can't. But I can say that I don't do the married guy thing." My voice fell. "Or any other guy, for that matter."

"Well, I know I'm just an old fogey White fellow, but I've always taken pride in being pretty trustworthy. Anything you told me would remain between the two of us." He held up his hand. "Scouts' honor."

"You're not just some old White guy, Rick. You're a kind person—my boss and my friend." I was thoughtful for a long moment. If I held it back any longer, I would burst. "If I trusted you with this and you told, it could put my mother's life in danger."

His usually smiling face was at once grim. "That serious?"

'That serious."

Just then a truck—Marty's truck—pulled up. And a man, but not Marty, hopped out and slammed the door. He was rather tall, rangy, slightly bow-legged, and wore Western-style boots with Indian designs.

He was firmly muscled, with a narrow Anglo nose in an Indian face. His untamed hair gleamed like shards of black ice with a sunset reflecting on them.

A mid-lifer, younger-looking than I had expected, he was really kind of handsome in a weathered cowboy kind of way. And he had just swung through the glass doors of Pik'N'Git. His eyes, holding the wild power of a pent-up storm, were riveted on me. And even though the brown hat with the beaded band nearly obscured his face, I knew immediately who he was.

A miasma of darkness and malevolence surrounded him. It choked the air and invaded the room like smoke. Rick must have seen the blood drain out of my face because he was looking at me as though I had morphed into a ghost.

My heart thundered, my stomach churned. My breath came in short gasps. I edged away as I eyed with barely restrained Terror this walking commander of the spectral realm.

"Dina, are you okay?" Rick asked. "You know this guy?"

I could hear the flailing of wings inside my head. Owls? I threw up my trembling hands to fend off my unseen attackers.

"No—get away from me!" I screamed, and the flailing tore quickly through one hemisphere of my skull and out the other. I gasped for breath as I held on to the counter. If I let go, I feared I would float off into another dimension. My knees began to give way, and Rick put his arm around my shoulder.

"Hey—let's get you into the office. You need to sit down and put your feet up. I don't want you passing out on me," he said.

We started toward the office, but our visitor had already incinerated me with those eyes: auburn, with sparks of jade and gold—a roaring kaleidoscope that raged and burned into me. I backed away from him, feeling my breath, my very life, being sucked into his forcefield. I held on to Rick for dear life.

But this customer just stood there, his gaze deadly, and studied me as if he were siphoning my thoughts. My Fear was palpable. He sensed that, I knew, and would go for the jugular— like a hungry wolf when he smelled the blood of his wounded prey.

But slowly, surprisingly, the stern mouth turned up at the corners, and a semblance of a smile chipped through the ice of his stony face. "You're Cheha's girl, aren't you? You look just like her. You know who I am?"

I gave a quick affirmative nod. "Yes. I know who you are." My voice was barely audible.

"Well, you tell Cheha that Jack Turner said hello—and that Bitterroot misses her." His voice was measured and calm, but I sensed that this rattlesnake could assume his striking coil at any minute.

I swallowed hard. "I can't. She left town and nobody knows where she is."

He began examining items on the shelves. "Kind of strange. A mother not contacting her daughter—ever—wouldn't you say?"

I shrugged. "She just left. We don't know if she's alive or—dead."

He was quickly in his coil and lashed out. "Oh, she's alive, all right. We both know that, now don't we?" He continued to smile that diabolical smile, while the top half of his face remained as motionless as death. He fingered a pouch of tobacco but placed it back on the shelf. "So, how's my little girl—my *tay-koo-che?*"

My throat went even drier. I was barely able to speak. "I—I don't know what you mean."

His voice exploded again. "You know exactly what I mean. Do not play games with Jack Turner. So, how's my girl—Little Chocolate Cheeks—the youngest? She used to sit on my lap when I brought food to your house!" He gestured broadly with his hand as he spoke, and it was then that I glanced at his left pinky. It had only half of a fingernail that was darker than the others.

Uncle John. Our benefactor turned tormentor...

I cleared my throat. "Shania is—out West."

"*Where* out West?"

Rick spoke up firmly. "Sir, I'll have to ask you to make your purchase and leave. You're harassing my employee."

Jack Turner eyed Rick for a long moment. Neither man wavered. "Okay, it's your store," Jack Turner said at length. He then turned to me. "Give me a couple of those beef jerkys and a pack of that tobacco. Oh, and a couple of those—" he rolled the words around—"Snickers bars." His eyes never left my face as he spoke.

"They're on aisles...," Rick began.

"I want the girl to get them for me," he said. "I fed her when she was hungry and barefoot and snot-nosed, and in dirty underpants. Fetching for me doesn't seem like too much to ask." He picked up a hand cart and banged it down on the counter. "Tell *that* to your mama!"

"Look, sir...," Rick said.

I threw up my hands. "It's okay. I'll get them for him." I located the items, placed them on the counter, and prepared to ring them up.

He then leaned forward with his face only inches from mine. "I would appreciate it very much if *you* would put them in my basket. *Then* take them out of the basket, ring them up, bag them, and place the bag in my hand. I always *handed* groceries to Cheha—in her hands. One bag at a time. *Every* time."

Anger began to replace my Fear. "Sounds like your problem is between you and my mother." I rang up the items, bagged them, and set the bag on the counter. "That will be $12.50. And if you want your items, pick them up yourself!"

He shrank in mock surprise. "Ooo-ooh, you have your mother's fire, *tay-koo-che*. But you would be wiser to learn fear!" His gaze held mine. "Okay. I'll pick them up. This time." He paid for the items and strode away.

When he reached the door, he turned and his menacing warning oozed with venom. "You tell Cheha—wherever she is—that all I want is what's mine. No more, no less. *Nobody* takes from Jack Turner. Or they will wish that they, *and everyone that they love, had never been born!* The grounds are filled with those who dared to defy Jack Turner—all from natural causes, of course. You tell that to Cheha for me!"

I grabbed the nearest object—a can of Campbell's Tomato Soup. "My mother doesn't owe you *anything,* and don't call me *Tay-koo-che*—I am not a little girl. And Shania is not your little girl, either!" As I prepared to hurl the can, Rick grabbed me and pinned both my arms to my sides.

"Let it go, Dina. It's not worth it," he said.

"Shania is mine, all right, in more ways than you know. But she's like her mother—grab and run. They both owe me!" Jack Turner said.

He started for the door but stopped yet again. This time he turned his gaze on Rick. "And you, White man, learn this. The next time I come into your store, you show me some respect!"

He then eyed Rick with evil so dark, so suffocating, I could literally *feel* the air being sucked out of the room.

Rick gasped suddenly. Blood gushed from his nose. He pinched his nostrils shut, stumbled over, reached under the counter where he kept tissues and other personal items and ripped out a wad of Kleenex. He held them to his nose with trembling hands. He stared at Jack Turner through eyes of Horror and Dread as his blood spurted through his fingers and streamed down the front of his shirt.

Jack Turner then turned on his heel, burst through the doorway, swung into the truck, and roared away.

I stood there, unable to control my quaking. A silence hung between Rick and me.

When the gush of blood eased and Rick collected himself, he eyed me warily. "You want to tell me what this is all about, Dina?"

I burst into tears. "I don't know what it's about. And I'm sorry I got you involved in this. All I know is that he is holding something over my mother's head. And that she was so scared she left town running from him. But he knows she's back. I didn't tell anybody, but somehow he knows. And he won't give up until he finds her!"

He handed me a Kleenex. "This sounds to me like a matter for the police to handle. I don't know who this guy is, but nobody is above the law!"

I shook my head vigorously. "The police can't help me. You don't know Jack Turner!" I dried my eyes and blew my nose.

"Well, if this torment is an ongoing thing, maybe you could get a restraining order. Take him before the Tribal Council or something—whatever you guys do. I mean, don't they have some means in the Confederacy to handle things like this?"

"Nobody will touch Jack Turner. He makes his own rules. He's a *witch*. What he did to you was just a small sample of his evil. He can kill people with his powers. Don't be deceived, Rick. The spirit world is very real—and Jack Turner knows how to command it!"

"Are you saying you believe he caused my nosebleed?"

"Well, what do you think? I saw the Fear in your eyes, saw your hands shaking. Did you ever have blood gush from your nose like that before for no reason?"

He shrugged. "Well, no, but it was probably just a coincidence. Too warm in here. Stress, maybe. I do have elevated blood pressure. And I—forgot to refill my prescription." His voice softened and he managed a smile. "Look, Rick will take care of you—and he's not intimidated by a fairy tale ogre."

I was standing at the window watching the parking lot just in case Jack Turner returned by the time Rick emerged from the bathroom. He had cleaned up, changed his shirt, collected himself, and by then was his usual upbeat self.

"People like this Jack what's-his-name create a *climate* of fear. And they prey on the superstitions they perpetuate. That's where they get their power—not through the spirit world. They're mental terrorists. Evil witches are characters in *Snow White* and *Hansel and Gretel*—figments of a writer's imagination. Like the big bad wolf."

I shook my head. "I can't make you believe anything that you don't want to believe. But we Indians are well acquainted with the spirit world, so don't cross him, Rick, please!"

He ran his hand over his thinning hair, in deep thought. "Look, why don't you take the rest of the day off? I don't think you're in any shape to finish your shift. Make it up tomorrow morning. Come in at six." He handed me an ice cold Pepsi. "Here. Go home. Chill out. Kick back.

Watch a soap opera or something. Get a grip."

I popped the can open and took a swig. "Thanks, Rick."

"Now, promise me you'll be careful," he said as I started for the door.

"I'll see you at six tomorrow," I said. "But listen, I'll be giving Sheila back her car this weekend. So I'll need to take the mid-day shift again, okay?"

Again, Rick was pensive. "You know, I have an old Vega. Nobody's using her and she'd probably come in third in a Miss Junk Heap pageant. But she's pretty even-tempered. Why don't you take her?"

I gave it brief thought. "Thanks, but I can't buy a car right now—not even an old one."

Rick shrugged. "What's it worth on the market—a hundred bucks? Take it for fifty. Pay it out however and whenever you can."

I chugged the rest of the Pepsi and tossed the can into the wastebasket.

The telephone rang then and Rick picked up. "Pik'N'Git. Could you speak a little louder?" He handed me the receiver. "It's for you." His eyes were glued on my face.

The voice on the other end was barely audible. "Dina, you gotta get here—quick…"

I held the receiver with both hands. "Uncle Donnie, what's wrong?"

"Having—trouble—breathing…"

"Hang on. I'm calling an ambulance!" I was near panic and guilt flooded my mind. I'd had to help Mama, and therefore had neglected him a bit lately. Now something had happened to him.

"No—ambulance—owls—outside…"

A chill gripped me. Uncle Donnie never locked the door except at bedtime, and everybody knew that. Everybody.

He was wheezing, gasping for air. "Get here quick. I have things to tell you before—I go!"

"You're *not* going to die. You can't. You hold on. You hear me? I'm on my way!"

Rick's voice was wary. "Dina, be careful. This could be some kind of trick. I think we should call the police!"

I hesitated for a second. "No. It would only make things worse.

Uncle Donnie is all alone, and I have to go to him!"

Jack Turner was tormenting us. But how do you fight the air? In his cunning, he knew I'd report what was happening to us to Mama, and eventually, she'd have to give in to him to save her family from his wrath. But would even he stoop so low as to hurt a harmless elder?

I grabbed my purse and headed for the door. "Rick, don't worry about me. I'll be all right," I called over my shoulder. My love and concern for Uncle Donnie far outweighed my Fear of what I would find—or of who might be waiting.

Rick yelled after me, "In fifteen minutes I'm going to call you. If I don't like what I hear or feel, I'm sending the police!"

The heat of the day was slowly giving way and dusk was hovering over the horizon. I fired up the Beetle and took off for home. As I rounded the corner, Uncle Donnie's house, always so familiar and comforting, now seemed almost sinister—like a hulking monster poised on its haunches; an old *halpatee* lurking as alligators do, in the deep shadows of murky ponds. Only this one had my beloved uncle inside its belly.

I jerked to a halt, leaped out, hurried down the shale rock driveway, and shuddered. The two owls—those sentinels of evil—were perched on a limb just outside the window of Uncle Donnie's room. Their low throaty calls wafted slowly and menacingly and filled the evening air with their eerie chant: "*He is with us—and you will follow, Dina. You will follow through the night's door.*"

Just then, every story I had ever heard about those omens of sickness and death came into sharp focus. But this time, my hatred of them overcame my Fear. I picked up a stone and flung it against the tree.

"Next time, it'll be the shotgun. Go on—shoo!"

The stone struck the trunk of the tree with all the force I could muster, but the owls merely fluttered, slowly, easily, to higher limbs. And they continued eyeing me ominously, as they resumed their terrifying vigil.

I felt wooden, devoid of my very humanity as I walked cautiously yet quickly up the steps. This could not be real, I thought; it had to be another nightmare. My heart drummed sickeningly, my temples throbbed. My stomach roiled inside me and burned like acid as I pushed open the screen door.

It groaned on its hinges like the moans of a dying man. A curtain of silence, a death-stillness, hung in the house. I flicked on the light. The shadows that hovered inside scurried beneath tables and couches and hid in corners.

The door to Uncle Donnie's bedroom was shut. Icy Terror so constricted my throat that I could barely speak.

I raced to his side and knelt beside him. "Uncle Donnie, it's me, Dina. Can you hear me? Tell me what happened!"

He lay on the floor flat on his back. His eyes, staring into mine, were glazed with Horror. His breath came in shallow quick snatches.

"I'm going; I know I am. He did it. I saw him, standing in the doorway. Blew something in the air—like dust. He did it…"

"Who? Tell me!"

"No—don't go—after him—he'll kill—you, too…"

I stroked his furrowed brow gently as countless yesterdays compressed into one terrible moment and rushed through my head.

Uncle Donnie, who had taught my brothers to hunt alligators, and each of us kids how to shoot wild game with his *efche esh fa yee kee*—how to catch garfish, trap birds, and plant a "wolf garden."

"You can always make it in the world if you know how to hunt and fish," Uncle Donnie had said. "Hunger is a wolf. And some beans and corn growing in the yard can keep him away from the door…"

Uncle Donnie, who taught us to drive that old truck, now as decrepit and helpless as the old man who owned it. Propped up on cement blocks, it was a monument to days past:

"Watch it. Stop sign coming up. Cut to the left—all right—you got it!" Then that squint-eyed triumphant bellow of a laugh that I had come to know and love…

I cradled his head in my arms. He was the only father I ever knew. How could it be possible that he was leaving me?

When it rained, it was Uncle Donnie who rumbled up in that old pickup to give us kids a ride home from school. "Hop in before you melt!" It was his tagline. And he'd grin from ear to ear, as a truckload of giggling, squealing, soaking-wet little Indian kids would pile in.

When his Jamaican friends from his bean-picking days brought him sugar cane and taught us how to chew it, it was Uncle Donnie who peeled it and handed the chunks to us along with a proverb: "You treat sugar cane like you treat life. Chew it up, swallow the sweet, and spit out the rest!"

But his still face was now wet with my tears. "I'm calling an ambulance right now. Hold on, Uncle Donnie—you hear me?"

Mustering all his strength he grabbed my arm and raised himself up on his elbow: "Doctor—can't help me. Call—the preacher." He pointed feebly toward the telephone. "Call—Aaron Burning Rain..." His breath then released in a long sigh and his words hung in the silence.

"No, no! Wake up, Uncle Donnie. Please wake up!" I rocked him back and forth while sobbing like a child. I lifted my eyes upward to the Christian God that the White preacher—and Aaron—said could heal. And raise the dead. "Please, God, make him well. Don't take him from me. I'll die, too, if You take him from me!"

The telephone rang. And rang. And rang. Probably Rick, but enshrouded in my panic and my disbelief and my sorrow, I did not answer it. And presently, the keening of approaching sirens grew louder and louder.

X

Samaritan One East

The doctors ran every appropriate test on Uncle Donnie, but their findings were inconclusive. None of his health problems—his diabetes, moderately high cholesterol, and slightly elevated blood pressure—were of sufficient magnitude to cause his coma.

Yet he lay there on his hospital bed, not dead, but not really alive either. He looked smaller and somehow older.

I had heard that some who had emerged from comas reported that they could hear what had been going on around them, so I had sat at his bedside every possible minute for the past two days. I spoke softly to him, stroked his brow, and caressed those work-worn hands.

"Double brown," he used to joke, "brown from birth and browner by the sun."

"Aaron will come," I said. "He's on the road preaching at the other reservations. I've left messages for him. I'm sure he'll be here as soon as they catch up with him."

But there was no sign that Uncle Donnie heard me. Nothing. Not a wiggle of a finger, not a flicker of an eyelid.

Yet I continued, "I want you to wake up. Come on, Uncle Donnie. You're a tough old redskin—stronger than whatever it is that is holding you down." A sob caught in my throat and I pressed his hand to my cheek. "Fight! We can't let Jack Turner win with his evil—by believing that there are no limits to his powers!"

My words rang hollow. Had I not felt the miasma of darkness that exuded from him at Pik'N'Git, by just being in the same room with him? He had strong medicine, because in spite of my prayers to God, Uncle Donnie was showing no signs of recovery.

Surely, Jesus had to remember me from Sunday school. Although it had been many seasons ago, it should count for *something,* I figured. But maybe God was mad at me. Perhaps He did not listen to those who never formally accepted Christianity, who turned back, or even to those of us whose involvement in The Indian Way was only marginal at best.

I had not mentioned Uncle Donnie's condition to Mama. She would only insist on coming to visit him and thereby risk being discovered. News of her return would spread through The Root and The Rez like a blaze kindled by lightning in dry woods. And anyhow, what could she do? Yet she had a right to know that her brother was dying.

"Sleep through the night in this world, Uncle Donnie," I said through my tears. I had the late shift, so I kissed his deeply etched forehead and left for work.

The weight of my world seemed to be on my shoulders as I pulled out of the parking lot in the maroon Vega. Just as Rick told me, it was no great beauty, but it was mild-tempered and reliable.

Uncle Donnie's doctors did not know why he was dying, but I knew. And though he could no longer speak, so did Uncle Donnie: the cause was rooted in the supernatural. If this suspended state did not smoke Mama—and the secret she had been concealing—from her hiding place, Uncle Donnie's death would certainly do that. Otherwise, Jack Turner's unrelenting pursuit of Mama would make no sense; and from the way things were going, it was only a matter of time before he would get what he wanted.

If he did not, then Mama would be in hiding for as long as Jack Turner walked the earth. Losing simply did not figure into his psyche.

Aunt Bett was finally able to locate Shania. She had moved from her home where she had been staying in Broken Bow, to California to pursue her modeling dream just as she had planned.

Along with her grade school friend Tracee, the two dropouts were now manikins in the glitzy world of makeup, clothes, photoshoots, and starvation diets. When I finally reached her by telephone, she was torn:

"I want to come home, but this is a cutthroat business, Deenie. Tracee heard that a casting director will be visiting soon. He'll be looking for new cinema talent. So I have to stay close. I can't miss out on an opportunity to be a movie star!"

"Shania, Uncle Donnie is *dying.* You will come home now, or you will never see him again!" For some reason I withheld telling her that Mama was back, or about her new baby brother. Somehow, the timing didn't seem right.

Whether or not she would come home was left to be seen, and I felt so alone. Johnny Hawk and FrankE stayed on the perimeter, as was their custom, during family crises; and as with Mama, they depended on me for updates on everything rather than becoming personally involved themselves: "It doesn't sound too promising. But don't let it get you down. There is only so much that you or any of us can do," JohnnyHawk would say in his fatalistic tone. FrankE, his big brother's shadow, echoed pretty much the same sentiment.

I drove home from the hospital on auto-pilot. I checked our mailbox and tossed the one piece of junk mail into the nearby trash can.

To make it to work on time, I would have to hurry and shower and change. Working at Pik'N'Git was drudgery, but right now it was serving two purposes: in addition to the much-needed cash, it was keeping my mind busy on something other than my beloved uncle's condition.

I pulled into Uncle Donnie's driveway and lurched to a halt. How still everything seemed! The owls had not yet posted sentry in the trees, but even so, as I entered the house it felt haunted.

I turned on every light in the house so the shadows would have no place to rest; although they filled every corner of my life, I could not let them win.

The cane-back chair still sat at the table in the same position he'd left it. I fought tears that stung my eyes. How empty the house, how empty my life was, without Uncle Donnie! He had always depended on me, and I couldn't shake the belief that I had somehow let him down.

And this time I would make no attempt to hold back the grief that I had kept so carefully contained. I allowed the sobs, wrenching and ugly, to eject fully from the center of my agony, spew through the dead silence, and simply have their way.

The force and depth of my grief both startled and frightened me. I feared how far it would carry me, because it seemed as though every emotion I had held back since the beginning of time rushed out like floodwater.

Terror and Grief having taken a hiatus, Confusion entangled me in its grip and rendered me helpless as he mocked, challenged, and taunted me.

"So you are an Indian! Yet you have refused our ways. And you have called on the White man's God. But He does not hear you.

"There are brothers from many tribes living on these grounds made sacred by Indian blood and tears. Many have attempted to share their tribal beliefs with you in a gesture of brotherhood. You have ignored them. But you willingly listen to the indoctrination of the White man's gospel."

I screamed out in the quiet. "Leave me alone!"

"No! You must listen, for you do not have the courage to choose. If you are an Indian, why do you hate Jack Turner, the keeper of the Indian's dreams? And why do you Fear Marty? Go to him; he will teach you the ways of the people. Now get up. Where is your Indian pride?"

I shook my head. "I will not listen!" And I lifted my eyes. "God, if You truly exist, take away this Confusion. And please—make Uncle Donnie well again so once and for all I can believe!"

The telephone jarred the stillness. The voice was crisp and professional, yet kind. "This is Samaritan One East calling. I'm sorry, Miss Youngblood, but your uncle is dying. If you would like to spend some time with him, you should come immediately."

"Thank you for calling. I'll be there," I said through my sobs.

Rick understood and expressed his sorrow when I called to tell him the awful news. The hood of the Vega, the best investment for fifty dollars I ever made, reflected the last of the late evening sunset as I left the house.

Did Mama have the right to know? I sat there behind the steering wheel, trying to decide if I should tell her or not. Finally, I concluded that, dangers notwithstanding, the decision to continue in hiding or to see her brother for the last time should be hers to make.

So I left the engine idling and barely noticed the black sedan parked across the street as I returned to the house. I dialed her number and even before she could answer I started to speak.

"Mama, it's me. It's about Uncle Donnie. He got sick a couple of days ago. He's in the hospital. Samaritan One East. They don't know what's wrong. But they say he's not going to make it."

There was a sigh and a long pause. "Cheha will be there to see her brother."

"I held back telling you because I was worried that it might not be safe. I try to be careful going back and forth from the apartment, but I just have this feeling that someone is watching me!"

Again the long pause. "Cheha Youngblood will go to her brother. She'll be waiting when you come for her."

"What about Chappy? He's too young to go up."

"You can keep him while I visit."

"Mama, listen—I'm sure Jack Turner knows you're in town. He just doesn't know *where* yet. So he has to know about Chappy, too. And I know he's the Uncle John that used to come to see us. I remembered that fingernail. But why does he call Shania his girl? Are they going together or something? What else could he possibly mean by that?"

She sighed and answered quickly, perhaps before she lost her courage. "He calls her that because she *is* his girl. He's her father—hers and Chappy's. But because Cheha's father was part Cherokee and part Apache, she named him Cherokee Apache Youngblood. Cheha's son will not wear Jack Turner's name, nor will he ever lay his evil eyes on him!"

"But how long can you run with him—hide him?"

She sighed. "Cheha was foolish. She never should have told Jack about this child being on the way. He insisted on her marrying him—moving out there in the hummocks with him. He wanted to swallow Cheha up into his life of evil and Terror. Well, the argument got more and more heated. And I guess Cheha wanted to strike where it would hurt the most:

"'Your demons don't know everything, Jack Turner. They didn't know about Shania!'

"'What about her?'

"Cheha stood right in his face: 'You mean your owls and your cronies didn't tell you? She's your daughter, O exalted-one-who-has-all-knowledge, who thinks he's as great as God. But little Chocolate Cheeks does not wear your name—and neither will this baby!'"

"He started raging then, and right before Cheha's face his eyes started to look like those of a—a—*snake.* He was going to shame me before the church. He was going to our newspaper; he was going before the Tribal Council. Anything to get his children. Then he started unleashing hell, tormenting Cheha with his powers!"

"Why didn't you tell us? Maybe we could have helped!"

"How? Cheha didn't want you involved. That's why she left. She thought it would be the only way to protect her family—and Chappy."

"Does Shania know—that he's her father?"

"Of course not. Would Cheha tell her and not you?"

"But she was at his house, Mama. And he bought her a car. She must know!"

Mama was momentarily silent. "Let's get to the hospital while there's still time."

I peered about cautiously as I left for her apartment; and I was equally watchful as we left for the hospital with Mama tightly gripping the handle of the hand-woven sweet grass bassinet.

As I pulled out into the street, a black sedan was parked in a space at the end of the parking lot. The brake lights were on, but because it made no attempt to follow I proceeded without thinking too much about it.

"Tell me—were you seeing Jack Turner while you were still married to our father?" I asked as I wove through traffic.

Now that she was able to talk about it at last, everything seemed to tumble out at once. "Only after your father refused to give *her* up—the woman he was seeing. Everybody knew Jack had an eye for Cheha ever since she was fifteen or so; he was always admiring her, offering Cheha clothes and money. But he was sort of a joke then, to Cheha and her girlfriends.

"But when Roy, your father, kept up his affair for two or three years, Cheha started encouraging Jack. Shania was her secret vengeance. Oh, it was okay for Roy to cheat, but when he found out about Jack, he walked out. And since Cheha was a member of the church, she had to keep it all inside. She had to keep Jack The Medicine Man her sordid little secret!"

I pondered her confession. "He wants his son, and he won't stop until he gets him."

"Cheha knows that. He had two girls of his own but placed all his desire for a son on Marty. Well, now Jack has that son. But if Cheha has to run forever, he'll never get his hands on Chappy. She will see them both dead and herself dead, too, before she will allow Jack's darkness into this baby's life!"

By the following morning, everybody on the reservation and in the Bitterroot Confederacy knew that Uncle Donnie was dying. So how much time would it take before they would also know that my mother was back in town? And with the infant son of one of the most feared witches in all of Indian country?

I felt sorry for Mama. After all her efforts to hide her secret, Cheha Youngblood would be the center of the gossip circus anyhow.

We always knew that Uncle Donnie had friends, but we never knew how many or how deeply he was loved until now. By the time we arrived at the hospital, the head nurse was expressing her concern about the fifty or so people that crowded the lobby waiting to visit; and the others who gathered outside, including the well-meaning medicine men wishing to combine their cures with the White man's therapies.

"Please tell your people that Mr. Jumper's condition is grave, and that we have other critically ill patients on the floor. We just cannot have all the commotion," the head nurse said to me. "You and the immediate family may visit with him as long as you wish, but please tell the others that they will have to leave. Hospital policy."

"I can't do that; they would be greatly offended. And you will have to make one more exception. When a man named Aaron Burning Rain comes, you must allow him in. It was the last thing my uncle asked for."

She sighed. "All right, one more. Mr. Burning Rain. If he appears." She melded with a host of other hospital denizens in white jackets and green scrubs, accessorized with stethoscopes and other medical paraphernalia.

I decided not to stay in the lobby with Chappy as Mama visited her brother for the last time. Too risky. Instead I looked about warily, then bundled him securely in his bassinet and headed for the parking lot.

He studied my face with his intense infant's gaze. He was a sturdy little guy, with ruddy skin, round cheeks, and spiky Indian baby hair. He also had a most serious countenance—and, I learned, hardly ever cried.

"Seems you know already that you're going to have to be a tough little redskin," I said gently. "Think you're up to it?"

One look at that wide, toothless grin, and I was forever hooked; so hopelessly was I in love, I would have willingly died for him—and would kill to protect him too, if I had to.

"Okay," I said, "I'll hold you to that."

I walked briskly across the parking lot to the Vega. My eyes darted about furtively. I shuddered. What could I do if Jack Turner leaped out of the hedges and demanded his child? What if he simply punched my lights out and made off with Chappy?

There must have been dozens of black sedans around—so the one parked next to my Vega, especially because it was unoccupied, did not raise any concern.

I laid Chappy's bassinet on the floor and headed for Mama's apartment. Every stranger's glance at me aroused my suspicion.

After quickly parking the Vega, I grabbed Chappy and, not trusting the elevator, hurriedly scaled the stairs to room 215. Ever vigilant, I set the bassinet down, let myself in and, sighing with relief, placed the baby in his crib at the foot of Mama's bed. "Okay, down you go," I said.

Because of all the stuff going on lately, anxiety worked overtime. On the verge of paranoia by now, I peeked between the opening of the curtains and was concerned about that black sedan that pulled in after me and parked on the far side across from us. Anybody inside would certainly have a crosshairs view of our window.

Like the one parked across from Uncle Donnie's and the one at the hospital, the windows were tinted. I chided myself for not taking down the license plate, or at least studying it more carefully to establish if it were the same car or not.

Presently a woman, youngish, dark haired, emerged from the sedan and began taking packages from the trunk. But as she started toward the complex, under the security lights, something rather odd happened—her eyes lingered at our window, then on the Vega.

I watched intently as she went up the stairs. At first I thought I was imagining things, but when she glanced up at our window several more times before she disappeared around the corner, I knew then that it was no coincidence. She was watching us.

Who was this woman? She had dark hair, but was she Indian? I could not tell. A Jack Turner informant? Obviously. I double-checked the lock on the door and kept an eye on the window.

Chappy started to whimper, so I changed his diaper. And in doing so, I noticed the corner of a notebook peeking from beneath the mattress of Mama's unmade bed. It was another journal. A new one, leading me to believe that she meant for the others to be found; apparently she wanted to explain the torment she'd kept bound in her heart for so many years.

Chappy lay on my lap enjoying his bottle, and with an urgency that was like hunger, I opened my mother's latest journal, the one she had kept during her disappearance:

August 17, 1980
Cheha had forgotten how hot Arizona is in the summer. She hates living in somebody else's house, but staying on the premises is the only way she can save enough money to take care of herself—and the child when it is born.

Mrs. Freese is one of the decent White people. She gives Cheha weekends off. Her father is ninety-something, but still lively enough for fanny pinching if Cheha gets too close to him! Cooking and caring for him is not hard. Mrs. Freese was surprised when she learned about the baby on the way. Before, she thought that Cheha was just a fat Indian lady—now she believes Cheha is a pregnant widow. Cheha feels so guilty deceiving her and misses the children. Especially Dina, who stayed close, the only one Cheha can trust to keep quiet about this—when the time comes...

I scanned page after page of her fragile, desperate thoughts. One about Jack Turner especially held my attention:

...he loves nothing more than being feared...

He and other powerful witches send strong curses on those who offend them, or on anyone who has an enemy and who will pay their fee....

I raised my eyes then, in deep thought: Uncle Donnie must have known about this. No doubt the destructive power these men wielded from the spirit world was the reason he tried so diligently to steer me away from Marty. And Jack Turner.

August 27, 1980
The midwife delivered my new son at 6:53 p.m. last night in the birthing center. Mrs. Freese was like a sister. Everybody pitied the "widow" of the husband who would never see the face of his beautiful son. It is true, in a way. Jack must remain dead to this child. But now Cheha wants to go home.

August 30, 1980
Called Dina tonight. Need her help, but how Cheha hated to burden her daughter with secrets!

August 31, 1980
Horrible dream that Jack knows where she is! Cheha knows now that she should have just left and never have told him about either of his children. But she was angry and wanted to hurt him—now she knows what the elders taught is so true, about words being like arrows and bullets. Once sent forth, you cannot call them back...

Chappy finished his bottle and began to fret, so I rocked him gently until his eyelids grew heavy, then placed him in his crib. It was dark by now, so I returned the journal beneath the mattress. Mama had been with Uncle Donnie for about an hour and a half, and it wasn't safe for her to be out much longer.

I transferred Chappy to his bassinet, being careful not to wake him. Before leaving, I peered outside. Every slow-moving vehicle and every loiterer was suspect. When it was at last safe as far as I could detect, I grabbed the bassinet and locked the door after me. "Okay, little guy. Let's make a run for it," I whispered and hurried down the steps.

As I drove through town, I glanced about frequently. And my watchfulness was not unwarranted. As I slowed down to make a turn, seemingly from out of nowhere, Jack Turner's green truck—the one Marty sometimes drove—suddenly roared into view. And it was coming up hard behind me. My heart drummed with dread. My throat went dry. *Oh, God*, I thought. *This is it.*

I floored the Vega's gas pedal. I knew I could not go back to the hospital. That would lead him to Mama and to who knew what kind of a confrontation.

So I raced for Uncle Donnie's house. I passed Pik'N'Git. Rick was ringing up a customer, smiling and chatting as usual. But charging through stop signs, Jack was gaining on me. Then, mercifully, a car entered traffic from a side street and nearly T-boned the truck. By instinct Jack swerved and slammed on the brakes. And it bought me a few seconds of time. But after that, it was no-holds-barred.

He roared through red lights and plowed down the shoulders of the road. He bullied his way in front of all who hindered him. Motorists slammed on their brakes. Tires squealed. Horns blasted. Insults flew. But nothing was going to deter him from pursuing me and claiming his son.

And there I was—desperately trying to keep one eye on the road, the other on the bassinet on the floor next to me, while at the same time trying to mentally scribble a strategy of escape on the suddenly blank page of my mind: *Pull into the driveway. Park. Jump out. Run to the passenger's side. Grab Chappy. Race to the house. Unlock the door. Then lock it again behind me.*

And all of it before Jack Turner could chase us down.

Over and over, I repeated: "Help me, God. Please help me with this baby. Help, me Lord!"

Nearly numb mentally, I slammed to a halt in the driveway, leaped out, and tried to grab the bassinet. It was stuck—wedged between the front seat and the dashboard and would not budge.

"Forget the bassinet—take the baby," a sane voice in my head advised.

So, keys in hand, I grabbed my tiny brother, now screaming in alarm, and fled for the house. The shale and gravel rendered me unsteady on my feet. I stumbled and skinned my elbow and knee, but managed to hold on to the baby, regain my footing, and continue my race against time to reach the house.

I had planned my strategy in my head, but carrying it out was another matter: I did not take into account that my hands would be shaking almost uncontrollably; that I could not find the key on the ring, and that I would feel like throwing up; or that it would take Jack Turner so little time before he appeared lightning-quick in the driveway.

He slammed to a halt and parked bumper to bumper behind the Vega. And he strode toward me with outstretched hands. "Give me my son. You don't have any rights to him. He's mine; *give him to me!*"

Eddie Was had been sitting and grooming himself. But when he saw Jack Turner, he eyed him, hissed, and growled. The fur of his arched back and his tail stood on end. His ears went flat against his head. He meant business.

"Scat—go on, now!" Jack Turner continued his menacing advance. Then he looked down at something beyond the cat—and halted dead in his tracks. For a brief second, a glint of Fear leaped into his eyes as the commander of the dark froze, and almost imperceptively, backed away.

I glanced down to where he was staring at the huge, black, glistening insect that scurried along and disappeared beneath the step. And in that half-breath of time I remembered Marty's words: *"Well, ol' John Turner is near terrified of cockroaches. I can vouch for that!"*

He recovered quickly but came no closer as he continued to hurl threats: "I'll tell you one more time—give me my son!"

Eddie Was continued his refrain from his tough tomcat stance.

Jack Turner glared. "I said, go on, now!" He then reached down and picked up a stone.

"No—please don't hurt my cat!" I said.

But hurl it he did, and it found its mark. Eddie Was let out a short cry and lay still.

"I hate you!" I yelled. I shouldered the screen door open, then dropped the keys; I tried to balance the baby and retrieve them at the same time. Everything moved in slow motion. I could only watch as poor Eddie Was lashed his tail weakly in his agony. I was sobbing and trembling. Chappy was screaming. I twisted the key, but the latch held.

Jack Turner's eyes blazed. His lips curled back in a snarl as he spewed orders at me. "I want my Indian son. I won't have you religious half-breeds, you *apples*—red outside and white inside—raising my little boy! You are traitors to your own culture, your own people!"

He started toward me. By the time he reached the first step, finally, mercifully, I heard the latch click. Balancing the screaming baby, I managed to shoulder open the door.

By the time he reached the top step, I was inside. Just as I was slamming the door he was grabbing the doorknob. I felt him tugging, but I pulled with all my strength and turned the deadbolt. He rattled the doorknob, banged on the door, and hurled curses and threats.

"Give him up, or I will hunt Cheha down and strangle the life out of her with my bare hands—right before your eyes. Then I will blind you, so that your mother's death will be the last image you will ever see!"

I sank to the floor behind the door and cradled the screaming baby close while I gasped for breath. "It's all right." I sobbed. "You're safe. I won't let him take you!"

As if he understood me, Chappy stopped crying then, and I could feel his tiny heart beating as I held him close. This helpless little human being had only me to stand between him and the darkness. And that I intended to do, even if it cost me my life, because Chappy deserved a future, a chance to make decisions of his own. My mother deserved to live freely among her own people without the Terror wielded against her that was Jack Turner's weapon. Like others packed guns and knives, Jack Turner brandished Terror.

As we sat huddled on the floor, he continued hammering with his fists and kicking the door with his steel-toed boots. And the tears that rolled down my cheeks were no longer those of Fear; but the hot tears of an impotent rage that had nowhere to go.

"Listen to me," he continued, "you tainted pretend Indian. I won't let you and your mother foul my boy with your White man's teachings. *I'm* his father, and he *will* wear my name!"

I summoned my courage. "He will *not!*" I yelled back. "He's Cherokee Apache Youngblood—my little brother, and he will never wear your name. You want to turn him into a—a broker of evil, and we won't let you! You want to kill us? Then go ahead. Be more of a murderer than you already are!"

He called my mother and me every foul name in his vocabulary. He kicked the door for emphasis with each item in his litany.

"My child will be brought up the *Indian* way." Bang. "*My* way!" Bang. "He will *speak* Indian." Bang. "*Think* Indian." Another kick. "*Look* Indian. *Live* Indian." He yanked on the doorknob. "Now, open this door and give me my son, Dina!"

"Never!"

An uneasy silence ensued, yet I did not hear him drive away. After a long moment, I peeked through the window. The truck was still in the driveway, but there was no sign of Jack Turner and, oddly, no sign of Eddie Was. In the twilight, though, I could see in every tree the chilling silhouettes of Jack Turner's owls as they continued their sinister chants.

Shuddering with Terror, I walked stealthily to every window, expecting each time for his face to pop up on the other side. Finally I crept into my bedroom to close the drapes. And as if materializing from the air, a gigantic owl alit on my window sill, and there we stood eye to eye. I screamed. It took off and vanished. Nausea nearly overtook me. My hands trembled uncontrollably as I yanked the curtains shut.

Jack Turner? Had he changed himself into an owl, too? Was it really true—could a person shape-shift?

The police. Maybe it wouldn't do any good. He had fearful cronies everywhere. But I would call anyhow. They would, by law, have to at least show up and chase him off. And it would buy me some time to take my mother home.

But Jack Turner seemed to have somehow read my thoughts. I picked up the telephone and was surprised to get a dial tone as I heard his truck roar away. And although I did not see them leave, the owls had vanished also.

"Let's go, little brother," I said in a quavering voice. I opened the door cautiously and glanced around for Eddie Was. He was nowhere to be seen, but the dimness of the streetlight revealed a small pool of blood where he had fallen. No doubt my best friend among the four-leggeds, a link to my childhood, had dragged himself off somewhere to die alone.

I choked back tears as I placed Chappy inside the car. Just as I was about the turn the ignition key, I heard the roar of Jack Turner's truck again. The headlights, like two giant owl's eyes, blazed through the darkness.

Jack Turner had U-turned.

Jack Turner was back.

He sounded his horn in one long, unending blast. I screamed and locked the doors as he tore around the Vega in mad circles and yelled over and over: "Give me my son!" He hurled curses in Indian.

The episode went on and on. Chappy was screaming. I was sobbing. And quaking with Terror.

Finally, Jack Turner lurched to a halt beside me, eye-to-eye. He rolled down the window. "Alright—keep him for now. But you tell Cheha this for me: If I don't get my boy before the sun crosses the sky twice, I will unleash the very powers of hell against both of you. I *will* get my son. Nobody takes from Jack Turner!" Then, still blasting his horn and yelling in Indian, he tore down the street like a madman.

I sat in the car with my head on the steering wheel, still trembling and sobbing and trying to compose myself.

The owls returned and resumed their threats. So apparently Jesus had not answered my prayers. Queasiness began to roil in my stomach, and I leaned out of the door as the contents of my stomach spewed out on the ground.

I sat there until the bout passed. *What next?* I wondered. Surely Jack Turner had to know by now where my mother was. And surely, without warning, when we least expected it, he would come in the dead of night for his son.

So it was time to do what I had to do. I felt like a robot, no longer in control of my own actions as I took the still whimpering baby and headed back into the house.

I tended my skinned elbow and knee and changed my blood-stained jeans. I crept into Uncle Donnie's bedroom—his adored Bible was still on the nightstand, his new eyeglasses were on top of it. A pencil between the pages marked where he last stopped reading. For all his seeking, for all of my prayers, I thought with bitter resignation, Jesus did not save him from Jack Turner. And apparently He wasn't going to save my mother, either.

Standing on tiptoes, I ran my hands beneath the tangle of Uncle Donnie's jeans and patchwork jackets on the top shelf of his closet until I felt what I was reaching for: the smooth handle of the *efche esh fah yee kee*. And now all that was left to do was to wait until the time was right.

Jack Turner had just pulled into Uncle Donnie's driveway. He swung out of his truck and started toward the house where Chappy lay inside sleeping. But he did not know that I was crouching, hiding, just beyond the hedges; that he was a dead shot as I peered across the barrel of the efche.

But just as my finger eased on the trigger, they came. Scores of them. Hundreds of them. Owls. Their great numbers blackened the sky as they swooped down upon me.

Their sharp talons tore at my arms as I shielded my face with my hands. One ripped the scalp of my forehead. I dropped the Winchester and, screaming, flailing my arms to fend them off, made a run for the house. But they closed in on me, ripping, tearing at my flesh. Owls. Jack Turner's owls.

"Call them off!" I screamed. "They're tearing me apart—eating me alive. Please! I'll give you your son!"

But Jack Turner just stood there and watched—and laughed. "Feed on her," he commanded, "like you feed on the flesh of rats!"...

I sprang bolt upright then, screaming in Terror as I fought my imaginary attackers. Then the walls of my own room slowly came into focus in the darkness of predawn. Gasping with relief, trembling, I collapsed against my pillow.

It had all been just a dream—a night Terror. But I could not help but wonder: *why, then, is blood oozing from a gash in my scalp?*

Could it be a self-inflicted slash from my own flailing in my dream war—or something beyond reality as I perceived it?

By the following afternoon, everybody in The Root and on The Rez not only knew about Uncle Donnie, but also about Chappy. As a young cousin cared from him in the lobby, between their wrenching sobs, gossips managed to corral their grief long enough to shoot quizzical stares at the baby and to speculate that perhaps Chappy was really Shania's son, the White boyfriend's baby; and that Mama was covering for her, taking the heat for her beautiful daughter so she could become the first Native American supermodel.

Meanwhile, upstairs in Room 307, Death, who could cleverly disguise himself as sleep, was now deceiving us with counterfeit snores as it rattled in Uncle Donnie's throat. Even though he was technically still alive, I had already worked through the agony of my loss.

My most bitter regret now was that he did not get to see Burning Rain. But it was just as well. It would only have given him false hope that his friend the preacher could call down the powers of heaven to save him.

I sat at his bedside watching as his monitor line grew weaker and weaker, and finally went flat. A doctor pronounced him dead. Then the wailing started. But even as it intensified and filled the room, I sat there dry-eyed. I had already done my grieving.

It was about a half hour after Uncle Donnie passed away that Burning Rain finally made his way through the weeping throng. I wanted to throw myself into his arms and sob out my anguish against his broad chest, but a cluster of prayer warriors—religious groupies I called them—who had come all the way from Oklahoma followed hot on his heels.

One, a White woman, middle-aged and attractive, was, I could see, fawning over Aaron's every need: bringing him a glass of water, carrying his briefcase. Smiling. Always smiling, even in this wailing throng. Always in his face. Things like that. Jealousy briefly pierced my heart even though he, on the other hand, regarded her with only a pastor's brotherly detachment.

With them, grim-faced, was the old woman in the black domed hat and traditional attire. The Mama Hat apparition was here. This time, however, it was obvious that she was very real.

I inched forward, straining to get a better look. She was moving among the crowd and I lost sight of her—same as in years before—as the group pressed in around the bed.

Burning Rain threw himself on his knees at the side of Uncle

Donnie's bed. "Lord God Almighty, in the Name of Jesus," he cried out, "let your Name be glorified. We ask for life for this brother. We ask you to raise him up off this bed to walk again in the land of the living. Call back his breath from the four winds, that he may live again and declare Your mighty works!"

The prayer warriors closed in then, all speaking at the same time, filling the room with unintelligible babble. How they expected God to understand with all of them talking at once was beyond me.

There was no Mama Hat, I decided, only someone who looked like her. As the praying went on and on, the nurses slipped out, their eyes averted, apparently embarrassed by this sideshow.

There was nothing more that I could do for Uncle Donnie now, except make sure that the one responsible for his needless death and responsible for the Terror dispatched against us got what he deserved.

And now was the perfect time. Nobody would miss me.

So while Burning Rain, his hair now undone, drenched in sweat and delinquent about his shoulders, cried out to this Christian God who obviously showed no concern for Indians, I eased my way through the crowd, down the corridor, down the elevator, across the parking lot, and into a fifty-dollar deal of shiny Vega metal sitting on good rubber. The loaded *efche esh fa yee kee*, wrapped in Uncle Donnie's favorite patchwork jacket, lay on the back floor. I would finish what I started with Jack Turner in that dream. Only this time it would be for real.

And there would be no owls to defend him.

XI

The Ancient Art of War

I started the engine and swung into traffic. By now it was late September, and a storm was kicking up in the Atlantic. Gusts of wind played havoc with the palm trees lining nearly every street. Mists of rain frothed on the windshield and drained down like rivulets of tears on a cold glass cheek.

My plan was set in stone. I would not be deterred. I would not be denied. As I turned onto the highway, I relied on my childhood memories when we would pile into "Uncle John's" car and head out for a visit in the hummocks.

My every nerve was fine-tuned to the slightest nuances of the road, the weather, and the howling winds that shook the Vega as if trying to rattle me back to my senses. But reason was suspended; for it was no longer I who drove, but Madness. When I reached the turnoffs that led to the hummocks, I slowed down.

There were no landmarks so, using reasoning, long-buried memories, and intuition, I chose the trail least overgrown with palmetto and sawgrass—the one clearly most recently traveled. I leaned forward, studying the narrow winding trail as I drove along. A half-mile or so down the path I caught sight of the hummock—the raised area where Jack Turner's house sat.

It was a fairly nice house, in the middle of a circle of chickees. It was smaller than I remembered it to be, but it was "Uncle John's" house all right. True to tradition, one chickee was reserved for cooking, but no doubt it was now just for barbecues—recreational purposes.

Another had a four-seater wooden swing; beneath still another, tools. Several "Indian cars"—without tires, rusted out—sat on concrete blocks, their former glory days long gone.

Last of all, beneath the chickee nearest the house, was Jack Turner's truck. I parked the Vega a safe distance away and sat there studying the scene from a past that was no longer a memory.

And it all came creeping back: "Uncle John" did not like indoor toilets. And I remembered one detached from the house—concrete block style like the main dwelling, but detached nonetheless with a bath, shower, and a flush toilet.

A thin black-and-white cur—a true Rez dog—dozed under the truck. He stood up, gazed in my direction, and started to bark.

Presently, the screen door creaked, and Jack Turner, the enemy of all goodness, stood there in the doorway. The storm winds carried his voice to me: "What is it, Watchtaker?" He peered in my direction and, for one terrible moment, my heart stood still. But he bent down and undid the dog's chain. "Quiet. Probably a raccoon or something. But just in case it's a panther, come in the house for awhile." He opened the screen door, but the dog continued to bark in my direction. "Come on, now—get moving, you ol' fleabag," he said with fondness.

I held my breath, hoping the dog would not decide to prove his loyalty by charging toward me. And I exhaled in relief when he barked one final challenge in my direction and loped inside.

Jack Turner shut the door after him and started across the yard then, carrying both a book and magazine as he headed for the bath house. He had planned, apparently, to sit a spell, I mused. My pulse quickened. Good. It would give me time. Carefully I unwrapped the *efche* from Uncle Donnie's patchwork jacket—the banner I was carrying into battle.

Quietly, I positioned the barrel in the wishbone of a small tree and waited in the misting rain. The ancient art of war. It was going to be fought my way. I would take the fight to the enemy in a surprise attack with my choice of weapon.

"Go get my *efche esh fah yee kee*," Uncle Donny had said that afternoon as he sat at the table only weeks ago. "Let's go hunting. I want to see if you still know how to shoot..."

"Oh, yes, Uncle Donny," I whispered in the blustering wind through clenched teeth as I crouched there in the brush, "I still know how to shoot. And the snake-blooded owl responsible for your death

146

will not go unpunished!"

Nearly a half hour later, the door to the bath house finally swung open again, and Jack Turner stepped outside. He coughed, cleared his throat, spat, and adjusted his belt. With the magazine and book still in hand, he strode back toward the house.

I had him in my sight. I aimed and braced myself. "Breathe your last, you son of the Devil," I whispered. I released the safety and gently placed my finger on the trigger. He would drop like a sack of potatoes.

Before I could fire, however, I caught a movement at my left, out of the corner of my eye.

Coming toward me was a young Indian man—flawless, handsome beyond description. He was clad in white buckskin...so white it seemed to glow.

Although short of being regalia in my estimation, his clothing was embellished with the most intricate beadwork made from tiny seed beads that shimmered and reflected the colors of an unseen rainbow. Unless your mama or aunt or somebody close made it for you, an outfit like this one would set you back five figures or more.

I released my finger from the trigger. Who was this stranger, and what in the world was he doing out here in the Everglades in an approaching storm?

He held some kind of notebook or tablet—white also, and made of leather also enhanced with beadwork of the most intricate workmanship. It was unusual to see such dress except at a powwow clothing contest. The tangy sweetish smell of new buckskin permeated the damp air.

When I caught his eye, he stopped short. I eased the rifle down, placed it on the ground, dropped the jacket over it, and started toward him to distract him from what I was about to do.

"Hello," I said and waved at him. "I don't think we've met before. You must know my Uncle Jack."

He came closer. His translucent skin seemed to glow, like a heat mirage was shimmering from within him. His glistening hair, raven black, was cropped shoulder length. His dark almond-shaped eyes were bright in his golden face—so bright they left me breathless...so bright they seemed other-worldly.

I took a step back as he approached.

He eyed me up and down but with a flat, inscrutable expression. He was definitely a looker but also disconcerting because he wasn't saying anything.

I tried to appear casual. "So, uh—do you live around here?"

"No. I go wherever the battle takes me." In the dying light, his teeth literally seemed to glow in their whiteness against his flawless skin and perfectly chiseled features.

And his voice—I had never before heard one like it. It was soft, while at the same time deep and commanding, like someone had tamed the thunder and tossed it into gently rushing waters.

I ventured a step forward. "You say you follow battles. What kinds of battles?" I offered what I hoped was my cutest smile. After all, hey, there was definitely a relationship possibility here.

"I do rescue work," he said.

I was curious. "Oh? What do you rescue out here—trapped and wounded animals?"

His words were matter-of-fact: "People. I rescue people."

"Well, you must have a lot of time on your hands because not many people live out here. Just my uh—Uncle Jack. And sometimes his stepson, Marty. Sam Waters used to, but he moved to Bitterroot."

Out of the corner of my eye, again, I saw my quarry slip through my fingers as Jack Turner made it to his house and shut the door behind him.

"So, are you going to visit my Uncle or what? I mean, you don't plan to stand here in the rain for the rest of the evening, do you?" I asked.

"I have done what I came here to do. To rescue your—*Uncle* Jack. And to rescue you."

"Me? From what?"

"From yourself."

Mine was a nervous giggle: "You're quite—interesting. Okay. So I've been rescued. Now what? Shall we go someplace for coffee?" I edged even more in front of the jacket to block him from seeing what was beneath it.

He did not respond but stood in the now steady rain. His gaze seemed to penetrate my skull and into my very thoughts. "You picked a bad night to visit your—uncle," he said. "Trees are down in town and the roads are going to be dangerous in another hour or so."

I noticed then that although he was standing in the now-driving rain that was glistening on my face, plastering my hair to my skull, and my clothes to my skin, *he was dry.* And so were his buckskins. Strange...

In the distance Jack Turner's telephone was ringing. My intended target, he was now inside his house and standing with his back to the window as he answered. *A dead shot,* I thought. Were it not for this handsome and intriguing weirdo, I could have taken him out minutes ago and been back at the hospital before anybody missed me. Nothing was working out.

It seemed obvious this cutie wasn't going to move. But if I left, he would see me take my weapon, and if he were one of Jack Turner's cronies, he would surely report it to him and make matters worse than they already were.

"Your beadwork is gorgeous. Are you on the powwow circuit?" I asked to distract him.

"There are many interesting things in the universe—things you cannot even conceptualize. Come with me, and I will give you a glimpse of the unimaginable."

I backed away. What kind of answer was that? I wondered. "Let me take a rain check. Literally," I said as I wiped the water from my face. My laugh was forced, artificial; and Fear was now a drummer in my chest. Maybe those owls told Jack Turner my plans. Or what if this guy standing before me was really a conjured spirit, sent to foil my plans and then lure me off to who knew what fate?

Just then, Jack Turner slammed down the telephone and burst out of the door. He was slipping on a patchwork jacket as he leaped into his truck. The brake lights flashed brightly—two flaming eyes in the dying light—as he backed up, turned around, and slowly negotiated the bumpy terrain. Wipers flying full speed, he headed for the one narrow path that led from his house back to the highway. He was sure to see the Vega.

A voice whispered to me: *"Take them both out. This stranger first, because he is a witness. You will never again have this chance. And You must avenge your Uncle Donnie, and your mother for the torment Jack Turner caused them. Nobody will know..."*

When the stranger shifted his gaze momentarily to the truck, I leaped for the rifle, turned to him, and I, Dina Youngblood, prepared to fire.

But he was gone. Just like that.

I looked around me, convinced that nobody could de-materialize in a split second right in front of your eyes. But vanished he had.

"Hey, I didn't mean to scare you. I just needed to keep the rifle dry and get back home—okay?" Nobody answered. I looked around, up, down, everywhere.

By now, the rain was pelting me in great drops. I put the safety on the rifle, tossed it on the back seat, squeezed the water from the jacket, covered the rifle with it and took off, grateful that Jack Turner slowed down apparently to adjust a radio station, probably to hear the weather report.

My Vega made it to the highway just as the truck's headlights rounded the last of many curves in the narrow pass. Wipers still going, still toying with the radio, he passed me easily in the driving rain without ever looking up.

I continuously scanned about for the stranger. But there was no sign of him. And I noticed that, as soon as I left the hummocks and turned onto the highway, the madness that had gripped me disappeared just as mysteriously as the stranger had. I was thinking rationally again and I started to tremble uncontrollably:

Dina, what were you thinking? Had it not been for that stranger's mysterious appearing—and disappearing—you would have murdered two people in cold blood!

Now my stomach was *really* churning. Bile in all its bitterness rose up in my throat. My head was spinning. I had tunnel vision—all around me was darkness. *Jack Turner's curse,* I thought.

Pull over. You're blacking out, my reason told me.

I swung the Vega over to the side of the road and lurched to a stop. I opened the door and leaned out until my nausea passed.

Afterward, I just sat in the open door listening to the wind howling like evening wolves. The storm was mirroring the same raging I felt in my spirit. I had no control anymore.

Dina Youngblood, the woman with two hearts, had finally split in two. And I realized that one was a calculating killer who wrapped her motives in the deep love for her family and her people; a warrior Indian of old who believed the ancient art of war dictated that you take out your enemy.

Within the other heart were the fragments of a memory of Christian teachings: to God alone belongs vengeance. Only He had the right to decide who should live and who should die—even someone as vile and wicked as Jack Turner.

How long I sat there parked on the side of the highway I do not remember. I dried my tears and, out of the corner of my eye, saw a figure clothed in white—the stranger in the buckskins—walking down the shoulder of the highway carrying that leather bound notepad. Surely he was no specter, I decided. Assured that the *efche* was still covered by the jacket, I rolled down the window, and honked the horn.

"Hey, want a ride?" I pulled up beside him. "That is, if you trust my driving." I unlocked the door and offered what I hoped was a reassuring smile.

He climbed into the back seat without looking at me. "Thank you, Dina Youngblood."

"You know my name," I said. "What's yours?"

"What I do is more important than what I'm called," he said.

"You said you rescued people. That's pretty vague."

"Specifically, I rescue people from strongholds."

Strongholds. Jails, probably, I figured. Lots of missionary types did jail ministry. A long silence ensued. I wanted to ask about the notepad he carried, but he was close-mouthed about his name and vague about what he did, so lots of luck, I figured, on his sharing what was in his notebook. "Well, you won't tell me your name. Perhaps you'll tell me something about strongholds and how you rescue people," I said.

"I command the fingers of the mighty to release their grip on the powerless."

He was good-looking, true, but we were definitely not hitting it off. So I decided that Marty was still the best-looking NDN guy on the East Coast, and definitely more accessible.

Aaron had more depth and compassion, and had scored lots of points with God, but as for this weirdo, I was sick of his cryptic double talk. And as he became less and less attractive to me, I could not wait to deposit him somewhere. Anywhere. I didn't want to spend one second longer than I had to with Mr. Conversationalist-of-the-Year.

"Well, you won't tell me your name or much about what you do. So at least tell me where I can drop you off," I said with a bit of a sting.

"I'm going where you're going," he said. "To Samaritan One East."

A chill raced through me as I pondered his words. *So I was right the first time. He obviously has powerful medicine, so it's best not to rile him. No telling what he's capable of doing.*

I chose my words carefully: "That's strange. My uncle crossed over a few hours ago, and my family and his friends are saying their good-byes. Do you have family there, too?"

"No. Just your Uncle Donnie. And the others."

It was a struggle to hold the wheel steady after that last statement, so we rode the rest of the way in silence. When I pulled into the hospital's parking lot, I turned to speak to him. But he had vanished. Again. And the only thing left behind was the lingering sweetness of new buckskin.

Still in my damp clothes, I was suddenly chilled to the bone. I refused to think, refused to speculate or to analyze. I just wanted to get upstairs to my family, where somebody could reassure me that I was not over the edge, and where people didn't vanish into thin air.

Could I be trapped in a night Terror again, unable to wake from it? I wondered. As I stood waiting in the lobby for the elevator, I kept looking about, hoping to catch another glimpse of Stronghold Rescuer. But as before, he was nowhere to be seen.

When the elevator finally arrived, it seemed to take forever for the door to open, another to close again and to reach the third floor, and an interminable time for the two chattering matrons to move off so I could exit. Even my feet seemed leaden as I made my last journey to Uncle Donnie's hospital room before they removed him from our presence to his new place among the dead.

The fragrance of fresh buckskin must have still lingered in my nostrils because it was not possible, I speculated, that it was also present on this hospital floor.

You're slipping—headed for deep black water, Dina. You need to admit to yourself that the stranger was only in your head, I thought.

When I entered Uncle Donnie's room, the mourners were starting their exits through the door. They hugged Mama, who was still weeping and kneeling at Uncle Donnie's bedside. They hugged me and wept on my shoulder. And they reminded me, "How you loved him. How he loved you!" But not a soul seemed to have missed me.

The old woman I glimpsed before was seated on a chair near the foot of the bed. Others of Aaron's prayer team milled about among the locals, offering condolences.

Aaron had secured his hair again and was mopping his face. And I thought with bitterness, *Well, score one more for Mr. Death, and zero for the Prayer Warriors, because Uncle Donnie is still dead.*

But I conceded that at least they had the courage to try, in spite of how others may mock their faith.

What really fascinated me, though, was that neither Aaron nor any of the warriors seemed the least bit embarrassed, angry, or disappointed that after all their loud pleadings to the Lord, their prayers had not been answered. The hospital attendants stood by, waiting politely for all of us to leave so they could do what they always did when all interventions failed: cover Death with a white sheet and wheel him to the morgue.

Even Mama, the last to leave the bedside, finally dried her eyes, too. It was over. Finished. Done. No power on earth could bring Uncle Donnie back. She hugged the old woman in the Mama Hat gear—and clung to her long and tearfully. Did they know each other? Somebody would have to tell me because I was done with speculating or trying to make sense of my world.

"Praise the Lord," Mama said softly. "What a blessing. I never imagined that I would see you again." She then turned to me. "This is Dina—all grown up now, as you can see."

Aaron came over and placed an affectionate hand on the old woman's shoulder. "Why didn't you tell me, after working with me off and on all these years, that you were kin to these people? You know what she did?" he said as he turned and addressed all of us. "She took Luke 9:62 in the Bible very literally: 'No man, having put his hand to the plough, and looking back, is fit for the kingdom of God.'"

Everybody laughed and interjected some rousing amens.

Aaron continued. "And there was another one she quoted about following the Lord's calling. I'll let her tell it!"

Mama Hat lowered her eyes demurely. "But Jesus said to him, 'Follow me; and let the dead bury their dead.'"

Aaron smiled broadly. "You hear that? That's Matthew 8:22. See? This warrior takes the Bible word for word!"

I went over to her chair, knelt at her feet, and took her small weathered hands in mine. "Mama Hat—my great grandmother. So it's really you. And you left everybody to go and be a missionary—a prayer warrior to the Indian nations?"

She sighed. "One night, I went to see what all the fuss was about at a revival meeting. I didn't go there to get saved, but I did. And later that night, the Lord spoke to my heart and said to work humbly and quietly and to intercede in prayer for my people.

"I knew if I stayed here or told anybody, they would think I was—" she smiled—"*on-na-hak-bee-pek.* I was an old woman even then. So I figured I had earned the right to do what I wanted. And I wanted to follow the Lord."

On-na-hak-bee-pek—it was one of the few words she'd taught me in Mikasuki that I remembered.

Aaron was loving every minute of it. "What really knocked me over was when I called out to Oklahoma for as many warriors as possible to come here and pray and encourage Brother Donnie, Sister Hannah Glory Cypress here—Mama Hat—was the first to volunteer."

His voice was mirthful. "She told me that Donnie was family. And when she got here, people started coming up to her talking about Mama Hat this, and Mama Hat that. I said, 'Who's Mama Hat?' Well, now I know!" he said with a laugh.

But just as quickly, he was serious again as he went and stood solemnly at the bedside. "Brother Donnie, I know you had a seeking heart for the Lord. I pray He will honor that and count it to your credit as a righteous man. And unless you stand up and start walking again, I'm trusting God that I'll see you in The Bright Place." He paused, quiet for a moment, then looked at his watch.

"Well, we haven't eaten since breakfast. Intercessory prayer is hard work. Let's go downstairs to the cafeteria and refuel with some of that great tasting hospital food," he said to his warriors.

154

People started filing out. Mama had her arm around Mama Hat. "You have another great-grandson to meet," she said as they headed out of the door.

I lingered behind for a last farewell. When they had all exited and the room was suddenly quiet and still, I took my uncle's cool hand into my own. "Good-bye, Uncle Donnie. I love you. I'll always love you." I stifled my tears.

And suddenly, there was again the tangy fragrance of new buckskin; at first it was faint, then it became stronger and stronger. My imagination again, I thought, and tried to ignore it. But a movement caught my eye.

Startled, I looked up, and the stranger in white was standing there at the foot of the bed holding his ledger, tracing with his finger down what was obviously a list of names. He stopped and fixed his intense gaze on the still form upon the bed. "Come back, Donnie Jumper. The intercessory prayers of the saints for you have been heard in heaven. It is not your time," he said.

Immediately, Uncle Donnie opened his eyes. He sat up, looked about, and appeared confused. "What am I doing in this hospital?" he demanded.

I could barely speak. "You're alive. Uncle Donnie, you're alive again!" I clasped my hands together and fell on my knees before the stranger. "Thank you—whoever you are. Thank you for bringing him back!"

"Get up off your knees, young woman. I am only a messenger. He is perfectly well now. Call the nurses and tell them to bring him some food."

He then walked to the door, stepped across the threshold, the portal that divided time from unseen eternity, and right before my eyes, vanished again into the spirit realm.

I stood there dumbstruck. Awed. Stock-still. Frozen. Petrified.

"Hey, over here. Of *course* I'm alive. So what are you doing standing there with your mouth open? And why am I in this hospital, aaay? If I passed out or something, for sure I'm okay now!"

But all I could say was, "Did you see him—the man I was talking to? He was Indian. Tall, beautiful, powerfully built, wearing white buckskin. Did you see him?"

"What man? Hurry up, girl. Get married before you die from a terminal case of Marty-on-the-Brain. I'll even hold my nose and try to tolerate him!" He paused and sighed. "Would be nice if you married up with the preacher, though." He sat on the side of the bed. "Well, since I'm here, where's the food? Don't they feed people around here?"

I stood at the door, looking up and down the corridor. "Uncle Donnie, didn't you see the man in white?"

He threw up his hands. "The only man in this room is Donnie Jumper. Maybe you saw a ghost, which is what I'm gonna be pretty quick if they don't get me some food!"

Holding his hospital gown in the back, he opened his closet, tossed out his clothes and those old alligator boots he refused to part with in spite of their scruffiness. "Nothing's wrong with me anyway. So this old Indian is going home, where you're gonna do me up some decent food, aaay!"

Having failed to locate the stranger, I went to the nurses' station. "There was a gentleman—uh, an Indian gentleman—wearing white Traditional clothes. I was wondering if he came this way. If you saw him."

The head nurse did not look up from recording something on her clipboard. "No such person has passed through these corridors. If he did, believe me, we would have noticed him."

I continued. "He said that the patient, Donnie Jumper in 307, needs to be fed now. But you need to hurry. He's determined to go home. He's getting dressed even as I speak."

She still did not look up. "Mr. Jumper in 307 expired at 5:27 p.m. They'll be taking him to the morgue shortly."

Just then Uncle Donnie's buzzer went off and his words echoed loudly in the nurses' station: "Could I get some dinner in here? A man's gotta eat!"

Then she looked up. And so did all of the other nurses—at each other, at me, and at each other again. Wordlessly, with their stethoscopes and clipboards in hand and with astonishment stamped on their faces, they tramped lock-step, like soldiers in jackboots, down the corridor toward 307.

Uncle Donnie was standing by the bed, clad only in his hospital gown and those old alligator boots. His Levis were in one hand, bare butt for all to see, and he was still pressing the buzzer.

"After I get my food," he yelled, "I'm checking outta here. And after I check out, I'm having this place investigated!" He then noticed that he couldn't pull up his jeans over those old boots, so he pulled them off again and started over. Jeans first.

One nurse just stood there dumbfounded. A young male intern pointed and whispered, "But—you're dead!" And passed out. Then they started rushing around at once, both taking care of the young intern, asking Uncle Donnie questions, and trying to coax him back to bed.

"Mr. Jumper, we need you to lie down and relax so we can check your vital signs," the head nurse said.

"For what—so you can pronounce me alive this time?" he said.

"The man in the white buckskin called him back," I said simply. "You don't have to believe it if you don't want to, but that's exactly what happened!"

I left then and headed for the elevator to tell Aaron and the prayer warriors the astonishing news. But the elevator was already on its way up and when the door slid open, Aaron and all the others poured out over the floor and headed for Uncle Donnie's room, where he stood perfectly well and appeared slightly perplexed at all the attention.

Aaron was ecstatic. "Signs and wonders!" he declared. "Praise the Lord. Praise the Lord! I will dance with the joy of King David!"

And dance he did. And laughed and sang and wept. Other prayer warriors joined in. Some fell prostrate. Others lifted their faces upward and spoke all at once in that strange babble. I just stood there, my mouth agape.

Somebody paged security.

Most of the prayer warriors swore they saw the man in white. Only a couple did not see anything, including the attractive blonde—the one I thought was paying too way much attention to Aaron, and she was clearly distraught. "I was sitting right *next* to Aaron. Why didn't I see him?" she asked.

"Well, he stood right next to me, and said 'Get upstairs. Your prayers of faith are heard and rewarded. Your brother is alive,'" another

Oklahoma warrior said.

"Don't you know what happened?" Aaron asked Uncle Donnie. "You died, Indian brother, and the Lord called you back. Wonderful—just wonderful!"

Uncle Donnie paraded around with the blood pressure cuff dangling on his arm, ignoring the nurse trying diligently to coax him to sit or at least to stand still.

His face seemed to glow from an inner light. "You need to listen to what I saw in the other place. I thought it was a dream till you told me I died. It was bright…filled with light. All the colors were like 3-D or something, shimmering and glowing, brighter and purer than I can describe. There was this gentle voice telling me I was chosen to leave the old place and come to that perfect place. But that I would have to go back and tell my people."

The head nurse pulled herself up to full height. "You were no doubt hallucinating, Mr. Jumper. That can happen with certain conditions—or medications. Believe me, you never left this room. You did *not* die. We were just…unable to read your vital signs."

And from that point on, she was in Uncle Donnie's crosshairs. "If Dina said a man in white called me back, then that's what happened! You can say what you want, but I know what I saw, and I know what I heard!"

The head nurse raised a quizzical eyebrow. "If a man from, uh—" she cleared her throat—"*heaven* called you back, why would he be dressed in an Indian costume?"

Uncle Donnie's reply was sharp. "He was dressed in Traditional Indian *clothes* because he *was* Indian! You think only White people are in heaven?" He eyed her. "Maybe you White people get favor here on earth, but God doesn't play that kind of stuff in heaven!"

158

XII

Another Tribe

Nobody cared who fell asleep on the floor, in a chair, or on Uncle Donnie's sofa. In the two days since he'd walked out of Samaritan One East, folks from all the nearby Indian reservations and communities had come to see the dead man who came back to life—with no sign of his diabetes.

Nobody went home, because nobody wanted to go home. Tents and tipis were pitched in the front and backyards. Somebody even erected a *chickee* on the side of the house.

Every day a large pot of *sofkee* somehow appeared on the stove, also frybread, venison, barrels of Kentucky Fried Chicken—all kinds of foods. Nobody really noticed who brought what. It did not matter.

We were unable to explain the feeling of closeness as we talked and sang and celebrated and gave testimonies and ate.Mama was sitting on the living room couch and little Cherokee—Chappy—was fast asleep across her lap.

"Anybody else have a testimony?" Burning Rain asked. "If you do, just get up and say what the Lord had done in your life." He held up his hand as he laughed. "No, not you again, Brother Donnie. Let's give some of the others a chance."

"I hear you, Preacher," Uncle Donnie said as he sat. "When I get started it's hard to stop, aaay!"

Mama stood up. "Cheha would—I mean, *I* would—like to say that I have never known such peace. Before, I had so much hatred in me for this child's father that it was burning a hole in my soul. I was so ashamed of the secret life I had been living, I just didn't think that the Lord would ever forgive me and accept me back. Now I know that His mercy is boundless toward us." She sat down and continued to lull her young son on her knees.

No more third person in reference to herself, I noticed. My mother was no longer "on the outside looking in."

"Amen!" Burning Rain said." Let's give this sister a hand for that wonderful, wonderful testimony!"

The applause was generous.

Burning Rain continued. "We are all new creatures in Christ now. We are no more Cherokee, Seminole, Navajo, Apache, whatever. We are all one tribe—both male and female, all are the called-out ones—members of the worldwide body of Christ. So we walk in the light and no longer have any fellowship with darkness."

I was bringing in two large cups of *sofkee* to a couple of the elders when Marty's truck pulled up in the driveway. But it was Tanya Willow, the office volunteer, who leaped from the driver's seat carrying a large platter covered with tin foil. Marty was on the passenger's side and, when he stepped out, he was also carrying a tray and a bundle of newspapers tucked beneath his arm.

True, it was my fault what had happened to us, yet I felt my heart bleed. I bit my lip to hold back the tears. I could not expect him to wait forever for me to make up my mind. For a fleeting second, our eyes met, and I jerked my gaze away.

"Where do you want me to put this? It's barbecued chicken and ribs," he said.

I pointed toward the table. "There, if you can find a space."

Tanya was practically glued to his hip and chatting brightly as both of them made space on the table for the additional foods. "I made cherry cobbler," she said. And as she glanced at me, I could have sworn she was gloating, for it seemed she had won the trophy.

"I tasted it and it's pretty good," Marty said. "I'd give it a B-minus." He smiled at her—that Marty smile. With that slight dimple in his cheek. And that sparkle in his eyes.

For a brief moment, Uncle Donnie's gaze shifted from Marty to me and his mouth tightened.

But Tanya was quickly making her way through the crowd, apparently straining to get a look at Burning Rain. "If I could ever get

160

through, I have some questions I would like to ask about this Christian miracle stuff."

Uncle Donnie walked over, put his arm around me, and steered me into the kitchen. "Marty's working on you. I know how you feel about him, but don't play into his game. Hold up your head. Not one tear for him, do you hear?"

"He's not doing anything wrong. I—said some things to him I shouldn't have. It was my fault what happened between us."

"Just watch it. He's up to something. I don't trust him."

"I can take care of myself." I managed a smile. "Don't worry, okay?"

He tossed Marty another disapproving glance and rejoined the group.

My bravado came off perfectly to the eye. Inside, however, I was heartsick.

And it was just after my conversion that took place on the same night that Uncle Donnie walked out of the hospital completely healed. We had all gathered in his house. I knew then that, more than anything, I wanted this Jesus that my beloved uncle couldn't stop talking about.

I had walked over to Aaron then, with every chamber of my heart crying out for this salvation that he preached. I had thrown my arms around him and wept.

"Do you repent of your sins and accept Jesus Christ as your Savior?" Aaron asked.

"Yes, yes—I do, with my whole heart. I give Him my whole heart!" I said, sobbing.

That had been two nights ago. Now, so soon after, jealousy and regret were like acid eating at my insides.

As though reading my thoughts, Aaron called out, "Be on guard, new saints of the Lord. Soon after your conversion, you'll most likely come under great spiritual attack. You may be tried in a way that blindsides you. Just know to stand in faith and to pray for the Lord's strength. The Evil One loves nothing more to prey on your weaknesses. So stay away from all people, places, and things that caused you to stumble in the past."

As much as I wanted to heed Uncle Donnie's advice, I retreated to my room, choking back tears because, in spite of everything, how do you stop loving somebody that you love? And Marty seemed to be going out of his way to avoid me.

As I made my retreat, however, to my surprise, he followed me to my room with that bundle of newspapers tucked beneath his arm. My door was open, but he knocked softly. "Okay to come in?"

I noticed then that he limped when he walked. "Sure. But what happened to your leg?"

"Just turned my ankle a little. I was playing basketball with some of the kids. It's pretty sore but I'm sure I'll live," he said.

"Did you apply an ice pack?"

"I did first off. The worst part is having to be chauffeured around till it stops paining me. Thanks for asking, Nurse." He smiled then. That Marty smile. With that dimple.

"I'm not a nurse yet—nowhere near."

He untied the bundle and handed me several copies of the newspaper. "The very first edition of *War Arrow*. I know you don't come around anymore, but you did a great job, so I thought you'd like to have some contributor's copies."

"Thank you." I spread open the paper. "Hey, this is super. I'm proud of you, Marty." Though the words nearly choked in my throat, I added, "Both you and Tanya."

"Well, writing is not her strength. She probably flunked third grade spelling to put it kindly. But she has lots of good ideas and she's really interested in seeing the paper succeed. She's worth her weight in seed beads, sweet grass, and patchwork."

He came closer and held my gaze. "But before you assume anything, let me say that there's nothing between us."

My heart leaped for joy, but I remained deadpan as I sat scanning the paper at my study table strewn with school work.

He leaned down and thumbed through the pages. "One article in particular I want you to read. It's by a Chippewa guy. He shares my thoughts on a lot of issues." His voice trailed then, his face was only inches from mine. And he smelled so good. It was just Dial bath soap I could tell, but on Marty Osceola right then, it was heady and intoxicating. He was looking at me and I was losing myself in those inscrutable dark pools that held so much mystery. He knelt next to me

162

and softly touched my cheek.

"Virgin of Bitterroot, may I kiss you?"

"Don't make fun, Marty."

"I'm not making fun. I have wanted to for a long time, but I won't do it unless you want me to. You want me to?"

The touch of his hand was electric, like gentle lightning. I allowed his kiss, which was surprisingly chaste and sweet.

"Why do you fight me so?" he whispered against my ear. "Was that so bad?"

I was breathless. "No…"

"Please stand up, Dina. Let me hold you."

He sighed deeply as I stood and surrendered to his embrace.

How I wished I could resist him, I thought, as Uncle Donnie's warning resounded, *"It's a game…"*

"You feel so good in my arms," he said. "You're in my dreams every night. Not seeing you or talking with you these past few weeks has been hard for me. I want you, Dina, in my life. Now. Tomorrow. Forever. Won't you say that you want me, too? I've tried to give you up, to forget you. But I can't. I just can't. You are my yesterday, my today, and my tomorrow."

"I don't know what to say, Marty. It's like a war inside me. We walk in different worlds. Besides, now, with the relationship between my mom and Jack, it's even more bizarre."

His voice was urgent against my ear. "None of that has to matter. They chose their lives. We have the right to choose ours. What's important is that we love each other the way we are; that we respect each other's values and beliefs. And I respect you and your values, Deenie—I do."

He was calling me Deenie. My childhood nickname. The memories came flooding back. "I care deeply for you too. I guess I always have, but…"

He drew me even closer and was kissing me as he spoke. "Let's not think on our differences. If we try hard, we can have a great relationship. We can make this work. I've loved you since we were kids. I've never loved anybody else. Without realizing it, you never had another guy because you were waiting for me, too. I know that. But I want to hear you say it. Say it, Dina. My heart aches day and night to hear you say it!"

I paced away and buried my face in my hands. "I do, Marty, I do, but I'm scared!"

"You must believe me. I would never hurt you. Let's get away, where we can be together. Alone. Now. Get reacquainted with each other." He stood behind me and held me, speaking softly against my ear. "It's been a long time since Girls Against Boys, and that last race to Panther Creek when I gave you your first kiss. Remember?"

I smiled wistfully. "Yes, it has been a long time. But you do know that I just gave my life to Jesus Christ. I'm a full-fledged Christian now. I'm going to be baptized next Sunday. And I don't know how that's going to play out in our lives in the long run. Even though you say there's nothing between you, I've seen the way you and Tanya..."

He turned me to face him and cupped my face in his hands. "Tanya helps at the newspaper office. That's *all*. She came here today to see what all the fuss is about—and took the wheel of the truck because of my bum ankle. You're the only woman for me, Dina. You have to believe that. And I would never stand in the way of your Christianity."

"But we would be what the Bible calls 'unequally yoked together.' That's when two people walk different spiritual paths."

"But doesn't your Bible teach you to love *everybody*?"

I brightened. "Yes, it does. So you've read the Bible?"

"Well, no, but that's what I've heard."

"I haven't read all of it either," I said. "Maybe we could study it together?"

He smiled. "Sure. Why not? I'll even be there Sunday for your baptizement. Would it be okay with you if I came?"

Aaron's idiom somehow slipped out of my mouth: "That would be wonderful—just wonderful!" I walked over to the dresser and dusted off the tiny Bible I had owned since Sunday school. "This is for you. Reading it would be the greatest thing you could ever do for me—for us. So you can understand. So we can walk the same path."

He tucked it beneath his arm without looking at it. "Sure, I have no problem with that. There's lot of good stuff in it, I hear."

I held him tightly with renewed hope. "Thank you, Marty. I can't wait for us to start studying together. And maybe you'll come to church with me sometime?"

I heard laughter, singing, and testimonies in the background, punctuated by loud amens and applause. Then the screen door whined on its hinges. The door slammed shut, and afterward—dead silence. A sudden chill stilled the laughter, the songs of praise, the testimonies.

After a long pause, Uncle Donnie's stilted voice broke through the silence. "Brother Jack Turner, welcome. Come on in."

"Let's go see what's going on out there," Marty said.

Jack Turner was just standing there in the doorway, saying nothing. There was a strange, inscrutable look in his gold-flecked eyes. And Mama just sat there, her gaze locked with his, petrified, speechless, helpless, as she held their infant son protectively to her bosom.

Nobody, not even Aaron, knew what to say. Everybody just sat or stood as they were, stock-still in silence. And every eye was glued on, arguably, the most powerful witch in all of Indian country. Dread hung in the air.

I stood rooted in my tracks. *God, why do you test me so soon? If he attempts to hurt my mother or take that baby, what choice do I have but to go for the efche?*

Neither Mama nor Jack spoke. Everybody there knew that this broker of bad medicine had always gotten what he wanted; knew that if this partner with evil, this sender of terrifying dreams who commanded the dark forces, asked you a question, he expected you to tell him what he wanted to know. And everybody in Indian country also knew that if Jack Turner demanded something of you, he expected you to give it to him.

Now he had come for his son. But only Mama and I—and perhaps Jack, too, by the look in her eyes—knew what she had sworn: that she would see him, the baby, and herself, dead before she would hand the child over to him.

I summoned the courage to come over and stand next to her. "Mama, you don't have to be afraid of him. If he tries to…"

"Call on the Lord, Cheha—call on the Lord!" a woman cried out. Then others began to pray in concert.

Jack Turner took one step toward my mother. And what happened next caused even the people of The Faith to gasp in disbelief.

It would become the stuff of local legend, for no doubt people would talk about it in Bitterroot and on the reservation for generations to come.

It was after ten in the evening. The novelty of the past four days—the celebration of the Days of Miracles, as The Rez and The Root folks tagged them—was finally wearing down. A sizeable number of people, however, were still filtering in and out of Uncle Donnie's house.

And because Aaron wanted to talk, we stole away, turned on the porch light, and sat outside on the steps.

"These last few days have been indescribable," he said as he toyed with a rolled-up day-old newspaper. "I just wish the world wasn't so hardened and unbelieving." He opened the paper again and strained in the dim light to reread the article:

"Officials at Samaritan One East attribute reports that a shaman dressed in traditional Indian clothing who raised a dead man to life and healed others to patient hysteria, tribal cultural beliefs, and a lack of understanding of medical procedures."

I sighed. "Well, I suppose we should expect that kind of reaction from the medical community. But it's making me rethink nursing as a career. I don't want to become cynical about the mysteries and miracles of life."

Aaron went on:

"Though questioned by the media from around the nation and several foreign countries, Samaritan One East's staff has so far declined to be interviewed individually as part of hospital policy.

"Officials further stated that comatose patient Donnie Jumper, a Seminole Indian who resides in the Bitterroot Confederacy, was never officially pronounced dead. Sources say that the medical staff merely had difficulty reading his vital signs because of equipment malfunction.

"Sources also state that other critically ill patients who claimed to have been healed were showing marked improvement even before the incident of the Shaman in White took place."

Aaron crumpled the newspaper and tossed it on the ground. "As an Indian, I've seen what powerful medicine men can do. But to see *God* work wonders like He did at Samaritan One, just as He did in the Bible…" He shook his head. "Wonderful—just wonderful. But, ah, the doubting world!"

Right then the headlights of Jack Turner's truck illumined the yard as he pulled into the driveway. He bent down and was busy with something on the floor of the truck. A few minutes later he stepped outside, carrying a box with several vents in it.

Aaron eyed the box, then stood and gave him a brotherly slap on the back. "'Evening, brother Jack."

Jack Turner nodded in response, rested his eyes on me, and lowered his head. "I—want to apologize, and I ask you to forgive me for everything I did. It was never my intention to harm this little four-legged. Or any animal. I only meant to scare him off." He knelt and opened the box.

I cried out with joy. "Eddie Was!"

He crept out, sporting a shaved spot on the side of his head. He purred gently as I picked him up and cuddled him. He had a small scab to show for his wound but otherwise was no worse for wear.

"I thought he had dragged himself off somewhere to die," I said.

"No, I put him in my truck. Then I took him home and made a poultice for him and took care of him. I'm a healer, too," Jack Turner said. "And that's all I'll be doing from now on—using plants and herbs the Creator gave to us, for only good."

"Thank you," I said. "I appreciate what you did, and what you're trying to do." My voice fell. "I do forgive you. And—I must ask you to forgive me, too."

He extended his hand. I took it and accepted it as a gesture of mutual absolution.

"I do want to ask you something, though, if you don't mind," I said.

I pondered how to phrase the question that had been teasing me. "How did you get those owls to speak to me—to do your bidding?"

He looked down at his feet. "It's...not something I wish to talk about anymore." He paused. But when he did speak, his answer chilled my blood: "Spirits empowered the owls. I summoned them out of darkness and commanded them to do whatever I asked. I planned to torment or even kill all of you until I got what I wanted." His statement settled like the reek of foul and stagnant air. "Well, I'll be leaving now. I promised to cook for my wife tonight. I make a mean barbecue. Come by sometime. Anytime. You too, brother Aaron."

I did not answer as he excused himself politely, got into his truck, and drove away.

Aaron sat watching as I idly drew figures in the dirt with a stick, lost in thought. "I'll bet you could be an artist if you really wanted to," he said.

"Aaron," I said at length, "do you, in the deepest part of your heart, believe that Jack Turner is *really* saved—that he *really* repented and gave his life to the Lord? I mean, he could be faking just to get his son and to marry my mom like he wanted to. All's fair in the ancient arts of love and war."

The events of two days ago still loomed fresh in my mind: how Jack Turner's signature terrifying stare was locked with that of the mother of his son, but that instead of holding their usual boast and swagger, this time, there was apprehension in those eyes.

And when he took that tentative step toward Mama, it was sort of like the unsure step of a baby just learning to walk, and how, without a word being spoken between them, as though she were in a trance, Mama had just stood up, walked slowly toward Jack standing there in the doorway at Uncle Donnie's house, and simply placed little Cherokee Apache Youngblood-Turner in the arms of his father.

Holding his infant son for the first time, cradling him gently, gazing into the child's tiny face, this most fearsome witch who struck Terror in all who opposed him, who could summon forces from hell, sank to his knees, and his shoulders shook as tears streamed down his face. His words choked forth in spasms.

"I believe!" He wept great shuddering sobs. *"I believe!"*

"Jack Turner," Aaron said gently as he knelt and placed his arm about him, "are you ready to repent, say the salvation prayer, and give your life to the Lord?"

Aaron sat there in deep thought as if he, too, were revisiting that momentous day. "You asked me if I thought Jack Turner was faking. Well, you were there when he crashed the gathering. You heard what he said, heard how he described what happened."

I paused, pensive. "That on the day of the storm, one of his informers called and said that Uncle Donnie had crossed over, and that Mama and the rest of us were at the hospital. He got into his truck and headed out to get his son. He said he had planned to kill us all if we resisted him.

"He passed me on the road that day. But he said that before he reached the hospital, a man in white buckskin stopped him and said: *'Turn around, Jack Turner. The Lord wants to manifest His power through you. You are to go to Donnie Jumper's house two days from now. There you will see your wife holding your son. You are not to speak to her or to anyone. You will stand still. If you obey this command, she will come to you. And she will place the child in your arms, that you might turn from your wickedness and believe!'*"

Aaron's gentle eyes met mine. "That's what he told us in his testimony. It's not my place to judge the truthfulness of it. His sins are terrible, sure. But if we believe that Jesus died to save the sinner, then we must believe that He died for Jack, too. And that He loves Jack Turner just as He loves you and me."

He stared off at nothing in particular for a long moment before he spoke again. "When Jack fell down on his knees and sobbed his heart out in repentance, I don't think he was faking. When he went and got all of his witch's paraphernalia and burned it in the yard right in front of us, I don't think he was faking. No way."

I shrugged. "Well, that quickie marriage sure seems to have made both Mama and Jack happy. For sure he isn't faking that. And Mama sure wasn't faking when she stood up and gave him that baby. Not after what she had threatened."

Aaron picked up a pebble, idly examined it, and tossed it into the darkness. "Few preachers get to see that kind of turnaround. That's why

I wasn't ashamed to cry along with everybody else when the two of them—with their baby—embraced and stood there weeping and saying over and over to one another, 'I'm sorry, I'm sorry, I'm so sorry...'"

I tossed away the twig I was drawing with and sat back against the step. "I have to confess, though, that after everything that happened between Jack Turner and me, I have a hard time accepting his sincerity. Part of me still thinks he could be taking the path of least resistance. He has never stopped short of getting what he wanted. I mean, a man who could do the things he did—*changing?*" I shook my head. "I don't think the powers will let him go."

"It was he who let go of the powers and allowed God to deliver him, just like He delivered me, Dina. So I know He can deliver anybody. And if I *had* to make a judgment, I would say Jack Turner is a saved man.

He looked at his watch. "Well, it's getting late. Doesn't look too good, a preacher sitting out here with a young woman till all hours. Especially one as pretty as you are." He took both my hands in his. "I want you to do something for me."

"Sure, if I can."

"Before you go to bed tonight, I want you to think on...my feelings for you. I'm sure you know it already, but I'll say it plain. I care very deeply for you. Before you were saved, I had to pray hard against my desire for you. It was so strong, it bordered on—well—lust and obsession. Now, since we walk the same path..."

I gently withdrew my hands and placed them in my lap. I considered his words and chose mine carefully. "Aaron, I think the world of you. I think you are the greatest man I ever met. I'm just not sure I would be right for you. Not now."

He looked down at his own big yet gentle hands that lay in his lap, his fingers interlaced. "I know I'm nothing great to look at. And I have a few years on you. Well, more than a few, to be honest. I'm close enough to forty to know what it's like. And you're barely more than a girl. I've told myself that it's foolish of me to desire you so much. If I could forget you, I would. But I just haven't been able to do that."

He looked at me, and his voice was soft. "Dina, even though I do okay, I'm far from being a rich man. But I offer you my whole heart and all that I have."

I sat there quietly. I had known all along that he had feelings for me; and I had to admit I felt strong affection for him, too. I could even love him without half-trying, I knew, if I allowed myself. But he was a *preacher*. And a traveling preacher at that.

"Aaron, I'm not what you think. It's true that I've never been with a man. But I've done other things. Wicked things. I almost murdered somebody—well, Jack Turner—in cold blood. I had him in my sight over the barrel of my uncle's hunting rifle because I hated him for what he was doing to my family. And it was my intention to kill a would-be witness, too. There was a great evil in my life, and it almost swallowed me."

"That's all forgiven, Dina, covered under the blood of Jesus, washed away the minute you repented and gave your life to Him. Hey, do you think I was always so upstanding?"

I glanced at him. "The worst thing you probably ever did was stick a wad of bubblegum under your desk at boarding school. Me, I even have doubts about what choices God wants me to make. I mean, have you ever asked the Lord to solve a problem, and then not know if the answer you settle on is from Him, the Devil, or yourself?"

He was thoughtful. "If the answer you settle on lines up with Scripture, you can be sure it's within His will. But we have to be careful, because the Devil's interference can also look a lot like God's will. What we have to look out for are the small deceptions—the things that are a wee bit off-course—the answers that have just enough of the truth woven in to look righteous."

I sighed. "What puzzles me is that after getting saved there are still things that won't let go of me."

He bowed his head and was silent for a moment. He did not look at me when he spoke, "If it's a wrong relationship, *you* have to let go of *it*. You know what 2 Corinthians 6:14 says about becoming unequally yoked together with unbelievers."

"Unbelievers can change. You said that you did. Jack Turner did," I replied quickly.

"True, but before either of us accepted the Lord, we caused many of the people in our lives a lot of grief. It's best not to become involved with those who are walking a different spiritual path. Extend God's love to him but do not become entangled. Love can become quite complex when it intertwines with physical intimacy. Sex completely rewires the brain. Once you become deeply involved in it with an unbeliever, it can be very difficult to break away."

So far, I mused, he was reading my thoughts perfectly.

"All things can be forgiven, Dina. But it's kind of like mending a dress or a shirt that has a large piece torn from it. We can patch it and make it wearable again, but it will never be quite the same," he said. "Marrying the wrong person can cause you to compromise your own spiritual walk with the Lord. In my marriage, for instance, my dear departed wife was the believer. And I was one of the most vile and despicable men you would ever meet." He was silent a long moment before he spoke again.

"She forgave me for all the pain I caused her, and she never talked about the old Aaron. But now and then, the things I did, the horrible words I spoke to her, would come to her mind. I know they did. Because I could still see the pain in her eyes. Wounds heal. Deep scars never go away."

I searched his eyes. "It's hard to believe you ever hurt anybody."

He lowered his gaze. "Do you want to know how many years she endured my abuse—my drinking, drugs, bar brawling, womanizing? Fifteen long years. Not including the two while we were only going together."

My eyes widened. "You ran around with other women while you were married?"

He shrugged. "To me there wasn't anything wrong with it, as long as you brought home your paycheck and your wife didn't know."

He shook his head. "I was corrupt fruit from a bad tree. To call my father an alcoholic would have been putting it kindly. He was a sot, a lush, a boozer. And when he drank, he often forgot his way home and ended up following some other woman to her place. Often we would go hungry because when he drank, wherever they sold booze, that was where his paycheck went—when he worked. When he drank, he was loose with his fists and his boots against us kids, against our mother, against his world."

He clenched his hands tightly together and I could see the pain in his eyes. He wasn't just telling this story. He was reliving it.

"About the worst thing I can remember, the thing that set me on a crash course of destruction, was the time some missionaries—White people—came to our community. They were concerned about so many kids producing other kids so, using the Bible as their source, they were teaching Indian parents how to explain to their kids the godly use of sex." He bit his lip and turned his eyes from me.

I reached over and took his hand. "Aaron, this is too painful for you. You don't have to tell me this."

"I know. But I want to. It'll just take me a little time." He cleared his throat and proceeded. "I guess I was ten years old, give or take. Anyhow, on the second night that the missionaries were there, they told the parents to bring their kids. So my mother brought us—my sister, my brother, and me."

He drew in a long breath. "Afterward, she was all excited. As soon as my father came home, she shared the teachings with him. Well, he hated all White people—missionaries and preachers especially. He believed their ultimate goal was to substitute their values and White religion in place of Indian cultures. And he hated Indians because he was one of them, and therefore powerless to have any say in his life.

"To make a long story short, after she told him what the missionaries said that they, as parents, needed to teach us about sex, he trashed the house. Called my mother a sellout…and much worse. He slapped us kids around—especially me, because I was the oldest and the biggest, and the one who talked back. He went out and got smashed on Nutty Gator, the cheapest booze you could buy back then. The firewater of legend."

Aaron paused. "Funny, but I've never told this horror story to anybody before—not even to Nate Bush, my prayer partner. But somehow I feel I need to share it with you."

So he continued. "Anyhow, when he came back home, maybe two, three in the morning he woke us kids up. He was dragging our mother out of bed by her hair. He…shoved her down on our old dilapidated couch in the living room and yelled, 'Aaron, Mitch, all o' you—get up! Your mama wants me to show you how babies are made. So I want you to watch. And don't you dare close your eyes or turn away. You do, and

I'll beat the hide off all of you—you dirty, snot-nosed, dumb, stinkin' little redskin brats!"

"He started ripping off her nightgown. She was crying and pleading with him, trying to get away, trying to fend him off. And we stood there screaming, begging him not to hurt our mama. But he...had his way. And he made us...made us watch. Something in me snapped then. I knew where he kept his shotgun, and he had taught me how to use it. I remember standing on a chair and fetching it from the top shelf of his closet. By the time I got back, he was staggering into his pants. I pointed that shotgun at him and I remember exactly what I told him: 'You ever touch my mama again, I'll blow your head off!'

"He stood there with one leg in his pants, and one planted on the floor. He looked me in the eye. I didn't blink. He didn't blink. But I think he knew I would have killed him. So he just got dressed, walked out, and never came home again."

I was choking back tears by then, but he just placed an arm around my shoulder and continued. "So I blamed myself because we could barely scrape by on what my mother could earn in town, and whatever odd jobs I could do now and then.

"It was only after I was a man that I understood why she seldom looked at me after that. I had run off the little bit of help she did get for us kids. So she kind of crumpled inside after that. And Nutty Gator became her refuge, too."

He wiped his silent tears and sort of collapsed against the back of the step. He had finally let go of the thing that would not let go of him. It was as though he had finally vomited up the rancidness that had been festering inside him for so long.

By then, unrestrained tears were streaming down my face, too. "I'm so sorry, Aaron."

He sighed deeply. "For sure, it was terrible. But for me personally, the worst part was yet to come. You know, it's strange how you can hate something you see somebody else do, then become powerless to stop yourself from doing the same thing to somebody else.

"Because after that, strangely, I hated my mother. Oh, I hated my father too. *Hated* him. For what he did to my mom, for what he did to all of us. But her I hated because of her defenselessness. Because in her frailty, I saw my own powerlessness, which the world had taught me all too well was my heritage as an Indian man. I felt that it was going to be the course of my life. Victim. I would always be a victim. Nobody could rescue me, and nobody could give me any power."

I lowered my head and wiped my tears. "Aaron, this is all so personal. Don't feel you have to—"

"No, no, I want to share it with you." He took my hand again. "I want to share *everything* with you, Dina."

A silence ensued between us before he spoke again. "Remember what I said awhile back, about a preacher not having many friends—people he can confide in?" He glanced at me. "Somebody he can trust? You don't mind listening, do you?" He was caressing my hand.

"Oh, no, not at all. I'm honored that you trust me," I said.

He continued. "You said you were troubled because you almost murdered two people in order to protect your family. Well, you're sitting next to a man who almost kicked and beat a woman to death with his fists because she didn't want to dance with him anymore.

"She was young, slim. Pretty. A lot like you. So how does that make you feel?" he asked with a quick sardonic laugh. "And I would have beaten and stomped her to death, too, if others in the bar hadn't pulled me off her.

"She was from one of the other nearby communities. Out riding with her friends, looking to have a good time. Flirting. Drinking. Laughing. Dancing close. But to a wicked man like I was, her actions meant 'hey, let's get it on.'

"So Aaron Emathla, *aka* Burning Rain, started really coming on to her, kissing her, and—well—putting his hands all over her. Doing things on the dance floor she didn't like. So she pushed me away and loud-talked me.

"And then—" there was a long pause before he spoke again—"I literally *became* my father. I heard my own voice coming from my mouth, and it was *his* voice. When he got drunk, nobody told *him* 'no,' especially not in front of a whole barroom full of his cronies.

"I was a big guy, too. Just like I am now. Tall, powerful—always been big. People often tell me I should have been a linebacker on somebody's football team. Never played, though. I guess in my prime, I enjoyed romancing Nutty Gator too much.

"Anyhow, I'd been drinking, and a couple of shots of booze under my belt was like splashing kerosene on a lit fire. I backhanded her clear across the room and I was all over her—fists, boots, a chair..."

"You said your name is Emathla?"

"Another story. A good story, though. But for later. Anyhow, for shattering her jaw, fracturing her skull, an arm, and two ribs, I served six months. But never once did I have a grain of remorse for what I did. The only thing Aaron Emathla regretted was that he got locked up. I'd even planned revenge on her after I got out, because according to my reasoning back then, it was because of her that I was in jail in the first place. As much as I hated the kind of man my father was, I had become him.

"Except I always brought my money home," he added quickly, "and I never raised my hand against my wife. Never. I crushed her with my putdowns and my lies and my drunkenness and my infidelities, but I never laid a hand on her. And I clung to that like it was sacred because it was the only assurance I had that a small part of me was still human.

He sat in deep thought for a long moment. When he spoke again, his entire countenance had brightened. "Then one day while I was locked up, an Indian preacher came to the jail. Before, I had seen only White pastors and I had the same hatred for them that my father had.

"But this Native preacher told me about Jesus, how He delivered him from drugs, alcohol, and a life of violence. His story was so much like mine. I believed I was too far gone, but he assured me that God is well acquainted with flawed and fallen and doubting men like I was." He pulled me close and wrapped his arms around me. "I hope this hasn't been too much for you."

"No, Aaron. You needed to get it out of you," I said.

He smiled. "You have a lot of wisdom for one so young. Anyhow, I figured if Jesus could save one Indian, why not give Him a shot at saving me? What did I have to lose? I was a walking dead man, bound for the fires of hell, trying to see how many more I could drag down with me.

"But that particular night in his jail cell, Aaron Emathla, the hate-filled, drunken brawler got down on his knees and asked Jesus Christ to be his Lord. It was then that I became good ground for the seed of God's word to grow in."

"So, that's in the Bible—good ground—seed?"

"The parable of the sower. Matthew, chapter 13."

"I remember something like that from a long time ago. In Sunday school." I leaned my head against his chest. "I'm sorry your life was so hard, that you suffered so much. My poor, gentle, sweet Aaron."

A long silence hung between us. I absently traced my fingers along the contours of his great hands as they rested lightly on his lap; I stroked them gently and examined them with interest. They could easily and completely envelop mine.

"Hands, especially men's hands, have always fascinated me," I said.

"Really? Why?"

"Oh, I don't know. I guess it's because they have such power to do either good or great evil."

He then closed that catcher's mitt over my hand and pressed it over his heart. "From now till the day I draw my last breath, these hands of mine will do only the Lord's work."

And what had been smoldering now ignited between us. His eyes were soft upon my face as he drew me gently to him. His kiss was urgent, hungry, yet a carefully tended fire that obviously was vigilantly contained; it was a sweetness both savored and shared, and I could feel his great heart beating against mine. I relished his nearness, the safety of his strength, the peace I felt being so close to him.

And although whatever I was feeling for him right then had no name, and my heart had no clear path to follow, I simply surrendered to this hiatus in time, kind of like one of those rare occurrences when a butterfly alights on your finger: and you just pause, stock-still, in awe, and allow the brief moment that leaves you breathless to have its course.

But he released me suddenly, surprisingly, and turned away. He buried his head in his hands. When he spoke again, his voice was quiet and thick with emotion. "I'm sorry, Dina. I shouldn't have done that."

"Why not? It was nice. Hey. Aaron. It's all right," I said as I leaned against his shoulder and placed my arm around him. "Even a preacher has feelings. You are a man. We like each other, so it's all right."

He all but leaped to his feet and shook his head. "No. We haven't made any commitment to each other. So it's not all right! Ever since that first night with you on the porch, I've wanted so much to hold you like a man holds a woman he loves.

"Yes, I wanted to comfort you then, be your pastor. But I also wanted you as a man wants a woman. And right now, I feel like—" he groped for words—"like I've been manipulating your feelings by telling you about my life. I should have waited for your answer first." He sat again, his head in his hands.

I inched closer to him. "Aaron, we just kissed. That's all. It's what men and women do when they like each other. They sit close. They touch. They kiss. We didn't do anything wrong!"

He drew in a long, shuddering breath. "Please remember what I asked you to do, and think on what I mentioned about my feelings for you. I need to know if there is a future for us."

"I...promise to think about it," I said.

He stood again and in his characteristic gesture ran his hands over his neatly groomed hair.

"I've been meaning to ask," I said, "even though you wear it in that bun, your hair is long, like a Traditional. I thought all Native pastors cut their hair. Like the White preachers do."

The question broke the tension between us. He smiled. "I spent all of my younger years being ashamed of what I am. I wear it long now because it's a statement both to myself and to the world. Aaron Burning Rain is unapologetically *Indian*." He rummaged his pocket for his keys and started for his van.

I stood with my arms crossed, smiling. "Okay. But don't you dare walk off without explaining to me about Aaron Emathla."

He stopped in his tracks and turned to face me. "I think it was my first revival meeting after I became a preacher. I had no idea what kind of impact I would have on the people. Most of them were Traditionals and not open to The Jesus Way. But after the service, during the altar call, an old woman who had been sitting in the back came up to me. She had been a witch with powerful medicine. Everybody in that community feared her—everybody.

"I'll never forget her name—Minnie Two Feathers. She said, 'Son, I came here to curse you. But your words fell on me like burning rain!' She accepted Jesus that night and she promised to pray for me every day until the Lord called her home to heaven.

"The word spread about her salvation, and by the time the revival ended, most of the people in that community had also accepted the Lord. One is still holding on to her witchcraft, though. But I think God is working on her, too.

"Anyhow, the name stuck. And it's official now. Aaron Burning Rain." He smiled. "Say good night to your Uncle Donnie for me."

It was just past eight o'clock the following night when I left Pik'N'Git. I stopped off and retrieved our mail from among the row of rubber stamp black boxes at the corner. I sifted through some flyers, a magazine, and the electricity bill.

Uncle Donnie was sitting reading his Bible and mulling over an unfinished study quiz. Eddie Was, fast asleep and purring gently, was curled at his feet.

As I closed the door behind me, Uncle Donnie looked up. "Shania called. Wants you to call her back." He finished filling in a blank on his Bible quiz sheet, stacked his papers, and pushed away from the table.

I plopped the mail on the counter. "Is she okay? Did you talk to her?"

"Yeah. She sounded—well, you know Shania. Always on edge. Anyhow, call her back. She's out in California. She didn't say so, but I know what she wants. To come home."

"How do you figure that? She loves modeling—the fast track."

He shook his head. "Something's not right out there with her. I've been praying about it, that the Lord would send her home. I don't like our Indian girls in that kind of business—parading around with price tags on themselves."

He gave the mail a cursory glance. "There's some more of that chicken and vegetables in the iron pot in the refrigerator if you're hungry," he said, then took his Bible and his papers and started toward his bedroom.

"Maybe later. What time did Shania call?"

"Around six." He glanced at me. "You're losing weight—need to eat more."

I smiled. "Look who's looking after whom." But as for that iron pot, I thought, had I not told him a dozen times it was too heavy for the refrigerator, and to store leftovers in plastic containers?

"Call your sister. Number's there on the table." He closed his door behind him.

When she picked up on the second ring, Shania's voice was stressed and she was near tears. "I need to come home. Deenie, they stole my car. That whole modeling agency thing is a sham. A lie. A front for a movie business...porn stuff. Tracee—she's making those movies. I tried to talk her out of it, but she thinks it will lead to something big for her!"

"Where are you?"

"I'm at a church, living in the basement. They let me stay until I can get a way home. I need you to send me some money for a ticket. Bus fare. Train fare. Anything!"

"I have a pencil and paper. Give me the address. Is it okay to wire the money there?"

"Yes, but I need it *now*. I just want to get out of here and go home. When I told that agency that I was quitting, they said I owed them thousands of dollars for promotional fees they say they paid to get my career started. But I can't pay them. I managed to run away from them and they're looking for me. Deenie, I'm scared. I want to come home!"

"Stop crying and don't panic. Just stay there at the church. And stay inside. You should be safe. Now give me the address."

As I was writing I said simply, "Mama's back. And I hope you're sitting down. We have a new baby brother. His dad is Jack Turner. That's why Mama left, running from him. Let's just say that they had custody issues."

"Really? Well, when I get home, I guess I'll have to hide too, from that Uncle John character," she said. "I saw him at a store downtown before I left. He asked if I remembered him. Anyhow, I said 'no.' And we got talking. He said he knew Mama, knew us when we were kids, and knew our family and everything. So when he saw that I was driving JohnnyHawk's old pony, he bought me a car and gave me some cash—for old time's sake, he said.

180

"He invited me to his house and asked me a lot of questions, mostly about Mama. Like, did I know where she was, had I heard from her and all. But now he may be after me, too, after I took the car and his cash and cut out on him."

"Cut out?"

"Yeah. I figured he was some dirty old man who sooner or later would try to put the make on me. So I took the car and the cash and split. I figured, hey, why not? Men use us for what they want, don't they?"

"Shania, Jack Turner's name is really John. As in *Uncle* John. They are one and the same person. And—he's your father, too. Your dad. Yours and Chappy's."

There was silence on Shania's end of the telephone. I heard her exhale loudly. "My father is a shape-shifting witch? You *are* kidding me, aren't you?"

"Sorry, little half-sister. I'm afraid it's the truth. Well, part of it, anyhow."

"Part of it? Does he know Mama's in town? I mean, he's not harassing her or anything, is he?"

"No. Do you want to know why?"

"Right now I don't know if I do or not."

"He got saved and they got married. And there's more—but I'll save it till you get home."

There was a long pause and a nervous giggle. "Right now, I'm not sure if it's safer to come home, or face the ones chasing me down!"

XIII

A Walk Through Fire

The day quietly stole away behind the horizon and Friday night settled in like a dark and gentle mist. Pik'N'Git was experiencing its usual weekend surge in sales of wine and beer and fill-ups at the gas pump. I had worked the early shift, so I clocked out, picked up my purse, and started out of the door.

"See you tomorrow," I said. Rick was on the telephone and waved absently as I headed for home.

"You ready for Sunday—we're getting baptized, remember?" Uncle Donnie said as soon as I cleared the door.

"No way could I forget."

"You wired her the money, so when's Shania getting in?" he asked.

"Tonight. And it was Jack that paid for the ticket. Her airfare would have cleaned me out. Looks like he's really taking his role as dad seriously," I said. "I never heard a man sound so happy to be forking over hundreds of dollars for an airline ticket before."

"Well, she is his kid."

"Maybe now she'll settle down and decide what she really wants to do with her life. This time, I hope it's the right choice—namely, school."

"I prayed for the Lord to put a glitch in that career if something wasn't right about it." Uncle Donnie glanced upward. "Thank You, Lord." He filled his water glass and headed for his room. "But don't tell her I prayed that prayer. She'd be mad at me."

The telephone rang once.

"Hey, what are you doing? Want to go somewhere?"

Marty. And immediately my spirit and my flesh were at war again. The flesh won. "Sure, but first I have to pick up Shania at the airport. She's flying in from California."

"Why don't we both go there and wait? We could grab something to eat at one of the coffee shops. And talk. Hang out. Do whatever. Hey, it's Friday night."

I did not want to say them, but the words rushed forth anyhow. "Sounds good. Give me thirty minutes."

"Twenty. I can't wait that long."

After a quick shower and change I was waiting in the living room when Uncle Donnie came through with his empty water glass. Somehow, whenever the telephone or doorbell rang at night, he got thirsty.

"Was that the preacher?"

"No. It was Marty," I said.

He refilled his glass with ice and water, came over, and stood in front of me. "You know, Dina, you gonna have to make a choice. You can't play with two men's feelings. Aaron asked you for an answer. You never gave him one. And that boy—I know you got a strong heart for him. But he's heavy into the Indian Way. How many times haven't I said it? Aaron is a strong, decent man of God. Why you doing him like this?"

I shrugged. "I told Aaron I would think about a relationship with him. And I have thought about it. He's a *preacher.* It won't work. I—just haven't told him yet."

"It's time you grew up. Every girl enjoys her short season of teasing men's hearts. Your season is over now. You are a young woman. You need to make a commitment to somebody. Marty will always be Marty. What you think is gonna change? Besides, Marty is family now, being that Jack is married to your mama. It's not right."

"He's Jack's stepson. It's not as though he's blood family—or our clan. We were seeing each other before Mama and Jack decided to marry. You can't expect us to just turn our feelings off like a faucet." And I played my trump card. "Besides, in the Bible, Sarah was Abraham's half-sister."

"Abraham and Sarah didn't live in Bitterroot! I get the idea you think Marty is going to shape-shift into a church deacon or something. If that boy was going to change, don't you think with all the miracles that happened around here lately, he would have done it by now?"

I shrugged. "I gave him a Bible. He said he would study it with me."

"Did he act interested, open it up, or did he just stick it in his pocket or under his arm or something?"

"Well...he didn't open it right then. But he'll get around to it. Look, he respects my faith. And whether you like it or not, he's coming to my baptism Sunday. We have strong feelings for each other. Maybe we love each other. I don't know yet."

"I'll tell you what you feel for Marty: plain old lust in a brown wrapper. All the women want him because of his looks and that wild charm. But what's beneath his skin—do you know? If you scratched him, would owls fly out? If a drop of his blood hit the ground, would it turn into snakes?"

My face crumpled and tears coursed from my eyes. "If what you say is true, then I'll find it out for myself. But don't ask me to stop seeing him. I can't!"

"You mean you *won't*."

"Okay, then, I won't!"

He sighed. His eyes pleaded with me. "He's playing a game, Dina, like you're playing games. But if you're bent on being with that boy in spite of everything you know about him, then you need to tell that to Aaron."

I shook my head. "I couldn't hurt Aaron. There's so much quietness and peace when I'm with him. Uncle Donnie, I love them both!"

His voice was quiet. "But you can't have them both. Remember that love isn't always where you look for it, but where it finds *you*. And you've heard it said before, Dina. If you cannot give up Aaron for Marty or Marty for Aaron, then you don't love either of them enough." He raised his glass and took a sip. "Ahhh...at least something is good around here."

Shania was clad in her Seminole patchwork jacket and jeans. Her roots had grown out several inches so that her now shoulder-length auburn hair was tipped with blond. She was even thinner than before, and there were dark crescents beneath her eyes. Gone were the glitz, the springy steps, the quick smile, the sassy courage that emboldened her to explore life beyond her own fence posts.

Once she spotted us, she dropped her one piece of baggage—a knapsack—and threw herself into my arms. "I just wanted to make something of myself," she said, sobbing. "I didn't want to spend my life stringing beads or weaving baskets. I just wanted to be somebody...do something on my own. But look at me, Deenie. I'm nothing. How can I face anybody? I'm so ashamed!"

My own tears streamed down my cheeks as I held her close. "You are somebody, Shania. You're my little sister. And you don't have any reason to be ashamed. How many of us have the courage to strike out on their own like you did? And there's nothing wrong with making our beautiful crafts. They help to define who we are as a people." I held her thin face in my hands and looked at her squarely. "So you hold your head up high and be proud of yourself, Shania Youngblood."

"Shania Turner," she said quietly. She dried her eyes and looked past my shoulder. "It's him."

Jack Turner was holding little Cherokee as both he and Shania—father-daughter reverse images of one another—stood face-to-face. Neither appeared to know what to expect from the other.

"They took the car," she said in a tentative voice. "They said I owed them money. They stole it!"

Jack Turner placed his arm about his daughter's shoulders. "You're safe at home now. That's the important thing. Cars—there are plenty more of them on the lot," he said and kissed her on the head. "But there's only one of you."

"We're going to take her to get something to eat, you two," Mama said to Marty and me. "I think Dad wants to spend time with his girl. And she needs to get to know her little brother."

I watched them walk away—a small family, fractured, trying to put it all together and make it work. Mama was on one side, Shania was holding Chappy, and Jack was in the middle, his arms about all of them.

As I watched that bright patchwork jacket meld into the crowd, I hoped that she would settle close to home now.

But how I would miss the hummingbird!

"Sixty-five souls!" Aaron cried out with exuberation after he and Nathaniel Bushyhead, who assisted him, baptized the last convert the following Sunday.

He raised his hands and looked skyward. "Hear me, O Lord. Thank You! And in the Name of Jesus, strengthen me and every pastor here that we might shepherd these precious sheep!"

He had avoided my eyes and treated me no differently from any other convert when he baptized me.

As I stood on the bank of Panther Lake and toweled the water from my hair, Marty stood back, watching me with an enigmatic half-smile, his thumbs in the belt loops of his Levis. He sauntered over.

"Nice ceremony. Let's go celebrate. Where you want to go eat? Chickee Choices okay with you?"

"Sure," I said. "But I need to go home and change first." I glanced about, secretly glad that Aaron was busy talking to a group of pastors and new converts and did not notice Marty or me.

But Uncle Donnie glanced at us with disapproval as I hopped into Marty's truck; I bent down lower than necessary to dry my feet so that Aaron would not see me as we pulled away. Marty seemed oblivious to the subtle drama going on around him as we headed out.

"That was quite a spectacle," Marty said at length. "The former lord of the medicine men standing in the water next to The Virgin of Bitterroot." He sounded angry.

"I think it took a lot of courage for him to abandon such powerful practices and embrace The Jesus Way," I said as we pulled into Uncle Donnie's driveway.

I leaped out and hurried into the house. I wanted to be out of there before Uncle Donnie returned, perhaps with Aaron. I did not want to face my uncle's disapproval—or Aaron's agony.

Marty followed me into the house. "Frankly, I'm still dumbfounded. I never thought my father would ever allow anything to dismantle his belief system. I mean, The Indian Way is what defined him."

"His spirit changed," I said. "You did hear about the miracles at the hospital, didn't you? And all the new converts' testimonies today? That proves God is more powerful than any Traditional Indian Way beliefs."

He shrugged. "The miracles were pretty awesome, I hear, but so are our traditions." He sank down on the sofa, picked up one of the ancient *National Geographic* magazines from the coffee table, and browsed idly while I went to my room.

I showered quickly, donned jeans and a T-shirt, grabbed my purse, and put on one sandal while hopping into the living room on one foot as I slipped on the other. "Let's go," I said.

As soon as we walked into Chickee Choices café, a voice called from a booth in the back, "Dina! Dina Youngblood! I haven't seen you in many moons!" A smiling young woman with a baby in her arms and several small children at her table in the back was waving at me.

"Emellda Tommie?"

She laughed good-naturedly as I came toward her. "Have I gotten so fat you didn't recognize me? But I bet you remember Girls Against Boys. We used to smoke them. But I was skinny and fast in those days."

"A long, long time ago," I said. "But you, Katey, and Mellinda were the fast ones. I never won a single race."

She eyed Marty loitering in the background. "Well, looks like you won *him*." She winked. "Definitely still the best-looking Indian guy on the East Coast."

"No doubt about it," I responded with pride. "So—are all these kids yours?"

"All four. Would be nice if I could find a good man that would stick around." When her baby began to whimper, she lulled him with a gentle sway.

"Is it a girl or a boy?"

"Another little warrior. Daniel Tommie. Are you still going to the Christian church? I know you used to, and I saw you at that revival meeting awhile back. So I guess that's why I'm sort of surprised to see you cozy with Marty. He's as Indian Way as they come. But don't get me wrong. You guys look cool together. It's just that I'm kind of, well, surprised."

"I haven't been going to church much. But I got saved and I'm starting back," I added quickly. "I got baptized today, along with Jack Turner, Uncle Donnie, Sam Waters—and lots of other people who were once Traditionals. Marty was there too, to support me. He's interested in Christianity. We're going to study the Bible together."

She shrugged. "Yeah, well, I heard about all the happenings at the hospital and at your Uncle Donnie's house. So miracles do happen." Marty waved at her and she waved back. "I think your sweetie is giving me the signal to sign off. Well, I hope it all works out for you," she said, a bit too tentatively for my comfort, I thought, as I rejoined Marty.

He ordered enough food for a banquet: frybread, gator nuggets, Indian burgers—the works. And more was being constantly brought out from the kitchen.

I patted my stomach after Round One. "I don't know where you expect me to put all this stuff. I can hardly fasten my jeans."

"This is a celebration. Open your mouth, Indian woman."

I did, and he dropped in another gator nugget. "Eat. I want to see how you are going to look when you're carrying my little warrior!" He made a circle as big as he could with his arms to demonstrate and dissolved in laughter.

When I didn't laugh initially, he began tickling me.

"All right, all right," I said and burst out laughing too. And as I did, I accidentally spewed a shower of half-chewed nugget into his face.

He really doubled over after that. "You—" He could barely finish his sentence. "You don't—" He was pointing at me and by then everybody else was laughing too, as he managed to choke out the last of his insult: "You don't—have any table manners!"

I elbowed him. "Stop it." Tears of laughter streamed down my face. "Indians don't carry on like this in public!"

"Rez Indians," he choked out between peals of laughter, "have a *public?*"

As the evening wore on, several others came over and joined us at our table. How long we stayed there, joking, enjoying the evening, each other, and the warmth peculiar to Root and Rez folks, I don't remember.

Marty never wore a watch. He lived by his own inner clock, so he never worried about the time. When he felt like leaving someplace he would leave, but not because a timepiece dictated it was time to do so.

I watched him as he interacted easily with his friends. How could such a comic—one who showed such obvious devotion to me—be as evil and calculating as Uncle Donnie accused him of?

The evening finally drew to an end. He boosted me into the truck, and we started down the highway.

"You've never been to my house. I built it myself, from cypress logs. Want to see it?" he asked. "It's in Big Cypress. You can be thinking on whether or not you want to live out there because it's w-a-ay back out in the boonies."

"How long will we be there? I can't stay late."

He shrugged. "Whenever you say the word, we'll leave."

"Sounds fair enough. But remember, I'm Christian. And we're family. So no—fooling around."

"Family? No, we're not. Only victims of other people's choices."

A silence followed.

As he'd warned, it seemed to take forever to reach his house in the deep woods. In the moonlight, the trees appeared like tall misshapen wraiths. Night eyes appeared and disappeared as animals, frightened from the roar of the truck's big engine, scurried to safety.

He parked beneath a *chickee*. His dog—a large no-breed brown-and-black creature with yellow eyes, bared his teeth as he snarled, barked, and lunged on his chain at me.

I gave wide berth to him. "He's not very friendly."

Marty called out firmly. "Coyote—*Ma-tee-nah.*"

Immediately the dog quieted down. He sat looking up at his master, eager, as if waiting for his next command.

Marty gave him a friendly scratch behind the ears and the dog stood on his hind legs, his paws on Marty's chest. "Down. Sit."

Coyote obeyed.

Marty turned to me. "Give him the back of your hand."

"Do I get it back?" I asked, only half-joking.

He threw back his head and laughed. "You will. I assure you, pretty Indian woman."

I extended my hand.

"Friend, Coyote," Marty said.

And Coyote immediately wagged his tail and licked my hand.

"Yech," I said. "Okay, I like you, too. But not your—slobber."

Marty smiled. "I named him Coyote because he looks like one, and I hear that the Navajo consider howling coyotes a bad sign. Since he's not actually a coyote, I figure his howl is a *good* omen, if reverse logic makes any sense." He pushed open the unlocked door of his cabin.

I looked around at the neatly arranged living room. "Hey, you're a pretty spiffy housekeeper. Somehow I never envisioned you with a dish cloth or behind the business end of a vacuum cleaner."

"Can't think in disorder," he said. "And since me no drink-um firewater, would some coffee be okay?"

"With one sugar only." I studied the rustic beauty of Marty's cabin, the handmade Native crafts. "You know—this reminds me of those summer cabins in the movies. Way off. Romantic."

"And with an indoor bathroom. They're a convenience to everybody—except my dad. Well, kick back. Turn on the T.V. Do whatever you want. Start acting like you're home."

I turned on the news, but neither of us really watched it. I was busy evaluating this beautiful being's every word and movement—and watching for any red alerts.

The Bible that I had given him lay on the kitchen table next to a bundle of sage, braided sweet grass, and a canvas bag that was padlocked. "So—uh—did you get around to reading this?" I asked as I picked it up and wiped away the thin film of dust.

He shrugged. "Nope. Not yet."

I tried not to sound preachy. "Like you said, lots of good stuff in it. It teaches us that smoke from burning herbs…smudging…doesn't purify us. Jesus' shed blood does that."

He handed me a cup of steaming coffee and kissed my forehead. "Hey, relax. Everything is okay. This may disappoint you, but Marty

Osceola is just a plain ol' Indian guy, one who has lots of respect for a Christian girl who's saving herself."

"Will you stop it? I'm not saving myself. I just haven't—had a man in my life."

He laughed. "Okay, whatever you say."

But as he turned back toward the kitchen his elbow caught my cup, splashing coffee down the front of my white T and onto my jeans. I yelled out, more from surprise than pain.

"Oops. Dina, I'm sorry. I'm so sorry!" He rushed toward me, panic in his eyes. "Did it burn you?"

I brushed at the stains on my shirt and jeans. "I'm okay. I managed to dodge most of it. I'll be fine."

Yet he seemed horrified as he rushed for a dampened kitchen towel, wiped at the stains himself, thought better of it, and handed the towel to me. "I could have scalded you. Look how I ruined your clothes. I'm sorry. Can I get you an ice pack?"

I wiped at the stains. "Stop worrying. I said I'm fine."

Uncle Donnie was wrong about him, I thought. Marty was really sensitive and concerned. He was also lots of fun and easy to talk to. I could tell him anything. Nothing upset him. His responses were easy and direct, and if he didn't know something, he simply said so. Before long, we were completely engrossed in, and comfortable with, each other.

But I discovered, too, that in addition to his characteristic of not wearing a watch, Marty also had no clocks in his house. Not one. And when I looked again at my watch, I panicked. How was it possible that seven hours had passed so quickly?

"Three a.m.? I can't believe this!" I exclaimed. "I have to call Uncle Donnie. He must be frantic!"

He threw up his hands. "Please forgive me. I'm in and out a lot so I don't have much use for a telephone. Look, just let me know and we'll do whatever you want."

"By the time we get home it'll be close to five." I sighed. "Then you'll have to drive back. I don't know what to do!"

"Well, I can sleep on the Futon and you can take my bed—or vice versa. Whatever you want to do, Virgin of Bitterroot. I would never do anything, or try to talk you into doing anything against your will.

Especially right after your baptizement."

"Bap*tism*."

"Oh? Okay, *baptism*. You should have told me the first time."

I smiled. "You take correction better than most men. The Futon is fine with me. I'll just have to explain what happened to Uncle Donnie tomorrow morning." But fat chance, I thought to myself, that he would believe a word of it.

Marty brought me pillows, a cover, and one of his shirts. "This will have to do for a nightgown," he said and cupped my face in his hands. "You have a sweet sleep. No dreams of storm skies, gray rainbows, or wild, painted ponies."

I stared at him. "I never told *anybody* about that dream. How did you know?"

He held me close. And as before, if lightning could be gentle, his touch was like that. "I know because I was there—in that dream." He looked at me and laughed. "Hey, when you go to sleep, don't you *always* dream about me?"

I managed a tentative laugh too, as he again cupped my face and looked deeply into my eyes. "Don't be so serious, I was only joking!" He took me in his arms. "You talked about our being family. We could be, you and I, you know. With our own life together and our own little warriors—yours and mine." His caress was warm and gentle and tender, and made me tingle all over.

"Marty, don't. We can't," I said.

But then he was kissing me, caressing me. "Yes, we can, Dina. But if you don't want me the way I want you, just tell me."

I wanted to say "no," tried to say "no," but I could not. Suddenly I was kissing him, too, and trailing my fingers through his heavy silk...Flutes were playing and birds were singing and the carousel in my head whirled us around slowly and gently. The jasmine blooming somewhere was sweet and intoxicating, his touch like gentle lightning, and the night was soft and tender and deep and black.

Time was standing still—and tomorrow seemed so far away...

192

XIV

Aftermath

The aroma of scrambled eggs, toast, and freshly perked coffee permeated the air the following morning. As I stepped out of the shower and toweled dry. I avoided looking at myself in the mirror. I refused to think on the previous night when all my resolve melted, and nothing else mattered except our desires that burned for each other.

I agonized: willing in spirit, weak in flesh. Only yesterday I was baptized into a new life, and today I was—here. Using Marty's soap, his towel, his Ban Roll-on. Having brought no change of clothes—mine were hanging out to dry on the wooden porch rail—I came to breakfast wearing his shirt.

He was already seated at the table, contented, bare-chested, barefoot, clad only in white drawstring pants.

A coldness crept over me: *Like the ones he wore in the gray rainbow dream...*

His night-kissed hair, delinquent and untamed, was tousled about his face and tumbled about his firmly muscled shoulders.

I noticed that he had removed the Bible I gave him and placed it on the coffee table in the living room next to a collection of magazines and Native memorabilia. The bundle of sage and the canvas bag with its unknown contents were nowhere to be seen.

I picked up the Bible and slowly drew it to my heart and lamented inwardly, *God, how did I fall from Your grace so quickly?*

Marty glanced up at me. "Hey. You look good in my shirt." He motioned toward the steaming plate of eggs and toast, then seemed to notice my reluctance. "Sit down. Eat."

I replaced the Bible on the coffee table, sat quietly across from him, and avoided his eyes as I took mincing bites. I had no appetite.

He spread some honey on a slice of toast and took a hearty bite. My silence finally attracted his attention. He reached over and took my hand. "Hey—you okay?"

I nodded. "I'm...fine." But my voice was barely audible. I covered my face and was unable to stop the sudden rush of tears.

He immediately came and knelt next to me. "Hey, Dina, what's wrong?" He smoothed my hair, took both my hands in his, and kissed them. "I know it was—your first time. Wasn't I—gentle enough? I would have waited if you'd said so, but we both..."

I shook my head. "I just don't feel very well," I said and wiped my eyes with a table napkin.

He leaned his tousled head against my shoulder and looked up at me with guileless eyes. "You still love me, don't you? You told me so last night. I sure love you. And I'll never, ever stop."

I kissed the top of his head. "Of course, Marty. I'm just so—confused. I just got baptized yesterday. I'm Christian. I was supposed to wait!"

He sat there quietly for a long moment, in deep thought. Then he stood up and gently caressed my shoulders. "You *did* wait, Dina. You waited for *me*. And you will always be pure and good and sweet and perfect in my eyes, beautiful Christian Indian woman. I don't want you to feel bad, like we did something wrong. Like you're a wicked person, or that I'm playing with your feelings." He tilted my chin upward and looked into my eyes.

"What we did is what happens between a man and a woman when they love each other. I want to marry you, and be with you and take care of you—always. Tell you what. I'm going out and buy you a ring. Would that make you feel better? Would you believe me then? You can come with me if you want."

Uncle Donnie's warning was like a ghostly presence: "*It's a game...*"

I looked down at his shirt that stopped just above my knees. "My clothes are still drying. I couldn't go anywhere like this."

He threw back his head and laughed. "That's for sure, pretty Indian woman. So it looks like I'll have to buy you some more clothes too, then." He held me at arm's length. "Let's see, five-four—and a bit on the skinny side." He drew me close and whacked me playfully on the seat. But we'll have to do something about that, won't we? Go eat." He headed for the shower. "I'll pick you up a—size six slim. How's that?"

"Pretty good," I acknowledged. "What did you do? Peek at the tag in my jeans?"

"You got it, Indian woman." And he flashed that smile that always left me weak and vulnerable.

He dressed quickly and headed out of the door. "Hey, feed Coyote for me, will you? He knows you now. He'll mind his manners."

I did not allow myself to think about how worried Uncle Donnie must be, how disappointed, or how disgusted with me. I had never previously stayed out all night. Maybe Aaron knew, too. Nothing stayed secret for long on The Rez or in The Root.

But I was caught up, swept away, and carried off in Marty's gravitational pull now, and nothing could turn back time. Sure, there were things about him that were distinctly Traditional. But love always prevailed, didn't it?

There was no use fighting it any longer. After all, he respected my faith—didn't he? And he was interested in studying the Bible—wasn't he? So if we gave each other space, like he said, respected each other's beliefs, like he said, and tried hard enough, we could make it work regardless of Uncle Donnie's and Aaron's dire warnings—couldn't we?

I brought Coyote his ration of dry nuggets from the wooden barrel in the kitchen and topped it with my uneaten breakfast eggs. True to Marty's prediction, the dog greeted me with a vigorous wag of his tail.

When he stood on his hind legs, he could look me square in the eye. His yellow gaze held mine, and he rewarded me with a drooling lick on the face.

"Okay, I like you too. Now please eat," I said and cautiously patted his head. I wondered jocularly what Eddie Was would think of this betrayal, my fraternizing with the enemy.

Morning quickly morphed into midday. I made the bed and washed the dishes. I searched Marty's closet, his bureau of drawers, and his bathroom medicine chest.

I wasn't looking for anything in particular—just curious, mostly. But I did want to know what was in that bag with the padlock. Search as

I may, however, I found nothing unusual in Marty Osceola's house.

And although I looked everywhere—beneath the bed, in the outside storage shed, and even in the trash can next to it—there was no sign of that canvas bag that had been on the table or the bundles of sage and sweetgrass. He must have taken them with him.

I ironed my jeans and T on the floor—Marty had no ironing board. I watched television, read, and faded in and out of sleep. I scrounged what I could find to eat: a slice of cheese and a left-over dinner roll. They were the best choices from among three brown-shelled eggs, an overripe tomato, and a half carton of orange juice well past its expiration date.

By the time the sun finally sank below the horizon, I was anxiously watching the windows. Without a telephone, if some emergency came up, I would have to walk the distance to the road through the woods, then down the highway—and then...

Stop it, Dina. He'll be here, my heart chided me, but I closed the curtains and made sure the doors were locked.

My watch showed 9:15. By ten I was close to panic. He had been gone almost twelve hours. I turned on all the lights, rechecked the locks, and turned off the television set. If something happened outside, I wanted to hear it.

I sat on the floor by the window peering into the blackness and listening to the cries of the night creatures. Suddenly Coyote began howling—a kind of wailing howl—as if fearful of some phantom in the blackness.

"What is it, boy—what do you see?" I asked as I eased open the front door.

The chirping of crickets was one with the night, and with each heartbeat I could hear my own blood pounding in my ears. Outlined by the moonlight, Coyote glanced back at me, then resumed his wailing howl. Though still tethered by his chain, he leaped and charged toward the road.

Then the night roared and sprang two great eyes as the truck's headlights tunneled through the darkness. Weak with relief, I sank down on the step with my face in my hands. "Thank God. Oh, thank God!" I whispered.

I sat there and watched as Marty, ever at ease, pulled to a stop. He leaped out and knelt next to Coyote. "Hey, you took care of things for me, didn't you? Good boy. Good boy." He then took several large bags from the truck.

When he saw me sitting there, he laughed. "Well, well, looks like you're going to fit right in out here. Most people from The Root or the city Rez are scared to sit outside alone at night."

"I had Coyote to protect me," I said and held the door open for him. He did not need to know how terrified I had been.

Both arms full, he kicked the door shut behind us, flung the bags on the Futon, then picked me up and whirled me around. "Ummm—missed you, pretty Indian woman." He planted a quick kiss, then produced the items from the bags. "Two pairs of jeans, size six-slims. Two shirts, two pairs of—uh, dainties—a toothbrush…"

I stood up and held the jeans against me. "You're a good shopper, Marty. You sure you haven't done this before?"

Without answering me, he took out a smaller bag. "Come here. Hold out your finger, pretty Indian woman. I've certainly never done *this* before." He slipped the ring—silver with three gorgeous turquoise stones—on my finger. "Be my wife?"

I was speechless. All my doubts about marrying him faded then. I loved him, and even though things were happening way too fast, I had passed the point of no return. Besides, maybe there was one thing that Uncle Donnie was right about: it was time I made a commitment. And the rest we would take care of one day at a time.

"It's lovely. Yes, Marty, I'd be proud to be your wife."

He stretched his hands upward, and let out a whoop. "Al-*right*!" He yelled. He held me and looked into my eyes. "In some Indian cultures, to win a bride, braves used to count coup—or bring blankets or captured ponies. Only then, after he'd proved himself could he take the bride he had won." He laughed Marty style and said, "This is too easy, so *White*. I should have to do more to win a woman like you."

He stood behind me, held me about the waist, and buried his face in the curve of my neck. "So, Mrs. Osceola," he said between kisses, "pick out something to wear tomorrow. I ran into my Lakota friend, Richard Eagle Feather, this afternoon. He's is in town from Pine Ridge and somebody requested a *yuwipi* ceremony for healing. He's going to

197

perform it. It'll be a good experience for both of us. You could do a write-up for *War Arrow*—tell about the rebirth of traditions and how intertribal brotherhood is uniting..."

I turned to face him. "A *yuwipi* ceremony? I heard Uncle Donnie talk about going to one of those. I can't participate in that. I thought you understood!"

"Dina, everybody knows you walk The Jesus Way. Nobody will try to change that. Look, Richey came all the way from South Dakota. He'll want to meet you. He's a powerful young holy man..."

"Marty, what about our Bible studies? You promised!"

"Is the world ending tomorrow? There will be plenty of time for that Bible of yours. Now pick out something to wear. And smile. Don't look so bewildered." He kissed my forehead. "I stopped by and told your ol' uncle you were with me so he wouldn't worry. I showed him the ring to declare my intentions and put his mind at ease."

"What—um—did he say?"

"Nothing. Just eyed me. Nodded. Closed the door. He'll come around. After all, to know me is to love me!"

"Was Aaron, I mean, do you know if Burning Rain...?"

"The preacher? He was there when I showed your uncle the ring. He shook my hand. Congratulated me. Then he left—said he was cutting his stay here short and heading back to Oklahoma." He reached into the shopping bag. "I almost forgot."

He withdrew another box, palm-sized, and opened it deftly with his strong slender fingers. "Turn around," he said and slipped the delicate silver chain around my neck. "Go look in the mirror."

The exquisite turquoise-inlaid cross rose and fell gently with each of my troubled breaths. I studied Marty's hands on my shoulders as we looked at our reflections in the mirror. They were gentle hands, as though he held a great treasure.

"Beautiful!" he whispered. "Turquoise compliments you."

I caressed those hands and managed a weak smile.

"Like it? That cross is my special present to you for your baptizement—uh—bap*tism*," he said.

I was barely able to speak. "It's—beautiful, Marty. Thank you."

"Look at us. Does a more perfect couple walk the earth?" He turned me to face him. "Hey, you must be pretty hungry by now. Let's go eat."

We ended up dining on hamburgers and coffee at a late café, with Marty jokingly picking on me as usual.

"Eat some more, skinny Indian woman," he urged after I downed two hamburgers. "I want to see that belly out to here!" He was laughing uproariously as, again, he made that ridiculous arm's-length circle.

Afterward we returned and sat on his steps under the moonlight, where he played his guitar and sang Traditional songs in the Indian languages.

I leaned against his shoulder and wondered in silence if he were honoring some ancient gods or traditions with his beautiful music. I wondered but did not ask—because I did not want to know.

"Dina, Dina, don't cry like that. Don't be so hard on yourself," Mama said as I sat on the floor at her feet. Her lap was drenched with my tears. I held her hands to my cheeks. I needed to see those hands, to feel them; for it was by her touch that I knew the love she had always had for me was still there.

She stroked my hair gently. "The feelings a woman has for a man and he for her are God-given. And powerful. And good. It sounds like Marty really loves you. But this conflict between the two of you is not about love or the lack of it. He walks a different path, Dina. And you cannot regard it lightly, or ignore how our family ties would affect your children."

"Oh, let people talk if they wish!" I toyed with his ring on my finger. "That's not important to us. We could move away if we had to. It's just that it's been two months now. I thought he would change. He doesn't interfere with my beliefs. It would be simpler for me to decide if he did. He's good and kind to me. But every day it seems, it's some other friend of his from a different tribe teaching him their Indian Way rituals!

"He's into this intertribal brotherhood thing. When I mention studying the Bible, or going to church together, he always puts it off. I don't know how to make this work. I've tried. Please don't tell me to break it off, I can't. I don't want to live without him. He's the only man I've ever been with!" I looked into her eyes as I sobbed brokenly. "Mama, how do you stop loving somebody that you love?"

She sighed deeply and paused in deep thought. "Love him if you must, Dina. But love God more. Enough to do what you know He would want you to do. Oh, Dina, when I saw you and Marty together, I hoped and prayed it would not come to this. My choices were easier. They were between protecting my son from a man I loved, hated, and feared, and baring my shame before everybody.

"With you, it's more difficult. You must choose between the man you love and your God." She continued to stroke my hair. "Pray for strength, Dina, the strength to make the right choice. Only you can do that."

The tears rushed forth again. "Uncle Donnie barely looks at me now—like I let him down. He'll never forgive me for not choosing Aaron," I sobbed. "I—I asked him if Aaron said anything before he went back to Oklahoma…if he left any kind of message for me."…

"What kind of message were you expecting?" Uncle Donnie was sitting in front of the television set and his eyes never left the screen.

"I—just thought he may have—said something."

"You let Marty ruin you. Now the whole Confederacy and every Seminole on The Rez knows what a stupid choice you made. What did you expect Aaron to say?"…

"Does it ever get easier, Mama—The Jesus Way?" I said through my tears.

She rested her hands on my head. "It does. But never for long. Challenges will keep on coming. Be strong. You are a new Christian; you won't learn it all at once." She sighed. "Only lately did I acknowledge the part I played in what happened between Jack and me. It was hard for me to admit that I wanted—well—*things*, and that I used him to get them.

"I guess we used each other, and when one couldn't break the other, we tried to destroy one another: I with words sharpened to wound like arrows, he with threats. And when his threats didn't work, he used Terror. Witchcraft. It took one of Aaron's sermons to remind me that God always forgives, if we ask," Mama said.

I dried my tears and sat there, thoughtful. "I need to know that there's still hope for Marty. Aaron changed. Jack changed, didn't he? And you ended up marrying him."

"Yes, but I didn't try to change Jack. He made that decision on his own. And you must not try to change Marty. If you stay with him, you must accept him the way he is. Be an example of The Jesus Way. Find your peace with God, in the quiet places within yourself. If change is to take place for Marty, let God do it from the inside out."

I dried my eyes. "I'll try to do that, Mama." I glanced at my watch. "It's almost three. I have to pick up Shania from her GED class. And please keep praying along with me for God to change Marty. Please tell Him to hurry!"

She sighed. "It doesn't work that way, Dina. Change could take ten years, twenty—even a lifetime. And there is the possibility it may never happen. Are you willing to sacrifice your precious youth for what you may never see?"

And I wondered: what if Mama were right, and Marty remained in the Traditions? Aaron had warned me what Scripture said about not forming love relationships with those walking a different path.

I remembered the uncomprehending look in Marty's eyes when he asked me to help him build a sweat lodge in the backyard for his Traditional friends for Indian Way rites....

"Marty, Christians are cleansed by the blood of Jesus," I said, "not by..."

"I have no problem with what you Christians believe. But what does that have to do with your helping me? I thought we were trying to build a life together. Didn't I read The Song of Solomon—and some of Proverbs, like I promised?"

"You did, Marty. But there's so much more. And it isn't that I don't want to help with the sweat lodge. I just don't think you understand. Certain Traditional practices contradict..."

"All right! You don't want to help. I understand that now."

So I watched him build it in the backyard by himself, in silence.

I dropped Shania off at home, and that night, before I clocked out from Pik'N'Git, I purchased a thick notebook like the ones Mama had. When the house was quiet, except for Uncle Donnie's gentle snores, I began to record:

October 29, 1980
Strange that I do not dream anymore when I sleep. I close my eyes, my spirit remains awake, but I have only thoughts—no dreams…

November 20, 1980
HE—I cannot speak his name!—did not invite me to go with him and his group to the Arizona Havasupai Indian Reservation to study their Native practices. Has he met somebody else? He never calls me Pretty Indian Woman anymore. And certainly not The Virgin of Bitterroot…

December 9, 1980
Went walking in the rain—haven't heard from him for a couple of weeks. Drove past his house at three a.m. His truck wasn't there. Wonder where he is, who he's with? Made an excuse not to be in Sheila's wedding. Brides and weddings I cannot bear right now!

December 25, 1980
Gave Uncle Donnie his gift, then went back to bed and slept all day. When I'm awake I see HIS face, hear HIS voice, can almost feel HIS touch. Will this pain ever end?

December 31, 1980
Took off his ring. I do not wear the cross anymore, either. Put them both in the top drawer behind my Bible that I am unable to read right now. Haven't been to church in a while…

It was now January 3, 1983. It had been three days since Uncle Donnie had the family over for New Year's prayer service. And although it was unlike me to procrastinate, I was just getting around to taking down the decorations. Just as I was placing the last of our special-occasion dishes back into the cupboard, the buzzer sounded for the last load of clothes in the dryer.

Chappy and his two younger brothers ripped through the house, squealing in little boys' glee, still enjoying their Christmas toys.

Uncle Donnie, rooted in his favorite armchair in front of a television football game, yelled distractedly, "You boys quiet down. I'm an old man. I can't hear over all that racket!"

I loved my little brothers, but I'd had it too with the noise. "It's almost sundown. I'm going to take them home," I said. "Okay, guys, pick up your stuff. Chappy, let's get going, buddy. Jack Jr., Little Paul—you guys are old enough to help a little, too. Come on, off the floor and into the toy box."

While the boys bickered, I took a bundle of clothes from the dryer, things I hadn't worn for a while and needed to give away. Among them, I noticed, were the two pairs of jeans—the ones Marty had bought me after our first night in his cabin.

I sat on my bed and began to fold them gently, slowly, as the echo of a memory, poignant, wistful, and bittersweet, played through my heart: the flash of a smile, a tender voice, a touch like gentle lightning, and those clear, dark eyes that drew me into their depths…

How long had it been? Two years ago—three? I wondered as I held the rough denim to my cheek. Sometimes it seemed only a day or a week had passed since we danced in each other's dreams. At other times, it seemed like a hundred years. Time, in the unconscious, is fluid and trackless, frequently with no demarcation between the now and the remote.

Shania could get some use out of the jeans, I decided, for they were a bit snug on me now. And as for the ring and the cross, they remained in their sacred place in the back of my bureau drawer next to my Bible, although I had not read it for a while.

The jeans, the ring, the turquoise-inlaid cross—they were all things of the past. I could not bring it back or change its outcome. So perhaps it was time to give serious thought to what I'd do with the rest of my life.

For ours had been a turbulent relationship: *"I can't stand this anymore. Your Pan Indian meetings—your friends always underfoot. I'm leaving you, Marty. You've made your choice. And this time, I'm not coming back!"* I threw some clothes into my suitcase.

"Try to understand. My father has abandoned the old ways. So who will carry on the Traditions if I don't? If we allow the old ways to die, then the White man will have truly succeeded in annihilating us." And his plea to me would be earnest. *"Where is the conflict, Dina? With your Christianity, our children would have the best of both worlds!"*

At other times, he simply took my feelings for granted.

Once some of his out-of-town friends dropped in unannounced, after we had already made weekend plans. And they had stayed for the entire time, with Marty participating with them in Indian Way rites and otherwise giving them his undivided attention. When they finally left, I exploded.

"This engagement is off, Marty. Why don't you just marry your friends since you love them so much?" Such scenarios had played out many times before between us, so he just sort of shrugged as, yet again, I flung my things into my weekender.

But this particular time, instead of pleading his case, shifting the blame, or insisting that I stay and work it out, Marty just lay there on the Futon. His voice was languid and self-assured as he half-watched some mindless wrestling match on the television.

"Hang that stuff back in the closet and chill out, Indian woman. You know you're coming back. You always do." He yawned and rolled over, his back toward me. *"'Cause we belong together. So why make extra work for yourself?"*

And he had again predicted rightly.

Yet, in spite of all the turmoil between us, there was still almost unbearable pain when I heard his name linked to Tanya Willow's. As I sat there on the bed, holding those jeans against my cheek, the memory of those times was as fresh as though it had happened a day ago.

Neither Marty nor I ever formally broke our relationship; we just hid our pain in the secret chambers of our hearts and kind of drifted. So there was the agony of renewed, then dashed hopes, each time he would continue to call from time to time.

On one particular occasion, Uncle Donnie avoided my eyes and handed me the telephone just as I walked in the door after work.

"It's for you," he said. It was going on midnight, and I was bone tired. Fridays were hectic at Pik'N'Git. But the busyness kept my mind occupied, for this time, I had not heard from Marty for over a month.

"Hello?"

There was a slight pause. *"Dina, I know it's late, but would you like to go someplace for a bite—maybe to Chickee Choices?"*

It was Marty. Just as if nothing had ever happened.

"I—okay. But I need to shower and change first."

"Twenty minutes?"

"Twenty minutes." I hung up and avoided Uncle Donnie's eyes, but he followed me to my bedroom and stood in the doorway.

"This is ridiculous. You've been on your feet all day, and it's late. Why are you letting him use you like this? Talk is that he's messing around with that Willow girl, too. And how long you been wearing that ring now? If he's serious about marrying you, how come you haven't set a date yet? This is foolishness. An elder is talking to you, Dina!"

"I know," I said and laid a fresh blouse and skirt across the bed.

My admission evidently caught him off guard, because there was a short pause before he spoke: *"What?"*

"I said, 'I know.'" Then I headed for the shower.

Surprisingly, he said nothing more then. But as Marty's truck headlights approached and I headed out of the door, I heard Uncle Donnie sigh deeply. I turned and saw him shake his head in resignation. He then filled his water glass, retreated to his room, and shut the door.

Marty and I said little during our drive. And once inside the café, we sat in the same booth as before. But this time, there was no laughter, none of our former joy.

"Just a hot tea for me," I said.

"Nothing to eat?" he asked.

"No, it's late. So. Why are we here?"

Marty didn't respond right away. He ordered my tea, and a Coke and chili-cheese fries for himself. When he reached over and tenderly took my hands, it was all I could do to hold back my tears and restrain from throwing myself in his arms.

"We're here because I miss you, Dina. You are the other half of my heart. It's killing me. It's not right, our not being together."

"I'm sure you have lots of—other interests to occupy your time."

He was quiet. *"You mean Tanya. It's a case where your perception does not line up with reality. It's not what you think."*

"And what do I think?"

He shrugged. *"That I'm sleeping with her."*

"Are you?"

"No. She'd probably like that, but no, I'm not!"

I inhaled deeply. How I wanted to believe him! *"Well, I've driven past her house after work a few times. And I've seen your truck there. So I suppose the two of you were up late playing Indian stick ball."*

His eyes held mine for a moment. There was a long pause before he spoke. *"It's only business with the paper, Dina."* He shrugged. *"Look, she's a night person—does her best thinking then. If she has a brainstorm that'll increase our circulation to keep our funding and asks me over to discuss it, what am I going to say—no? Dina, if you had stayed with the paper instead of walking out, we wouldn't be having this conversation."*

The waitress brought our order. *"Have some,"* he said as he ladled the chili and helped himself to his cheese fries.

I nibbled a few and studied his casual posture. *"Why should I have stayed, Marty? I mean, no matter what suggestions I made, she always came up with some idea to counter it. I didn't agree to work on the paper just to spend most of my time arguing with her. And whenever you weren't there, she treated me like I was her employee. Or worse, invisible."*

He looked surprised. *"I didn't realize that the two of you weren't hitting it off. And I certainly didn't think that Tanya's working there would come between us."*

"Marty, you are so blind." I sighed deeply and managed to keep the tears at bay. *"I don't know what to do. I really don't!"* I paused in deep thought. *"Remember space? You told me once that any relationship could work if people had space. Well, you have your space, and I have my space. So why are we so miserable? Why do we fight so much?"*

"If you don't care, you leave. But we love each other, so we stay and

fight. We do it, because neither wants to let the other go." His eyes held mine for a long moment. *"I don't want things between us to continue like this, Dina."*

"*But what about what we talked about…fought about, the last time we split?*"

He pondered my question. *"You mean church."* He heaved a deep sigh. *"Don't I go once in a while? Have I ever stopped you from going?"*

"*Well, no. But. That. Is. Not. The. Issue!*"

He shrugged, perplexed. *"Then what is? I give you all the freedom you want to do your thing, but you try to stop me from the Indian ways, our Traditions. I told you. When I'm ready, I'll do more about going to church. Look, I've read some of your Bible—Song of Solomon—nothing to argue about there. And Proverbs…lots of wisdom…so much, an Indian elder must have written it."* He smiled that Marty smile then—guileless, with that slight dimple in his left cheek. And my heart simply melted with longing for him.

So we ended up at his place—again.

On my way from work the following day, I passed by a men's shop and there was this blue shirt in the window. It had some beadwork on the collar and I could just picture Marty in it. It was kind of pricey for my budget—almost forty dollars.

But I decided he was worth it, that our relationship was worth it, so I splurged and bought it. His eyes brightened when he opened the box.

"*Hey—it's great. Perfect. I'm wearing it tonight. So dress up or dress down, pretty Indian woman. But let's go eat."*

"*Let me iron it a little first…"*

"*Nope. I'm wearing it just the way it is, with your fingerprints still on it,"* he said and took me into his arms. *"Know what? You're never going to get away from me. Remember what I told you? Half of my heart beats in your chest and half of yours beats in mine. We split up, we both die."*

The evening was perfect. And the following morning he wore that same shirt to work—over my protests, because there was a small coffee stain on the cuff.

"*I'm wearing my new shirt, Indian woman—so deal with it,"* he said with that Marty grin.

But by the following afternoon, his friends started coming over again: some for the sweat lodge, some just to hang out, this time for three days. And there was the smudging and the constant pressure to get Marty and me, over my protests, to attend the summer Ute Bear Dance social in Colorado—to my understanding, a kind of Indian Sadie Hawkins Day.

And whenever I visited, no sooner than my feet had crossed the threshold, the telephone—Marty had finally gotten one installed—would start ringing. Tanya. Morning, noon, or night, the telephone gave us no peace: Tanya. Or his Pan Indian friends. All constantly calling or underfoot. Church? I didn't even attend anymore.

The final blowup, however, happened when Tanya Willow showed up at Pik'N'Git late one evening, cover-girl stunning in poured-on jeans. She was driving Marty's truck. And she was wearing that blue shirt with the beaded collar I'd bought for him.

"How's it going, Dina?" she said as she loaded items in a hand basket. *"Miss you at the paper."*

I tried to sound distracted and perfunctory as I rang up the next customer in line.

When it was Tanya's turn, she flourished her long silver nails as she took the items—all Marty's favorites—from her basket and placed each on the counter for me to ring up: canned peaches, Del Monte brand, cranberry juice, cashew nuts, buffalo jerky.

"Marty has a lot of great things going on at the paper. I keep telling him he doesn't need me with all the ideas he has, but he insists on my staying. So, how's Pik'N'Git treating you?" she said with a saccharine smile.

She's pushing my buttons, I thought, *spoiling for a reaction.* And it was all I could do to keep my cool as she chattered on and on, baiting me. I avoided looking at that shirt and seeing that smirk of satisfaction on her smug face, because all I wanted to do right then was to leap across that counter and rip out her blond-streaked hair by its black roots.

And when Marty phoned me later that evening after work, as soon as I heard his voice, I was still so furious I slammed down the receiver without speaking to him.

He did not call back.

But by the week's end, I had simmered down and was close to madness to hear from him. But days later, after I had finally swallowed my pride and called him, his phone was disconnected. I lamented many times and was even physically sick that I denied him the opportunity to explain—if indeed, that was why he called. Besides, knowing Tanya as I did, it was possible that she took the shirt without his knowing it.

But days without hearing from Marty turned into weeks, and weeks into months. Tanya kept *War Arrow* going for a while. A couple of times she called me on the pretext of business. I could tell that she was trying to extract information, because she was too proud to admit that she did not know where Marty was, either. So I was purposefully vague and answered with double-talk. No way was I going to give her satisfaction by admitting that he had walked out of both of our lives.

As time went on, I noticed I wasn't receiving my *War Arrow* subscription anymore. I called the office. The phone there was now disconnected, too.

It was as Marty said—half of my heart was missing, lost someplace. And in addition to that pain, it broke my heart that, for all of his efforts, his dream to unify all the tribes apparently had simply failed to thrive, too. Like our love. Like my very life.

"Eat something," Uncle Donnie would insist, and he would place food before me that he had prepared with his own work-roughened hands—he, who all but hated cooking. But all I could do was to take those loving old hands in my own, press them to my cheek, and weep. He never withdrew them during those times. He just allowed me to cry until I had no more tears.

And there were his other efforts to pull me out of the depths of my depression when he'd knock on my door:

"I'm going to church. Why don't you get dressed, too?"

But each time, my answer was the same as I lay in bed: *"I'm too tired. Maybe next Sunday—okay?"*

And if Uncle Donnie invited the church's visiting committee, I would lock myself in my room and feign illness. Mama tried to get me to re-enroll in school. I had no more interest, because at Pik'N'Git, there were no demands on me except to perform my duties with robot-like precision. Working gave me a reason to get up every morning.

Rick came in occasionally whenever I needed time off. He promoted me to manager in order to devote full-time to some kind of home-based business he was running.

So there was babysitting my nieces, nephews, and much younger brothers, and taking care of Uncle Donnie. I dropped the kids off to church sometimes, but I never stayed.

I did get to know Jack Turner, though, and in spite of myself enjoyed his testimonies. He had become a popular speaker in the churches, explaining how he came to power as a witch, and how he abandoned all his practices to walk The Jesus Way:

"As a medicine man, I would fast from food and water for three days for a spirit guide to appear to tell me what I wanted to know. And that was what I placed my faith in."

His voice would rise to full power: "I did not know anything about God's plan for our salvation, had never read a Bible. To me, Jesus was a White man, who was God of the White man. And as an Indian, I figured I wasn't bound by any of His teachings.

"I had the spirits. They were powerful. They gave me everything I wanted—everything except the promise of salvation. But God heard my prayer and forgave me. And if He forgave a man as deeply mired in wickedness as I was, Indian people, He will forgive you, too…"

I found his Christian testimony comforting, reassuring. Yet, for me, everything was still colorless: the bougainvillea, the periwinkles, the crotans, the sky. I, myself, was now little more than a walking, speaking shadow, as gray as that rainbow of my long-ago waking dream.

Whenever Uncle Donnie saw me wistful, he would remind me: *"You should have married Aaron, so I could leave here in peace! How can I have peace, seeing what you have become?"*

One of the boys was crying. My reverie ended then. The cares of the day yanked me from the painful past and back into the numbing agony of the present.

"What's going on out there?" I yelled.

I tucked the folded jeans and other give-away items into a bag. "Okay, boys, line up and let's go. No pushing, no running. Papa Jack and Mama are waiting for you…"

The boys spilled out over the yard as soon as I parked in front of the cooking *chickee*. Jack was busy at the barbecue grill, and family and friends milled about.

"Pull up a chair; grab a plate," Jack said.

Even after all this time, I still found myself eyeing him warily now and then, secretly watching for some clue that he was still the East Coast's most powerful witch. But all I saw was a man turning steaks and chops on the grill, with a look of peace on his face and a doting love for his family in his eyes.

Mama came over and gave me a hug. "Thanks for bringing the boys home. Did they behave?"

"They were fine," I said, and sat at one of the long tables set end-to-end. But for all the family togetherness around me, I felt strangely detached. Jack came over and placed a plate before me, piled high with corn on the cob, steak, and of course, Mama's frybread.

"Enjoy!" he said.

I could only nibble at the feast in front of me. I tried to make merry, but all the laughter and noise of life being lived that spilled over from the house and into the yard contrasted much too sharply to the emptiness of my own existence.

I surfed the radio stations on the way home, not looking for anything in particular—just some nice music, anything to break the humdrum and the silence.

But instead, a portion of a radio preacher's sermon caught my attention:

"So I say to you, if you are bowed down with a spirit of heaviness and oppression, Jesus can lift that, if you give it that burden to Him. Open your Bible to Matthew, chapter 11. Read verse 28. What did Jesus say? 'Come unto Me, all ye that labor and are heavy laden, and I will give you rest.' But you have to bring Him your oppressions and command all the mountains in your path to move!"

For the first time in many months, I felt pent-up tears sting my eyelids, for I was indeed burdened. And tired—so tired of smiling when I was dead inside; of laboring to appear to the world to have it all together, yet at the end of the day, barely having the energy to do anything more than go to my room and crash.

I was tired of wanting to do something with my life, but not knowing what; and of watching those around me pursue some destination; of wanting to go someplace too, but not knowing where. Maybe it was too late for Matthew 11 to help Dina Youngblood. Perhaps she was too far gone.

When I reached Uncle Donnie's, I just sat there in the car for a while with the engine idling. Thinking. I was a waste on the earth. Just breathing in and breathing out, and only appearing to be alive. I even thought about the pills—not just the one I sometimes took when I had trouble sleeping. All of them.

Uncle Donnie must have sensed that I was at the lowest point of my despair as I sat there in the driveway because he came and stood on the steps until I switched off the engine. By the time I reached the house, he was holding the screen door open.

"Okay, I know I'm late. But I stopped for Jack's barbecue. He sent you dinner. Give me a few minutes and I'll have it on the table," I said as I headed for the kitchen with the foil-wrapped plate.

He followed at my heels. "When will you speak to your mountain?" he asked in a loud voice.

I turned to face him and stood there speechless in his unwavering gaze. Had he somehow been listening to that radio sermon, too?

"Go in your room and get your Bible. Open it up. Read it. Cry out to the Lord. He is as near as your prayers, and His Word will not return void. Do you believe that?" I had never seen such intensity in his eyes.

"Uh—what's this all about?" I asked when I found my voice again.

"You, Dina. It is about you. You are a born-again baptized Christian. Yet you have allowed the spirit of heaviness to defeat you. You have allowed the past to imprison you. You have made the promises of God null and void, that you can come to Him for the peace and the rest you seek in your life. Didn't our Savior say that all power is given to Him in heaven and in earth? Is there anything that He can't do?"

I could only stand there and grope for words that would not come.

"Answer, young woman! Do you believe that the power of God is stronger than the power of evil? Answer this elder!"

I choked back tears. "Yes. Yes, sir. I believe it."

"Then show your faith, and speak to your mountain!"

I lay awake that night. That sermon and Uncle Donnie's confirmation continued to echo in the quietness. They were right, of course: I had settled into a lifestyle of drudgery and defeat. Revisiting dreamscapes that existed only in memories could not be the extent of my existence. If I continued on my present course, no doubt I would wake up one day and discover that I had missed life.

I thought of the past three years and all the turmoil that had surrounded it. Surely, after all this time Marty had married, someone else had borne his little warriors, and I was probably nothing more than a distant memory. And as for Aaron—what a treasure he must be for the lucky woman he had surely chosen by now!

Uncle Donnie's commanding words edged again through my thoughts: *"When will you speak to your mountain?"*

If Pik'N'Git, babysitting, and caretaking were to be all God intended for me, then why was this longing for something else continuing to burrow in my spirit? It was a new year. If things were ever to change for me, I would have to take the first step toward regeneration.

I switched on the lamp and quietly took Mama's old Bible from the back of my drawer, from the dark recesses where it had rested unread for the last three years…where I had also hidden Marty's ring and the turquoise-inlaid cross.

"*When will you speak to your mountain?*"

I remembered the words in their essence from Sunday school, and thumbed through the pages until I found the passage—Matthew 17:20. It said that if one had faith even as small as a mustard seed, he could command, and mountains would move. That radio preacher's challenge in Matthew 11 to seek rest from labor and heaviness—it seemed almost too easy. But how I wanted that rest!

Then the tears came—hot, rushing, dammed-up tears that finally overflowed the wall I had erected around my heart. I forced myself with all the faith I could muster and spoke into my own darkness: "Mountain of ashes and despair, spirit of heaviness, I command you—move." I paused then. "In the name of Jesus," I added.

I climbed into bed and lay there in the stillness for an interminable time. No bolt of lightning struck, nor did any voice rumble from the heavens. Yet I felt compelled to act—to do something.

It was past midnight, but I reached for the telephone at my bedside. I had my own line now. I dialed Rick's number, even though I had no clear thought of what I would say to him. But when he answered, I opened my mouth and the words were somehow there: "I'm sorry to bother you, I know it's late. But could you come in for me tomorrow? There are some things I have to do…"

It was midmorning the following day. I fingered the small box in my pocket for the last time. Inhaling deeply for courage, I walked into the quaint, dimly lit shop with the wrought iron bars on the windows whose sign stated simply:

JEWELRY
Bought and Sold

The proprietor was a small man, ancient, balding. And his impeccable manners were a throwback to an earlier age in America's evolution when such things were valued. He briefly examined the three-stone turquoise ring and the inlaid cross.

His voice was kind. "They are of great sentimental value, I'm sure. How much is the lady expecting?"

"Anything. I—don't want to know their value. I just can't keep them anymore."

My downcast eyes told the story. He pressed several crisp bills into my palm and I stuffed them into my purse without counting them. He patted my hand with compassion as I left the ring and the cross on the counter.

Choking back my tears, I walked out of the shop without looking back.

January 4, 1983

Sold the ring and the cross. I won't count the money—I can't! I'll stick it in an envelope and put it on the church collection plate. It tore my heart out and I cried. But they were tokens that tied me to a past that is like "water spilt on the ground, which cannot be gathered up again..." From 2 Samuel, chapter 14. Mama wrote something similar to this many years ago. I did not know then that it was from Scripture.

January 5, 1983

I dreamed last night for the first time in three years! I was dressed in dazzling white and running toward a rainbow—not gray this time, but glorious in all its hues and brightness. There were no storm skies, no owl creatures, no strange painted horses. And no HIM. Though it does not make me happy, I do feel liberated now—and at peace.

January 6, 1983

Since I had the bright rainbow dream, my spirits are lifting. I can barely keep my feet on the ground—almost walking on the air! I feel as though I am waking up after a long sleep. The world isn't gray anymore. The sky, the flowers, the trees are all alive and blazing with color!

XV

The Way of Blessing

s we sat at the table eating supper the following evening, I looked up a couple of times and caught Uncle Donnie studying my face—actually *looking* at me for the first time in many months.

A smile toyed at the corners of his mouth. "I feel a happy spirit in this house. Perhaps you have spoken to your mountain. Perhaps I can finally make my journey in peace?"

The blood rushed to my face and could feel the refreshing in my spirit. "I had this dream—the first dream I've had in years. It was about a rainbow, radiant and brilliant. And as I ran toward it, this dazzling white dress I was wearing started to reflect all its colors."

"Is that all?"

I dropped my head. "No. Also, I-I sold his jewelry yesterday. His ring and his cross."

"Whose ring and whose cross?" His eyes were fixed on my face.

"You know—the ones *he* gave me."

"The ones *who* gave you?"

I bit my lip and lowered my eyes. "Marty. I sold Marty's ring and Marty's cross. I'll put the money on the church's collection plate."

He leaned back in his cane back chair. "Good! You're finally able to speak his name again. I think you're ready to go forward now."

I grasped his calloused, work-worn hands and stroked them gently. "Uncle Donnie, I must trust you with a big secret. I quit my job. I feel a pull on my life to be a missionary. I'm going to Oklahoma, to Broken Bow, where I can stay with Aunt Bett for a while. Later I can find a job and work in some little church. Teach Sunday school. Do whatever until the Lord reveals to me if there's something else He wants me to do. But I don't want the family to know—not yet, anyway. They would try to talk me out of it. They would think I'm," I pointed to my head, "*on-na-hak-bee-pek.*"

He took a sip of water to calm his wheezing cough, smiled, and studied my eyes. "Well, looks like one more Youngblood woman will walk through the night's door."

"Think of it this way," I said. "Outside the night's door is the morning."

He nibbled a bit of baked potato. "Aaron is pastoring a church in Broken Bow. Thought I'd tell you that."

"Oh, how do you know? I thought he was an evangelist that traveled around."

"He still travels. Just not as much. Calls me now and then. Keeps me informed." He breathed deeply, coughed again, and took another sip of water.

"Really?" I held his eyes for a long moment and swallowed hard. "Does he ever—ask about me?"

"No, Dina. And probably for the same reasons you couldn't talk about Marty."

I could barely speak. "How come you never told me?"

"Because. You were walking through the fire. It is a terrible journey, and each person that walks it must make it alone. It is one as gray as that rainbow you dreamed about; as gray as that mountain of ashes that was in your path. But I know the Lord was with you, because I prayed night and day that you would be able to overcome. But you hurt Aaron really bad, Dina. Gut-kicked him. Led him on, and then on the same day he baptized you, spent the night with Marty.

"No, I didn't tell you we talked. I didn't want you calling him, involving yourself in his life—not before you were both ready for the green grass of new ground."

I sat there, pensive. "You have to believe me, Uncle Donnie. I never meant to hurt Aaron." I sighed. "But I'm not going to Broken Bow to see him. He's probably married again by now, anyhow. And even if he isn't—he wouldn't be interested in me. Not after what I did to him."

Uncle Donnie pushed aside the last of his largely uneaten baked chicken. "Well, I know for a fact that he never remarried." He lifted his eyes to mine. "The rest—who can say? The end of this story is for the two of you to write."

A smile started in the pit of my spirit and tugged the corners of my mouth almost from ear to ear. I rested my elbows on the table and cupped my chin in my hands. I studied every feature of my Uncle's craggy, adorable face. It was as if I were imprinting it on my mind for all time.

"Know what? I love you, you crafty old redskin. Listen, I contacted a nurse, a good friend of mine, to look in on you after I leave. She'll take good care of you. And make sure you tell her about that cough—and don't give her a hard time. Do what she says."

He sat stock-still and studied my face. "Nobody will ever take care of Old Donnie Jumper the way you did, or love the old snapping turtle near as much. Now, go get my Bible. Do it now. An elder is speaking."

I did so without asking questions. He took it from my hands and turned through the pages, apparently already sure of the Scripture he was seeking. "Sit down. I want to pray you a blessing," he said.

This was a first. But again I obeyed without question. I sat before him and he rested his right hand on my head.

"'He that dwelleth in the secret place of the most High shall abide under the shadow of the Almighty...'"

Tears were streaming profusely down my cheeks by the time he completed reading Psalm 91.

"And there's one more," he said and thumbed quickly back through the pages. When he found the Scripture, he again rested his hand on my head. "'The Lord watch between me and thee, when we are absent one from another.' Now, you go in the peace of God, Dina Youngblood."

He placed the Bible on the table then, and when I stood to my feet again, there were tears in his eyes, too. I clung to him and we wept together.

"Don't you worry, daughter. You go where you feel a pulling. And remember what I taught you about life—and sugar cane," he said.

"I remember. Chew out the sweet, spit out the rest."

"Good," he replied. "Always remember that. As for me, my own journey awaits. I began it once before. This time I must finish it."

He had always been a father to me, the only one I had ever really known. And now, for the first time, he had called me his daughter. I smiled and dried my eyes. "Don't you dare go running off too," I said as I cleared away the dishes. "I couldn't live without knowing that I could always come back to you."

He filled his glass with ice water. "Nothing that we see in this old world is permanent. It will all pass on." He coughed again and took his signature swig: "Ahhh, g-o-o-o-d water." He then took his Bible from the table, went to his room, closed his door after him, and went to bed.

The next morning, I made enough oatmeal for the two of us and served cantaloupe chunks—something a little special, something he loved, since it would be our last meal together before I headed for Oklahoma.

"Breakfast, Uncle Donnie," I called out. It wasn't like him to oversleep, especially with the aroma of freshly perked coffee in the air, but perhaps with my leaving, he didn't fall asleep right away the night before.

So I knocked softly. "Come on out. Don't pout, now. You know I'll stay in contact with you." I opened the door a bit.

He lay in bed with his Bible open and facedown across his chest. His hands were folded over it. His peaceful face bore the sweetest of smiles. I went back into the kitchen and waited a few minutes for him to end his quiet time. He had not stirred by the time I returned, so I went over and shook him gently.

"Breakfast, Uncle Donnie—I fixed you some cantaloupe."

He remained unmoving. It was then that I noticed a fragrance—one familiar in my memory, the tang of new buckskin—lingering in the air. My eyes combed the room. I swallowed hard. My heart drummed with an almost paralyzing sense of the awe of anticipation.

"Man in White—I know you're here—please, show yourself," I said in a barely audible voice. And I stood there, unmoving, scanning every corner, every space. But this time, the being from across the portal hid himself from me.

On the floor beneath the window, however, a tiny round object shimmered and reflected the light of an unseen rainbow.

I picked up the tiny seed bead and pondered it with wonder. It was like the ones on the garment of the Man in White. I turned again to Uncle Donnie. The same smile was gently etched on his face. And in the half-light of early morning, time itself seemed to hold its breath.

"Uncle Donnie?" I called out again, in a choked whisper.

My answer was an encompassing hush—and a great stillness.

XVI

Good Ground for the Seed

Just before dawn, clad in jeans and a comfortable denim shirt, I loaded my new pony—a pre-owned Caprice—with only my barest necessities. I placed the ancient Samsonite hardside in the trunk, wrapped Uncle Donnie's old *efche esh fa yee kee* in his favorite patchwork jacket, and placed it on the back floor. He had wanted me to have it. I would stop by the mailbox on the way, one last time before I headed out because I had not checked it for a while.

As I started the engine, a quick shadow caught my eye. Eddie Was dashed from the hedges into the driveway.

I sat for an instant pondering what to do. There was nobody to take care of him now, for in the blink of an eye, Uncle Donnie was simply *gone.*

It had been two weeks since his gentle passing, and although I was slowly accepting that grim reality, I struggled with it: how could a person be part of your life for as long as you have existed and then, just like that, simply disappear from it so suddenly? And it was so very, so awfully *final.* I sighed deeply, swallowed back my tears and switched the channels in my brain.

"Okay, E.W., you're not going to like this," I said as I left the engine running and rushed back into the house. Ringed tail held high, Eddie Was dashed in after me, no doubt anticipating his chow; and before he could back-pedal in protest, I plopped him in the wooden crate Uncle Donnie had made for him years ago for his vet visits and placed him in the car. With the chow.

He yowled for a short time, and then resigned himself as I pulled out of the driveway for the last time. A few minutes later, I heard him crunching on his breakfast.

I parked beside the mailboxes and left the engine idling while I retrieved our mail for the last time.

The two fliers I tossed in the nearby trash can. The letter I held close to my eyes, straining to see in the dim light from the lamp pole. It was hand-addressed to me and thick, obviously several pages long. Return address: *M. Osceola,* and postmarked in Spokane, Washington, eight days ago. For a brief moment, my heart seemed to actually stand still in my chest.

Marty had spoken infrequently of his friends on the reservation in Wellpinit, and also on the Yakima Reservation. Now, from the far away Northwest, he was once more reaching out to touch my life.

My hands trembled and my mouth went dry as I opened the envelope. An undated photograph fluttered to the ground. I retrieved it, and a thousand dreams and memories ago came rolling back like the tide on a seashore. It was just as though he had never gone away.

His hair was now well past his shoulders. Coyote was nearby. They both stood in the half-shadows in some unnamed place and time. Marty's thumbs rested casually in his beaded belt in that typical Marty pose.

The boyish face I remembered was now a bit more chiseled and angular, but he had to now be the best-looking Indian guy on the West Coast. A beam of sunlight caught that slight dimple of his left cheek and the glint of those dark, bright eyes that pierced straight through my very heart. I could almost hear his laugh.

Slowly, I unfolded the letter. What could it possibly hold? I wondered, and as I walked slowly to the car, turned on the dome light, and sat reading the greeting of that letter, I could have sworn I heard his voice: *Dina, My Dearest...*

A stab went through my heart. "No—no, Marty," I whispered. "Why, after all this time? I can't—I can't!"

So without reading further I refolded the letter with hands still shaking, and almost reverently, slipped both it and the photograph back inside the envelope.

I do not know how long I sat there in the car, holding that letter pressed against my breast, fighting the image of those dark eyes that had forever seared their impression into my heart.

Was he was on his way back to Bitterroot, to try again to rekindle what we had lost? Was he asking me to join him somewhere in a new adventure—and to give it one more try?

I had only to open the letter—right there in my hands—to find out. My question asked out of a first love's anguish and heartbreak played over and over in my head: *"How do you stop loving somebody that you love?"*

Perhaps he was telling me that he had finally abandoned Indian religions and now embraced The Jesus Way. All I had to do was peel back the flap of the envelope, read those words so carefully scripted by Marty's own hand, from Marty's own heart, and I would know.

I then remembered Uncle Donnie's warning: *"He is walking a different path..."* And the insistence of my young heart in the throes of first love: *"Anyone can change..."*

But in spite of everything, it was my mother's words that reminded me of why I was leaving for Oklahoma: *"You must love God more..."*

Morning was lifting her shades on Bitterroot. I remembered my plan to be on the road before sunrise. I was running late, I reminded myself, but I stepped out of the car and reopened my suitcase in the trunk.

I steeled myself, mustered all my discipline and courage, and placed the unread letter beneath my wallet, T-shirts, and jeans.

I ached to know what he was saying to me, and one day I would know. But not today. I could not chance being deterred from my mission.

So I snapped the lid shut and stood there momentarily with my hands on the trunk, fighting to suppress the image of that slight dimple when he smiled, the echo of his voice, and the memory of his touch—like gentle lightning.

And as I pulled into the street, I watched all that was familiar—Uncle Donnie's tan and brown house, so small and so quiet now; Pik'N'Git on the corner; The Root; The Rez; all the things embedded so deeply in my heart—grow smaller and smaller in my rearview mirror as I headed for Broken Bow.

Good ground for the seed...

BONUS FEATURE

Taking It Deeper
Helps for Teachers and Leaders

The "Bonus Feature" items are designed to help a teacher (public, private, or homeschool) as well as leaders (book groups, discussion groups, or study groups) take the concepts of *Gray Rainbow Journey* deeper. They can also be used by individuals to further deepen their reading and understanding of the book.

The "Discussion Questions" require a variety of reading, writing, and literary skills aligned with the Florida Comprehensive Achievement Test (FCAT) and most other state standardized reading assessments. Skills include discussion, making predictions and inferences, reading for details, making comparisons and contrasts, recognition of different dialects, and identifying universal themes and character types. Students have the opportunity to relate what is read to their own experiences and feelings. Additional activities also strengthen students' research and writing skills.

For the "Discussion Questions" section, students could read a chapter, then answer the questions for that chapter individually, as homework, or as part of a review group in class. Or the students could read the entire book, then break into review groups to complete the chapter-by-chapter questions together; and afterward discuss the answers and points of view as a class. Suggested answers are provided for you at the end of this book.

The "Vocabulary Enrichment" exercise is designed to help students determine the meaning of words in context, a skill required by Florida Comprehensive Achievement Test (FCAT) and most other state standardized assessments. The worksheet also requires students to use dictionaries (to determine the definition of the word, the part of speech, and the pronunciation) and to incorporate new words into sentences of their own. Responses will vary greatly, so no answers for teachers are included for this section.

However, for the Vocabulary Extension question, "Why do some Native Americans reject the term *Native American?*" on p. 265, students should consider that the term originated only in the late twentieth century (1960s) and base their responses on additional information from their research.

Discussion Questions
Gray Rainbow Journey

Chapter I: Bitterroot: Angry at the Sun

1. Why did Dina read Cheha's journal? Give at least two reasons.

2. What frightened Cheha so much that she dropped her beads and loom?

3. Do you think the incident really happened, or was it a dream?

4. Why was Cheha angry with the sun?

5. Name two things Dina would do if she could disappear from Bitterroot.

6. In what point of view did the author choose to tell this story—and why do you think the author chose it?

Chapter II: Home Before Dark

1. Why did Dina choose to pursue a nursing career?

2. What kinds of crafts did Cheha make for the tribal fair and powwow?

3. What kinds of creatures perched in the mango tree outside the kitchen window?

4. How did Dina feel about these creatures?

5. How did Cheha feel about Shania's chosen hair coloring? Why?

6. During their childhood, how did the girls manage to win all the foot races against the boys?

7. Why did people fear Jack Turner?

8. What relationship did Jack have to Marty Osceola?

9. Different ethnic groups as well as people living in different parts of the country have their own dialects, including some vocabulary

unique within their groups. When Shania said, "My Greyhound ticket left me busted, and I needed a few bucks to water the pony," what does "pony" mean in this context?

10. Why did Dina hide their mother's journals from Shania?

11. When she ran away, why did Cheha take the crafts with her?

12. What kind of career did Shania plan to pursue?

13. What news did Shania share with Dina that caused Dina to reflect on the past?

14. Why do you think Shania is so thin?

Chapter III: The Scent of Twilight

1. How did Dina feel about meeting Marty again after not having seen him since grade school?

2. Why did Marty want to unite all the Indian tribes under one standard?

3. Why did Uncle Donnie believe that Jack Turner was "bad medicine"?

4. How did Uncle Donnie feel toward Marty?

5. In this chapter, how did Uncle Donnie feel about Christianity?

6. What was the relationship between Dina and Uncle Donnie like? Explain.

7. Why did Shania cancel the meeting that she and Dina had planned together?

8. Where was Shania headed when she left Bitterroot?

Chapter IV: Ghost Town Spirit

1. What made the relationship between Uncle Donnie and Dina special?

2. Why do some aspects of Indian spirituality cause its followers to live in fear?

3. How did Dina feel about abandoning the spiritual beliefs of her ancestors for the Christian faith?

4. What did Cheha stop doing that she once did on a regular basis?

5. How did Dina's non-Christian friends feel about her choice to abandon Native Spirituality (Indian religion)?

6. How did Reverend Ward, pastor of _____ Church, feel about all Indian religion (Spirituality)?

7. What annual activities drew the largest crowds of both Christians and non-Christians to church?

8. Why did the four Traditional men and the teenage son attend church that Sunday?

9. Who did Dina believe that she saw sitting on the front row at the revival meeting that night?

10. Google the word *simanooli* at: simanooli – bing.htm. What does the word mean? In what ways were both Cheha and Dina runaways?

Chapter V: Patchwork, Rainbows, & Hummingbirds

Are the following statements true or false?
Mark T for true; F for false.

1. Shania owned a red horse that she nicknamed "The Pony."____

2. Uncle Donnie needed to eat lots of Snickers candy bars because he was a diabetic.____

3. Shania gave Dina one hundred dollars in twenty dollar bills.____

4. Uncle Donnie bought Eddie Was from a pet store.____

5. Eddie Was received his name because of Shania's speech impediment. _____

6. Shania took a part-time job in order to pay for a Mustang. ____

7. Uncle Donnie encouraged Shania to pursue her dream to become a super model.____

8. Dina believed that rainbows and hummingbirds described Shania.____

Chapter VI: Painted Horses

Fill in the blank with the appropriate word or words for questions 1 through 4.

1. JohnnyHawk told Dina that he wasn't a_____when he insisted on paying for her Coke.

2. The Traditionals believed that one could not be a real_____ and a_____at the same time.

3. The word *gospel* means "_____ _____."

4. In Marty's editorial, he believed that White people wanted all of the Indians'_____, _____, and other _____ _____.

Answer questions 5 through 18.

5. How did B.J., the proprietor and a non-Christian, feel about advertising Christian events through his smoke shop?

6. What did Marty want Dina to do to advance the causes of Native people?

7. What historical figure did Marty believe the Native people should pattern after to empower themselves?

8. Based on his viewpoint as stated in his editorial and conversations with Dina, what do you believe was Marty's basic

reason for wanting to unite all the Indian tribes under one standard? Explain your point of view.

9. How did Dina feel about the role Marty wanted her to play?

10. Marty makes his intentions to marry Dina clear. What is your opinion of his proposal?

11. What **fear** does Marty reveal to Dina?

12. Why do you think Dina cries when she leaves Marty that evening?

13. What do you think Dina's dream means?

14. The title is first mentioned in this chapter. What do you think *gray rainbow journey* means?

15. Do you think Marty drugged her or put a spell on her; or do you think the dream came from her own fears?

16. Who telephoned Dina the following day?

17. What clues does Dina pick up from the phone call?

18. Make three predictions of what will happen in future chapters.

Chapter VII: Truth Crushed to Earth

1. What incident did Dina keep from Uncle Donnie because she didn't believe that the time was right?

2. How did Dina's feelings toward her father change after she read her mother's journal?

3. What income level does the story indicate for Uncle Donnie? Give evidence to support your view.

4. Based on Dina's investigation, who was "The mystery guy—Mr. Terror himself"?

5. After he returned from town, what did Uncle Donnie do that Dina found unusual?

6. How did Dina feel when she discovered where they were going that evening?

7. After Uncle Donnie revealed his Big Secret, what did he believe it would teach him?

8. Who did Uncle Donnie invite to dinner at his home?

9. How did Dina feel about her role in preparing for the dinner party?

10. The yuwipi ceremony is most closely associated with which American Indian tribe?

(Hint: Google yuwipi *for further information.)*

11. Burning Rain tells Donnie this: "Dryden, a great thinker, said that truth is the foundation of all knowledge. Bryant, another great thinker, said that truth crushed to earth will rise again. Pilate asked, 'What is truth?' And Jesus Himself said, 'I am the way, the truth, and the life.'"

Who are these men (look them up on the Internet if you don't know) and what does this conversation reveal about Burning Rain?

Chapter VIII: Speaking Spirits

1. What did Dina do before she went to bed to prepare for the dinner party the following night?

2. When Cheha called, what did Dina hear in the background?

3. What was peculiar about Cheha's speech?

4. What did Cheha ask Dina to do for her?

5. What was Cheha's reaction when she discovered that Shania had visited Jack Turner?

6. Why did Dina need to earn extra money?

7. What did Dina wonder about Marty?

8. Why was Cheha afraid to give Dina her telephone number?

9. What does Marty do that reinforces Uncle Donnie's view that Marty is learning "bad medicine" from Jack Turner?

10. What was Uncle Donnie's secret motive for giving the dinner party?

11. Aaron Burning Rain believed that power came from what two sources?

12. What did Dina believe that her life would be like if she married a pastor?

Chapter IX: Noonday Nightwalker

1. Where did Dina go the following morning?

2. Why was Bitterroot founded?

3. Why did Uncle Donnie think Burning Rain would be a good match for Dina?

4. Why did Burning Rain decide to stay in Bitterroot longer than he'd planned?

5. How did Sheila Marston, Dina's best friend, help Dina?

6. What did Cheha have with her as she exited the train?

7. Who entered Pik'N'Git as Dina was explaining her dilemma?

8. Explain how his presence made Dina feel.

9. What happened to Rick as a result of the visit?

10. What was Uncle Donnie's description of what happened to him?

Chapter X: Samaritan One East

1. What or who did Dina believe caused Uncle Donnie's medical condition?

2. What was Shania's initial response when Dina told her of Uncle Donnie's condition?

3. Under what condition would Dina believe in God?

4. Why did Cheha wish to keep Jack Turner from seeing Chappy?

5. What was the head nurse's attitude toward Uncle Donnie's friends as they crowded into the hospital lobby? Why?

6. What were Dina's feelings toward Chappy?

7. How did Dina find out about the details of Cheha's stay in Arizona?

8. What happened as Dina headed back to the hospital with Chappy in her Vega?

9. After Uncle Donnie was pronounced dead, what did Dina decide to do?

Chapter XI: The Ancient Art of War

1. What was the weather like as Dina headed to Jack Turner's house?

2. What kind of pet did Jack Turner own?

3. Describe what Dina saw in the woods before she could fire the <u>efche esh fah yee kee</u>.

4. What were her initial feelings toward what she saw?

5. What made her fearful?

6. What did Dina's Christian memory remind her about vengeance?

7. How did Uncle Donnie describe his death experience?

8. What was the head nurse's explanation of Uncle Donnie's experience?

9. How did Burning Rain explain what happened?

10. What was Uncle Donnie's attitude toward the head nurse?

Chapter XII: Another Tribe

1. What did Cheha's testimony reveal about her?

2. How did becoming a full-fledged Christian interfere with Dina's feelings toward Marty?

3. What does "unequally yoked" mean?

4. Before Jack Turner becomes a Christian, what is he told to do to let the Lord manifest himself?

5. How did becoming a Christian change him?

6. Why did Dina find it difficult to believe that Jack Turner had changed?

7. How did Aaron Burning Rain feel about his own life before he became a Christian?

8. Before he became a Christian, what were the two things that Aaron never did that made him feel that part of him was still human?

9. Why did Shania want to come home?

10. What was the real relationship between Shania and Jack Turner?

Chapter XIII: A Walk Through Fire
Fill in the blank or answer the question.

1._____ was happy to pay Shania's airfare from California back to Bitterroot.

2. Uncle Donnie preferred _____to Marty for Dina.

3. Dina believed that Uncle Donnie was wrong about Marty. Why do you believe she feels this way?

4. Emellda Tommie is surprised to see Dina with Marty. Why?

Chapter XIV: Aftermath

1. How was Marty dressed at breakfast the following morning?

2. What was missing or moved that had been there the night before?

3. When he realized that Dina was unhappy, what did Marty promise to do?

4. When Dina searched Marty's house, did she find anything unusual?

5. How did Dina feel in the house alone as night fell?

6. Name the two pieces of jewelry that Marty gave to Dina.

7. What does Marty believe about the mixing of Traditional Spiritualism and Christian practices?

8. As the relationship fell apart, how did Dina react to it?

9. What items did Dina sell in order to break the hold that the past had on her?

10. Describe Dina's dreams before and after she sold the items.

Chapter XV: The Way of Blessing

1. What did being able to speak Marty's name again demonstrate?

2. What path did Dina choose for her life?

3. Why didn't Uncle Donnie tell Dina that Aaron had kept in touch with him over the years?

4. Do you agree with his decision? Explain why or why not.

5. Who was going to take care of Uncle Donnie after Dina left?

6. What happened to make it unnecessary?

7. What is the meaning of the tiny seed bead Dina finds in the morning?

Chapter XVI: Good Ground for the Seed

1. Who did Dina decide to take with her to Oklahoma?

2. What did she find in the mailbox when she checked it for the last time?

3. What did she remove from the item?

4. What did she decide to do with what she found?

5. Why did she make that decision?

6. Do you believe that she will be able to keep the promise she made? Why or why not?

7. What do you believe will happen once she arrives in Oklahoma?

Culminating Projects

1. Compare and contrast Aaron and Marty. What traits do they share? What traits are opposites?

2. The initiation theme archetype consists of separation, transformation, and return. How does Dina go through each of these stages?

Separation:

Transformation:

Return:

3. Match the archetype to a character in the novel. There may be more than one right answer!

a. Hero. A larger-than-life character that often goes on some kind of journey or quest. In the course of this journey, the hero demonstrates the qualities and abilities valued by his culture.

Gray Rainbow Journey character: _____

b. Shapeshifter/Trickster. These archetypes can be virtuous or nefarious. The Shapeshifter's mask misleads the Hero by hiding his intentions and loyalties. These archetypes can be virtuous or nefarious.

Gray Rainbow Journey character: _____

c. Wise old man. Typically represented by a kind, wise, older father figure that uses personal knowledge of people and the world to tell stories and offer guidance that illuminates to his audience spiritually a sense of who they are and who they might become.

Gray Rainbow Journey character: _____

d. Shaman. A helper who aids the Hero in his seeking of a guiding vision to help him/her on the journey. A shaman can also wield great power for good or evil.

Gray Rainbow Journey character: _____

e. Villain. The Adversary who represents power and strength. Both strength and fortitude are required to do battle with him; submission to him leads to death of the self.

Gray Rainbow Journey character: _____

f. Helper, Giver, Caretaker. Compassionate, thoughtful, and generous, this type can also be passive-aggressive, clingy, and manipulative. May be motivated by a great need to be loved and needed and fears being deemed unworthy of love.

Gray Rainbow Journey character: _____

Extra Projects

Choose one or more of the following projects to extend your learning. Some of the projects are best done individually; others lend themselves to group work.

1. Illustrate a scene from the book that you found especially captivating; or create portraits of what you believe certain characters look like.

2. Research Traditional recipes and prepare some Native American dishes to serve to the class, such as frybread or <u>sofkee</u>.

3. Find three examples of Native American poetry and share these with the class.

4. Aaron lists his three reasons why he is Christian. Interview an adult Christian and ask them for their three reasons. Are they similar or different from Aaron's?

5. If you can play a flute or any other instrument, learn a Native American song and perform it for the class.

Choose one or more of the following research topics to share with the class. You may want to prepare a webpage, a PowerPoint presentation, or a written report, depending on what equipment you have available.

1. The setting for the story is the Florida Everglades. Research the water system, wildlife, and environmental problems the Everglades faces today.

2. Research the Native American traditional ceremonies mentioned in the novel. Include the Green Corn, Sun Dance, and yuwipi ceremonies.

3. Research social problems on reservations today.

4. Based on research, describe how Indian-owned casinos have affected the lives of Native Americans.

Vocabulary Enrichment
Gray Rainbow Journey

Read these sentences from the novel and try to determine the meaning of the underlined word on your own. Then look up the word in the dictionary to see if you are correct. Also write down the part of speech and the correct pronunciation using diacritical marks. Finally, use the underlined word in a sentence of your own that shows you understand its use.

1.   They were seeds she hoped would **germinate** in us and keep the ancient ways alive, for they were tales Mama Hat feared would become like many perceived the Indian people to be: existing, yet somehow extinct.

Definition:

Part of Speech:

Pronunciation:

Your Sentence:

2.   I dusted it off and read the title. The King James Bible. Mama's. But I seldom saw her pick it up after her **hiatus** from church and, consequently, mine from Sunday school.

Definition:

Part of Speech:

Pronunciation:

Your Sentence:

3.   The crinkly furrows around his eyes, he had to know, were consequences mostly of many years of squinting—because he conveniently "lost" every pair of eyeglasses he ever owned. When his **ophthalmologist** asked why he refused to wear them, he muttered once, "'Cause they make me look old."

Definition:

Part of Speech:

Pronunciation:

4.   I can take care of myself. And I'm not a <u>tay-koo-che</u>. I'm a young adult. An **emancipated** minor, if you will.

Definition:

Part of Speech:

Pronunciation:

Your Sentence:

5.   I was totally **infatuated** with Marty, but it couldn't hurt to look, I figured, for who knew which way this new relationship-of-sorts was going to go?

Definition:

Part of Speech:

Pronunciation:

Your Sentence:

6. I spruced up the house, **marinated** some Spam in canned tomatoes, put fresh towels and a new roll in the bathroom, and made a "do" list for the following day:

Definition:

Part of Speech:

Pronunciation:

Your Sentence:

7. Whether or not she would come home was left to be seen, and I felt so alone. Johnny Hawk and FrankE stayed on the **perimeter,** as was their custom, during family crises; and as with Mama, they depended on me for updates on everything rather than becoming personally involved themselves.

Definition:

Part of Speech:

Pronunciation:

Your Sentence:

8.   Other prayer warriors joined in. Some fell **prostrate**. Others lifted their faces upward and spoke all at once in that strange babble.

Definition:

Part of Speech:

Pronunciation:

Your Sentence:

9.   He was looking at me and I was losing myself in those **inscrutable** dark pools that held so much mystery.

Definition:

Part of Speech:

Pronunciation:

Your Sentence:

10.   "No, I put him in my truck. Then I took him home and made a **poultice** for him and took care of him. I'm a healer, too," Jack Turner said.

Definition:

Part of Speech:

Pronunciation:

Your Sentence:

11. As I stood on the bank of Panther Lake and toweled the water from my hair, Marty stood back, watching me with an **enigmatic** half-smile, his thumbs in the belt loops of his Levis.

Definition:

Part of Speech:

Pronunciation:

Your Sentence:

12. So when Mimi-the-Waitress with the **saccharine** smile came back over, Sheila was ready.

Definition:

Part of Speech:

Pronunciation:

Your Sentence:

13.   Again, Rick was **pensive**.

Definition:

Part of Speech:

Pronunciation:

Your Sentence:

14.   I **pondered** her confession. "He wants his son, and he won't stop until he gets him."

Definition:

Part of Speech:

Pronunciation:

Your Sentence:

15. "All Indian religion is **animistic**—rooted in superstition and demonic spiritism."

Definition:

Part of Speech:

Pronunciation:

Your Sentence:

Vocabulary Extension

Denotation is the dictionary definition of a word. **Connotation** is the emotional meanings attached to a word. While two words might have the same denotation, they may have different emotional meanings and show differing degrees of respect.

Think about the different emotions that a woman might feel after a man calls her these different terms: *a lady, Indian woman, my woman, my female, chic, squaw, slut.* Which terms have positive feelings attached? Which ones are negative?

Terms to refer to ethnic groups also have different connotations. Think about these terms and discuss the connotations:

Indian

Native American

Injun

Why have some Native Americans rejected the term *Indian?* What is the history of the term?

Why do some Native Americans reject the term *Native American?*

Note: You can find out the history of any word at **www.etymonline.com.**

Answers to Discussion Questions
Gray Rainbow Journey

Chapter I: Bitterroot: Angry at the Sun
1. Why did Dina read Cheha's journal? Give at least two reasons.
A: She wants to find her mother and hopes the journal will reveal her whereabouts.

2. What frightened Cheha so much that she dropped her beads and loom?
A: The dark shadow of a winged creature.

3. Do you think the incident really happened, or was it a dream?
A: Possibly a dream—or a night terror sent by an evil medicine man. Answers will vary.

4. Why was Cheha angry with the sun?
A: It continues to shine on the world outside while she lives inside in stillness and dark despair.

5. Name two things Dina would do if she could disappear from Bitterroot.
A: Finish school, get a job, buy nice clothes, party, socialize.

6. In what point of view did the author choose to tell this story—and why do you think the author chose it?
A: First Person. It makes the story more personal. The reader can more easily get inside Dina's head and perspective.

Chapter II: Home Before Dark
1. Why did Dina choose to pursue a nursing career?
A: She dropped out of school to take care of a diabetic grandmother and later moved in with her Uncle Donnie to care for him. She won respect and approval from the elders, felt it was a way to contribute to her people, and grew to feel that caretaking was her destiny.

2. What kinds of crafts did Cheha make for the tribal fair and powwow?
A: Beadwork and patchwork cloth.

3. What kinds of creatures perched in the mango tree outside the kitchen window?
A: Owls.

4. How did Dina feel about these creatures?
A: She feared that they were bad omens.

5. How did Cheha feel about Shania's chosen hair coloring? Why?
A: She felt angry because her daughter had rejected her own heritage by trying to imitate White people; she interpreted her daughter's choice as a kind of self-hate.

6. During their childhood, how did the girls manage to win all the foot races against the boys?
A: They chose a boy they knew they could beat, although Dina's choice of deceptively strong Marty earned her continued defeat.

7. Why did people fear Jack Turner?
A: He was thought to be a shape-shifting witch.

8. What relationship did Jack have to Marty Osceola?
A: He was his stepfather.

9. Different ethnic groups as well as people living in different parts of the country have their own dialects, including some vocabulary unique within their groups. When Shania said, "My Greyhound ticket left me busted, and I needed a few bucks to water the pony," what does "pony" mean in this context?
A: A car.

10. Why did Dina hide their mother's journals from Shania?
A: Shania and their mother were at odds, so Dina felt that she would use

the journals to expose her mother to ridicule. Answers may vary.

11. When she ran away, why did Cheha take the crafts with her?
A: To sell them to support herself.

12. What kind of career did Shania plan to pursue?
A: Modeling.

13. What news did Shania share with Dina that caused Dina to reflect on the past?
A: That childhood sweetheart Marty Osceola is in town.

14. Why do you think Shania is so thin?
A: She diets to excess to maintain what the modeling industry and popular opinion believe exemplifies beauty.

Chapter III: The Scent of Twilight
1. How did Dina feel about meeting Marty again after not having seen him since grade school?
A: She acts cool, but he has never really left her heart.

2. Why did Marty want to unite all the Indian tribes under one standard?
A: So that they would gain political power. He's employing the same tactics as did the Blacks in history.

3. Why did Uncle Donnie believe that Jack Turner was "bad medicine"?
A: He blames Jack for Sam Waters' illness because of the rumors of his great powers to do evil as a medicine man.

4. How did Uncle Donnie feel toward Marty?
A: He believes that the Indian activists are largely a group of rabble rousers headed for trouble, that Jack Turner has schooled him in his ability to do evil; and that he could influence Dina or cause her harm.

5. In this chapter, how did Uncle Donnie feel about Christianity?
A: He largely regards it as "the white man's religion," but being unsure of

268

its power, regards himself as "half Indian and half Christian," in the event the stories about Jesus are true.

6. What was the relationship between Dina and Uncle Donnie like? Explain.
A: They love each other in spite of being aware of each other's flaws. She feels that she has contributed to the "learned helplessness" he wields to manipulate and get his way; and he loves her in spite of her strong-willed nature that sometimes lead her into trouble. They employ humor in their interactions with one another.

7. Why did Shania cancel the meeting that she and Dina had planned together?
A: She has to select a new car.

8. Where was Shania headed when she left Bitterroot?
A: To California to become a model.

Chapter IV: Ghost Town Spirit
1. What made the relationship between Uncle Donnie and Dina special?
A: They take care of each other, and have each other's best interest at heart. He is a father figure.

2. Why do some aspects of Indian spirituality cause its followers to live in fear?
A: Traditional spirituality permeates their lives, and they believe some of the spirit beings can cause them harm.

3. How did Dina feel about abandoning the spiritual beliefs of her ancestors for the Christian faith?
A: She is in conflict because giving up Indian beliefs seems like denying her identity and her heritage.

4. What did Cheha stop doing that she once did on a regular basis?
A: She stopped going to church.

5. How did Dina's non-Christian friends feel about her choice to abandon Native Spirituality (Indian religion)?
A: They regard her as having betrayed her identity and cultural heritage.

6. How did Reverend Ward, pastor of **Hope for Tomorrow Independent** Church, feel about all Indian religion (Spirituality)?
A: He believes that it is all animistic, and rooted in superstition and demonic spiritism.

7. What annual activities drew the largest crowds of both Christians and non-Christians to church?
A: The Christmas pageant, Easter service, and the Thanksgiving community meal.

8. Why did the four Traditional men and the teenage son attend church that Sunday?
A: They came to disrupt the sermon because it challenged their beliefs and lifestyle.

9. Who did Dina believe that she saw sitting on the front row at the revival meeting that night?
A: Mama Hat, her great-grandmother.

10. Google the word *simanooli* at: simanooli – bing.htm. What does the word mean? In what ways were both Cheha and Dina runaways?
A: *Simanooli* means "runaway." Cheha ran away literally by leaving town, while Dina fled emotionally by withdrawing into herself when the circumstances of her life became too much for her to bear. Answers will vary.

Chapter V: Patchwork, Rainbows, & Hummingbirds
Are the following statements true or false?
Mark T for true; F for false.
1. Shania owned a red horse that she nicknamed "The Pony." **F**

2. Uncle Donnie needed to eat lots of Snickers candy bars because he was

a diabetic. **F**

3. Shania gave Dina one hundred dollars in twenty dollar bills. **T**

4. Uncle Donnie bought Eddie Was from a pet store. **F**

5. Eddie Was received his name because of Shania's speech impediment. **T**

6. Shania took a part-time job in order to pay for a Mustang. **F**

7. Uncle Donnie encouraged Shania to pursue her dream to become a super model. **F**

8. Dina believed that rainbows and hummingbirds described Shania. **T**

Chapter VI: Painted Horses
Fill in the blank with the appropriate word or words for questions 1 through 4.
1. JohnnyHawk told Dina that he wasn't a **Rockefeller** when he insisted on paying for her Coke.

2. The Traditionals believed that one could not be a real **Indian** and a **Christian** at the same time.

3. The word *gospel* means "**good news**."

4. In Marty's editorial, he believed that White people wanted all of the Indians' **land**, **gold**, and other **natural resources**.

Answer questions 5 through 18.
5. How did B.J., the proprietor and a non-Christian, feel about advertising Christian events through his smoke shop?
A: He believes in keeping a good relationship with the entire community and all of his customers happy, so he allows it.

6. What did Marty want Dina to do to advance the causes of Native people?

A: Write for his newspaper.

7. What historical figure did Marty believe the Native people should pattern after to empower themselves?

A: Dr. Martin Luther King, Jr.

8. Based on his viewpoint as stated in his editorial and conversations with Dina, what do you believe was Marty's basic reason for wanting to unite all the Indian tribes under one standard? Explain your point of view.

A: To regain power to build better lives for the Native American people. Answers to the point of view will vary.

9. How did Dina feel about the role Marty wanted her to play?

A: She is attracted to him and wants to please him, but she is torn between duty to Uncle Donnie, finishing her degree, finding her mom; and feels conflict between the Indian Way and Christianity.

10. Marty makes his intentions to marry Dina clear. What is your opinion of his proposal?

A: Answers will vary.

11. What fear does Marty reveal to Dina?

A: That he would die without his being here on earth ever having mattered, and without having done anything to better the condition of the Native people.

12. Why do you think Dina cries when she leaves Marty that evening?

A: There is confusion and conflict between her feelings for him and her Christianity--also perhaps a fear of losing herself by being drawn into his sphere of influence. Answers will vary.

13. What do you think Dina's dream means?

A: Dina both loves and fears Marty. She senses danger in a relationship

with him. Answers will vary.

14. The title is first mentioned in this chapter. What do you think *gray rainbow journey* means?
A: A rainbow should be colorful, but Dina senses a darkness (a grayness) entering her life. Answers will vary.

15. Do you think Marty drugged her or put a spell on her; or do you think the dream came from her own fears?
A: It seems quite possible that he drugged her. The author leaves this up to the reader. Answers will vary.

16. Who telephoned Dina the following day?
A: Cheha, her mother.

17. What clues does Dina pick up from the phone call?
A: She hears a baby crying and the voices of a man and a woman.

18. Make three predictions of what will happen in future chapters.
A: Dina will find out where Cheha is. Dina will turn away from Marty in the end but not until he hurts her. Shania is going to get into trouble. Answers will vary.

Chapter VII: Truth Crushed to Earth

1. What incident did Dina keep from Uncle Donnie because she didn't believe that the time was right?
A: That Shania was at Jack Turner's home.

2. How did Dina's feelings toward her father change after she read her mother's journal?
A: She no longer views him as a hero.

3. What income level does the story indicate for Uncle Donnie? Give evidence to support your view.
A: Low income. He has no money to fix his truck.

4. Based on Dina's investigation, who was "The mystery guy—Mr. Terror himself"?
A: Jack Turner.

5. After he returned from town, what did Uncle Donnie do that Dina found unusual?
A: His door is closed, and he's reading a book that he has bought.

6. How did Dina feel when she discovered where they were going that evening?
A: She doesn't want to attend, can't understand why her uncle kept it a secret, and possibly fears the power of Burning Rain's message. She's also aggravated that her uncle expects her to ask his questions.

7. After Uncle Donnie revealed his Big Secret, what did he believe it would teach him?
A: How to get rid of "bad medicine."

8. Who did Uncle Donnie invite to dinner at his home?
A: The preacher, Aaron Burning Rain.

9. How did Dina feel about her role in preparing for the dinner party?
A: Annoyed.

10. The yuwipi ceremony is most closely associated with which American Indian tribe?
A: Lakota/Sioux.
(Hint: Google yuwipi for further information.)

11. Burning Rain tells Donnie this: "Dryden, a great thinker, said that truth is the foundation of all knowledge. Bryant, another great thinker, said that truth crushed to earth will rise again. Pilate asked, 'What is truth?' And Jesus Himself said, 'I am the way, the truth, and the life.'"

Who are these men (look them up on the Internet if you don't know) and what does this conversation reveal about Burning Rain?
A: John Dryden was an influential 1600s English poet and playwright.

William Cullen Bryant was an 1800s poet. Pilate was a king named in the Bible, and Jesus is the Christian Bible's prophesied Messiah. Burning Rain's ability to quote from them shows that truth is of great importance to him and that he is educated in a wide range of philosophies.

Chapter VIII: Speaking Spirits
1. What did Dina do before she went to bed to prepare for the dinner party the following night?
A: She "spruced up the house, marinated some Spam in canned tomatoes, put fresh towels and a new roll in the bathroom, and made a 'do' list."

2. When Cheha called, what did Dina hear in the background?
A: A crying baby again.

3. What was peculiar about Cheha's speech?
A: She writes and speaks of herself in the third person.

4. What did Cheha ask Dina to do for her?
A: Find an apartment where she can return home and live in secret from Jack Turner.

5. What was Cheha's reaction when she discovered that Shania had visited Jack Turner?
A: Helpless fear.

6. Why did Dina need to earn extra money?
A: To help pay for her mother's apartment.

7. What did Dina wonder about Marty?
A: The extent, if any, of his involvement in the terror campaign against her mother; and if he had used "medicine" or drugs on her the night she had the terrible dream.

8. Why was Cheha afraid to give Dina her telephone number?
A: The number would show up on her telephone bill, and Jack Turner's spies would relay the information to him.

9. What does Marty do that reinforces Uncle Donnie's view that Marty is learning "bad medicine" from Jack Turner?
A: **He brings exactly the items she needed—plus Snickers, which keep cropping up as something sinister associated with Jack Turner. The owls that frightened Dina retreat at his approach.**

10. What was Uncle Donnie's secret motive for giving the dinner party?
A: **Matchmaking and learning how to break curses and spells.**

11. Aaron Burning Rain believed that power came from what two sources?
A: **Light and darkness.**

12. What did Dina believe that her life would be like if she married a pastor?
A: **That she would live under great restrictions and be hindered from realizing her goals and dreams.**

Chapter IX: Noonday Nightwalker
1. Where did Dina go the following morning?
A: **To Pik'N'Git to buy a newspaper and search the want ads for a job.**

2. Why was Bitterroot founded?
A: **To provide a community for those who wish to stay connected to the Native community but don't want to live "The Rez experience."**

3. Why did Uncle Donnie think Burning Rain would be a good match for Dina?
A: **His belief was that "He's a decent man and not bad-looking. He would treat you good. You would get a chance to travel with him. And listen good now." He squinted and pointed his finger for emphasis: "No owl in his right mind would come near you ever again with the preacher around!"**

4. Why did Burning Rain decide to stay in Bitterroot longer than he'd

planned?
A: He's in love with Dina.

5. How did Sheila Marston, Dina's best friend, help Dina?
A: Sheila loans Dina a car.

6. What did Cheha have with her as she exited the train?
A: Her infant son and a suitcase.

7. Who entered Pik'N'Git as Dina was explaining her dilemma?
A: Jack Turner.

8. Explain how his presence made Dina feel.
A: Fearful. Terrified of his powers.

9. What happened to Rick as a result of the visit?
A: Blood spurted from his nose.

10. What was Uncle Donnie's description of what happened to him?
A: That he saw owls, and that Jack Turner blew a powder into the air that caused his condition.

Chapter X: Samaritan One East
1. What or who did Dina believe caused Uncle Donnie's medical condition?
A: Jack Turner

2. What was Shania's initial response when Dina told her of Uncle Donnie's condition?
A: She didn't want to leave her career. She believed that if she left, in such a cutthroat business, she might miss her opportunity.

3. Under what condition would Dina believe in God?
A: If he would take away her confusion and heal Uncle Donnie.

4. Why did Cheha wish to keep Jack Turner from seeing Chappy?

A: She wished to rear him as a Christian, which she knew that Jack Turner would never agree to.

5. What was the head nurse's attitude toward Uncle Donnie's friends as they crowded into the hospital lobby? Why?
A: That there were too many, and they would disturb patients and hospital business.

6. What were Dina's feelings toward Chappy?
A: Great love and protectiveness.

7. How did Dina find out about the details of Cheha's stay in Arizona?
A: She read her new journal.

8. What happened as Dina headed back to the hospital with Chappy in her Vega?
A: Jack Turner chases her down and threatens her.

9. After Uncle Donnie was pronounced dead, what did Dina decide to do?
A: Go to Jack Turner's and kill him.

Chapter XI: The Ancient Art of War
1. What was the weather like as Dina headed to Jack Turner's house?
A: Misty rain.

2. What kind of pet did Jack Turner own?
A: A dog.

3. Describe what Dina saw in the woods before she could fire the efche esh fah yee kee.
A: An Indian in white buckskin.

4. What were her initial feelings toward what she saw?
A: She finds him handsome.

278

5. What made her fearful?
A: **She became afraid that he was possibly a conjured spirit sent by Jack Turner.**

6. What did Dina's Christian memory remind her about vengeance?
A: **That it belongs to the Lord.**

7. How did Uncle Donnie describe his death experience?
A: **He was in a place full of light and indescribable beauty, but a gentle voice told him to return and tell his people of what he had seen.**

8. What was the head nurse's explanation of Uncle Donnie's experience?
A: **An equipment malfunction.**

9. How did Burning Rain explain what happened?
A: **He believed that the Lord had called Donnie back, and called it a sign and wonder.**

10. What was Uncle Donnie's attitude toward the head nurse?
A: **He felt that she was haughty and condescending and responded by being contrary and confrontational.**

Chapter XII: Another Tribe
1. What did Cheha's testimony reveal about her?
A: **That she was willing to admit her own guilt in having used Jack Turner for revenge against her cheating husband, for needed cash for her children; and for having goaded him toward violence.**

2. How did becoming a full-fledged Christian interfere with Dina's feelings toward Marty?
A: **She is heartsick because she is unable to lead him to The Jesus Way.**

3. What does "unequally yoked" mean?
A: **Not walking the same path with the same beliefs.**

4. Before Jack Turner becomes a Christian, what is he told to do to let the

Lord manifest himself?

A: To go to Donnie's house, stand still, not say a word, and Cheha would willingly place his son in his arms.

5. How did becoming a Christian change him?

A: He burned his witch's paraphernalia, renounced the practice, became a devoted father and husband.

6. Why did Dina find it difficult to believe that Jack Turner had changed?

A: She didn't believe the powers of evil would let him go, and was afraid that he is faking to get what he wanted.

7. How did Aaron Burning Rain feel about his own life before he became a Christian?

A: He called himself corrupt fruit from a bad tree. He was a drunken, violent bar brawler who blamed others and his past for his state in life.

8. Before he became a Christian, what were the two things that Aaron never did that made him feel that part of him was still human?

A: He never beat his wife and always brought his paycheck home.

9. Why did Shania want to come home?

A: She had found out the modeling was a sham, a front for porn operation.

10. What was the real relationship between Shania and Jack Turner?

A: Daughter and father.

Chapter XIII: A Walk Through Fire

Fill in the blank or answer the question.

1. **Jack** was happy to pay Shania's airfare from California back to Bitterroot.

2. Uncle Donnie preferred **Aaron** to Marty for Dina.

3. Dina believed that Uncle Donnie was wrong about Marty. Why do you believe she feels this way?

A: Part of it is that her lust has blinded her eyes. Also, she loves him and is unwilling to believe anything negative about him; and because he agrees to read the Bible, she believes that she can lead him to become Christian. Answers may vary.

4. Emellda Tommie is surprised to see Dina with Marty. Why?

A: She knows Dina is Christian, and Marty is Indian Way.

Chapter XIV: Aftermath

1. How was Marty dressed at breakfast the following morning?

A: Bare-chested in the white drawstring pants from her dream.

2. What was missing or moved that had been there the night before?

A: The Bible, the bundle of sage, and the canvas bag

3. When he realized that Dina was unhappy, what did Marty promise to do?

A: To participate in Bible study.

4. When Dina searched Marty's house, did she find anything unusual?

A: No.

5. How did Dina feel in the house alone as night fell?

A: Scared and isolated.

6. Name the two pieces of jewelry that Marty gave to Dina.

A: An engagement ring with turquoise stones and a silver and turquoise inlaid cross.

7. What does Marty believe about the mixing of Traditional Spiritualism and Christian practices?

A: He believes if he reads the Bible to please her, she should help him in Traditional practices, too.

8. As the relationship fell apart, how did Dina react to it?

A: Recorded it in a journal, just as her mother journaled her relationship with Jack.

9. What items did Dina sell in order to break the hold that the past had on her?

A: The ring and cross.

10. Describe Dina's dreams before and after she sold the items.

A: Her early dreams contained a gray rainbow, which represented her depressed state of mind. The new dream has a colorful rainbow and she is running toward it in freedom.

Chapter XV: The Way of Blessing

1. What did being able to speak Marty's name again demonstrate?

A: She has broken his hold on her.

2. What path did Dina choose for her life?

A: To become a Christian missionary like her great-grandmother.

3. Why didn't Uncle Donnie tell Dina that Aaron had kept in touch with him over the years?

A: He felt that neither was in the frame of mind to proceed with the relationship.

4. Do you agree with his decision? Explain why or why not.

A: Yes, because his decision had the best interest of both parties in mind. Answers will vary.

5. Who was going to take care of Uncle Donnie after Dina left?

A: A nurse.

6. What happened to make it unnecessary?

A: He dies peacefully once he knows Dina is going to Oklahoma and will possibly become Aaron's wife.

7. What is the meaning of the tiny seed bead Dina finds in the morning?
A: Uncle Donnie has been led away by the same being through which he was previously brought back to life.

Chapter XVI: Good Ground for the Seed
1. Who did Dina decide to take with her to Oklahoma?
A: Eddie Was.

2. What did she find in the mailbox when she checked it for the last time?
A: A letter from Marty.

3. What did she remove from the item?
A: A photo of Marty that reminds her of the relationship that they shared.

4. What did she decide to do with what she found?
A: She decides to read the letter only after she arrives in Oklahoma and is established in her ministry.

5. Why did she make that decision?
A: She feared that any level of involvement with Marty would awaken old passions that would interfere with her mission to serve God.

6. Do you believe that she will be able to keep the promise she made? Why or why not?
A: Yes, but with great difficulty. Answers will vary.

7. What do you believe will happen once she arrives in Oklahoma?
A: Answers will vary.

Culminating Projects
1. Compare and contrast Aaron and Marty. What traits do they share?
A: Both are passionate—Aaron for his God, and Marty, for the Native people and their traditions. Both have good looks and charisma.

What traits are opposites?
A: Aaron draws power from the light while Marty draws at least part of his power from darkness. Aaron is kind and considerate, and does not manipulate to get his way; Marty places his agenda above all else and, because of his upbringing, feels he has to constantly demonstrate strength through getting what he wants at any cost. Answers may vary.

2. The initiation theme archetype consists of separation, transformation, and return. How does Dina go through each of these stages?

Separation:
A: When her mother leaves, Dina is separated from her Christian-based love and guidance, leaving an emptiness in her life, and her glamorous sister's escape further deepens this void. Left with only caretaking to validate her existence, these occurrences could have contributed to Dina's subconsciously making choices that convince her she is still lovable and desirable.

Transformation:
A: Through the tough choice she makes between Marty and Aaron, Dina's beliefs are put to the test. She makes the wrong choice for a while and suffers for it.

Return:
A: In the end she comes back to the values that her mother and the Christian church instilled in her.

3. Match the archetype to a character in the novel. There may be more than one right answer!

a. Hero. A larger-than-life character that often goes on some kind of journey or quest. In the course of this journey, the hero demonstrates the qualities and abilities valued by his culture.
Gray Rainbow Journey character: **Dina**

b. Shapeshifter/Trickster. The Shapeshifter's mask misleads the Hero by hiding his intentions and loyalties. The trickster deceives others to get them to do what he or she wants. These archetypes can be virtuous or nefarious.

Gray Rainbow Journey character: **Jack Turner, Marty Osceola**

c. Wise old man. Typically represented by a kind, wise, older father figure that uses personal knowledge of people and the world to tell stories and offer guidance that illuminates to his audience spiritually a sense of who they are and who they might become.

Gray Rainbow Journey character: **Uncle Donnie**

d. Shaman. A helper who aids the Hero in his seeking of a guiding vision to help him/her on the journey. A shaman can also wield great power for good or evil.

Gray Rainbow Journey character: **The Indian in white buckskin, Aaron**

e. Villain. The Adversary who represents power and strength. Both strength and fortitude are required to do battle with him; submission to him leads to death of the self.

Gray Rainbow Journey character: **Jack Turner**

f. Helper, Giver, Caretaker. Compassionate, thoughtful, and generous, this type can also be passive-aggressive, clingy, and manipulative. May be motivated by a great need to be loved and needed and fears being deemed unworthy of love.

Gray Rainbow Journey character: **Dina, Cheha**

Note: Although Dina loves and cares for her uncle, she also feels put-upon, trapped, and taken for granted sometimes. But she also enjoys being esteemed by the elders and others and doesn't want to do anything to lose anyone's approval. Cheha could also fit this archetype if her actions toward Jack Turner within their relationship were fully examined within a broad range of possibilities.

<u>Extra Projects</u>

Choose one or more of the following projects to extend your learning. Some of the projects are best done individually; others lend themselves to group work.
1. Illustrate a scene from the book that you found especially captivating; or create portraits of what you believe certain characters look like.

2. Research Traditional recipes and prepare some Native American dishes to serve to the class, such as frybread or <u>sofkee</u>.

3. Find three examples of Native American poetry and share these with the class.

4. Aaron lists his three reasons why he is Christian. Interview an adult Christian and ask them for their three reasons. Are they similar or different from Aaron's?

5. If you can play a flute or any other instrument, learn a Native American song and perform it for the class.

Choose one or more of the following research topics to share with the class. You may want to prepare a webpage, a PowerPoint presentation, or a written report, depending on what equipment you have available.
1. The setting for the story is the Florida Everglades. Research the water system, wildlife, and environmental problems the Everglades faces today.

2. Research the Native American traditional ceremonies mentioned in the novel. Include the Green Corn, Sun Dance, and <u>yuwipi</u> ceremonies.

3. Research social problems on reservations today.

4. Based on research, describe how Indian-owned casinos have affected the lives of Native Americans.

About the Author

"*Gray Rainbow Journey* introduces America to Native Christians in their unique struggles and attempts to balance the often-opposing worlds of Christianity and the Traditions," says debut novelist **K.B. SCHALLER** (Cherokee/Seminole).

A member of the Native Christian Church, Schaller organized and served as playwright/director of an ensemble theater for Native American Youths at the former Chickee Christian Academy on the Florida Seminole Indian Reservation.

An independent journalist, Schaller has contributed articles to *The Good News,* and to *Indian Life* and the *Seminole Tribune* Native newspapers. She is also a poet whose poems appear in several anthologies.

She and her husband, Jim, a design engineer and also a lay minister, have a blended family of four children and three cats. Chief, the most recent addition, is "a rescued Rez cat who curls up at my feet during my long stints at the computer—and who is a prototype for the feline character Eddie Was," she says.

Schaller is hard at work on the sequel to *Gray Rainbow Journey.*

For more information:
KBSchaller.com
www.oaktara.com

LaVergne, TN USA
22 September 2009
158592LV00002B/2/P

9 781602 902206